Blue's
Coach
Works

Blue's Coach Works

Neal Graham

CREATIVE ARTS BOOK COMPANY
Berkeley, California

ISBN 0-88739-262-8 Paper
Library of Congress Catalog Number 99-61097
Printed in the United States of America

To my son, Damon, whose energy has served as an inspiration for this book; and to Robert Gover, a bold writer and supportive friend.

Blue's
Coach
Works

Chapter 1
The Five-Minute Hero

S he certainly knows how to turn herself out. A different perfume for this unexpected visit to my office, bolder than she ever used to wear. And how else has she outfitted herself today? Long, elegant dress, a queenly deep purple color, as well as that jade necklace, the one I bought her to match her eyes. That was when she turned forty and business was good at Pollution Resolutions. And when I went along with her idea of paying her a hefty salary as my office manager to improve our household cash flow. Prosperity with a cost though, bringing me to where I am now: Martha's votes of no confidence in me. My son Ryan running the roads with his shady friends. The EPA that has me by the neck and is sucking the blood out of me. And now my last fortification, the company, crumbling around me like a walled city under a round-the-clock barrage of cannonballs.

"What are you looking at?" Martha asked, without facing me yet, looking at herself in the mirror as she fluffed up her still naturally golden hair.

"That painting you have your hands on. What are you doing with it?"

"Don't you agree it's a little out of place here in your office, now that you're in a downsizing mode?"

FIVE O'CLOCK SHADOWS, the perfect name for this painting I've finally learned to see clearly, and she's pulling it off the wall! I've been looking at this picture long enough to understand it, to see the human workers as worker bees, and now she wants to haul it away. Not that I see myself as one little person in a queue of office workers, traveling on escalators and elevators behind glass walls. 100 years from now I can't believe Gaylord here in the state of Maine, snow and moose country, could possibly attract enough migrants to turn us into such a city. Or maybe I've become a northern species of a worker drone, more similar to the big city workers than I care to admit. Which could explain why I disliked this painting so much when she first brought it home from the auction. Far preferring then to see myself once more as a fast and agile goal maker who could bring a crowd to its feet with applause.

"You enjoy teasing me, don't you? I like that painting where it is, Martha," I said as she was removing it from the wall.

"If I didn't know you only tolerated it all these years, I wouldn't be doing you the favor now of getting it out of your life, dear. Besides, we need to sell it and I have a buyer."

Not worth fighting with her over the damn thing! Too many things to keep track of already. I don't care that she's taking this painting, so much as how she's doing it—like a creditor seizing assets. I don't really know what's most worth saving, let alone exactly what I must do to save it, but I will!

"No, I want it to stay right here with me."

"Don't worry. I've brought the one from home that was hanging in your study that you liked so much of the barns and the cows in the heavy gold leaf frame," she said. With both hands I gave it a sudden yank to pull it back from her, in the process knocking it into the table, chipping a corner of the frame. "Ned, this isn't the time or the place for horseplay," she said with a wink. "And I certainly don't want to play tug of war with you."

"I wish I knew after all these years what your game really was, Martha. Why are you here. today? Didn't we agree a long time ago that you'd never have to set foot in this office again?"

At this point Rachael, the office manager, joined us. "Great, you're just in time to help, since no one else at hand will," Martha said.

What a charming smile she has when someone else is in the room. Now that we have company she knows I won't fight her for possession of this painting of the city, and she thinks instead I'll hang a paint-by-the-numbers type scene of a farmhouse, pasture, red barn and dairy cows, which she bought when we were first married, at a garage sale for twenty dollars. The kind of horse trading in which she excels.

"Isn't there something timeless about this scene?" Martha asked her, as they both held it, and for a response Rachael nodded in agreement. "It's something simpler and more direct, which I'm sure Mr. D'Amour can better relate to, especially these days, and a small fraction of the value of my cityscape, which he's been hating to see on this wall for too long. Don't you agree the old world craftsmanship of this traditional piece could prove more soothing to all of you in this office who remain to appreciate it?"

"Don't worry, Martha, I have no plans to go anywhere else," Rachael said.

"Now, please excuse me, dear," she said, brushing past me, holding the skyscraper painting. "But if you're unavailable to help, don't bother," she said as she stood in the doorway, looking up and down the hallway for someone else.

Now that she has her hands on the painting, she'll probably take it to her dealer friend and sell it to raise money. But from now on I must cut my losses. Should get everything out of her reach that isn't nailed down. But today, no time to argue with her, especially not in front of Rachael. No one else has to know any more of our business than they already do. But now that she's appropriated the painting, hopefully she'll soon be gone with it.

"Excuse me! Hello! Anybody home!" she called from my office door into the hallway. Then after no response she walked down the hallway, peering into different rooms, stopping immediately when she found Don Peters, of all my employees her favorite. "If you'd be good enough to help me carry something to my car, Don, I'd be much obliged," she said, jingling her car keys.

"That's the least we can do," Francis Yankovich offered.

Peters must have some useful work to do. I wish he'd go away. No doubt she wants me to disappear, but it's my office, not hers, and I won't oblige her.

"Ah, Francis, how thoughtful."

He's made his way into the room, joining her and Peters. She's not even glancing at Francis. Though she's standing before the three of us, she's focusing her attention on Peters' mannequin face and his hair, without even a trace of gray, black as the first day I hired him. She turns back and forth between the two of them, ignoring me the best she can. The shiny white gold of her jade necklace is catching the light in brilliant reflections every direction she turns.

"Mrs. D'Amour, I'll never forget when I was fresh out of school and first came on board here, and you made me feel like a personal guest, rather than an employee," Peters said, leading her toward his office, Yankovich and myself as well following.

"And I'll never forget the wonderful Queen Anne reproductions you were buying before Mr. D'Amour thought the company could afford it," Yankovich said. "Then I remember you went on to redo the reception area in kelly green, with mauve accents. The Queen Anne motif you chose is so much warmer and soothing than that hard black steel furniture Mr. D'Amour had in place before he invited you to join us."

"Francis, good catching up with you. Thanks for offering to help, but I don't think Don and I will be needing it. Meanwhile, won't the staff meeting be starting shortly?" she asked, escorting him out of Peters' office, then closing the door behind just the two of them to keep me away.

Martha can see me through the glass window of Peters' door, but she's continuing to flirt with him anyway, as if I were invisible. But I'm not only watching them, I've activated the room monitor function on the the the new phone system installed by Cyrus Langway my right-hand man. Only he and I know the access code. Now I can hear what they're saying without their knowing, and I can glance from time to time at them through the glass.

"Perhaps I should feel encouraged, but he can see every move we make," Peters said. "It's been a while. Are you here because you need me?"

"Not you, just your bull strength and ignorance."

"Even more promising." Peters grinned.

"Shut up, Don. I'm talking about your back. I need you to lug one item down to the car. Next time I might do some more house-cleaning here."

"I was never hired to do that kind of work," he smiled at her.

"You were only twenty-one and barely out of school when we hired you, and even then you managed to get out of assignments you didn't like. In hindsight, not such a good idea to have taken you on in the first place," she said.

She's bracing her arms on his chair, and leaning over him so he can look better at her chest. Now she's straightening up, and if I'm not mistaken, she closing a button on her blouse.

"I should have quit a long time ago, when he put you out of the office," I heard Peters say.

"Now you tell me! If you would have done that, then I probably wouldn't have taken the blame and lost my job here to save your job. No way will I repeat that little adventure, not with so much to lose. Don't forget that I have a marriage. Besides, rumor says you have a girlfriend."

"Why don't we talk about all that some evening, depending on your boss's schedule, Martha?" Peters asked.

"First of all, he's your boss, not my boss. I come and go as I please. Second of all, I'm here for the painting, not for old times, not for you."

"Look, Marty, just because he writes my paycheck, he doesn't own me any more than he owns you."

"I won't hear any more disloyalty!" she said, her hands clamped over her ears. "I can feel sorry for my husband, not being able to hire anyone more loyal than you or Francis. Now will you grab your end!" She took the other end of the painting herself.

"It looks like you two need help," I said, having intercepted them, accompanying them down the hallway. I pushed the elevator button to hold the doors open, but they malfunctioned, closing solidly on the big picture frame.

"Now look what you've done!" she said. "Is someone going to help me free it!"

"An elevator should never do that," I said. "I'll have to call for a repair. I'm lucky it wasn't one of you injured."

I let them yank the painting free and descend with it. I might have left them alone, but I wasn't done with them. I ran down the stairs. When they came to the landing, and maneuvered the painting to the outermost door, Langway was waiting for them.

"Don't let me keep you from something important, General," Martha said. Adjutant General Cyrus Langway, the state's most important Air Force National Guard officer until he retired, now my most loyal engineer and advisor, had at my request been loading banker's boxes of files into his own car, but he stopped immediately to take over from Peters the task of loading the painting into her vehicle.

"Not at all. I've been told to drop what I'm doing and put you on first priority until you get underway."

"Assigned by the boss? To get rid of me? Don't bother yourself."

"I make it my business to stay clear of personal details, Mrs. D'Amour," the General said.

". . . Don't worry, Martha," I said, breathing a bit heavy from my sprint down the stairs after them, "if Cyrus can keep the code to World War III in his head, your unclassified secrets should be safe with him."

"Peters, you can go now. We've got this under control," the General said.

"Excuse me, not that it's any of my business, but how can you tell what you're hauling off if none of these boxes is properly labeled?" Peters asked. "Since we have an appointment next week with Mr. Borak and his assistant Moretti at the Environmental Protection Agency to look at our barge canal files, I would feel a lot more comfortable if we left all our files in place until after they're done—"

"I believe they have a fishing expedition in mind, but they're not sportsmen," I said. "Wouldn't those lazy bureaucrats love us to stock our pond for them? Think of this as early spring cleaning, if you need to think about it at all, Peters. No need to look so concerned. For your information, these are my own personal files with receipts for coffee, ribbons, pens, paper and the like—dustcatchers, nothing of any importance to anyone, understand? You can return to the office now. Glad to see you're on the ball though. "

Rachael's been watching us from the first story window, but good office manager that she is, doesn't want to miss the action. So she's scooted downstairs to join us and is standing quietly while the General and Peters arrange the booty in the back of Martha's vehicle.

"Oh, Rachael, why didn't you let me know you were waiting for me? No need to stand there. I'd like to catch up with you now, if you care to join me for a few minutes," Martha said.

She's invited Rachael to sit with her in the front seat for a chat. Rachael, my office manager, has always treated this business like her own. When I first hired her, she acted like a nanny to the business, her baby, giving it extra attention by finding things, tasks to do for it evenings, unpaid overtime. Hardly necessary now that we've drastically cut back. Now she seems to be very concerned about the business in a different way, as if she were nursing a terminally ill child. Rachael knows all our secrets, which I hope she's not sharing with Martha, who hasn't been working here since I got Rachael to replace her. I notice Martha's gone out of her way to leave her car windows rolled down for my benefit, again treating me as if I'm invisible. She's past the point of pretending to be polite, and it doesn't matter anymore to her what I hear or don't hear and what nonsense she tells my employees.

I wish the General had covered the labels to the file boxes that we're removing, the ones that Borak has no business using for his ridiculous investigation. "OK, General, you can continue with the file boxes for the time being, until staff meeting," I said. I then sat in the front of his vehicle and read the morning's paper while listening to Rachael and Martha.

"I'm sure you've had a lot on your mind lately, right?" Martha said to Rachael.

"Yes, if you mean Bernard. He moved out of the house last month."

"I'm so sorry to hear that. But from what you've been telling me over the last few years, that must come as a relief."

"Not for my little girl Patricia. She was daddy's girl, and she's been taking it hard. As for my son Paul, I'm concerned about him, because he's become quiet and moody. He's always wanting to see his father. I believe he blames me for the separation, rather than Bernard."

"No, Rachael, I won't let you be so hard on yourself. From what you've told me, you've done everything humanly possible to keep your marriage together . . . But if there's anything at all I can do to help you through this, don't hesitate—"

"If you think it's easy to feed the three of us now on the one paycheck I take from here, rather than the two paychecks we used to have—" Rachael said.

"Now as far as Bernard's concerned, if he isn't contributing what he owes you, then maybe you need to get after him," Martha said.

"It's not like Bernard doesn't have his own expenses, like rent for his apartment. Like your son Ryan living by himself, he's having a hard time surviving on his own."

"Apples and oranges. One big difference: my Ryan's a kid; Bernard's your husband. Now woman to woman, I'd suggest that you don't feel too sorry for Bernard, if he doesn't care to stay around long enough to act like a father. The way I see it, once a man makes his bed, whether in your house or another, he'd better sleep in it. Rachael, if you're talking survival for you and your kids, then all's fair between you and Bernard. If you plan on being the survivor, you do what you have to do, if you know what I mean. Take into account that any of us is worth only so much in the marketplace. I hope that's helpful."

"I always knew you were on my side from when you first trained me as your replacement. You're very fortunate, Martha, to have been able to stay home all these years in that beautiful house with your family. I haven't been very fortunate with Bernard, you know."

"We do have a unique house, if nothing else. As for your family, Martha, have you been been getting along any better than I have with mine?"

"Sounds like we could compare notes about stressful family situations. Like Bernard, my husband's created a stressful situation for me, and now he's going to fix it."

Martha glances at me, checking to see if I'm overhearing her complaint.

"I don't understand, Martha."

"My situation at home and yours with Bernard—we each need to know more. I wish I could stay longer, but Mr. D'Amour is out here, impatient as usual, shifting from one foot to the other, and I'm afraid he'll have an accident if I don't go soon and let him relieve himself. We must get together again soon at a better time. But when we do, let's be sure we have an agenda and a purpose. If you promise to keep me up to speed with your life, then for my part, I'll do what I can to advise you through your domestic skirmishes. OK?"

"I wouldn't want to be a bother though, Martha."

"Of course not. I'm always available to help. By the way, the best time to reach me is mid-morning, any working day when I'm alone at home. We can talk much more freely without worrying about anyone eavesdropping at my home," Martha said, then gave her an embrace goodbye. "Now don't forget who your friends are. I'll be expecting your call."

I realize I've got more important business than keeping myself up to speed on Martha's gossip with my crew. I need to get back up to the office to make an important call to the town manager wanting me to clean up his mess. A contract with him would certainly help.

Volatile hydrocarbons, that's our specialty . . . Leaking landfill . . . ? High water table, no problem . . . After that point, cost plus . . . Of course we're bonded . . . No, I wouldn't pay attention to those press releases . . . Liability? I told you we're bonded . . . Others bidding, really? On a high risk operation like that . . . ? If you believe it's that easy, why not clean it up yourself . . . ? Good, if you can find anyone to do it at a better price, go ahead . . . We're going to remain in business a long time . . . Excellent, now you're doing the right thing . . . See you three o'clock Tuesday. I'll be out there with the backhoe and the engineer and we'll poke a few holes, see what kind of mess you've got . . .

He talks like he knows all about doing the job himself, another city manager wanting to cover his butt. He has backhoes, a bucket loader, dump trucks and equipment operators, and I believe if he weren't afraid to do it with his own men and equipment, he wouldn't be calling me. Knows damn well insurance means a little bit more than nothing in this case, that if I screw up, it's my neck, not his. But at this point risk doesn't scare me. I have nothing to lose. If I can win bids on a few more tough jobs like the one for this bureaucrat, I'll have at least a fighting chance to keep this dog and pony show together here at Resolutions, Inc. Which would probably be a better deal for these employees still left on the payroll than for me personally. If it weren't my name and reputation at stake, I could have folded up, but I'll never let the bastards walk over me now! Maybe I've been too kind-hearted, protecting these last few from the axe, just because they've been working here the longest. Especially since their poor judgment got me into trouble with Borak and the EPA in the first place. On the other hand, what if my own judgment wasn't as good as it could have been, should I fire myself as well, lay down and give myself up to them for dead? I suppose that if I did take my eye off the ball, and I did help bring us into Borak's grip, then I shouldn't be too quick to blame and discharge the last of my troops. After all, Borak and the EPA exist to prosecute. If they can't find legitimate reasons to go after companies such as mine, they don't hesitate to fabricate them. Borak's ruler of this New England territory for the EPA and doesn't hesitate to use his power to make a bigger feifdom for himself.

If nothing else, the members of this crew of mine are stubborn survivors like myself. If they weren't working for me, I could even grow fond of them, with the exception of Yankovich. Wish I never hired him, though he can draw better than any of the engineers or draftsmen that ever came through my doors. If only I knew how well he regarded his extra talent at the drawing board, and how sensitive he'd become once he came out of his closet. He's become not just my cross to bear, but everyone's! Morale would improve drastically, if only I could figure out a way to to get that prima donna out of this office. Then maybe I could I could get them to work better with each other and, more importantly, with me, and get it through their heads I'm their employer, the one who cuts their checks every Friday. They've got to understand I'm not their father and not their keeper and had to furlough those three employees last month to save Resolutions, Inc. and salvage their jobs with it. Yankovich has been doing his best to turn them against me, not understanding what I've done to insure our survival!

I'd cut out these weekly staff meetings, if I had any other way to keep track of them. If only they'd stop inventing so many plausible reasons for how they've marched us to this treacherous pass! Sorry explanations for habitually snatching defeat from the jaws of victory, how they've brought us to this state of siege. They may be able to live in their fool's paradise, dreaming up their sort of mushy excuses, but I'm at the helm and cannot afford delusions. Look out Feds! Look out Borak! Resolutions will prevail!

I must lead them and stand strong, no matter how this all ends! I need to think what I want to say to them this morning. Talk to them about sacrifice and triage, using our more limited resources most efficiently. On second thought, not such a good idea, considering how worried they've become over the company's prospects, and theirs with it. Probably best to reassure them. On the other hand, a little insecurity might focus their attention and help them improve their performance.

To the lion's den, the conference room. A fine spread this morning, I see. Maybe I can't offer them any long-term guarantees or pay any more than what they'd fetch on the open job market, but feeding them well should improve their attitude today. Bagels, pastries, cheese, juice and coffee.

"Nice food, Rachael," I said, once in the conference room. "Even if you're running us over budget, I'm sure everyone appreciates being able to eat breakfast here. The top of the morning to you all!"

"No matter to me, Mr. D'Amour," Yankovich said. "Personally, I'd just as soon have my own breakfast at home and come in at 9:00 instead of 8:00 to get ready for a 10:00 staff meeting."

"We all have our challenges, don't we?" Rachael said, taking him aside. "This morning I had to feed the kids breakfast, then get their books and clothes together and drive them to school a full hour early, then pick this up at the deli by 7:30."

"God," Yankovich said, "I can't even imagine being a parent like you, having to deal with car pools, fresh kids, a cranky husband, and I'll bet you'll have college bills the size of the national debt," Yankovich said.

I can see by the expression on her face, Rachael's annoyed by the little twit. She's taking Yankovich further aside where she thinks no one can overhear. I'll be damned if I'm going to allow any key information to pass me by today. But there's little that I can't hear when I set my mind to listen:

"Well, believe it or not, I like my expensive family. . . . Of course, you and your friend Sizemore will never have kids to trouble you. The two of you must be happy living so carefree."

"Rachael, I could always confide in you, but now I wonder if my confidence was misplaced, whether you really wish me well."

"Hey, I don't think you can afford to distrust me. We need all the friends we can get, especially someone as special as you."

"I think you're damning me with faint praise. But we haven't any more time to chitchat," Yankovich said.

The others have arrived, and Yankovich is trying to get our attention:

"For today's staff meeting I'll have to divide you into three camps, if you'll take my lead. We have the bagel eaters, the pastry eaters and the beef eaters, not to mention the abstainers. The choice is yours this morning."

"OK, folks, help yourselves, grab a seat, and let's get underway," I greeted them. "The bad news is the Apaches won't go away. The good news is we're tough and we're fighting them off."

Yankovich threw up his hand, as if he were trying to get a teacher's attention. "Excuse me, sir, I'm not native American in origin but for any of us Americans, whatever our origin or background, we have the right to be properly addressed, and I don't think—"

"Quite right, you're not thinking. As your leader, I need to lead you as best I can, away from unnecessary battles. We have more pressing challenges to deal with than the name we choose to call our elusive enemy."

"I'd have to call the Feds our masters, the way they're making us scared of our own shadow," said Lewis, our engineer who would much rather be in a space ship than in the pollution business.

Lewis is crazy if he thinks I'm running scared. His imagination's gotten weirder since I first saw those spy novels on his desk, and I bet he's reading them during his working hours, not just his lunch hour. If he's not finding enough challenge in his job, he, like Yankovich, could be replaced. Not too likely though, and they know it. If I fire Yankovich he'd slap me with a discrimination suit, and Lewis I can't afford to hand a pink slip because, in spite of his big mouth, I've never had anyone on the payroll who knows more about soils and hydrology.

". . . Yes, Environmental Protection Agency, I listed as the first item on your agenda," I said. "Their Superfund Program, through which Washington has been dumping mountains of money into cleaning up the worst toxic pollution sites in the country, such as Medford Pond, which we've been helping fix. Any updates, insights or suggestions to share?"

"Whether I'm a PRP or not, they scare me," Peters said. "Though I've never had to deal with them, other than for signing off on their inspections, I understand they can swing a heavy bludgeon. They have the power to condemn a site and hire an army of new contractors and bill all the PRPs for all the new work, as well as charge them penalties for their part in creating the mess in the first place."

"*PRP's*? One of the *Potentially Responsible Parties* the Feds are calling us. I call it *Proven Ridiculous Policing*? Don't you gag on their alphabet soup?"

They're looking at me like I've gone over the top, lost my mind. Sitting there very quiet and very nervous, like they're seeing the emperor with no clothes. Like they're waiting for class to start, only I didn't study up the night before to make them a lesson plan. To hell with them—that's why I hire them, to deal with these little details. And fortunately, Rachael has the important details at her fingertips, a list of PRP's she hands me, just in case I might forget one or two of them.

"Are we afraid we're really PRP's, boogiemen? No way! They have us confused with boogiemen! Do we plan to let them scare us? No way! I mean don't we all like to travel down the highway of life at a good clip, carefree, humming a tune, top down, wind in our hair, without even bothering to glance at the rear view mirror. But all good things have a way of coming to an end. When we're stopped on our joyride by the long arm of the law, our initial emotion: fear. We come up with all kinds of reasons why we were traveling 100 miles an hour in a sixty-five zone. Then we realize our fears were unnecessary. The reason? We've been stopped not by an authority in uniform but by a PRP, a *Possibly Related Policeman*. We won't go to jail. We won't even get written up, and we shouldn't because we're not criminals!"

I've got a captive audience here, but not an appreciative one, judging by their half-dead response. Not fun to be caught in the same room with them. I'm seeing their teeth, but they can't bring themselves to smile at a good joke, to laugh at their boogiemen.

"So where does that leave me, in the vehicle, or road kill?" Don Peters persisted, and this drew a sympathetic laugh from my employees.

I thought Peters could understand my little comedy, but evidently he missed the point entirely. Even after so many years here, he's still desperate for security, and expects me to somehow guarantee him safe passage.

". . . And the winner is," I continued, reading from Rachael's list of EPA targets, other than ourselves in the Medford Pond fiasco, "Citizen's Gas, Rushford Concrete or Rushford Construction —I can't remember which . . . Plus we have Medford Precision, the Central Railroad, Adco Oil. And most interesting of all, the state's also named itself as a PRP."

"No, sir, the Feds struck a deal for the state's assistance, so the state's off the hook," the General corrected me.

"Ditto for the railroad," Rachael said. "They were never officially designated a PRP, although its railroad cars were carrying hazardous materials on the tracks right by the pond, and sometimes cleaning the residue out of the cars and into the pond. As well as carrying in close proximity to the canal potentially polluting materials—"

"General, why don't you look into that angle further," I said. "It could help our cause if we knew why Borak's ignoring some of the obvious candidates."

"It seems to me," Peters said, "we've entered the picture after the fact, that we've simply been hired as subcontractors to reverse the toxic condition by removing the toxic materials left by the PRPs."

"Why wouldn't they come after us?" Lewis asked. "After all, while we were pulling out that 1500 tons of sediment, coal tar and contaminated soil from Medford Pond, all the neighbors living south of the Pond, suddenly took sick, ended up in the hospital, and had to boil their water."

As my best engineer, I'd expect him to stick closer to the facts. But I must stay cool. Be careful not to shame him, but show this nerd we have to be careful not to make others believe the site is any more noxious than it already is. As far as I'm concerned we've already cleaned up the pond and now need to focus on what we've accomplished.

"How can we have made people sick by removing contamination? What do those events prove? Nothing at all, in my opinion.

So if I were you, I wouldn't be too quick to confuse coincidences and symptoms with causes."

"I believe that by our digging we put more contaminants in the drinking water than—" Lewis said.

"Keep in mind that over the past fifty years, there were car repair garages, an auto body shop, gas stations, a dry cleaners, a photo lab, a welding shop, and a machine shop, all in the general area where those people reported bad water. And not until very recently was there ever a program in place for people to collect used oil and solvents, rather than dump everything on the ground. So did it ever occur to you, you might be drawing some extra speedy conclusions, Mr. Lewis? I mean whose side are you on? Our policy in this organization is that we deal with fact instead of fantasy. We need to get our facts straight, and we need to work as a team! My point is if we don't know—really know—that we're completely innocent, then how can we possibly convey our innocence to anyone else? We have to continue to walk tall here at Resolutions! Show Borak and his pack of lawyers any doubt or any hesitation, and they'll jump all over us, feed on us, and pick our bones clean!"

"Mr. D'Amour, if danger's so close at hand, would you give me permission to work on a more immediate project?" Lewis asked.

"What's that?"

"Not only would it place us out of the danger zone, but we could tap into an unlimited market. I know chemically how the best shark repellents work, and I could make us a lawyer repellent!"

Does Lewis know or does he care how repellent he is to me? He has a big grin, playing the clown, a role that doesn't suit him. I like him a lot better with his head in his sci-fi books and his mouth shut. I'm glad Rachael's hustling him out of the room, but why is she whispering to Yankovich? I don't trust them together.

"OK, Peters," the General said, "do me a favor and go to my office and bring in the barge canal file that's lying on my desk."

Suddenly Peters, Yankovich, Davis and the other new employee aren't talking anymore. But even if I can't get their attention these days, they seem to listen up to the General. He must have some papers in mind that will get us a little closer to the truth this go-around, to pull down the sandbags this gang's piled up between me and the looming disaster. Now's the time for a thorough accounting and certainly time for a more effective plan of countermeasures.

"Before I can fetch those records for you, sir," Peters said, "I would like to know why I'm named as defendant and why the authorities request me to appear in court."

"Don't trouble yourself, Peters. Mr. Davis, would you get the General's file?"

Pretty boy Peters throwing us one of his curve balls. No matter to him though how he performs; he thinks he has a permanent place here on the team. He wouldn't be here today if Martha hadn't offered to quit the office and in return I hadn't promised not to retaliate against him for playing with Martha by firing him—ever.

Just one more bad deal I still have to honor with my wife, the Deb Queen. It all started when we were in high school and I responded to her flattery, telling me I not only looked good, as plenty of the other girls had told me, but handsome as a god. How her opinion of me has declined with the shrinking of our bank balances! She'll never dare do any more with Peters than flirt with him, probably to annoy me as much as anything else, but seeing her with him in this office this morning makes me uneasy. Peters, who looks unnaturally young, ten to fifteen years younger than his true age, looking not nearly as old as his gravelly voice sounds. Time to swing at that slider or sinker or curve ball, whatever it is, and send it in a direction that will improve my score in this game.

"Why are you involved in our skirmish with the authorities —is that the question, Don? Because your name's an important one in our organization. Remember that as one of the project engineers for the barge canal project, you signed off on all the compliance report audit sheets that Borak's been scrutinizing."

"Be that as it may, sir, I don't believe they can hold me accountable as a PRP."

"You do understand that as the engineer who happened to sign off on most of the audit sheets, they want to speak with you. No problem. Go take another look at these papers, and you'll see you're hardly alone, that you have plenty of company. You'll see that Resolutions, Inc. and my name appear much more often than yours," I said, grabbing the stack of reports from Davis, dumping them on the conference table, and in the process spilling the cup of coffee he had set on them. Rachael worked quickly to wipe up the mess and contain the damage, which, once again, wasn't entirely my fault. "No, I wouldn't trouble myself too much about what these documents say about us. These reports are really driven by Borak trying to get reappointed as regional environmental commissioner. Or for him to go back to Boston where he belongs and run for dogcatcher. He needs us. If he didn't find us, he'd have to invent another villain. He needs to win over the voters, and what better and safer way to do that than to tar and feather and run me out of town on a rail! To him we're just some dumb country engineers from Gaylord, Maine! These papers don't need to make any sense, because he's just using them to harrass us. They're worth no more than the pulp they're printed on. I can't decipher them, and you certainly don't need to, not so long as we're retaining Chip Thompson, who's a damn good lawyer and a personal friend of mine, to do that for us. He assures me that we're all covered, OK?"

"Covered just like the Americans had the French covered in Dienbienphu, if memory serves," said General Langway with a laugh which no one shared.

Oh, this is dandy, now Langway's mocking me in front of my own forces! He looks the part of the leader, authoritative. Hasn't lost much of his military bearing, works on staying fit. I see him in the park jogging in good weather and bad weather, and in the gym on the machines. But keeping himself fit to take over my command? Never! We go back a long way and he's been loyal to me to a fault. I know he's in my court.

"What exactly do you mean, General?"

"Mr. D'Amour, I think you'd have to agree that the Americans either couldn't or wouldn't help the French who were under siege. . . . The French at Dienbienphu in Vietnam were on a flat-topped mountain, shot up from all sides by the gooks, but the Americans were holding back their air power because they were afraid to become involved. To be fair, the strategic errors rested with the French. They couldn't believe the gooks with just muscle power could jackass all that artillery through the jungle and up the mountain, any more than they could anticipate losing the battle."

More of the General's wartime fables, apparently making the point that I'm not offering them reliable backup. He wouldn't be so quick to correct me, especially in front of the staff, if he cared to remember what I did for him when we first met. That was a dozen years ago, which was three years after he'd taken his retirement from the Air Guard, having climbed the ladder to adjutant general. Coming to me as an unemployed civilian with bills to pay, a fish out of water, until I took him on and retrained him. I don't expect thanks, but do expect a better show of respect.

"I believe we'd rather hear about commitment to our cause, rather than about the remote possibility of losing, General."

"I do have experience in the air flying missions, and on the ground deploying troops. Until you've worn the uniform, sir, you cannot really know how costly it is to lose," Langway said to me, calmly, but angry enough at me for his face to turn red.

He's a hard act to follow, a genuine, decorated military hero, who's played in higher stakes games than I ever knew as a young man. Just the same, I'm not about to retreat. I've still got the hunter instinct, if not in warfare, and no longer in football, then in business—still!

"I'd have to believe, General, you're dying to talk to us about bravery under fire. So before we move on to other business on the agenda, let me ask all of you what's the difference between a coward and a hero?"

"It would help if you defined your terms, Mr. D'Amour," Peters said. "I mean a reasonable person who assesses a danger-ous, life-threatening situation wouldn't necessarily be . . ."

I had originally hired Peters to keep the books, but after his fling with Martha, haven't trusted him near them for many years. Makes me uneasy with his nose in files that don't pertain to him.

"The difference between a hero and a coward—anyone have a clue . . . ? A hero needs to be brave longer. A hero needs to be brave only five minutes longer than a coward. So hang in there. Now does anyone else care to share an opinion with the rest of us?"

"I believe," Rachael said, "If Mr. Borak is reassigned along with his staff or retired, then our troubles are over."

Rachael, the peacemaker office manager, has always been un-comfortable with dissension in her domain, though I'm beginning to suspect she's been forging alliances to secure her own position.

"No, I don't believe it's a top-down thing, that Mr. Borak is following orders from his superiors," the General said.

Everyone knows the General's in charge of operations when I'm not available. The way he always carries himself as a com-mander, some of them must wonder whether, in fact, I've become just a figurehead who answers to him. Wrong!

"I think if he weren't making freelance decisions to attack us," the General continued, "we wouldn't find ourselves in the middle of this snafu, which they're trying to bury along with our bodies."

"That's sounds like a victim thing, and I'm not into that," Yankovich said. "Thanks, but no thanks. I, for one, don't plan to be anybody's scapegoat—"

"*Scapegoat*, yes, Francis, I believe you're a perfect goat" Lewis said. "You can take that as a compliment, because goats are pretty hardy. They feed off vines, roots and thorns. Or, better yet, if you were to come back to us in the next life as an animal, you might revisit us as an excellent grain-fed chicken."

"Are you listening to Lewis harassing me, Mr. D'Amour? In the workplace aren't we all legally entitled to the same respect?" Yankovich asked, then left the room. He came back with the Civil Rights Commission workplace rules and threw it on the table beside the court papers.

"Certainly, Mr. Yankovich, we do things by the book here at Pollution Resolutions—I mean Resolutions, Inc.," I said. "For the record we don't tolerate discrimination based on race, creed, religion, et cetera, et cetera. Rachael, read that thing. And don't forget the sexual orientation part. Read him his workplace rights out loud and put it in the minutes."

"That won't be necessary, sir. I simply meant to point out—"

"Did you hear that, Rachael? Record that he declined for us to read back the rules which we had posted and which he removed from display. Now with your permission, Mr. Yankovich, we have some business to discuss."

"If you ask me, Mr. D," Yankovich said, "aren't we all about looking at the problem without solving it? My mother taught me that compromise is all about dividing up a birthday cake so that each one thinks she's getting the biggest piece. I have a friend who works as a mediator. Instead of blaming someone and pointing fingers, I thought mediation—" Yankovich said.

I wish I could figure out what Yankovich's gripe really is. He's an artist more than a draftsmen. If I could simply write him a loan check to send him to art school, with a binding agreement that he would never return, so I'd never have to hear his increasing complaints, I'd do it. But I believe he enjoys it at Resolutions too much playing the fey gadfly, that with his poor attitude he'd have a problem holding a job anywhere else.

"Do I understand correctly that you're suggesting an arbitrator?" I asked.

"Sometimes a third party can find a compromise. The difference between an arbitrator and a mediator—"

"Never mind, either way—no way." I said.

Now this twit's not only calling me *Mr. D* in front of the others, but he's telling me how to run my business. I'd do anything to get him out of my life! I'd like to ignore him, but I can't allow his nonsense to go unanswered in front of the others.

". . . If Borak and the EPA really wanted to end this fairly, I'd negotiate," I continued. "But they're not interested in talking— they really want to gobble us up. And if we prove too big for them to swallow, they at least want to eat our lunch. That's what their trumped-up Medford Pond case is about—an attempt to destroy us! Did your mother also tell you discretion's the better part of valor? Mine did, and that's why we're going to continue to keep our distance and certainly won't be reaching out to pet these monsters. They have power, and they have the appetite to grab a lot more, and this mediation, or whatever you care to call what your friend does to earn a wage, would play right into their hands. So do you understand now why I don't want to hear any more about it?"

"Bravo, sir, bravo!" the General applauded. "We'll give them hell!"

The General's saluting me. I'll count him solidly on my side. But that damn Yankovich still doesn't get it. He's shaking his head no, just to be obstinate. A burr under my saddle, but I'm going to ignore him for the time being.

From the far end of the table, opposite me, Davis stood up to speak: "I haven't been here very long, so I'm not up to speed on these legal questions, which I don't believe are any of my business anyway. But with your permission, Mr. D'Amour, I would like to make a suggestion." I gave him a nod of approval. "It would seem to me that we're taking valuable time from this meeting, which should best concern itself with day-to-day operations and making ourselves a better, more profitable organization. If we have legal questions—now correct me if I'm out of line, sir—couldn't we be writing those questions down on paper for you to review and answer at your discretion? Or, perhaps, after gathering enough of these questions, if you see fit, you might consider bringing in Mr. Charles Thompson, our attorney, to respond to those questions that he feels are appropriate for him to answer."

"Excellent idea," I said. "But in the meantime, before we get Chip Thompson here, write me a memo, or leave a voice message, or send me an e-mail."

"If you're not here or there, then how could we find you, Mr. D?" Yankovich asked. "Would you intend to become a virtual boss?"

Ignore Yankovich. Focus instead on the brightest hope of this bunch, Davis. He seems very attentive, may have potential. The General did well to recruit this young man from the Guard. As long as he remains a temp, we don't have to pay him benefits. So far he seems grateful for the job and hasn't been complaining about anything. Hope Yankovich's and Lewis's bad habits don't rub off on him. At least this young man appears to be in my corner.

Probably because Peters attitude is positive and he looks good, he doesn't win any popularity contests in the office. If looks could kill, Peters would have been struck down dead, just because he made a well-meant, though impractical suggestion. With the exception of my top man the General, and maybe Rachael, they're probably jealous of him because they're worried he's got more talent. Good, at least I've shaken them up enough this morning to get their attention. Now let's send this motley crew off with an inspirational bedtime fable:

"You know, it's not easy to run a business. It can be a lonely and thankless job. That's why I like to spend some time at my camp to unwind. I won't tell you on which lake I built it, because, no offense, I never want any of you good people to find me up there. Well, that's where I was headed last weekend. My wife and I were cruising down the road, enjoying the scenery, when this chicken runs down the shoulder, and passes my car like I'm standing still. Its legs were pretty much a blur, but I knew I was seeing three of them! My car rides pretty smooth at any speed. Martha was busy doing a crossword puzzle, so she wasn't noticing anything out of the ordinary, not until we were flying down the road at eighty or ninety miles an hour on the straightaways, trying to catch this chicken running on all threes. She began to scream, then threatened to hit me or jump out. It didn't matter to me what she wanted—I kept going in a kind of trance, witnessing a miracle of God or the devil.

"So this three-legged chicken I was following, she turns the corner off the road and then into a farmer's yard. I was still trying for all my car's worth to follow her. Why? Because I was awful curious to know whether I was getting bested by a young pullet or by an old hen. But I couldn't see this three-legged bird, not with the cloud of dust she was stirring up in front of me. As I was driving blind into the cloud of dust, I drove off the road altogether and took out this farmer's mailbox in the bargain."

"But if the dirt road had no other houses on it," Yankovich said with a mischievious smile, "and belonged to just the farmer, wouldn't they have placed the mailbox at the head of the road by the state highway, instead of where you said you struck it?"

"Very clever, very logical . . . At any rate, the farmer was watching me from his porch, rocking in his chair, smoking his pipe. *You saw a chicken come running down the road five times as fast as a race horse?* I asked him."

"*Ayup,* he said.

"A chicken with an extra leg? I've never seen one before with three legs.

"Nope, I reckon you didn't.

"And I never saw one that could outrun a car. Who's he belong to?

"Me. Ain't she something? She belong to me. I bred her special with three legs.

"Three legs? Why three legs?

"Well, first off, there's the wife—she won't eat nothing with scales on it. And then there's junior—he won't eat a creature he knows by name and travels on hooves. Plus there's me. The only thing we agree to feed on at the same time's chicken. Fact is, we don't like nothing better for Sunday supper than a stuffed roast chicken, swimming in gravy and maybe some dumplings and cranberry sauce on the side. Trouble is, we each want our own drumstick. So that's how come I bred me a chicken with three drumsticks.

"So how does a three-legged chicken taste, any different?

"I don't know. I can't rightly say, 'cause I ain't never caught her ..."

End of the story, and they don't even realize it, the dead heads! Finally, the General's laughing and poking Davis, both smiling now. At least I reached the two of them. The others, meanwhile, are looking at each other for cues on how to respond to my tale. They're looking at me strangely again, embarrassed, as if I've lost my mind. Maybe someday, if I don't get rid of them first, I'll make them think for themselves. Now there's a funny noise coming out of Lewis, low and rumbling like gas—no, a laugh, while the others are still sitting there dumb as posts.

"What's the point, sir?" Yankovich finally asked.

"What would I do without you trying to keep me on track? Why have I shared with you my life-changing encounter with that superhen? Because she frustrated me. I got a glimpse of her, and she was gone. She made me feel mighty foolish, like I was seeing a mirage. Tell me, don't you see how here at Resolutions we're all bothered about a strange bird who doesn't really have anything to do with us?"

"A red herring, sir," the General finally responded, "like when we send out junk information to throw off the enemy's decoders, or if we're in the air, like when we're jamming the enemy's radar so they don't knock us out of the sky before we've had a chance to drop our ordnance."

"Yes, General, precisely," I agreed. "Goats, three-legged chickens, Borak, pick your beast, the point being that we keep our attention on what's running beside us, in front of us, and running circles around us, animal or human game. In the process of running away from us they can blind us with their trail of dust. Then we give them chase, trying to keep up with these critters, and if we don't watch where we should be going, then we're bound to crash and hurt ourselves. In other words, we can't be certain of who or what we're seeing.

"Let's close out our session with this thought, cowboys: *Shoot lower, sheriff! They must be riding shetlands!* So if there's nothing else . . ."

"Excuse me, Mr. D, but I need to speak with you about this crash thing," Yankovich said to me before I could leave. I took him into another room and closed the door. ". . . Can't afford a fatal crash, and bottom line neither can the Yankovich family."

I thought we covered all the important business at the staff meeting, yet he insists on speaking with me some more. He talks too much, which is probably why I know as much as I do about him, about his background more than what motivates him now. The Yankovich family, third-generation Russians, he once told me when we trusted one another. He had a grandfather who survived a slave labor camp in Siberia, and came to this country hopeful for his future in this country. After his persecution his grandfather justifiably bitter, a state of mind which evidently Francis chooses to revive, though he has no czar and no gulag labor camp to protest, nothing but his own private demons troubling him. Too much politics of entitlement in his brain, too quick to play the victim. If only I could have forseen ten years ago before we first let him though my doors to draft the intricate plans it would take the others twice as long to complete! The dissention he's been causing! He's not only unpleasant company now, but a liability, and I don't know how I can rid myself of him.

"I assume you're still concerned about the EPA witch hunt against us, Francis. Let me worry about that. We're traveling together in the same boat, after all. So let's concentrate on getting our bearings, laying out our course, and heading in the right direction, OK?"

"I'm more worried in the short run about how we'll be able to handle the work load you've dumped on us."

"I don't think you're up to the impossible. I'm not asking you to attempt more than you're capable of doing."

"I mean if we get all those contracts the General and you are bidding for, we don't have enough manpower to do the work, not with those of us left."

"No problem. Keep in mind since we've tightened up, we've paid you out a lot of overtime in the form of extra benefits, even though you're on salary. Look at it this way: a big project or two or three could prove to be a cash cow for anyone in this organization who's ambitious. From adversity springs prosperity."

"But still, if we don't have enough qualified engineers—"

"Then we'll recruit us some fresh ones! Think of our projects as building pyramids: they were going to get built, no matter who was on hand to build them."

"Sounds like slave labor to me," Yankovich said. "And, besides, I wouldn't want to spread myself too thin. When I do a job, I need to focus."

There's no way to get him to back off, and stonewalling doesn't work with him either. This guy's impossible to ignore. I have enough problems to deal with besides answering his dumb questions and reassuring him.

"Not to worry. I'll be working right beside you, shoulder-to-shoulder. Butthole . . ."

He's scowling at me. Must think I'm insulting him, too bad. Pitiful excuses for his laziness. He can leave us anytime he wants, but he must know not many employers would babysit him like I do. And now to qualify my words before smoke comes out of his ears. "Working with you . . . butthole . . . to elbow."

"Mr. D'Amour, I don't like being called that."

"What?"

"You know," Yankovich persisted.

"I don't. I do know I can't speak with you right now." I said. "But, remember, if you have any more concerns, talk to me first so I can straighten you out."

"And I don't like being treated as a child."

"Oh, sorry if I've been doing that. I must have had your parents in my mind, trying to guess what it would be like to reason with them and you at the same time. Imagine, three Yankovichs together in one room!"

Chapter 2
Resolutions, Inc.

S ix A.M., just a few hours of restless sleep in my absent daughter Erica's bedroom. Lately I don't feel welcome in the master bedroom with Martha. To tease me she leaves her door open, so I can see her by the night light as I pass. As I'm looking at her from across the threshold, I can still appreciate her good looks, her best asset, bathed in soft light, glowing pink from the pink curtains and the floral pink wallpaper, an ornate boudoir of her own design. If I could get a bit closer, she'd probably smell as sweet as Cleopatra, with her perfume, bath oil, and moisturizer. If we were new lovers and I were there beside her, I'd press against her, slide within her, and she'd certainly welcome me to make love to her, no matter how deep into her dreams. In my bed where I belong, if only she hadn't such long memories for every disagreement we've ever had, usually about money. The money I once had, the money I've tried to make back, and now additional borrowed money I'm not repaying. But no need to play her game, continuing to make love to an indifferent wife who dwells on past frustrations. Or maybe I have it all wrong, and she hasn't really left her door open to tease me, to lure me back with her pink light. Perhaps she just prefers a little bit of light so she doesn't feel alone, keeping her night light burning like a child would.

Fear of loneliness, fear of the dark, fear of tripping and falling. Could be she's more reasonable and practical than I've been giving her credit for, using a night light so she won't stumble into furniture again like she did five years ago when she broke her toe. I know how lightly she sleeps, so I'm not about to disturb her and then have to listen to complaints about how I've awakened her. That's why I'm going to leave Martha be and let her dream on, undisturbed and alone the rest of the night.

If I were sleeping in Ryan's room I'd have to respect his privacy and not look at the pinups he hides under his mattress. But I'm not there because I wouldn't want to take the chance of losing my temper with him if I were to catch him rolling in before dawn after one of his nights on the town with Blue Littlehale. A drug dealer and thief, a common criminal, Ryan's somehow been hypnotized by that lowlife, and one way or the other, I'm going to break the spell!

So that's why I'm in Erica's little girl's bedroom, trying to forget about my wife in the next bedroom and my son who's probably running the roads with Blue's gang. Erica, who's now a grown woman and doesn't see us more than once a month. She hasn't slept under this roof since she first met Derek, now her husband. Strange that she sees us so little, yet insisted on getting her mother to help her redecorate this bedroom of hers back to the way it was when she was ten years old, crowded with dolls and stuffed animals. Why, to recall her long-vanished childhood?

Martha could be alongside me right now in our little girl's room, for all the images of her that are passing before me. Tonight I'm remembering some good times we had together, like when I first knew her twenty years ago just after I rebuilt the Indian motorcycle. Her hanging onto my waist, shrieking at first as I'd speed into the deep turns, then after that laughing and loving our fast rides outside Gaylord. Thrashing my powerful machine over the back roads, making good on my pledge to her we'd keep the Indian away from the paved main roads, the ones which Dr. Aldrich, her father, traveled in his new Cadillacs. A man who stopped making housecalls, who traveled for thirty years between home and the hospital. A predictable main road circuit, leaving us to run the less traveled dirt and gravel roads, the woods beside them, perfect for picnics when we were hungry, as well as lovemaking. Except for the weekends she'd spend at her family's Boothbay Harbor house on the sea, where she'd grown up riding in yachts with her wealthy friends.

My motorcycle had to go to pay for college. And too bad midway through college football had to go, due to injuries. Now at this stage of the game I may have to give up my wife. But no need right now to think of what I've already lost and what else may be slipping from my grip. Now that I'm out of bed and dressed, I'm careful not to wake up Martha on my way to my basketball court. A good place for me to go times like these when I want to put business and personal betrayals out of my mind, a wonderful place for forgetting. Basketball, a young man's game, and like football, a team effort. But not the way I play it here on my court, solo, running, jumping and shooting by myself to keep myself intact. Once I learn the moves in any game, no one can ever take them away, whether or not my body can do what my mind asks of it. A football athlete, pro material, now two decades slower than my college prime. A natural athlete, good enough even in basketball to run with most any of the guys in pickup matches at the Y or at the health club. But I don't have anything to prove anymore. So instead of playing sloppy mismatches with whoever might want to challenge me, I play here against myself, running, jumping and shooting, no more playing to the stands for score points.

Hard to believe though, as fast as the money's hemorrhaging lately, that this three-eighths basketball court made perfect sense at the time I built it. That was when I was flush with cash to build the Deb Queen the dream house I believed she deserved. And along with it, a court where Ryan and I could play together, not just a hoop in an asphalt driveway, but a special place where we could play all year long, allowing us to shoot baskets out of the weather and on a hardwood floor with some spring under our feet, rather than on concrete. But now that the kid's gone, looking for trouble and doing a good job of finding it, that leaves me alone in this mini-gymnasium, the part of my wife's dream house I've reserved for myself.

I miss some baskets. Sink one. Run myself across this baby-sized court to the other basket, shooting until I sink one. Back over to where I started. Run. Shoot. Retrieve. Run. Shoot. Retrieve. No penalty zones in my solo games because I make the rules as I please, the rules this morning being to dump as many balls in the basket as I can. Playing against myself, the greatest challenge I'll ever confront. Take out ten minutes every half hour.

Sunrise coming through the windows. What better do I have to do with today than shoot baskets? An endurance test, seeing how long and how hard I can keep going. Planned on being alone, but I'm not. Thought this was a one-man show today, but now I see a challenger, Chip Thompson, my lawyer, a man who customarily rises early enough to match his huge ambition. I'm glad he's on my side in the Medford Pond war, not my interrogator.

"Good morning, counselor. Weren't we scheduled for this afternoon at two? This is a little bit early, even for you. Did you come out to play with the big boys?" I asked.

As long as he's here, fire the ball at him. He doesn't expect it, and I catch him in the stomach, knocking the wind out of him.

"Better take off that suit jacket so you don't muss it up, if you want to go a few rounds with me and don't wan't to get any bloodstains on it."

"This isn't supposed to be a contact sport. I know you took a few blows to the head, Ned, but I can't afford an injury if you're going to play dirty."

"We'll take turns, shooting, starting with you, Chip. Go ahead."

The harder he tries, the further from the basket he's throwing them. He takes a dozen bad shots, getting more aggravated with each miss, not used to failing. He's walking away, ready to give up already.

"I've got to be back to the office by eight," Chip said.

"You're aiming too high. Loosen up. If you don't throw it so hard against the backboard, it won't come back at you over the rim."

Move him back to the foul line. Show him how to shoot. Much better, now that he's trying it my way. Now he's putting it through the hoop every third time.

"A little change makes a big difference. I can hardly believe it," Chip said.

"That's because you've been trained to doubt," I said. "If I didn't know you were such a skeptic, then I'd feel a lot more insulted by that crack you made about the lumps I've taken on the head. With all due respect, skeptics like you exhaust themselves so much with unproductive questions that they have no energy left to even begin working on solutions."

"Ned, my logical approach has kept you afloat in the deepest and most treacherous waters, so to speak. And if you identify me as a skeptic because I don't immediately implement your suggestions, then keep in mind that tennis, not basketball, is my game. In that game I bet I can run circles around you. If you care to challenge me to a few matches, then let's set a time."

Much more pleasant now that we're taking turns shooting, him sinking one every now and then. But he's losing interest, looking at his watch and stopping, raining on our parade, obviously wanting to do something different. I'll have to invite him into the house to see why he's really here.

"I've never been able to understand, unless temporary insanity —why on earth you risked it all to chase that one Medford Pond contract with the Feds. Didn't you know that once you contract with them, in effect they own you, lock, stock, and barrel?" Chip asked.

"Did you come here today to give me that advice for free? Or is the meter running right now?"

"How would that matter to you, inasmuch as you don't have change for the meter?"

He makes me so angry I slam down my orange juice, spilling it on the stone counter top, then drip it onto my shoes.

"If you're implying that my credit isn't good—"

"Ned, what I'd like to do and what I can do are two different things. My accountant tells me we need to clean up our books, that we should write up our losses for last year. On one hand he won't allow me to carry an open balance for Resolutions, Inc. On the other hand, I'm not willing to write off Ned D'Amour because I have too much respect for you."

"Yes, your associate Denise Pendergast did mention my account balance."

"You know, she's quite a competitor at racquetball, but she can't find women that can challenge her. Maybe that's another match you'd enjoy playing, Ned."

"What do you mean?"

"Nothing more than figure out what your best game is and stick to it. Racquetball's really your game, as tennis is mine."

Now I know he's here this morning to dun me! Then let him line up behind my other creditors! I wouldn't be surprised if he's running his meter to charge me more billable hours as we're speaking, judging by the way he keeps talking and looking at his watch.

"I hope I'm not keeping you from something important."

"Actually, I am in a time crunch. Since we're not going to have sufficient time to resolve a repayment plan for the debt you've undertaken—"

"Then don't let me keep from a more important account, if there's a more profitable client you could be seeing instead of me."

"Fine! If you think that alone, with neither Denise's nor my help, you'll be able to handle a fresh legal matter to which you, the defendant, will need to respond personally this morning, I can leave right now."

Chip's acting on his own suggestion by walking out on me and back to his car. I'm following. Must be careful not to get rid of him too soon. I may still need him. Must be polite to him.

"Nice metallic paint. It sparkles in the sunlight," I finally said to Chip through his car window. "Aren't these big Beemer seven-series good for about a hundred-sixty, or is that the Benz six-series?"

"I wouldn't want to attract the attention of the authorities by any such stunt."

"Of course you wouldn't, not in your line of work. But I mean with twelve cylinders under the hood, the beast must run!"

"Not this particular model. With that bigger engine they run about ten thousand dollars more, a bit out of my reach," Chip said.

"And I'll bet this rig's all paid for, knowing how good you are in handling your accounts."

Chip has burst to his feet, flinging the car door open hard enough to slam it into my arm.

"Coming from you, my friend, I'll choose to take that as a compliment."

"Of course. Don't you think I appreciate your work for me?" I then pulled Chip's plaid suspenders with my thumbs and released them with a snap. "Very snazzy for a trial lawyer. Will you be wearing a jacket to cover these up while you're in the courtroom?"

"Does that concern you, Ned? Afraid these suspenders might cost me your case? If I do decide to wear them to trial, will you promise to fire me, please?"

I can't gain anything by showing him how much he's annoying me. Could be worse: he could start charging me interest on top of his billable hours. I didn't think Martha was up and about, but she's once again inserted herself into my business. She's in a trickster mood, sneaking up behind Chip and quickly putting her hands over his eyes. How playful she can be with almost anyone but me!

"Guess who!" Martha whispered in a guttural voice.

"Who else could the lady be but your wife, Ned?" He then slipped underneath her arms. "Wonderful. Now I have an admissible sample of your fingerprints, Martha," he said holding up his smudged eyeglasses.

"Never mind about that. Use your imagination if the view's blurry. Can you see something pleasing through them?" she asked and stood before him.

"Just Martha Aldrich D'Amour in front of her house."

"What else? We go back further than here and now. When you look at me what do you really see?"

"I wouldn't want to embarrass you."

"Try me."

"The Martha I remember? OK, here goes," he said, squinting and walking around her. "High school graduation weekend, I see you diving from the rocks of the gorge, swimming underwater, then resurfacing, diving, and swimming deep again and again because Ned and I and some of the other boys are watching you."

"You were only curious to see whether I'd come back to the surface," Martha said.

"Not exactly. You knew full well you'd gotten the attention of quite a few of us, and we were more than curious. You moving in the clear blue water, a sliver of pure white flesh, disappearing and reappearing. Then you sunned yourself on the rocks," Chip said with a wide grin. "That was before you two were a number, Ned."

"Then what?" she asked.

"Then I jumped in, but you were a little too elusive and wouldn't let me catch you. Eventually you got her though, Ned."

"Don't worry about me," she said with her charming smile. "I've never been anyone's property."

"Well, let me tell you what I don't see: from your shoulders down not much different than when you were eighteen and swimming like a mermaid. You're a fortunate man, Ned."

She's turning red, enjoying the attention. She can kill two birds with one stone, encouraging him to keep flattering her, while at the same time annoying me.

"You're too kind, Chip. What else do you see through your dirty glasses?"

"Your unique home."

"Then you're impressed?" she asked.

"And a bit perplexed. I can't tell whether the builder tried to figure this out as he went along, or whether he was working from an architect's plans."

"Perplexed?"

"Yes, because most people would not have chosen to build an expensive custom-built house at this location. Not here on the bedrock of a mountain."

"Oh, I agree. If I had my way, we'd be living at a lower elevation. I get terribly cold in the winter. The winds slice through me up here. Did Ned ever tell you this was once a quarry that belonged to one of our business accounts? And it will storm up here while it's pleasant down below," she said with her palm upward to test for raindrops.

"I'm sure Chip doesn't care about any of that," I said.

"When this client of Ned's got himself into money trouble," she continued, "we were there with cash to help him out from under this property. We really thought we got a great deal, considering the view, but before we could start construction, we had to blast a big hole in the mountain, and still we couldn't put in a basement. So when all's said and done—"

"Martha, excuse me, but I believe you've told Chip all that at last year's Christmas party," I said.

"Well, if I have been embarrassing Ned and boring you, Chip, by repeating myself, then I won't take any more of your time. It's been a pleasure," she said, extending her hand to him.

"*Au contraire.* Always a pleasure, never boring listening to you, Martha."

"Well, then you shouldn't act like such a stranger, coming by only on business," Martha said.

"I wish I didn't have to work 80 hours a week. I wish I had more time to socialize with good friends like you, but I had to make the time in my schedule to talk to you because—"

"Any other reasons for staying away so long, aside from too much business on your plate?" she asked.

"Well, to tell you the truth, you folks never invited my wife Jane, nor Jane and myself, since your last Christmas party."

"If we've hurt your feelings we do apologize," she said.

Why is she looking so sternly at me? We haven't been socializing with anyone lately, not since the newspapers have made me so famous. I hate those smart remarks and questions they have for me at parties. I don't know who's side she's on, besides her own, but she certainly isn't on mine. And I can't believe she's complaining to him about this palace I built for the queen herself.

"Oh, dear, I do believe it's raining," she said, removing her sunglasses and wiping them on her silk scarf. "Well, in case your mama never taught you to come in out of the weather you might want to get in your car, or else follow me."

Very inviting, even charming, but only when the mood strikes her. From her mouth I haven't heard such friendly words for me lately, not that I need to pay much attention to her moods any more. But look how well this professional skeptic's following her lead, trailing her to the house like a chick following his mother hen.

She took Chip by the arm, led him to the kitchen table, where she poured him and herself coffee and left me to pour my own. "Without your help I truly don't know where Ned would be."

"Well, you're not out of the woods yet," Chip said, waving his hand, which she caught in her own to get his attention, and then slowly released it.

"I certainly enjoy visiting with you. But since in no way does Ned's legal strategy affect me personally, should you really be speaking to me about his problems? Of course, if Ned had the good sense to keep me on as his office manager, rather than Rachael, he would never have gotten himself into this quagmire."

Provocative, throwing me her bait, but I'm not about to jump for it. And treacherous, turning on Rachael who just spilled her heart out to her about her domestic problems! As rude as she's acted, I'm not about to lose my temper, especially in front of someone else, nor hand her another little victory at my expense.

"Are you done, Martha?" I asked.

"But ever since Ned's kept me off the payroll and out of the office," Martha continued, "I make it my business to stay out of things over which I have no control. While I'm sure Ned tells me no more about Mr. Borak and the other watchdogs he's managed to antagonize."

"Dogs. You got that half right anyway," I added.

Dogs? I could warn him about her bite, but Chip himself could prove even more dangerous to someone who gets on his bad side.

"Unlike my husband, I make it a point not to call or name names, especially when that person isn't on hand to defend him or herself."

We were in the family room, and she sat Chip beside her on the leather couch. "I get the very best view from here," Martha said, adjusting the cushions behind her. "Look," she said, and took his head in her hands and gently turned it in the right direction, trying to duplicate her own perspective for him. "From here I can see the world. I can see in advance anyone coming to my front door, then further a half mile down the drive, and on a clear day ten miles in each direction up and down the valley."

"Although you did say it's too cold so high up on the mountain, I think, on balance, you like to look down on the world from your dream house here." Chip said, then turned his attention from the outside to the floor. "At the Christmas party Jane noticed this pale red ceramic tile. We're redoing our kitchen and she made me promise to find out where we can get it."

"Actually this is natural quarry tile."

"That's just what I told Jane, not baked tile, but real stone, of course. And you probably removed it from this old quarry."

"We couldn't find the right hue anywhere but offshore. This is so much subtler than any shade we could find domestically. We were working with a wonderful supplier somewhere in Italy—Mefli or Terni, or maybe Chieti or Rimini. Can't you remember, Ned?" she asked me earnestly.

I'm not able to help her, so she leaves, then returns with a piece of her monogrammed note paper, writing out the number of the tile distributor in her favorite gold writing instrument. Blotting the ink to dry it off, she places it in her matching lavender envelope, licks it shut, and slides it into Chip's planner, the full VIP treatment.

"Is it cold in the winter walking on a stone floor?" Chip asked.

"In the winter it's so toasty I love to walk barefoot on it. I insisted that we have special radiant heat built underneath it, the kind I had growing up."

As I remember at the party Chip wasn't focused on anything but collecting business cards, trolling through my guests, my own clients and friends, to land them as his own accounts. If I could only find a way to charge him for the goodwill of my client list, then get him to account for it and deduct his benefit from my bill he keeps building up! I also remember how busy his cute wife Jane made herself, circulating with the best-looking men and encouraging them to refill her wine glass. If he doesn't pay closer attention to his wife, someone else probably will. And this guy's giving me advice on how he thinks I should live my life!

"I love the way this warm stone plays against the cherry cabinets," Chip continued.

"Really they're teak, nearly impossible to import. Overseas if they catch you cutting down a teak tree, they cut off your ears, or your fingers or some other extremity. Rather draconian, kind of an eye-for-an-eye thing. Ned and I sought out this teak because we thought ordinary oak cabinets would spoil the look we were try-ing to achieve."

I got up and drew back the curtains of a half-dozen windows. "From here we can see in almost all directions," I said, "and almost forget about most of what's going on down below there."

"Well, if nothing else, you've bought yourself a view, and a lovely sweep of the horizon, a very big investment, or a liability, depending on how you analyze it."

"Chip, I don't understand," she said, "you just told me you'd love to live here yourself, and now you say my home's a liability. I know my husband's paying you well for your advice, but why don't you tell me what you don't like about what you see?"

"Not at all, Martha, I love what I see here . . ."

I must be careful of a man like him who knows the price of everything and the value of nothing, even if he's my advisor. And I won't attempt to figure out whether Martha likes or hates this home I built for her, because it's too late to concern me anymore.

"Martha, I hesitated to come here this morning to talk to you two about a personal matter, namely Ryan, which perhaps can wait until this afternoon's scheduled time, Ned."

She's walking right up to Chip and doing her stare-him-in-the-face routine. She thinks she can psych out everybody at will, yet keep all her secrets behind a pretty face. But, regardless, I can tell most of the time what's going through her mind. I can see by looking at her she's really scared about what Chip might have to tell us.

"Ryan, he has such high spirits! I wish I could stay to fill you in, but we're entertaining this evening, and I need to run out to the store and buy a roast," she said, car keys in hand.

In a flash I snatched them away. "If you need to speak with both of us, she's not going too far now," I said to Chip.

She lunges at me to retrieve her keys. I swap them to my other hand before she can get to them. She's retaliating by stepping on my foot with her pointed heel, damn it! Shooting pain! Clench my teeth, won't show her my pain!

"Ned's certainly not a gentleman!" she shouted, and ran away from me, leaving us both alone in the family room.

"With Martha you got yourself one fast-running filly," Chip said once she was out of earshot. "You must have fun keeping her pace."

"Fun? To tell you the truth, we've had our challenges in this house the last couple of years."

"With Ryan especially, I would think," Chip agreed.

"What do you know about him anyway? I don't believe I've spoken with you about him."

"No you haven't lately, but in my line of work I need to read the police blotter column in the paper to keep track of my current clients, as well as the bad guys who may come to me to represent them. And it seems that over the last couple of years I've seen Ryan's name half a dozen times. Does he enjoy getting caught, or does he just do it for the attention?"

"Maybe you shouldn't believe everything you read."

"I'm not suggesting you're responsible for his felonies and misdemeanors, though obviously the boy does need someone's attention as we speak. Now if you'd care to give me a chronology of his prior arrests."

"No, I'd rather not, because, as I told you, he's none of your concern!"

"Oh, really? Don't you realize that our firm has been dealing with the Aldrich family before either of us was born!" Chip shouted.

"So do you believe that gives you a proprietary interest in me, in my son, or in the D'Amour family as well?"

"You bonehead, if you won't take my advice, that's your stupidity, but Ryan can't afford—"

"Let me worry about my son, OK?"

I must be careful not to show Chip how much he's bothering me, intruding in my family life.

"Well, we don't need to deal with your son for the moment. I'm not here to worry you, but to get your personal and business affairs on track."

He was born with a silver spoon in his mouth and walked into his daddy's law practice, while I've had to build my business from the ground up. He just knows how to sue and defend against lawsuits, nothing about running a business other than his law office. But I must be careful not to underestimate him. Maybe I can't afford him anymore, but I can less afford to ignore him.

"Really? Aside from the Borak problem, which you're going to solve, my business is doing fine, thank you."

"Ned, I respect you too much not to tell you what I've observed."

"I'm all ears."

"It would seem that if you were minding the store more closely, you would be able to manage your employees better."

"Now let me guess: on one of your scouting missions to my office, you crossed paths with Yankovich. Am I right?"

"Not exactly."

"And then I'll bet you let him buttonhole you and recite to you a new installment of his sad story."

"In essence, though not in fact," Chip said.

"Now he's griping to you, an outsider! He must be leaking company secrets, not only to you but to who else?"

"In your sort of business, Ned, you have tricks of the trade, not proprietary company secrets. Since you have nothing to steal, I wouldn't be worrying about—"

"That's easy for you to say, but I refuse to tolerate spies! I'm going to boot him out!"

"On what grounds?" Chip asked.

"Poor performance. That's enough."

"I'm afraid not. You're already fighting battles on two fronts, personal and business, and you don't need a third. He'd make too appealing a victim. "

"On what grounds? How about incompetence!"

"Not a good enough reason, I'm afraid."

"Who's side am I paying you to take anyway? I can fire them as I please!"

"Then have I reason to believe you've terminated at least one employee without cause?"

"Hey, I'm not on trial!"

He's not listening to me, but playing one of Ryan's discs in the stereo. He's moving to the music, doing a twenty-year-old dance to new music, sliding his soft loafers over the stone floors at half-tempo, then full tempo. His hair was very light when he was a kid. With a towhead's very fair complexion looked like a choirboy, an innocent look some of the girls liked, the ones who wanted to mother their boyfriend. Hard to tell now whether it's sun-bleached, or whether it's turned white. And if I hadn't grown up with him, not sure whether he'd appear to me today more as a young man or an old man.

"*Hip-hop,* is that what they call this sort of music?" Chip asked. "I refuse to let my daughter listen to this sort of thing in the house, which may be why she goes to the clubs. And to find dancing partners and other partners, as well.

"Ned, you could have saved yourself a whole lot of trouble and money if you'd been following my advice instead of your whims."

"For instance?"

"Like two years ago after Borak first smelled blood and started the action against you and despite my advice to the contrary, you metamorphosed from *Pollution Resolutions* to *Resolutions, Inc.*"

"Seems to me as long as it's my company I can name it any damn thing I want!"

"You still don't get it, Ned. Let me explain it to you once more. By appearances you were reregistering yourself in order to somehow avoid answering to the charges outstanding against you."

"What's in a name? You were born *Chester*, but now you go by *Chip*. Same case with *Pollution Resolutions*. *Resolution, Inc.* or *Pollution Resolutions*—who cares? Why should I be stuck with a bad name? It seemed to be giving potential clients the wrong idea that we were in the sewage processing business. And with all that bad publicity Borak was throwing at us, I didn't think a new name could hurt. I was simply trying to win over the new customers I had to find if we were going to stay afloat, Chester."

"You realize that no one except you has ever called me by that name, not even my mother."

"Not quite true! I remember that Felice Harrington, the one whose father owned the truck company in Lewiston, she called you Chester all the time, and back then when you didn't take yourself so seriously, you didn't mind it a bit. Now lighten up on your old friend, Chip. Is that name more pleasing to your ears? I understand how you born-to-the-manor attorneys think, even though a guy like me was born to bang together two-by-sixes and pour concrete. Maybe you're too good to work for me, except on your own conditions."

The fair-haired boy's face is red, and, as usual, he reveals his anger. He'll need to do a better job keeping a lid on his true feelings when the time comes for him to represent me in court, provided that I can't shake the EPA loose myself before then. But regardless of how poorly he may respond, I'm going to continue calling it like I see it.

"Getting back to our account," I said, "let me make you this offer so that we can get ourselves back to zero, provided you fail to win your legal fees back from the EPA for their false charges."

"It will take a very convincing argument, Ned, to get you off with less than a six-figure fine; a minor miracle to win a dismissal. If you think I can accomplish a major miracle, to get a government agency to compensate you for wrongful investigation, you're deluding yourself."

"Hey, don't worry, pal, I never ask for something for nothing. I've come up carrying bricks and mortar since I was twelve years old and only know about working for everything I have. All I'm suggesting is we trade horses instead of dollars."

"If you're talking about bartering your Pollution Resolution services, if my septic works were to fail I certainly wouldn't call anyone but you. But I don't need that work, nor can I think of anything else you could do for me."

Not much of a vote of confidence from my own lawyer. Regarding me as no more than the guy who cleans up other people's crap! Look at that sheepish grin! After all the years we've known each other, he should know that I don't pump septic tanks!

"Let me ask you this: wouldn't you like to be a better father?" I asked.

"Based on your phenomenal success with your own kids, what are you suggesting?"

"Ducks or goldfish. Kids love them. Especially if they can swim with them."

"You think I should take them to a petting zoo or buy them an aquarium?"

"Not quite, Chip. But I am suggesting that with my equipment I could dig them a good sized pond in that marsh behind your house."

"I'm afraid that wouldn't make good use of my resources."

"A practical man! Then stock it with trout and eat them three nights a week!"

"And I'm not sure you're qualifed to engineer such a project, Ned."

"How so?"

"I'd never let them swim in bog. Polio lives in stagnant water."

"A cautious man! OK, so I won't build you a pond that would be the envy of your neighbors, not if you don't trust me any more than the Feds do! So why don't we figure out a plan B? Like what about the five-car garage you're planning to build, now that you added this Beemer to the fleet?"

"Four-car."

"Then the fifth stall I'd guess you're using for storage of your golfclubs and the kids' bikes and where your bride can pot her plants."

"I never showed you the plans, Ned, and we haven't even broken ground yet, so how did you know about it?"

"A suspicious man! Just like you read the court reports, I read the building permits."

"I'm afraid not."

"A reluctant man! Not ready yet to make a fair deal? How would we call it if we were on equal footing, not lawyer-to-client, but lawyer-to-lawyer: *quid pro quo*? OK then, how about a Plan C? I know we can work together to reconcile the amount due to zero."

"Fine, so long as you're not asking me to be your banker any more."

"No problem. I'll give you your fair share and then some. You can take that to the bank."

"Not where I bank, not if you aren't willing to make me a better offer than the last ones, Ned. Like my banker, I prefer to deal in good funds, not promissory notes."

"My word is my bond. You didn't like my offer of quid pro quo in the form of my personal services, so what the hell do you want from me?"

"Cash would be best. A good check for $76,000."

Maybe he's not as flush as he appears. In another month he could need the cash to make tuition payments for his two children at Redfield Academy and one at Bowdoin College. No, I don't owe him cash money, any more than I owe Ryan anything.

"Speaking of Ryan, Ned . . ."

"No, let's forget about my son for a while! Let's get back to my proposal, my very best and final offer. Once again, and probably for the last time today, I'm offering you a piece of the company in the form of shares."

"I've already told you I can't get too excited about non-voting shares, which could prove worthless."

"Meaning that you're even doubting I'll still be in business, Chip?"

He's not answering me, which makes me wonder if he still thinks I can survive, whether he represents my best interests. He acts like the doctor assigned to a patient on his last legs, who he doesn't think can make it through the night, not very optimistic about my future prospects. He knows I see the doubt in his face. Instead of looking at me though, he's thumbing through one of Martha's coffee table books, this one with photographs of spectacular beaches on Carribean islands. If Denise and I can match up our calendars, I'd love to take her to an island, diving on a reef, fishing for marlin, dancing through half the night, making love the other half. On second thought, this is not a good idea. Could be walking myself into a trap. A fair chance that one of Martha's vacationing friends, or worse, her parents' Doctor friends, might me spot with Denise. But I shouldn't be planning my life around unpleasant events that might never happen. No more than I should worry all the time about short bank balances. Apparently the Deb Queen doesn't. With the kids out of the house our expenses could be much less, but the only changes I see in her is that she complains more and spends more. As for Chip he's another one with his hand in my pocket. I'm tired of always being the last one into my own wallet!

There Chip goes again, jumping up to watch out the window, acting like a lookout for a band of robbers. Maybe I've made him nervous, the deeper I get into his mind. But he's still working for me, so who cares what he thinks? It's time to get him back to the business I hired him to do.

"So why else are you here, besides to tell me what I should do with Yankovich and Ryan?"

"Missing records."

"What kind of records?"

"Records pertinent to the barge canal, records I need to see and which the court will surely demand."

"You mean old, expired ones?"

"In particular, files from eight-and-a-half years ago to the present, Ned."

"Of course, you wouldn't find papers that old in the office. We had to give up some of that extra space we had and get rid of the dead files, or else we'd be working in very cramped quarters. Most likely the old records would have been pulled from the inactive files."

"And where do you keep the inactive files?"

"Off site."

Why's he's smiling at me like the cat that swallowed the canary? I can read faces, and I know he's not telling me something. He's really fishing for information way past the statute of limitations to which no one has any right—not Borak, not the court, and certainly not my own lawyer.

"I'm afraid that's not good enough."

"So what were you looking for that you couldn't find?" I asked.

"The records showing exactly how many truck loads, the contents of those trucks, and site samples."

"That was ancient history, almost ten years back. I was hired by the city at that time, then the state got into it, then Borak. Old news. The issue's between the EPA and me, going back five years, not ten. We'll take a hard look and see what we can come up with, Chip."

"I'm afraid if you don't, I can't in good conscience, represent you."

"Wait a minute. Don't misunderstand me. Just because you can't find what you're looking for doesn't mean it doesn't exist. Did you ever think to ask before you helped yourselves? If you can't find something all that important, why not contact my office manager Monday morning, OK?" He's shaking his head no. He has his heels dug in the dirt. The missing records could be a convenient excuse to jettison me.

"No problem. I'll continue consulting with Ms. Pendergast, seeing how you're too busy for me."

"Off the record, how much has been consulting and how much consorting with her?"

There he goes, again crossing the line into my own personal business. If Martha were to overhear him, she might get the wrong idea. Old friend or not, I'd better keep him out of my house from now on. And I'd love to get him off my case, if there were some way I could replace him with Denise.

"You're full of advice for me, Chip. Now it's my turn. The smart master understands when the apprentice has passed him, like General Cyrus Langway has, in some ways, surpassed me in my organization. If I were you, I'd let her do her job without interfering. She's outstanding, your best. Leave her alone."

I hear yelling from outdoors. I look. Martha's shouting like a crazy woman, trying to force open the door of a van with a crowbar she's grabbed from my workshop.

"What the hell's going on down there?" I shout to her from the window.

"I want my boy back now, Mr. Fitch! Where's his father hiding!" she calls in all directions.

"At your service, Deb!" I say.

"If you ever call me that again, it's all over! Act like a father! Get your son out of there!"

She always makes sure there are plenty of people around before shooting off her mouth to me. I don't like her throwing a fit and issuing me orders. With her bad temper I don't like that iron bar in her hand. I rush out of the house to prevent her from doing anything more foolish than she already has.

"Drop it!" I say.

I grab her arm, bend it backward, and she drops the crowbar. Ouch! Hits me hard in the face! Her little fist packs a punch, which she knows I can't return.

"Jumpy, ain't she?" Sheriff Fitch says to me, having emerged from the police van, leaving Ryan shouting within it. "Maybe that's where the boy gets his mean streak from."

"I won't condone handling my client in this manner!" Chip says loudly.

"I thought you were working for the boy's old man, not for her," Fitch whispers.

"If you don't get off my property immediately, I'll call the authorities!" Martha threatens.

He responds with a guffaw so big that his gut quivers and tears fill his eyes. "Mr. Thompson, couldn't be you told her that I am the authorities. Of course, Mr. & Mrs. D'Amour I could turn him back over to the state police, who've been arresting him near as many times as us county cops. Your choice. Quite a little fighter, ain't he?" Fitch says smiling at my son Ryan, his captive, who returns the compliment with more curses and obscene gestures.

A three-fingered wave and an embarrassed grin to me from Ryan. An obnoxious kid. Not proud that he's mine. Won't do him any good in the long run if we rescue him again.

"Better do what you have to do. Take him away, Mr. Fitch," I say.

"How can you live with yourself as a father conspiring to lock your only son in there like a common criminal?" she asks.

"I don't make the laws, Mrs. D'Amour, I just enforce them," Fitch says. "Ain't nobody's about to accuse me of going soft on the perpetrators who come into my custody. And I wouldn't be using up half my day hauling this kid of yours back and forth, if I wasn't a nice guy, a father myself, trying to help out your prominent family as a special consideration to Mr. Thompson."

"Now you're not implying consideration in the form of property or any manner of payment, are you?" Chip pointedly asks.

"Is the Pope Catholic? Like I was saying, we been giving this kid of yours the red carpet treatment, leastways compared to how we like to move the average offender."

"What he means is usually they'd transport them to the station in a secure police cruiser, rather than in this civilian vehicle," Chip explains to Martha. "Because I thought you'd like to see him in a less restrictive environment, I've especially arranged that—"

"Chip, how could you let Ned talk you into pursuing and cap-turing my son like a puppy in a leghold beaver trap? Did it occur to you that by taking away my poor boy's rights, by teaming up with Ned and this bounty hunter you're behaving like a gang of vigilantes?"

More belly laughs from Fitch, quite jolly for a peacekeeper who, more often than not, sees people at their worst moments. But his mood suddenly changes, and he seems nervous now that he's checking on Ryan, pulling his automatic three-quarters out of his holster.

"I agree with you ma'am," Fitch says, having returned to the adults, "let's put this critter out of his misery."

Martha looks horrified, thinks he's talking about Ryan, but I see him nod toward Chip, his subject.

"You must understand, Martha, that we have Ryan's best interests at heart," Chip says. "He's been arrested for a burglary and resisting arrest, yet, as a special concession, we've brought him to your home. And if I weren't a friend and advocate of this family, then why else would I prevail upon you to bring Ryan here in your own personal vehicle rather than in an official vehicle? And why wouldn't Sheriff Fitch simply keep him in the lockup with those common criminals to which you were referring?"

"Speaking of rest, Mr. Thompson," Fitch says, "you want me to bed him down now, or should I just stand guard over him out here? No matter to me. Either way I get paid the same."

"For God's sake, let's act humanely!" Chip says. "Of course we're going to let the young man stretch his legs and fill his lungs with fresh air! I'm sure, Martha, you appreciate the good faith effort and the special arrangement we've made to allow him to visit with his family. But now we must ask for your cooperation by allowing us to use the most secure space available for his over-night stay."

"Bed me down!" Ryan bellows from the van. "No, forget it! It's daylight, and I'm not a baby who needs a nap! Go jump in a mud hole, piglet! Oink! Oink!"

"Excuse us, ma'am," Fitch apologizes, tipping his hat to her. Again he pulls Chip aside. "Ain't he a touchy little bastard? If he don't shape up, I go along with what Mr. D'Amour wants, and I'll lock him up with the convicts."

"That's not an option anymore," Chip says. "I'm afraid we're committed here for the night. We'll get him to the courthouse to-morrow afternoon," Chip says.

"No can do. Can't leave him inside there more than six hours without no chow and a toilet, or I'll get myself into trouble. Rules and regs."

"Frankly, Mr. Fitch, I don't care about your dumb rule book," Martha says, having overheard them. "I insist you let me see my son now."

Fitch slides open the van door a crack to allow her to visit with his captive. "Good looking kid, if nothing else, Mrs. D'Amour. A lot better looking than most of the ones they give me to process. With his curly hair and the dimples in his cheeks, if he was a girl, he'd be pretty, kind of like you ma'am."

She still has great power to distract men. Ryan seizes the opportunity to bolt, tumbling the big man backward.

"How the hell did he slip out of those handcuffs? Grab him, boys!" the sheriff bellows as he lies on the ground stunned, his head bleeding.

Ryan's headed down the mountain, fast as he can move. No way will I let him get away from me. The kid's got some speed from his baseball days, but his stride's too short to win this sprint against me. He's pouring on the steam, but I'm closing on him fast! Intercept! Got his jacket, his pants, taking him to the ground, rolling with him! Rolling over and over, off the road and down the embankment!

"Shit, Dad, are you trying to kill me or just beat me up!" Ryan shouts, out of breath.

"If you don't like it, then next time don't—"

"That's your trouble, Dad, always full of don't do this and don't do that! Real smart, aren't you, tearing up your business shirt and your business trousers and your business tie and your wingtips. So how much you figure this stupid little game of hide and seek's costing you?"

"More than you're worth," I say once we climb back onto the road.

"Well, damn it, Dad, for you doesn't everything have a price? Wasn't that why you always wanted me to become a businessman like you? You can keep your money and your lawyer!"

"It seems every time I look, you mess yourself up, Ryan!"

"Then stop looking so hard! It's my life!"

"OK, so what did they haul you in for this time? Theft? Disorderly? Possession? And, tell me, how did Chip Thompson know about all this before your mother and me?"

We're getting too close to the truth, for his comfort. He's too ashamed to look me in the eye.

"Just a second, Dad, I'm splitting a seam. Nature calls, unless you think you can control that too," he says.

As he's peeing he's walking. With a yellow stream, he's running down the hill! Short memory, already forgot he lost the first race! I'm closing faster on him this time and dump him on the ground again!

"Can't you give it up, Dad!" he yells, pulling up his zipper. "Can't you get it through your head I'm not ever going anywhere you want me to go! Bud Fitch doesn't really want me in his jail any more than I do!"

When I take him by the neck and begin walking him back up the hill, Ryan shakes himself free.

"I told you and that oinker up there I'm not some kind of a baby! I'll go by myself, unless you think you're tough enough to knock me out and throw me over your shoulder and carry me!"

I'm tempted to lay out cold this loudmouth son of mine, and he's asking for it, but he knows that if I lose my temper, I'll make myself the bad guy. I let him walk ahead of me far enough so I don't have to speak with him, but not so far ahead that he'd attempt losing yet another footrace against me.

"Now look what the cat dragged in," Fitch says. He tips his hat to me, grabs Ryan, slaps a handcuff on a wrist, to which he handcuffs himself. "He ain't going too far too fast too soon," Fitch laughs as my boy tugs on the manacle.

"Get this off me! It's too tight!"

"This time let's see you break loose of the cuffs. Ain't you figured out by now, the harder you pull, the deeper the teeth dig into you? And worse, you've tightened up my side at the same time." Fitch takes his key to loosen up his own handcuff. "Feel kind of like a bass fighting a hook in your mouth?"

"You don't know anything how I feel. This hurts!"

"I won't tolerate any more of this abuse!" Martha shouts and pushes me toward Fitch. "Not in my house! If you're any kind of a father, stop him! Get him out of here now!"

"Martha, you're more than half his problem," I say. "If you personally can't tell the difference between right and wrong anymore, and if you're covering for all his little crimes, how do you expect him to ever take responsibility for himself?"

"If you had paid more attention to him and less time to business projects over your head, then having to clean up the messes you've created, Ryan would be a different boy today. He's probably been living on the streets, or in the woods and got hungry and took some food to eat just to survive. Can you blame—"

"Actually, ma'am, this time we caught him stealing computers," Fitch explains, "most likely he's getting into the bigger stuff with the higher street value. Of course, I'm not at liberty to discuss how, who with, or what he might be doing with the stolen property."

"But that doesn't seem to stop you from playing judge and jury," Martha says, "rather than your mission today, which I thought was as Chip's hired moonlighting security man."

Fitch clenches his teeth and shakes his head, looking very angry, still holding Ryan by the belt, with both Chip and me by his side. "You got a heavy cross to drag, Mr. D'Amour, with her hitched to it," he says, pointing to Martha, who's angrily left us for the porch. "I got some police business and can't be fooling with the boy right now," he explains as he snaps the cuffs off his wrist and onto mine, attaching me to my son this time. "Stay put, gentlemen." Then he turns his attention to his two-way radio. *"Tied up here overnight,"* he says into the microphone attached to his epaulet. *"Better hunt up the deputy on call. . . . OK, if they act up that bad, use a whip and a chair . . . !"* Now he steps back a couple of dozen steps and turns his back and speaks very low, not realizing I could still overhear him. *No, they ain't going to break if you have to handle them. . . . Don't let them act so tough they think they're in charge. . . . Do what you have to do to get their attention, Smitty. Remember I'm behind you 100%.*

"Well, Sheriff Fitch, since you appear to have everything under control, I'll be on my way," Chip announces, having stepped away from the rest of us on the way to the house.

"PSST!" Fitch whistles and trots after Chip to catch him before he can get to his car down the driveway. At the same time Martha converges on the two of them, leaving me alone with Ryan, manacled to him. "If I don't take the boy to my facility," Fitch says loud enough for everyone to hear, "I suppose as a favor to Mr. Thompson, I can hold him here in a room in the house with one bed, one door, a TV, and a chair or two, with windows that lock."

"I'd rather die than turn my home into a prison!" Martha says.

"As they say in the taverns, ma'am, *your place or mine?*"

"How can you allow this terrible man to talk to me that way, Ned!" she shouts back to me.

Silently I lead Ryan to a spare room with a bedroom suite and an ironing board standing in the middle of the floor, the other three following.

"They used to have a full-time maid," Ryan tells them. "This was her room, but now they don't use it because they can only afford a cleaning service every other week."

Fitch unlocks the handcuffs, thumbs through the Bible on the bureau, then takes Ryan aside. "You're a kid only a mother could love, and I'm not too sure about her."

"Goddamn—" Ryan starts to say before Fitch can throw his hand over the boy's mouth to silence him.

"I bet your daddy read to you from this book, like my father read to me the commandment about not taking the Lord's name in vain."

"No, because this is the maid's room, and she forgot to take her Bible with her when they fired her."

"Mr. Fitch, we don't appreciate your trying to lay a guilt trip on my son," Martha says. "For your troubles my husband is going to escort you from my house. I won't have any part of this!" Martha insists and leaves me alone with my son.

A TV news report from the other side of the world showing lootings and reprisal killings in the aftermath of a riot in Malaysia. One more place an American shouldn't be visiting. Their problems aren't mine, just because our banks control theirs and they sell us VCR's and clothes. I've got to worry about the revolution at home. Don't need this. I turn it off.

"I want the fucking news!" Ryan shouts, flipping it back on.

"Ryan, I've heard enough from you for one day. Quiet!"

"And don't tell me you don't recognize him, just because he's from somewhere else! I mean look in the mirror at a dictator, someone who wants to control others! But you found out the power game doesn't work if you can't take prisoners! The secret is, Dad, that Mom calls your tune, and now Fitch has made you his prisoner as much as me! Can either of us leave this room? So why don't you get yourself free of Mom and Fitch by setting me free first?"

"*Prisoner*, you damn fool! I've been doing everything possible to keep you alive and well!"

"Bullshit! Where were you when I needed you—in your office in your leather chair, drinking coffee and ordering people around?"

"I'll make believe I didn't hear that."

Now Ryan's found a broom in the corner, but has to take the ironing board and iron out of the way to get to it. He's acting strange, sweeping the corners all the way to the ceiling.

"What are you doing now!"

"Cleaning cobwebs."

A low pressure system heading in a southeasterly direction . . . At times precipitation may be heavy . . . Showers expected with some flooding in low-lying areas...

"Shit," Ryan says, "not a good night for travelers."

I shouldn't have to speak over that noise. I lunge for the TV cord and yank it so hard I snap off the plug.

"Wish I didn't have to do this, Dad! Pleasant dreams!"

As I turn around I see him above me, bringing the iron crashing on my head.

My head's spinning and hurts. I should have cold-cocked the creep after our little foot race. It was a mistake turning away from him, trusting him for even a second. He's left me on the floor my back, looking up on the ceiling, Fitch standing above me, talking into his radio.

No, ain't got much of a jump on us. . . . No, don't want the state police in on this. We're keeping it in our jurisdiction, if possible, so no APB, not yet. . . . He's in his father's dark blue Cadillac. You got the VIN and number plates. Best bet, try cutting him off south and west, and the minute you apprehend him, hold him for me to process, understand?

"He tapped you easy with that iron. Could have broke your skull if he half tried. I don't think you been out more than ten or fifteen minutes."

"What's all the commotion!" Martha says, arriving as I ease myself onto the bed. "What have you done to yourself?" She pokes at the bleeding cut on my head. "Have you been fighting with him again? Can't you brutes pick on someone your own size? What did you do with him? You're bleeding all over the comforter! Here, let me help you." She throws me a wet washcloth.

"Martha, you're giving me a headache worse than I already have. Do us all a favor and shut up already!"

"Next time we apprehend him, he won't slip away," Fitch says. "I'm losing time. If he sneaks back here, ma'am, be sure to call me immediately. You don't want to be found harboring him."

"But it's our car. We lent it to him. He didn't steal it," Martha says.

"Right, I'll see what I can do for you about grand theft. See you soon, I'm sure."

"That man enjoys his work too much," Martha says to me once he's gone. "I believe he's dangerous. Next time there's no telling what he might do to your son if he catches him with no one else around."

Fitch is barreling down the drive in a hail of gravel, his blue lights whirling. Back in our big house now, Martha's cries silent sobs, having curled herself into a ball on the sofa. That's the difference between a father and a mother: she feels hurt, while I'm not sure whether I want to strangle him or just disown him. What does she want from me anyway, to be a friend, a husband, a lover, nothing at all? If only we could get him completely out of our lives, then maybe we could still have a life together. Time to pull together, reach out and hug her, which only makes her curl up tighter and sink deeper into her corner of the sofa.

"I'm in no mood for that. How can you be so calm while your son's running for his life from those mercenaries? If you're any kind of a father, you'll get moving and find him before those terrible cops lose patience with him and hurt him."

"I think that's a bad idea."

"Go now! And don't come back unless you come back with Ryan!"

She's shoving me very hard, throwing in a few slaps. She doesn't care about my aching head. Patience. As the Chinese know, crisis is opportunity riding a dangerous wind. Tonight I need to ride high—go which way the wind blows! So let her push me out the door to the four winds, and let them carry me out of here so I may land on friendlier territory! Fine and dandy, now I'm headed to Denise!

Chapter 3
Playing for Fun

My frantic wife, so anxious to shield Ryan from his own stupidity, has prevailed upon me for three days now to drive her through the worst neighborhoods to find him. I think she's more interested in retrieving him than Fitch is. She has too much invested in our delinquent boy to risk losing him. My role, as she needs it: someone handy to blame for his crimes, his arrest and now his escape. I never volunteered to lead her search party, and I don't appreciate serving as her all-purpose scapegoat. I'm certainly not obligated to drop business (or pleasure, for that matter) to find him and rescue him yet one more time. Truthfully I don't think I'd care if Ryan vanishes out of my life, not after he sneaked up behind me and knocked me out cold.

But now that the weekend's here, Martha's thoughts turn from Ryan to her social life. That leaves me alone while she's out of town visiting one of her equestrian friends. All the more reason to see Denise early, rather than wait until our attorney-client meeting we'd set for the middle of next week. I'll be getting with her this evening at her health club to work out with her. To find out whether she's as good at racquetball as her boss Chip says. And see how much of her support I can enlist.

Mid August, the first signs of fall here in the north country, the leaves heavy on the trees, some of them already dried out and on the ground. On the road there are cars full of parents and children, seizing a warm and fair weekend before school begins, boats and campers in tow. Plenty from Quebec and Massachussetts to moosewatch and play in our backyard. I like the flatlanders best as tourists at play. Families with destinations, enjoying each other's company, unlike the D'Amours lately. And me driving out of town to get away from my crazy family, or what's left of it. But forgetting about them during this drive's not so easy, and lately I'm pulling up pieces from my memory better off forgotten: I've failed to match, much less surpass, the life Martha had as a doctor's daughter before marrying me. We've produced Ryan, a public safety hazard, especially when he's hopped up and hot-rodding down the road in some stolen car. And Erica, about as unpleasant toward me as her mother, who Martha insisted go to art school, and is now running a boutique, largely dependent on these flatlanders. A woman who like her mother, has become an artist in spirit but not in practice, somehow unable to make the time to sit down at an easel. Leaving myself, without much of a household, a man with a business under siege and defending the enterprise for what reason? For my family which has little understanding, much less respect, for what I've done for them.

Is it time to develop a new business plan? A personal plan? Contingency plans? No, forget those unpleasant details for now. Instead this weekend I'll create a pleasure plan with my phantom friend and assistant advisor, Denise. Strange how it took a full two years after Borak and the EPA began suing me for me to find out she was one of Chip's staff lawyers. A fortunate coincidence I bumped into her in the corridor. Glad we found each other again, and often I regret that thirty years ago I let her father get between us and break up our friendship.

Now my pager's beeping, like a truck signaling me it's backing up where I'm standing, warning me to do something fast. I thought I had it in my jacket pocket, but I can't find it and it won't quit beeping. Must have left it in the trunk. Stop the car, pop open the trunk! There, found it, and it's displaying Keystone Bank's number for me to call back. Another creditor who's going to have to wait his turn in line. Damn thing's an electronic leash and they're calling *Here doggie*, trying to get my attention! I may not be able to run away from everyone dunning me, but I don't need them ringing for me day and night! Bye bye beeper! Kill this thing once and for all! Lay it to rest behind this back wheel. Back to the driver's seat. Roll the car over the damn thing, once backward, then forward. Crushed like a bug under the front wheel. Now I can pick up the broken pieces and hurl them into the woods. Let those vultures try to find me between now and Monday morning!

It was no accident Denise recently joined the Fair Oaks Club. She told me she chose this health club so far from Gaylord to avoid meeting people she knew from work in order to be able to unwind. But we both know full well it was largely on account of me, so that I could remain anonymous out here where Martha's country club set would be less likely to venture. This renovated building with its steel roof and large, unobstructed freestanding span, an alteration from a furniture warehouse. Within it now weight and exercise machine rooms, racquetball courts, a pool and lockers, as well as a snack bar.

A silver-haired man shook my hand as I stopped at the entrance desk. "Mr. D'Amour, you've been here before, I see. The name's Bill Chatsworth."

Friendly fellow, but I didn't come this far out of the way to meet people. A familiar face: square jaw, invisible eyebrows and fair reddish complexion.

"I've registered before as a guest, as you can probably see."

"Yes, but you've also become rather famous," Chatsworth said. "I've been following you in the papers. Kick them where it hurts. Besides, my brother prints your brochures."

Too many people know too much about me, even forty miles from Gaylord here in Bath, a tough shipyard town the yuppies are struggling to prettify into a postcard seacoast town like Camden.

No, he's not done with me yet. He's followed me into the locker room. He's hanging around while I'm changing clothes, apparently ready for another round of talk. This time though I need to turn the subject away from myself.

"What then was your trade?" I asked.

"You mean before the Ironworks lost its shipbuilding contracts to the Japanese and I picked up this building at auction? I'm in sales, always been in sales. I used to tell my staff when I was active in the printing business with my brother, they're all salespeople, whatever their job description, with the exception of the back office people. I trained them to know that sales are the life-blood of commerce and made them work for their keep by becoming good with the public. So tell me, Ned, what's the secret to your success?"

Reading his face, he doesn't seem sarcastic, but dead earnest. Could he possibly take me for a success, simply because I've survived so many attacks by overwhelming forces? A perverse spectator sport, cheering for the underdog, and the newspapers have certainly made me out to be not only the villain, but a longshot bet. In any event, this conversation has gone far enough.

"I don't want to lose my court," I said, looking at my watch.

"Don't worry, we got the best one reserved for your lady-friend, the one with the resurfaced floor. She told me you'd be here about now and to send you through. If I were you I wouldn't keep her waiting. I'd hop there in the corral."

"Then you know Miss Pendergast?"

"Not that much anymore. I gave up bronc riding. Too old for that kind of sport. Hey, racquetball or tennis or business: we chase a fuzzy ball, or a smooth ball, or we chase a dollar. Only a blind man could miss that she's one pretty lawyer. She made her career out of reading laws, and in my case read me her own set of rules."

He knows her schedule quite well, and it also seems he's been waiting for me to arrive to look me over. I can only guess how well he knows Denise. Or maybe that's his true game, to make me guess and sow the seeds of doubt. But instead of leaving me alone now, he's following me, all the way to the court where she's been warming up without me. I suppose as the owner of this club, he can trail after me as he pleases. I suppose I could ask him to get away from me, but I won't give him the satisfaction that he's rattling me. She's pounding the ball hard. White tennis outfit with a contrasting blue scarf holding back her long hair. She's worked on keeping herself trim, and it shows.

"I don't imagine I'll be seeing you, unless you decide you like my courts here enough to come back again. Go get her!" Chatsworth said.

I must have distracted her by whistling at her because she misses her return serve. Just wanted to let her know I was behind her so she wouldn't run backward into me. But now that I'm in her practice game with her I've managed to take control of the ball. Volley the captured ball, send it against all the walls and back to her. Don't run her too hard, not in the warm-up volleys. And now send a high slam into the glass directly in front of Chatsworth, who's retreated above us into the spectator seats, watching us.

Volley's over, and now she takes a break. I'm not going to stop her from giving me our usual long kiss hello, not on his account.

"If you're ready, Ned, let's go to the main event."

I need to feel out her game, play to her strength for starters, make her run hard out of the gate. I know my limits: not to get stupid and not to even think about playing full out for more than forty-five minutes total, or the pain in my knees will overcome me, and those nylon braces won't be enough to keep me in the game. But if I keep an eye on the clock, and play smart, my injuries won't catch up with me and sideline me.

Let her knock herself out, running to all corners of the court to give herself a three-point lead over me. Take control. Now make her run like a rat in a maze, chasing a reward. Send her here, there and everywhere. Let her go after the ball on any of the four walls, as well as the ceiling. Make her spend her reserves to return my fast balls, allowing her to initially stay just ahead of me in score. So far, so good, I haven't shown her my hand. Build up ball speed gradually and don't use the ninety mile an hour serves yet, not until she believes she'll take the game.

She's slowed down, but I have plenty of energy. The endurance part of this match is over. Now keep delivering these projectiles at 90 or 45 or 180 degrees from wherever she's last placed her shot. A barrage of shots coming from any direction, too fast for her to anticipate, just beyond her reach, now pushing me into the lead, nineteen to sixteen. On to the second game; first game my win. Fine. I'm ahead of Denise, where I belong, but not too far ahead to appear ungracious or discourage her. I'll let her pull ahead of me this second game and then take the third for the match.

"You're playing surprisingly well," Denise said as we were taking a break, drinking cold juice. "If I didn't know better, I'd guess you've been practicing long and hard, just to beat me."

"I haven't practiced in weeks, but I'm practicing with you today."

"So that's your purpose, and I thought it was because you missed me."

"That too," I said.

I rub Denise's back and her arms, which were tight and muscular and look at her strong profile, deepset dark eyes and black shiny hair. A powerful and graceful body, whether in motion or at rest. She's damp to my touch and sweet as I'm smelling her. But when I draw myself to her again and kiss her cheek, she pushes me away. Too bad, because this time there's no one in the seats to watch us.

"Or are you really here because you're in trouble again?" she asked me, drawing back.

"Trouble? Me? I wouldn't want to spoil our weekend, bothering you with those details."

"More importantly, are you also going out of your way not to bother Martha with details, such as where she stands?" she persisted. "Or is it just me you're showing this extra consideration?"

"I'll tell you what, I'll forget about Chatsworth; you forget about her. Ready for one more game?"

"Didn't Bill tell you we have to be out of here by 6:30?"

"We both know I shouldn't believe what you tell me, Ned," she said, taking the initiative and kissing me on the cheek this time.

We're back to the game, I take my serve, then give her a couple of points, but not any more that would risk her overtaking me. Now she seems to be playing an especially fast game and it's time to use finesse to overcome her advantage of uninjured legs to take me to a lead that I won't allow her to overcome. She has a tall woman's legs, proportionately longer legs than mine, a man's, longer than the average woman of even her substantial height, the legs of a marathon runner. I need to make sure I place my shots well, so she's doing most of the running, not me.

She always had natural talent as an athlete, even when I first knew her skating in college. Plenty of push and a graceful glide, good speed on the ice. It shows on this court, certainly for her age. If she'd listened to me rather than to her skating coach, she would have tried out for long distance track after the skating season. Naturally fast legs are one thing, but she would have neeeded the will to match. It was obvious she didn't want to become a decent athlete nearly as much as I did. She used her wonderful legs winter seasons as a skater, never taking on running during the other seasons.

"You gave me a run for the money. Excellent game," I said with a handshake when it was over.

"You move better than you have a right," she said looking at the braces on both my legs. "Here I thought you had a handicap, but perhaps I should be the one asking you to give me a handicap."

"Too bad that you didn't see these legs sprint down the football field in college. Not to boast, but twenty-five years ago it took a pretty good man to stop me."

"So now that you've slowed down, you prefer to play with the girls?"

"Whenever you care to play with me, Denise."

"Then first you'll need to feed me. I told Bruno I'd be there at 7:00. Chatsworth doesn't take me there any more. Care to join me?"

Bruno's Restaurant, only eight tables, the most exclusive in Bath and Denise's choice. This building used to be a boat supply store and overlooks the water. With only us and one other couple at the far end, we must speak very low. Violins through the speakers, candlelight, white linen. Coq au vin for me, rack of lamb for her, not a night to order from the right side of the menu. Our waiter staying at a discreet distance, watching, ready to respond with more wine when I nod my head in his direction. She probably doesn't really know yet about my reduced circumstances, and I'm not sure how to best tell her, certainly not now, risking an otherwise promising evening with her.

"What happened to your knees?" she asked. "Tell me about the braces."

"Let's just say an especially mean football player, Doug Koroleski, who played for UMass went on a search and destroy mission whenever he played against me. That could have something to do with the games where I'd managed to snatch the ball from him and make some touchdowns that they liked in the grandstand, which got him in trouble with his coach. So he waited for his chance and to get back at me and took me down by the knees, even after I'd passed off the ball. And he didn't come at my legs straight, but rammed into them sideways to do the most damage. Referee never saw it. The medics hauled me off to the hospital. That was the first patch-up job done on my right knee, and operation two followed it the next season. Then a guy even bigger than him, Billy Sweeney, busted up my left leg, which was the end of my football career."

"I wish you'd invited me to see you play. I might have been your cheering section, if I didn't mind the violence and the blood."

"I never did enjoy getting hurt, but I'd never run away from a challenge either."

And if she had stayed in state with me for college, she could have watched me in practice before those gorillas busted me up, or seen me run 10's in the 100-meter time trials. At one game she could have seen me do an end run around a charging 300-pound defensive end trying to get at me to take me down before I could snap off my long, dead accurate forward passes. If she better knew the fighting side of me, it might not surprise her so much that I'm very difficult to beat when I'm determined to win.

"My father found out just how good you were at butting heads. That could have been the reason you never got further with him."

That wasn't the reason at all. It was Denise's choice, not her father's, to break it off with me. She didn't have to listen to her parents when they told her that seventeen was too young for her to be spending so much time with me alone. And neither did she have to believe them when they kept telling her my prospects weren't good, that I was destined to work with my hands like all the other men in my family.

"Or because you preferred to listen to your mother and father rather than to me."

"You do know my dad died about three years ago, don't you?"

"Sorry to hear that."

"No you're not. Don't lie," she said. "And before you ask me, my mother's moved to where it doesn't ever snow, outside Phoenix, to help her arthritis. So, for all practical purposes, they're completely out of the picture. Lucky you."

"Yes, we're back together. The flame's rekindled."

"In all the years since we first knew each other and you were making your valiant efforts to keep your marriage together, and even after we ran into each other at my our law firm, I've never spoken to Martha. I've recognized her, but I doubt she recognizes me. My friends were certainly not her Boothbay sailing crowd. Like your family, mine had to work hard for a living. But from what I hear of her, it's best to keep us far apart. I understand she travels with a firetruck and carries a very big firehose, that she enjoys throwing rain on parades."

Agreed that Martha, given a chance, would throw a heavy wet blanket on our picnic this evening, if somehow she knew about us. I've managed to forget about Chatsworth and his obnoxious interview. So for her part she can forget about Martha, at least for tonight.

"As long as we're each trying to figure out who's in the picture and who's not, I'm sorry that Steven didn't work out."

"No, you don't miss him any more than you do my father, but thanks anyway."

"I do have to admire him, smart as he was in geology."

"No, physiology and microbiology. In the labs Steven generally came to the right conclusions, but I suppose I came to the wrong conclusion that he was going to move on to become a well-paid consultant."

"None of my business, Denise, but maybe you should have stayed married to him a little longer."

"How do you figure that?"

"Didn't you tell me he finally got tenure at the university? If it's security you were looking for, it would have been pleasant living off a position where, you can't possibly get fired, unless you hold up a bank."

"Or hump a girl student, in a public lounge at 4 A.M.! I still can't believe he got himself terminated over one not very attractive granola-eating chick, not when there were so many others available to him, and not to mention myself, his trusting wife!"

Insane, Steven losing as fine a woman as Denise. But maybe I should be careful passing judgments on another man, because there may be other men out there somewhere saying similar things about Martha and me.

"I didn't know. Sorry. We've been out of touch too long. Too bad it had to end that way."

"At least it ended, unlike the match made in heaven you made with Martha."

"She's the mother of my children, if nothing else."

"That's something Steven and I never got around to do, an accomplishment. I presume Erica's grown up by now. And you have a son, don't you? Is he out on his own, out of the house? And where does that leave you?"

"I'll let you know as soon as I figure it out."

"Out of curiosity, what were you thinking when you first traveled with Martha, that as an Aldrich she'd lead you down the road to riches?"

"That had nothing to do with it. Whatever I've got, I've made on my own."

"Really? I thought during the summers you were able to work for your father in his construction business."

"I could have worked for a dozen others, but he needed me, not the other way around, if that's what you're getting at. In fact, working for him, I worked a lot of unpaid overtime, which would have never happened with any of the other contractors. A couple of times when Dad would get behind on a job, and I missed practice, the coach threatened to cancel my football scholarship. I may not have been born with a silver spoon in my mouth, but you'd never find me asking anybody for anything, and I never expected—"

"Expectations. Funny the way things turn out as we'd least expect. At the time neither of us expected my parents to return from that wedding at 8 P.M.," she said.

"But that's all the time your old man needed to get himself stinking drunk and downright mean!"

"Not fair! Just because he caught us *in delicio*, and just because he then arranged that you should never touch me again while I was living under his roof, that doesn't constitute sufficient cause for you to demonize him!"

We must have been speaking louder than I realized. Now there are three couples here besides us, and two of them are looking our way. One man, older than me, but not quite retirement age, with a chunky gold watch with sparklers, is half smiling at us, no doubt imagining us thrashing around together in bed.

"That sure got his attention, Denise," I whispered. "I think he could like you, almost as much as I do."

"That's not funny. I'd think you men would get tired of ogling women that are wrong for you!"

She didn't have to shout that in the poor fellow's direction. He's taken that comment personally, has turned red, and is now returning his attention to his own dinner companion, not mine.

"If you think I'm wrong for you, Denise, you should have considered that before."

"I didn't have to. My mother did that for me. She had her doubts whether you'd stay loyal to me."

"I think she kept too close an eye on you."

"Remember the date when you took me to see that Italian movie in Portland, the one with the titles, *The Defector*, where the soldier manages to find new lovers between battles and who defected from the army just before the truce was declared in order to live with the red-haired one in Switzerland?"

"A deserter, yes, but from the fascist Italian army, which made him a hero," I said. "And it was called *The Patriot*. To me a hero has to answer to higher principles than survival. I thought he crossed the border after the war was over. And I don't know how you can tell from a black-and-white movie that her hair was red."

"You do have an incredible mind for detail, Ned, but only when it suits you. I'm wondering though whether you recall what we did afterward?"

"Not much. You were always kept under tight curfew."

"Remember how you couldn't get it together after the movie to get me home until after 1:30 A.M.? And are you forgetting that you dropped me off at the curb to walk up to face my mother alone? You couldn't have missed her waiting up for me on the front porch."

I don't know why she has to dredge up that disastrous date, unless she's looking for more reasons why we've stayed apart for twenty-five years now. She can only blame her parents and me until she runs out of reasons and has to go to the mirror to see the important one. I should probably look at myself as well, for giving up on her too soon and not pursuing her after she left home.

"Then maybe you should have explained to her that I ran out of gas and that we had to walk a couple of miles each way to the nearest open station. I told you to show her your dirty white shoes in case they questioned the story."

"Incredible memory! But I remember distinctly that she thought I'd scuffed them frolicking with you on the beach. She didn't believe me, and that night was the perfect excuse they needed to keep me out of your clutches, Ned."

"Then for parents like yours with so little trust, you could have walked in with a torn dress and barefoot, and they wouldn't have thought any less of me," I said.

"That was your trouble, Ned, you never gave them credit for being able to see the forest from the trees."

At this point I could care less about what her parents did so long ago to discourage her seeing me. *The forest from the trees*. She's throwing words at me. I don't know what she really means. I touch her beneath the tablecloth to see if tonight the magic is there between us.

"You know I'd rather you don't, not right here," she said, placing her hand on top of mine. "What kind of man are you?" she asked me, smiling.

"A sociable one, just right for you, Denise. And one who, with your help, is going to forget all these sad stories. I have you in mind, nothing more."

"The sooner you pay the bill, the sooner you can bring me home. It seems we have so little time together."

"Yes, let's make the best of what little we have."

———————

A sign ten feet across announces we've arrived at *Chelsea Estates*, and behind it lies a massive fieldstone entry arch and a wall stout enough to support a sentry tower. Of all the houses in the compound I like Denise's the most—turrets, gables, dormers everywhere. A large house big enough for six, useful for their entertaining, but otherwise it seems very big for just her and Steven. She told me he left this place to her free and clear, only requiring now that she keep it in fresh paint and decent repair and pay taxes on it. But I'm still not clear why now she wants to stay here. She also said she hasn't been entertaining her old friends, who seem to have made themselves scarce after her separation. Their plan was to split them up fifty-fifty, but in reality they proved to be fair-weather friends who could only relate to them as a couple, no longer as individuals. Her friends were the movers and the shakers. Unlike her husband's faculty colleagues, the academic types, the men in beards and the tweeds; the women, in print dresses and sandals. So she's lost her husband and his income and friends, but she got to keep the house. Another good deal for a good negotiator. I just hope I can get her to negotiate for me with Borak and the Feds as well as she's done for herself.

Now that we're standing inside the door, we're done with talk, time for a kiss. Denise's kiss is much more than a friend's— a lover's, with a restless and probing tongue. She puts her arm around my neck, shifts her weight to one foot until I take up her cue and pick her up off the other foot to carry her to bed, as she's come to expect during my visits of the past months. I set her on the corner of the bed. She turns her back to me, allowing me to reach around her, unbutton her, and pull her blouse over her head. Now she turns back to me, takes me once again in her arms, pulls my face to her breasts so I may kiss them. Gently she pushes me back and stands naked and lovely before me. We're going to have another fine night together.

"What do you think?" she asked me.

Now she's on her feet, walking around the room lighting a couple of candles, really modeling herself for my appreciation. Beautiful breasts, which jiggle just a little, but still firm, even compared to when she was a girl and I saw her for the first time when we were playing in the forest on a mat of ferns. Her legs are now more feminine, less athletic than when she was a slender kid practicing her ice skating four months out of the year. Time's changed her, but hardly for the worse. She's taken good care of herself. Of course, it helps that no baby's ever passed through her body.

"Are you looking at just me?" she asked, glancing behind herself.

"I don't see anybody else."

"Except for the one you allow to look over your shoulder."

"Who might that be?"

"I know I'd rather forget about her," I said.

"Should I help you?" she asked, then dropped to her knees alongside the bed and rubbed the inside of my legs, as she always did.

"If you'd like," I said.

"Is that a command or a wish . . . ? Say it right so I can start on you."

"Let's do it."

"Do what, Ned? What do you want to do?"

"Come on, sweetheart. You needn't ask me."

"Tell me what you want. Say it!"

"The same as the last time," I said, hurrying to remove my own clothes.

"Not so fast! I can't be sure you're the same," she said, pushed me back, and began undressing me herself. "Do you eat the outer leaves on an artichoke, the spiny ones, just because you get your hands on them first?"

"No, but on the other hand I don't peel a tomato because it's too thin-skinned. What do you want to know?"

"I need to know once and for all whether this is about habit, convenience or about love. I need to know whether we're talking about friction and fire, or about a meeting of the minds. I need to know whether—"

"Words! If I wanted to account for every breath and every step I take, then I could have stayed at home with Deb Queen this weekend. If I wanted to get ready for a cross-examination, I could have made an appointment with your boss Chip."

I then began to pace about the room. She waited until I came within reach, lunged for my legs, and with a sudden burst of power tripped me up so that I fell on top of her on the floor.

"I'll have to tell Chip he pleases you more than I do, unless, of course, you'll let me make it up to you. She began pumping me up. ". . . Ah, now I see I have your increasing attention." Gently she pushed me onto my back. ". . . Or do I? What are you look-ing at besides me? Because if I can't get your full attention, I may have to quit," she said.

"OK, I've got my eyes on you. As well as behind you on your new wallpaper. And above your head that purple and blue border."

"Then are you telling me you admire my handiwork?" she whispered and placed her tongue in my ear.

"Did you hire a decorator to cut and paste and match these patterns, or do you know how to do it yourself?"

"Do I know how to do it? I'll let you be the judge. I've got the time if you've still got the ambition."

She's touching my chest with her fingertips, playing with my tiny male nipples. She draws away, returns, teases me. My turn now for the love game. Exploring her with my lips and a little bit of my teeth, finding her nose, her ears, down to her breasts, then past her belly to her sweet inner taste. She responds with a murmur, pushes my head away for the moment. But I believe she wants more. No more interruptions, won't stop now. Her breathing speeds up, a shudder passes through her body.

I've moved her along too quickly, taken her further along than I intended. I'll leave her alone now to her own pleasure. So I lie beside her, touch her from time to time to keep her awake, but won't play with her anymore.

"Close your eyes, Ned, so we can move to the same place at the same time."

I do what she says, quietly holding her hand. I work at putting all words out of my mind, words that can't help me align my feelings with hers. I've done this before with her, *opening me up*, as she once called it, putting ourselves together in a wonderful trance. This time I see her traveling with me in space:

We're traveling to the same destination on two tickets, flying on a very fast plane. We're leaving the ground, leaving behind our bodies. No longer bound by the pull of the earth. Moving between clusters of stars, through amber plasma clouds, seeing worlds building and decaying. We have within us the power to sail like this together, forever, no reason to stop this beautiful journey, flying naked in tandem as a perfect pair of lovers, so fast and powerful no force can pull us off track. A celestial journey of two warm creatures, joined. I'm entirely separate from Denise and united with her at the same time.

Back to earth, back to Denise, our earthly bodies, lovemaking. Take the lead again. Timing's everything. Get back in synch, stay with her, or better yet, hold back a little behind her. I hold a pace that's just a little slower than she wants, holding back enough to make our pleasure last as long as I can. She's completely with me, throwing up her legs, wrapping them around my neck, pulling herself off the bed and half onto my shoulders.

"Oh, yes! We're almost there! Don't stop, not now!" she shouted. "Run with me! I'm crossing the line! Ohhh!"

She's finishing with a shudder more violent than the last one, followed by another, then still another, long after I'm spent. Now she lies in my arms, content.

The sport of love we run together. I go across the finish line, then she follows. If the race is about speed the man wins. If it's about enjoying the journey along the way, the woman's advantage. Who cares who comes first and who comes second and who's ready to run a rematch? No more, because I want to please her more than myself. Unlike my younger days when I would keep tallies of my success with women, a time when my own pleasure meant more to me than pleasing someone else.

I should have left my cell phone in the car, because it's ringing and I hate to answer it now. It's hanging from my belt on my pants, draped on the chair on the other end of the room. I hope whoever's trying to reach me gives up soon.

"She's checking up on you? Next time you see me, you might want to come by yourself."

Denise is driving me crazy, hinting about Martha again. I should be able to put Martha out of my my mind, if only Denise could forget about her. And now that my thoughts are increasingly linked with Denise's, I too am having trouble completely ridding myself of Martha's image. I imagine her face: pert nose, very fair skin, and her father's determined mouth.

I wish Denise wouldn't lead me to compare the both of them, making me look backward to my life with Martha rather than forward, wherever my reunion with Denise may take us. If I'd made my children with Denise instead of Martha, they couldn't have failed to turn out better than our last-born Ryan, who's got as poor an attitude as his mother's.

"It would be lovely if you could give me your full attention. We'll work on it."

Troublesome words again, lovers' word games. It's too easy for lovers to say more than they need to and look for unnecessary words of reassurance from one another.

"By the way, I saw your friend Barbara Evans the other day in the mall. She was shopping for a dress for a charity event, and she wanted to know all about you. She sends her love. I take it she's not siding with Martha."

This isn't the kind of pillow talk I like, distracting me rather than helping me focus on just Denise. Maybe though I should be flattered that she believes I'm like the ice man, an itinerant lover. Our making love today doesn't give her the right to know what I did a year or ten years ago. For my part, I don't care to know about Steve Pendergast, nor about any boyfriends she might have subsequently had. All that matters right now is the magic between us.

She's done talking and turns toward me, belly to belly. I'm strong, but not ready for another go right now. The years have made me a better lover for her, though a bit slower one. I must be aware of how I approach her, not act too eager, never make myself heel at her command. She wouldn't respect me if she could walk me on a leash. Nor am I a bull on service duty. So I'll let her know when I'm good and ready, and maybe that's going to take me a little more recovery time than when we were both eighteen, new to love, and could go at it like marathon runners.

Chapter 4
Sunset Motel

Martha acts like the house is hers alone, the way she gave me her ultimatum after her equestrian weekend to either find Ryan or for me not to bother returning. A relief in a way, no longer having to confront her every day. And maybe I'm comfortable staying in this motel because, like myself, it's seen better times. By its looks no one's bothered to replace furniture or carpets or paint for a couple of decades. I'm holed up here, not because Martha has any chance of winning her claim for the house, but for the time being, I find it very convenient to live in peace by myself. A motel nine-tenths vacant, with this fine pool, without little ones to pee in the water. Can't remember when I've had as much time to myself, and I'm enjoying it as best I can. I'm seeing a lot of bad movies, reading books of little more value than the nonsense I see in the newspapers and on the TV in my room. Another reason for staying in this B-grade motel, rather than one of the better ones closer to Gaylord: I know too many people in town and wouldn't care to bump into one of them in a lobby and letting them suspect why I'm living in a motel room instead of at home.

So while I've temporarily lost my home with the view, I've gained a pool. *Quid pro quo*, as Chip would say. It's easy to swim in my marked lane, sliding lap after lap through the water, emptying my mind of troubles. Good thing I'm flexible, able to adapt to any new environment. And I've equipped myself with two sets of goggles, one clear for dull days and one tinted for brilliant, sunny days like today, far too nice a day to spend indoors behind a desk at Resolutions, Inc.

I'm a swimming machine doing laps: Stroke. Kick. Stroke. Kick. Stroke. Breathe. Three more cycles, and I'm up against the wall again. Prepare for fast reverse. Dive now. Twist a quarter turn. Plant feet against wall. Push off for all I'm worth. Surface and grab a gulp of air. Start the cycle again. Puts me in a mindless trance, exhausting and boring, so I'm careful not to ram the wall with my head.

Swimming, strictly an endurance sport. The swimmer's face and body's visible to the crowd only a moment or two at a time. A sport unsuited for grandstanding. A game for boys and girls with big ducky feet and hands and long legs and arms, and more endurance than finesse. A sport someone can do without an elaborate game plan. But I suppose I shouldn't be criticizing anyone else for lacking a plan, since right now I don't have a workable one of my own. I believe I do my best planning these days underwater, in between my gulps of air, swimming in the pool of this neglected motel. So my plan for today: to figure out whether I should move to a more suitable place, an apartment where I'd have to sign a long lease, thus extending my retreat. But staying away from home for too long might not be too smart or make any sense, that is if Deb Queen ever decides to surrender this latest skirmish and give up her stupid claim against our dream home, which I built mostly to please her! I know that she's been hatching a plan to grab it from me, while trying to force me to maintain it for the parties she'll never stop throwing for her friends, who have always been more important to her than her husband. The ones who with good reason always looked forward to the spreads of meats, fish, and desserts. Entertaining lavish enough to impress the Aldriches, her parents, through which she knows most of these people in the first place. Parties she refused to believe we couldn't afford anymore, yet kept throwing until I pulled money out of the account to stop the hemmoraging of my fast dwindling funds.

I'm swimming laps to unwind and forget about my headaches with Martha. If only by willpower I could put her completely out of my mind. Now what am I seeing out of the corner of my eye every time I come up for air? A pair of long legs and a butt. A big floppy hat and oversized sunglasses. Attractive breasts, which must have been gorgeous ten years ago. Age 30, judging by how they droop ever so slightly. This woman's body looks very familiar from the shoulders down. I can't quite catch a glimpse of her face. She could be one of my old girlfriends, who I just can't recall at the moment. She seems to be trailing me, walking a couple of stroke lengths behind me on the concrete. If this lady's trying to get my attention, she shouldn't wait to call to me when my head's underwater and I'm in the breath-holding part of my stroke with my ears filled with water. But this is my workout time, and I won't let anyone distract me. My calves are aching a bit, a good workout, but I must push a little harder. No pain, no gain if I want to build up my swimming muscles. Fifty more laps, and I'm done for today. By then this woman should get tired of her little cat and mouse game.

I'm finished for now and hoist myself out of the water. Why's she now doing her toe touches here in front of me at the edge of the pool? Why's she keeping her butt pointed toward the sky four times longer than it takes her to get to the upright position? Is she doing this for my benefit? If she wanted to get my attention, she's succeeded. No, I already have enough women in my life. I just need to get out of here. Too late, she's turning toward me. I'd better get that towel over my suit before she sees my visible appreciation of her attributes.

"Mr. D'Amour, the General knew I'd catch up with you if we persisted," the woman said. She turned to face me and removed her sunglasses and outsized straw hat.

"Rachael! I would have said hello sooner if you'd made yourself known! I certainly wasn't expecting you to find me here. Either this is a hell of a coincidence, or you've been hunting me down."

Then too it would have helped if she weren't skulking around the pool this morning traveling incognito. She looks much better out here in her shorts and halter top than she does in my office in a business outfit, and she knows it. She's certainly caught me off guard. My face feels hot now. Probably too much sun. Shouldn't be showing her my embarrassment by turning red from the inside out. She's my employee. Oh, hell, what do I care what she thinks?

"The General can always find what he's looking for," she said.

"So the General and you are in charge now?"

"Of course not, sir. But you've been gone well past the return date for your vacation. We began to wonder whether you were back in town. Last week one of us thought he saw you on the highway somewhere near Chelsea. We've been calling your home, but Martha doesn't seem to know anything."

I'd like to tell her how good it's been not seeing the crew and how much I'd enjoy making this unannounced vacation permanent. But I have to be careful not to make her morale any worse than it already is, though it's seemed to improve in my absence, making her appear to be very cheerful today.

"What do you care about my wife? She has nothing to do with Resolutions, certainly nothing to do with your job, since the day she left and I hired you as our office manager. The organization once ran like a well-oiled machine."

"Mr. D'Amour, I truly hope I haven't hurt your feelings."

Feelings? I wish she'd cut out that touchy-feely stuff. I'm talking job description, performance expectations, facts, not feelings.

"If I caught you at a bad time, I apologize. If I didn't have a couple of messages to deliver, I suppose the General could have waited until you got tired of your holiday. But we all know he's second in charge only when you're not available, and when he told me to do a reconnaisance mission and use my network of friends to find you, I had to stop working on all my important projects and come to your aid."

"And snoop around to hunt me up, is that it? Congratulations then! Mission accomplished! You've chosen a beautiful day to look for me, and at the same time work on your tan. Sure beats staying back in the office and talking on the telephone and tip-tapping on a keyboard, right?"

"If I'm catching you at a bad time, I can come back when you have less on your mind."

"My mind's fine, thank you, Rachael!"

"I didn't think you'd mind if I dressed casually today. But if you're not comfortable talking business while I'm wearing this outfit," she said, crossing her arms over her chest, "I'll go to the car and put on a wrap."

"Don't worry about my comfort either because, to tell you the truth I'm damned uncomfortable no matter what position I get myself into these days!"

"I'm sorry to hear that, but if it's any comfort we're all in this together, no matter what happens. I hope I can be useful to you," Rachael said, breaking into tears.

Oh no, crying, a lady's ultimate defense! And worse, sincere tears! I have to believe she takes her responsibilities seriously. I wonder if she and the General would remain so loyal to me if they could find another employer willing to pay them as much as I do. Perhaps I'm paying them top dollar for the wrong reasons, to have them on hand to keep me company. Or, bottom line, maybe I'm hanging onto Rachael because she's so good at soothing and mothering everyone in the office, including me.

"I'm so happy that I've found you today!" Rachael said, once she had stopped sobbing. "The General wasn't sure whether you'd want to join us at today's meeting, but it doesn't matter either way. What a relief that I've gotten to you so you can sign off on some papers, before you disappear again," she said and handed me a clipboard with sheets of unsigned checks, as well as a pen.

Strange how she's all business, yet dressed for the beach. Even stranger how the bulk of our checks are being written for pond-digging projects. We're fast becoming ordinary contractors doing low-value homeowner work, rather than public works projects.

"The numbers aren't working. Time to prune the tree," I mumbled to myself while looking at the paperwork thrust at me showing me our rapidly declining fortunes.

"Excuse me, Mr. D'Amour, were you saying something?"

If I'm the boss, I should be able to run a few numbers in my head without having to explain to her. So I'm not going to answer her. Now where was I? It looks like thirty-five grand a month just to keep these clowns on my payroll punching keys and shuffling papers! I bet my staff sit on their asses behind desks six hours for every one hour they're in the field getting their shoes muddy and their fingernails dirty and actually doing some useful work.

"I know what you're wondering, sir: are we holding our own, or are we slipping further behind?"

She's smiling at me like a school nurse, trying to distract me, calm me down, or fool me, and I don't like it. Or maybe it's just me feeling like I'm her fifth grade schoolteacher trying to find out why she didn't do her assignment right, and these papers she's throwing at me is her unsatisfactory homework. Now she's producing a bank deposit zipper purse, from which she pulling deposit slips. She's not seeing the big picture, and here she's trying to sugarcoat this bitter pill and have me swallow it.

"Yes, I was curious why we have more dollars going out than coming in, Rachael, and what you and the staff plan to do about it."

"I have to disagree, sir, because I know in my heart of hearts we're more than holding our own. Here, you be the judge," she said, putting the deposit slips in my hand.

Now I get it. She had to track me down, not to get my approval for any particular business decisions, much less the way they're doing business, but rather to get my signature for checks. Tomorrow I should take a day off from this annoying little holiday and pay them a surprise visit and sort them out, to see who's working and who's pretending to work. If they think they can replace me with a rubber stamp with my name on it, let them see how long they can survive without me!

This is interesting, a charge of eight hundred bucks for office supplies. And now I see a couple of hundred more for travel mileage than I've never authorized the General to take! I need to calm down now and not show her how much these red numbers are provoking me.

"OK, Rachael, let's see how well you've been running the store. Follow me inside."

Now I've got her full attention, judging by the concerned look on her face. Whether or not she's going to turn on the tears again, it's time to take control, make her accountable for any bad news she came here to tell me. How have I managed to surround myself with these prima donnas?

———————

Once we were in the my motel room she stood at attention while I spread out the slips on the little motel-sized desk. "How about if I call off the deposit or withdrawals, while you punch them in the calculator," she suggested.

Afraid not. Let the numbers speak for themselves. Tally the deposits, then the withdrawals, with none of her help. I don't need any fresh bad news from the office today.

"The General and I calculated we've hit $57,000 in revenue, and we have another week of the month left. So overall, sir, wouldn't you agree we're holding our own?"

She's trying to cheer me up, but she's not amusing me. If he'd teach her how to read an income sheet, then she might understand how fast we're falling behind. But most likely in my absence he's enjoyed assuming full command. And to exercise his authority, I'll bet he's been holding back key information from her, as if he were still handling classified documents.

"Seems to me you're comparing apples with oranges, net with gross. I'm confused with what you've shown me. But I hired you as my office manager, to eliminate confusion from my business life so I can get a life outside of business!"

"Oh, Mr. D'Amour, has it come to that? I'm so sorry," she said with her eyes tearing again, sympathetic to my situation. "Life doesn't always treat us fairly. I know how the kids can upset us, and how this money thing must annoy you just that much more. I know from my own experience that kids without a father or a strong male around can run pretty wild and challenge us, can't they?"

She thinks she knows much more than she actually does. I don't need to hear updates on her personal life, and for her part, she's seen and overheard much more about me than I trust her to keep to herself. I'm not looking for sympathy, but she's given me a dose of it, regardless. Look at those furrows in her worried forehead.

"Certainly if there's anything I can do to help with any personal problem, please ask me anytime," she offered.

"You don't mean talking about Martha?"

That's exactly what she means because she's shaking her head yes. This time she's overstepped her bounds.

"Thanks, but no thanks! I hope you don't plan to advise her, because she won't listen to anyone, including me."

"Precisely. That's why sometimes a woman will only listen to another woman. On the other hand, as a woman your man's perspective doesn't make sense to me. But please tell me if I'm interfering in your personal life, sir."

"You wouldn't be interfering, Rachael, if I needed a marriage counselor. I remember my grandmother would say because God gave us two ears and one mouth, we should listen twice as hard as we speak. That's quite a challenge for someone who loves to visit with people as much as I do."

"Absolutely, sir. As my mom used to tell me, we sleep in the marriage bed we make. So, if with the best of intentions I've said too much and hurt your feelings, can you forgive me now? And I promise now I'm all ears, Mr. D'Amour. If I interrupt again, please jump on me."

Jump on her? That might be fun for a few minutes, but afterward she'd have me in her grasp. No, rather than jump on her, she might benefit a whole lot more from lighthearted behind-closed-doors corporal punishment. I can imagine laying her over my lap, pulling down her drawers, and slapping her pretty fanny.

I better be careful now, in case she can read my thoughts. That's why I'm glad she retreated when she did. She must know by now I may like a lady's pleasant words and flattery, but I'm no fool. But the way she's smiling at me so sweetly, she makes it hard for me to set her straight. If only she weren't working so hard to charm me, then I'd be in a better position to tell her why I hired her. Which was to arrange personnel, pay bills, shuffle papers and play with the computer, not to stuff herself into her pretty little shorts to chase me all over town.

"I'm glad you brought me this receipt, Rachael. This one has a government seal on it, but the print's so tiny I'm having trouble reading it. Are we playing guessing games, or are you going to tell me which agency it came from?"

"EPA, sir."

"That's peculiar, since for the life of me I can't remember authorizing you or the General to give those bastards any more information without consulting me!"

"Well, Mr. D'Amour, I don't believe you can fault the General, and I must remind you I was on vacation that very date."

I must have doubt written all over my face, because now she's showing me the empty page in her date book, the dates she took her vacation, as if that could somehow prove she wasn't in the office at the time and had nothing to do with caving in to the EPA.

"And, sir, I almost forgot this paper, which is really part two of the receipt."

Another paper with the government's seal, but bingo—Borak's signature with Yankovich's authorization below it!

"Ah, Mr. Yankovich! No, I won't fault him, but I will eliminate him! It's time to drain the little toad's pond and bake him in the sun!"

"Remember, you're talking about a person with feelings; those were just papers."

"He had no right to collect these records, which he's gathering to use as information against Resolutions! Either he walked into Borak's trap unknowingly, or he conspired with him!"

"Don't you think that's a little extreme?" she asked.

"Neither of them had any right! Get those documents back!"

"I think it's out of our hands, sir, but the General and I knew you'd want to do something, so we set up a get-together to discuss it."

"Why don't you ring up my right-hand man right now so I can give him my recipe for frying a toad?"

"I'd rather not, sir."

"Rachael, no offense, but why don't you get going right now before I get ugly?"

"If you talk to the the General he'll confirm everything I've reported. And if you choose to come to the meeting with me, he'll insist that we're not late. We had a heck of a time booking Mr. Thompson to join us, but we were lucky that someone cancelled and he gave us the time slot. He must be a good lawyer if he's that busy."

"Do you know how you tell the difference between a good lawyer and an defective airbag?" Forget it. She's not even listening. I won't waste a good lawyer joke on her today.

While I'm dressing I can hear her whispering something on the phone to the General, but I'll be damned if I'll ask her why she had to wait until I was out of range, unless she's reporting to him on my general appearance and state of mind.

"If we can head out now, I can brief you along the way," she said, taking the mail away from me that she had just delivered and which I'd begun opening. There would be no need for her to drive me to the office if Martha hadn't claimed both cars for herself. Now that we're in her car together, she's suddenly become quiet. Rather than speak any more, she's playing a motivational tape, *Abundance is a State of Mind*, recorded by a psychologist with a convincing voice. Good intentions if she wants to improve herself, but the wrong message. If everyone had abundant intelligence and abundant confidence and abundant ambition, all of which I myself used to have until recently, then people would reap as they sowed. Instead we study how to siphon grain off from the community's silo. A plausible theory for how people behave. I'm thinking differently now. What's come over me? I've always been a man of action, who had little time for big theories. My staff may be making me crazy, but I must be careful in this staff meeting not to yield them the upper hand and let them think they've ground me down!

Chapter 5
Medford Pond

The motel is only forty minutes from the office, but Rachael allowed twice as much time as she needed to drive us here, which leaves just her and me waiting in the conference room. The General's off to lunch, and neither Chip nor Yankovich have shown up yet. While we're waiting I'll find something else to talk to her about, other than business.

"Tell me, Rachael, what do you usually order for lunch at Monica's?"

"Why do you ask, Mr. D'Amour?"

"Because I thought I'd take a client there."

"The women tend to eat salads; the men, beef."

"Strange that when it changed hands a couple of months ago, they kept the old name."

"Monica's daughter Janice told me they kept the name the same when Monica sold it to keep the old customers," Rachael said.

"I hear that now for the first time they're serving up jumbo shrimp. Doesn't *jumbo shrimp* contradict itself? Life is full of contradictions. Lately I've had time to think about foolish things like that. Big shrimp or jumbo shrimp, they're Martha's favorite. Were they nice and plump at Monica's?"

"I like mine with hot sauce, the hotter the better."

"And how does Martha like hers?"

"You should know your wife's habits by now, sir. Nothing personal, but it might help you to pay better attention. She likes hers with just a twist of lemon. Because I like mine so hot, she calls me the wild one, and she tells me she wishes she could turn the clock back to my age."

"And if she could, what would be the first thing she'd do to make herself happy?"

"I believe we can be most happy when someone near and dear pays attention to us."

"What? Now didn't she tell you what her fantasy was, the dream that keeps on jumping into her mind every morning before she wakes up?"

"Isn't that rather personal? She's still your wife, sir. Shouldn't you put it to her yourself?"

She's playing cagey, trying to avoid what she knows about Martha that I should. "What has she told you about the dream, damn it!"

"No need to abuse me in that way, Mr. D'Amour!"

I guess what she means by *abuse* is simply asking her questions she doesn't care to answer. I could call her on this game she's playing with me, but instead I'll apologize and let her win this round.

"I'm sorry, but I really would like to know."

"If you absolutely insist," she said. "If, as you would have me believe, she's shared her dreams with you, there couldn't be too much harm in repeating it to you, Mr. D'Amour, even though I believe I'm Martha's only friend in the world she's shared this dream with. . . ." She closed her eyes, as if to imagine better herself. "Martha told me she'd ride a big chestnut stallion on a path through a forest of huge oak trees, dripping with Spanish moss. A fine summer day, dawn. Her horse carries her through the fog to the river bank, and they swim across it to the far bank, where a very handsome man's waiting for her with a long towel."

"And did she tell you what she was wearing?"

She's smiling back at me. I think she knows a lot more than she's willing to admit, and she's throwing me a crumb of information at a time.

"Nothing, nothing at all. And neither is the man waiting for her. That man in her dreams wasn't you, if that's what you really want to know," Rachael said.

Suddenly without warning she gets up and leaves me alone in this conference room, hoping no doubt that I won't make her explain any more. She didn't have to rub it in that Martha's dream lover didn't resemble me in any way. And, worse, to deliver her message with a smile, as if I'm supposed to be happy hearing from Rachael what I've suspected, that they've been meeting continuously, up until now, talking about Martha's hot fantasies. And, doubtless, about how my marriage, or what's left of it, fails to match up to the Deb Queen's fantasies. What an unlikely pair of friends: Martha, a prominent bone doctor's daughter, and Rachael, a hardscrabble dairy farmer's kid, hardly like any of Martha's tennis and horse friends. Martha always plans her moves in advance, leaves little to chance. Knowing Martha, I can't believe theirs is an accidental friendship. I bet Rachael's been her source to keep her posted on the state of my business and my life.

Now she's returned, knocking on the door trying to get my attention. I must have been daydreaming. Did she lock herself out inadvertently, or did I lock it because I'm sick of her? Has she been gone a minute, a quarter hour, who cares? Time and schedules don't matter to me like they once did.

"Mr. Langway would like to make himself available," she announced as the General followed her into the room and took his place at the head of the table directly opposite my seat.

He hadn't sat down a moment before he got up to sit beside me to speak directly to me. "Damn good to see you back, sir! If you don't mind my saying so, you're looking damned good, considering. Off the record, it's none of my business, really, what you've been doing the last couple of weeks, but rumors have been flying about your son. I know what you must be going through with a youngster that won't mind. Sometimes you need to put the fear of God in them, unless of course, they never learned what God was in the first place. I used to be a troop leader, so I could reactivate myself if you need me."

"I'm going to get a whip and a chair and tame him myself. Thanks anyway."

He then returned to his position at the other end of the conference table. "Well, we have a business to run, so I'm going to cut to the chase, sir. We got a situation on our hands here, but nothing we can't master. I've seen my share of action, but the battles are won in the barracks, every bit as much as on the battlefield. I've worked with a lot of good men, excellent men, and even a couple of genuine heroes. I've gone head-to-head with bullies,

sneaks, and grandstanders, and I've also dealt with fakers, pan-
sies, 4Fers, cowards, traitors, and featherbedders. But this son-of-
a-bitch Yankovich—excuse the French, Rachael—he's the poorest
excuse for a man I've seen since I had to throw a couple of dope-
dealing AWOL's in the brig."

"Yankovich—is he the reason for this emergency meeting?" I
asked.

"Like I said, nothing I can't handle," the General said.

"Excuse me, but I thought the purpose of the meeting was to
discuss Francis' grievances. If I knew you were so hostile to him,
General, and were going to persecute him, I would have never
worked so hard to bring Mr. D'Amour to this inquisition."

"Rachael, we're not taking an opinion poll, for Christsake. We
got ourselves a situation and zero minus fifty-seven to get ourselves in formation. We best be drawing up a game plan before
the Huns come over the hill, if you get my drift."

Rachael had briefed me in the car that Chip Thompson would
be joining us, though I'm not sure why he should be sitting in on
our staff meeting. Especially since the last time we met he threatened to cut me and Resolutions loose. But now that he's arrived
he seems to have one foot out the door, standing in the threshold,
hands in the pockets of his beige Italian cut suit, rattling his change
and keys, looking bored.

"What a pleasant surprise," I greeted him. "I wasn't sure
you'd make it."

"My office is only five minutes from here. Rachael seemed so
intense on the phone when she invited me to sit in on your pro-
ceedings, that I accepted her request to administer first aid."

"I'm sure you don't have anything in your first aid kit that
the lady needs. We're quite robust here, especially her," I said.

"Could you ask Mr. D'Amour exactly what he means, Mr.
Langway?" Rachael said, blushing.

The General's signaling me to be quiet and stop bantering
with her, but I won't. If I want to lighten up this wake, it's none
of his business. So now I'm going to try to put her at ease by letting her tell me a little more about herself, since she seems to know
so much about me, though not here where the others can overhear.
I must be careful not to compromise the details of her personal
life in front of her co-workers, in case I know more than they do.
Since Yankovich isn't here yet, and they're not ready to get started anyway, I'll speak with her in privacy.

"If you'd step outside with me, Rachael, I'd be glad to explain," I said and took her to an empty office. "The grapevine has

it that you have a new boyfriend." Rachael nodded. "Drives a big truck . . . ? Short haul or long distance?"

"Long."

"Then he stays on the road overnight?"

"Only because he wants to. It's his choice."

"Rachael, lately you've been guessing my motives and have made suggestions regarding my personal life. Now tell me if you mind if I take a look at yours."

"Of course not, Mr. D'Amour," she said warily.

"With your truck-driving boyfriend, I'd have to believe he really could work closer to home, but running cross coutry he gets more hours and more pay."

"He bought himself a brand new Peterbilt and now he has to make big payments," Rachael said. "I told him he cares more about the debt service than about me."

"About service to you?"

Now she's red, blushing a brighter shade than she forced on me when she first cornered me in the pool. I said *service*, and she must think I mean the kind of service a bull does to a cow. Once again I've been betrayed by words, this time my own. Though she can annoy me, I'm not vengeful and I really don't enjoy making her uncomfortable. But if those tender feelings she's always speaking about get in the way, that's another of her problems. Oh no, I see tears, which she's doing her best not to show, turning away from me as she dabs at her eyes with her tissue.

"They can't start without me," I said, "so you can stay here to compose yourself, until you're ready to join us. If I've accidently said something you don't like, if I stepped on your toes my apologies. OK?"

"I would appreciate it if we could get on with business without any more investigation into my personal life."

"Investigation, that's a strong word." I said.

"Investigation or inquisition, just as you're about to do to Francis."

This seems more like an insurrection, the way she is questioning my right and the General's right to make tough decisions at Resolutions. I don't like my office manager interfering with policy. It could set a dangerous precedent.

"Obviously there's been a misunderstanding, Rachael, so why don't you let me make it up to you? Go ahead, enjoy the rest of the day on me," I said.

No response from her. She's doing her best to ignore me. I don't have to explain myself, but I do need to get out of the same

room with her before I show how much her unbusinesslike behavior is annoying me.

I quickly left her to return to the men in the conference room.
In half a minute she had joined us. "I'm afraid as office manager
I should stay here. I insist," she announced her arrival, speaking
directly to Chip, though she knew full well he had no power to
decide anything for the company.

"I can do no more than advise," Chip said, pointing to the
General and to me. "It is the officers who must decide."

"If you force me out that door, you'll miss me, gentlemen."
This time she used the General's tissue to dab away her silent tears.

"We won't miss you if you came here in behalf of Mr. Yankovich. If that's the case, you're free to go as you please," the
General said. "But keep in mind the door swings both ways."

"He means to say the company plays no favorites and evalu-
ates everyone by performance, as defined in the procedure man-
ual," Chip said.

I liked the old conference room better, the one we used to have
before we had to sublet out our extra office space. Here we have
filing cabinets that get in the way and probably have been con-
cealing Yankovich for who knows how long! I know he's seated
behind the files listening, because his foot's giving him away. I see
his clunky tan shoe, a cross between a hiking boot and a work-
man's shoe. I know he's there, but they don't yet. This conversation was never meant for his ears. I now go out one door and
reenter through the other, sneaking up behind Francis, startling
him, bringing him forward.

"We've taken this sort of thing long enough," Yankovich said
once I seated him before everyone.

Chip's looking at the both of us, speechless for once. Looks
embarrassed. Not one who appreciates surprises.

"*We*? Define your terms," Chip said.

"With all due respect, you don't realize how we serve you,
even when we don't get any credit from you," Rachael said.

I don't know what she means by *we*. I had no idea she was
dissatisified at work. It's one thing to deal with one renegade like
Yankovich, another to lose a competent manager like Rachael.

"What sort of thing?" the General asked. "Keep in mind,
Rachael, that my people can always feel free to come forth if they
have a legitimate beef."

"I get very uncomfortable when I see one of our creative people being persecuted," she said. "And I have a problem with some
of the sexist attitudes around here."

"Rachael, make up your mind," I said. "Either come or go, but do something already before you make me crazy!"

"You can do that without us. But you'd be amazed at what we can do on our own! You'll see," she said and rushed out, tears beginning to well up in her eyes. Yankovich was directly behind her.

––––––––––

After she left the General, Chip and I sat looking at each other. "I don't know what kind of fit she took," the General said. "But I'm guessing it happens every month. Ever notice that's the time they like to cry?"

"After Yankovich gave up all those Medford Pond records to Borak," I said, "I can't trust him anymore, but Rachael's behavior I have trouble explaining . . . ? Maybe her monthly kicked in when she took that day off a few weeks back and Borak used the chance to raid our files."

"Gentlemen, I won't even attempt to save you from your blunders if you persist in this line of speculation!" Chip shouted, throwing his hands over his ears.

A wasted performance. Rachael might have been impressed with his righteousness, but she's gone. His grandstanding won't work with me or with the General.

"I don't mind helping you with honest mistakes, but your stupid blunders are something else," Chip continued.

"Now please don't act righteous; it's too out of character." I said.

"I can't fix the abysmal morale I see in this place. If we were alone, Ned, I might make a personal suggestion."

"Make believe it's just you and me, counselor," I said. "Don't mind the General."

"Sell out," Chip said. "I suggest you bail out. Get out. But don't cash out, because you'll need it for your penalties and fees, if you want to avoid—"

"I meet the opposition head-to-head," the General said, "not avoid it, whether it's Borak with his regulations he bends to suit his purposes, or the enemy shooting at me. We're not retreaters, are we?" He then looked at me for approval. "Mr. D'Amour and I know that if we plan to win, we'd better be prepared to take a little flak."

"Let me caution you, gentlemen, Mr. Yankovich is far from dead."

"Very true, you can count a man as a casualty without waiting for him to take the last trip," the General said.

"Or think of him a rotten tree in a forest that needs thinning," I said.

"I refuse to take part in this collusion," said Chip.

"Sure, Mr. Thompson, let your conscience be your guide. I have no problem with that," the General said. "But seems some people who don't mean us well play by a different set of rules."

"I don't know what you're referring to," Chip said cautiously.

"Those code red files that are missing, the ones that were robbed," said the General.

"Stolen? Where precisely?" Chip asked.

"Mr. Thompson, I wish we knew. I was hoping that you or one of your assistant lawyers who was looking them over before they went missing, might be able to lead us in the right direction" the General said.

"I don't follow," Chip said with a blank look.

"After you lawyers were done looking through the files and got what you needed, I moved them to my fireproof cabinet in my office at home, where I didn't think they could get into the wrong hands." the General said, evenly and deliberately. "I thought the papers were safe in my own house, but I guess I was wrong! I don't know how the hell Yankovich knew to look for the key to the files behind my humidor," he now said with more conviction, "or whether he forced open the lock. But however they did it, somebody knocked out my window and busted my lock. Or it could have been a woman small enough to slide through my tiny basement window who left behind a small tan glove. Or else a small man about Yankovich's size. Seems to me breaking and entering's a crime. But I'm not about to ask the law to help me track the burglar down, especially if it's an inside job we can handle ourselves."

"Code red because they were red hot, in a manner of speaking?" Chip asked. "Now you wouldn't be talking about the documents showing numbers and contents of truck loads, as well as site samples?"

"Yes, those papers, and then some."

"But this does bring us to a contradiction, Ned," Chip said to me. "You told me some of your records were lost, but now are we to understand that before they were permanently lost they were temporaily lost, so to speak, by Mr. Langway, who willfully moved them to his home?"

"Your conclusion, Sherlock. As I recall, I just told you I couldn't remember who moved them or to where."

"Because if so, those key files relating to their investigation may prove to be a smoking gun, particularly if they have been hidden or destroyed. They would be looking at intent."

My own lawyer, trying to make me out as some kind of criminal, his intent that I hire him for more hours. But since when is it a crime to keep my files where I need them? I don't believe he cares at all about me, but about his $76,000, which he's probably jumped to $96,000 by tacking on interest on top of interest, the damn shark.

"The boy wonder's back," the General whispered to me as Yankovich returned.

Is this man with Yankovich who's shaking my hand trying to impress me with his vice grip? He has a square jaw, heavy eyebrows and a stern demeanor. His tie clip has the official state seal on it, which could mean he has connections at the state level.

"Sizemore, Frank Sizemore. I'll be representing Mr. Yankovich today."

"We won't be very long," the General said to him, trying to lead him back out the door. "We have a little company business to discuss here during business hours. We'll give Francis back to you when we're done."

"What firm do you represent?" Chip asked.

"I'm representing Francis Yankovich independently."

"You're repeating yourself," the General said. "State your business."

Just what we don't need, another legal battle. I could throw him out, but we're probably better off letting him stay so we can at least find out what he's trying to get from us for Yankovich. "We know you have your agenda, but we first wanted to open up Francis' schedule book so we can count up his sick days," Sizemore said.

"You've got the key to those records, General, so why don't you get them for us," I said.

"May I have your card?" Chip asked as we waited.

"I'm sorry, not with me. May I have yours?" Sizemore asked.

Chip's trying to get my eye, wanting to talk to me alone, probably doubting Sizemore's lawyer credentials because he can't produce a business card, but that could be what Yankovich wants, that we leave him alone with files again. The weasel's up to something, but that wouldn't make any sense, even for him. Most likely the two of them are here to demand irrelevant paperwork. Rachael must have alerted him that he would be the subject of this meeting and to prepare for it in advance.

"Mr. Yankovich, I was just wondering why Rachael drew up this month's schedule and gave you all this time off without consulting me," I said, once the General had returned with the attendance sheets and I had a chance to read them.

"Well, Mr. D'Amour, with all due respect, it would be easier some days consulting with a ghost, since you're not here at all," Yankovich said.

"In the last four months, it looks like you've been out forty days," the General said. "Feeling very sick?"

"Mr. D'Amour, to answer your question," Sizemore said, "he simply collected some overdue sick days, long since overdue, to which he was entitled. He's been under the weather lately. Would you like to know why?"

I must steer clear of any health questions, in case it's AIDS. Whether he really has it or not, if he tells me he does, then he can nail me for discrimination if I fire him. I liked it better when I first hired Yankovich and he had the good sense to remain in the closet. How times have changed!

I can see in their smug faces they think they've got me by the short hairs. Need to pry them loose.

"Mr. Sizemore, you're casting a shadow," I said, holding the papers up to the window light. Now he's standing over me, arms crossed defiantly, reading my documents over my shoulder.

"I think you've got to move on, because you're blocking my light. Maybe I'm not explaining myself too well. You need to move the other way. We need to take care of business right now, Mr. Sizemore."

"I'm sorry, we will not go away. I am here today to represent Francis."

"Represent in what capacity? If you are not an attorney, then you are misrepresenting," Chip said, but received no further explanation.

"I say we throw this imposter out!" said the General.

"Forgive me, Yankovich, but I must have missed something," I said. "Has something been bothering you lately?"

"Well, I'm surprised Rachael didn't get you up to speed. After all she's in charge of personnel, and I'm a person, even though you sometimes treat me beastly."

He probably thinks because he works here he has the right to haul in and open up his footlocker full of personal problems, which I truly don't care to know about.

"Didn't you think it was just a tad funny that she dragged us all to the same table? Or did you think we were going to discuss the wind and the weather, sir?"

Tacking on a *sir* doesn't impress me in the least. He's completely out of line.

"Actually I was hoping you were going to explain to me about some decisions you made on your own without consulting with me. You know full well, Mr. Yankovich, we do have a chain of command here. The General is in charge when I'm not here."

"And all these years, sir, I thought General was a make-believe title."

Now he's pushing his luck. The General's eyes are bulging out of his head.

"Make-believe, my ass, son! Excuse the French, Ned, but these armchair, popcorn-eating civvies never have a clue who is keeping the peace, because they've never met the enemy on their own ground! They've never had mortars explode next to them, seen their pals taken out by shells, grenades, artillery. Their kind never sees action, so the likes of them hadn't ought to be bad-mouthing my rank!"

"Would you care to explain what you mean by *your kind*?" Frank Sizemore asked.

"He retracts that comment," Chip said.

"Yeah, why don't you quit picking words, Frank, so we can fix whatever's bothering the both of you, or else just take your guy somewhere and get him fixed," I said.

"I'm sorry, Mr. D'Amour, as the owner of this enterprise and as Frances' boss, until this very moment anyway, we have cause to show that you have been harrassing him," Sizemore said.

"I treat anyone who works for me the same. We have a real simple policy here. You work, you get paid. You screw up, you own up to it, or else you pay the price."

"*Pay the price*? That sounds so final," Sizemore said.

"Damn right! Like I tell my own son, you lie down with dogs, you're bound to get fleas!" I said.

"Lie down? Francis has documented many occasions like this in which you've made such references to his personal life."

"Mr. Yankovich, Mr. Sizemore, gentlemen, Mr. D'Amour simply means to say that he wants to know precisely the nature of your complaint," Chip interrupted as he looked through their folder. "I see you have in your records dates and descriptions of events that have nothing to do with sick and vacation days. Why don't you let me have it for a minute so I can copy it for our records?"

"Mr. D'Amour, we suspected such tricks," Sizemore said to me.

"Tell your friend, Francis, I don't play tricks. I'm a straight kind of guy."

"*Straight*? How are we supposed to take that?" Sizemore asked, making a notation.

"Straight as an arrow, straight shooter!"

"Ned, as far as I'm concerned, you're done responding in any way, shape, or form to this fraud," Chip said. "This man's no attorney!"

"I'm serving you notice there are going to be consequences to your actions, Yankovich!"

"Consequences?" Yankovich asked.

"Not only fraud, but sabotage! Insurrection! Back where your Yankovich clan came from I bet you stepped out of line once and you were shipped off to Siberia! Here we've been paying you very well for what work you used to do, but the party's over!"

"Are you threatening me?" Sizemore asked.

"No, he's not," Chip said, unsuccessfully trying to move Yankovich out of the conference room.

"I've heard enough out of you guys!" I said.

"Then you don't want to hear Francis' grievances?"

"On the high seas they called it mutiny! The captain had a right to deal straight with mutineers!"

"Are we talking corporal punishment, Mr. D'Amour?" Yankovich said. "We have our rights. They outlawed slavery and they outlawed flaying a man just out of spite and malice."

"Let me remind you the skipper has the duty to run his ship safely and on course, and if one particular scoundrel stepped out of line—" I said.

"If anyone stepped out of line he had the right to throw him over for the sharks to eat," Yankovich said.

How lucky for them we're here standing on solid ground in a civilized country.

"You obviously do want to fire him," Sizemore said. "On what grounds?"

On the grounds that if he insists on staying within arm's length, someday I might lose my patience and use my hands on him to repay him for what he's done to us.

"I don't think you got the idea, Mr. Sizemore. We want you out of here!" the General said.

"Not just yet!" I shouted, coming between the General and Sizemore. "We want to know about breaking and entering!"

"I don't know what he's suggesting," Yankovich said to everyone but me.

"Then how about aiding and abetting?"

"One more word from you, Ned, and I am walking out of here!" Chip said.

"Or should we talk about unlawful trespass? Or about being a burr under my saddle for too long?"

With no further explanation, Chip leaves. I know the meeting is going nowhere, but I can't help challenging Yankovich's treachery myself.

"Or how about theft of trade secrets?" I continued.

"Now isn't this talk of stealing some files a wee bit far-fetched, sir?" Yankovich asked sarcastically.

"I wouldn't be talking to Mr. D'Amour in that tone of voice, so long as you're drawing a salary here," the General said, putting his huge hand on Yankovich's small shoulder.

"You knew damn well that you were not authorized to give up any of our tax records to the revenuers," I said.

"Revenuers, Mr. D'Amour? Aren't we exaggerating just a tad, making them sound like the G-men who break up the bootleggers' barrels with hatchets?"

"In this office never under any circumstances, not until the day before it's due, which is when we put it in the mail, do we give up tax information of any kind!"

"But those papers were old, from about six years ago, well before this whole sludge thing, papers just like an old Sunday newspaper that's only useful for lining a birdcage. Mr. Borak said it was routine, that we shouldn't have anything to worry about."

"Well, he lied. Start worrying!"

"But he said if we didn't do anything wrong, then we had no problem."

"Then are we to understand that because Francis cooperated with an official investigation, now you're getting rid of him?" Sizemore asked.

He's trying to lead me into a trap. I didn't fall off a turnip truck, and I'm not going to answer that dumb question.

"So what other promises did Borak offer you?" I asked Yankovich.

"He doesn't have to answer such a provocative question," Sizemore said.

"What's Rachael been saying to you?"

"Stop harrassing me!" Yankovich shouted.

If they push me much further, they'll see some serious harrassment. They love making themselves victims.

"And what did Borak whisper in your ear?" I continued.

"Just as I have the right to free speech, I'm proud that I have the right to free silence! "

"General, they're wasting our time and we can't accomplish anything on our agenda with them on hand," I said.

"What exactly was that agenda, Mr. D'Amour?" Sizemore asked, continuing to make notes on his pad.

"OK let's close out this meeting," the General said.

"You're done, Francis! Go!" I shouted.

"Are we talking termination?" Sizemore asked expectantly. I now took Sizemore's yellow pad of notes, opened the window and threw it six stories below into the parking lot. "I wish you hadn't done that."

"Consider yourself lucky it wasn't you!" I said.

"Careful now, Ned," said the General.

"Yes, he's fired!"

"Are we talking about terminating now, with no notice?" Sizemore asked with a smile. "We'll be in touch."

Chapter 6
Quid Pro Quo

It's been several weeks since I've seen Denise, that night I stayed over after our dinner in Bath, too long without her, and certainly too long by myself in the Sunset Motel. As competitive as she is, I'm surprised she hasn't tracked me down for a rematch of our racquet ball match. The truth is Martha's knocked the props out from under me, that I've probably needed this time to myself at the Sunset Motel. I hope she doesn't believe that because I haven't stayed in touch with her that I don't value her, or value her as no more than a convenient lover. In these silent weeks she might have gotten the wrong idea that I've abandoned her. Better to just show up, explain face-to-face why I haven't been too sociable lately.

If Chip as a lawyer were braver and if he truly had the hunter instinct and didn't mind going for Borak's jugular, I would have worked to patch up our differences and still be using his services. He's wrong if he thinks I'm going to miss him, because I believe Denise will take me on, even if Chip attempts to interfere. Too bad I hadn't gotten her to work as my lawyer before Martha put me out of the house. Now I'll not only have to explain my disappearance but explain why I need her to defend me.

When I see Denise I must be careful not to appear too apologetic, with my hat in my hand. I ring the bell, but no answer. What do I do now? Go back to the motel? Not an option. Through the living room window I see a couple of pairs of rollerblades in the hallway. If one set's hers, the other must belong to a guest. And through the kitchen window on the floor behind the door I see today's newpaper, and even from here on the porch I can see the newspaper front-page orange photo of last night's North Country Hotel fire in Gaylord. An old wooden firetrap gone up in flames. Maybe that's what's destined for me—going up in flames. No, I can't afford to feel sorry for myself just because I'm in trouble. I'm not close to retreating. Defeat is not an option, but I do need Denise to help me stand strong.

Although there's no telling when she'll return, I don't care to be anywhere else but here, certainly not by myself another evening in my room at the Sunset Motel. If I hang around outside her house any longer though, I'm bound to excite the neighbors' curiosity, especially that one across the street who's studying me behind those avocado vertical blinds. So I'll back away from her porch, move out of her sight.

I drive back down the road to the gold-leafed *Chelsea Estates* sign and take a right turn out of the development, then another right and jump the curb and drive between the trees so no one can see me, and conceal my car behind the trees. Now I can approach her house from the rear where only one neighhbor's house faces me. I try the back porch window, which is locked. Then her bedroom, also locked. But the bathroom window is open. I boost myself in over the sill.

I make an awkward landing, head and elbow first onto the tile floor of the bathroom. I draw the curtains in the rooms facing the street so they can't see me, even though I only turn on lights in the back rooms. My next order of business will be to prepare a decent dinner for two, since I have nothing more to do than wait for her and have no reason at all to rush tonight.

Not much food in her refrigerator. I wonder whether she ever eats at home. So I'll cobble together what I can find. A little chicken, some broccoli and beans. Cut it all up. Stir fry it. Now thicken and flavor it with some corn starch, soy sauce, wine, salt, pepper, garlic. Perfect timing, rice done at the very same time. Set it all aside in covered dishes. Light those fat Christmas candles that can burn for ten days and ten nights, and wait for her.

On the table by the bed a book to read to keep myself awake, a biography of Amelia Earhart. The pictures don't reveal the huge fuel compartments in the wings. Amelia's flying game of fuel consumption versus time. Forcing herself to stay awake. Flying across the ocean in a slow, heavy plane whose entire cargo was barely enough fuel for the trip. I bet this appeals to Denise because she herself would like to fly high, to fly away from her desk full of dreary legal papers. Maybe Earhart needed to fly the most dangerous routes in order to outdo the flyboys. Denise, a strong woman following a strong example, yet still the little girl doing daring tricks on the jungle gym, unafraid of falling off now and then. Someone who can be a great help to me, once she decides to take up my cause. I know my players, and I'd say discipline in the face of deadly boredom is her strongest attribute.

Then I take a look at her environmental lawbooks to see if I can find something helpful about who gets blamed for long-term pollution from multiple sources. It's past midnight, I can't find anything that I think would help my cause, and I'm still waiting for her. My brain can't deal with any more fine print, so I slide between her sheets, and turn on the TV and watch cops and criminals shooting at each other. Then I find something better, old film-clips where I watch Hitler invading Russia in the winter, a similar miscalculation as Napoleon's, trying to move men and equipment great distances in a hostile environment. Hitler's men in forty below zero weather, the survivors retreating over soldiers who froze to death in place. Man at his worst, yet an inspiration, leaving me to know without a doubt who the heroes are and who the villains are. Enough amusement for my brain for one day. Denise's books closed, television off.

"Oh my God!" Denise shouted, having turned on the light and pulled back the bedsheets to look at my face. "I can't believe it's you!"

"Dinner's served, madam!"

"You shouldn't be in there!"

"No? There's no place else I'd rather be, dear. Should I go to the kitchen and serve us? Or would you prefer I put on an apron first?" I threw back the covers and stood before her naked, my arms wide open. She stepped back, until she collided with the wall. Then she giggled, covering her mouth with her hand.

"Denise, who's in there?" her friend called to her from the other room. "I'm coming."

"Don't you dare. I'm getting dressed," she said, changing no more than her sweater.

"Who's been cooking?" the guest asked.

"Take-out, delivered. I know them well enough to leave them the key."

"Looks like he's turned on the microwave to heat it. Do you always entertain your take-out boys in your bedroom?"

"Yes, as a matter of fact, Roger. Maybe we should call it a night," Denise suggested.

Roger's knocking on the bedroom door, and here I'm standing in my underwear. Don't need to fight with a jealous lover, could get nasty. She's going to have to choose up sides right now.

"Why don't you start eating without me," she said. "I'm not terribly hungry."

This friend of hers is obedient as a blind man's dog and leaves her alone as instructed. As we sit on the bed I slide one hand under her blouse, the other beneath her skirt. This time the door flies open and I meet him face-to-face. He has nice blonde curls, a bowtie mouth. I try to figure out whether his cute boyish looks makes him look much younger than she is by fifteen or twenty years, or whether he's really the boy he appears.

"Roger, you should have knocked. You're embarrassing me and must leave at once," Denise said.

"Nothing personal," I said and shook his hand to let him save face.

"I'm not into threesomes! This is disgraceful!" he complained.

"You know how it is, Roger, when you get to be our age, you get bored with the same old twosomes," I said.

He lets me escort him to the front door, but I make sure in my underwear I stand discreetly to the side of the doorway, out of sight of the neighbor with the avocado blinds, in case she's still watching.

"A pleasure ," I said to Roger, who leaves with no further protest, a calf, not a bull.

Denise was waiting for me in her nightclothes. "Next time you might call in advance beforehand, as a courtesy" she said, once we were alone again.

"If I've interrupted something important, I should get out of your way."

"Too late now. Stay put. We have some unfinished business, Ned."

"My feelings entirely," I agreed.

"Don't talk to me about your feelings. I admire not only strength in a man, but sensitivity and understanding. That's why I've just about given up trying to comprehend your state of mind, stranger."

"I came here to explain why I had to stay away for so long. I didn't want to. It had nothing to do with you, but with needing to sort out my problems. You might be able to help me."

"So you've crawled into a cave somewhere, and now you've come out to crawl next to me," she said and pulled me close.

————————

I can't let her believe I've come here to escape my problems, rather than to enjoy her company. Words can't begin to help me now. Denise's warm and inviting body is the true object of my desire, which has been dormant for so long in the same house with Martha. But now, pressed against Denise, I feel strong and content, with an overwhelming dream overtaking me. Without exchanging words I am free to feel, rather than think, and to rest. I close my eyes, though I'm not sure how long I nod off to sleep. She awakens me gently with her sweet scent, a new perfume she must have put on for me. She's tickling my face with the lace fringe of her pastel blue nightgown. And she stands before me as she slips her nightgown over her head, after which she slides into bed and presses herself against me.

"What are you here for, my body? Free legal advice?"

Though she's trying to be cheerful and may be joking, I sense she suspects my motives, no doubt trying to psych me out with that sticky ESP gift she's used with me since we were little. With Denise, you can run, but you can't hide. Maybe that's why we never got together sooner, because I've always placed a great value on dreams I didn't care to share with her.

The phone began to ring. "You don't mind if I kill it, do you?" I asked after a dozen rings, then picked it up and immediately set it down again.

"At this hour only lovers, insomniacs and third-shifters are awake," she said.

"And drunks. This one's probably dialing us from the bar, mistaking us for his taxi ride home. Don't you hate distractions, Denise?"

"Here, let me help you concentrate on what's at hand," she said.

She's pulled back from me and makes me close my eyes to focus my attention on her caresses. She starts with my knees, slowly working her way higher on my body. Her mouth is close to my ear, and I feel the flick of her tongue. I am breathing fast, and now that I'm fully swollen, she uses my piece like playing a tune she's careful to leave incomplete, not wishing bring on the finale just yet.

She knows how to tease me, to bring me to the brink of climax, but no further yet. She pauses, waits for me, closes her eyes. My fingertips explore her full breasts, her taut stomach, padded buttocks, powerful legs and muscular arms. A body within which no baby will ever be conceived and grow. A contradictory and thrilling body, the feminine competing with the masculine, a first-class brain ordering it. And controlling her brain, an intuitive and extrasensory power. Without words as we make love, I feel very close to a strong and kind woman, one I would have done well to pay better attention to twenty years back.

"If you're ready, I am," she said.

No guessing Denise's intentions, a woman who bluntly speaks what's on her mind, she's unmistakably ready for me. I'm here to please her, a lovely assignment. I'm about as excited to be inside her as the first time. Our breathing grows faster, in synch with our back and forth strokes. As the first time making love with her on the beach, I'm hearing the same music, chorus and pipe organ! Religious—sacreligious, I don't care, the song comes from us, our bodies are our instruments, and our music plays to the heavens! And as I felt when I was a naive boy, these bits of joined flesh change forms! We follow our notes toward listening angels— away from this world! Intense! Yes, the finale, climax!

I arrive just before her first shudder, after which another follows. I feel the pull of gravity, falling back to Earth from the heavens. In my own body I feel a warm glow after our perfect performance together. I'm glad she's quiet right now. I believe she's as content as I am, without needing to account for her feelings with unnecessary words, just as I wouldn't care to explain to her the new images filling my mind. I now imagine I'm at my very peak, running. I'm eluding all the players desperately trying to take me down. After a hundred-yard sprint I fly through the end zone, winning the game for my college team and a fat contract with the pros for myself, a double victory. An old dream of glory I've forgotten for so long but which has now come back to me.

"I'll never understand men," she said into my ear suddenly, startling me from my dream.

"You should know me by now."

"Were you thinking I have just you in mind?"

"Apparently not," I said. "Before I arrived there was Roger."

"And by bullying him you quickly saw to it that he was gone. Actually you men are predictable: fight or flight."

"Then blame yourself for being worth the fight."

"And what about Martha—are you still fighting for her? What is she worth to you?"

"It's been a lovely evening. How about keeping her out of this bed, where she doesn't belong, and for your part you can keep out your ex-husband Steven. Deal?"

"*Quid pro quo*, but not so fast," Denise said. "I'm a little bit confused. I thought Martha was out of the picture. Or rather, she put you out. So is that why you're here, because you've become lonely and homeless? Should I feel sorry for you then?"

She's certainly setting her net, but I'm not obligated to swim into it and become dinner on her plate.

"You know, sweetheart," I said, "I'm not very good at these cross-examinations at 2A.M. Can we adjourn? Isn't it predictable that we get some sleep when we're tired?"

"That's one good way not to have to talk about your issues."

I know I can avoid this discussion by saying nothing, but now I'm curious how I can annoy her so much and attract her at the same time.

"What issues?"

"I mean who controls you?"

"Nobody!"

"Doesn't your not-quite-former wife?"

"Ridiculous!"

"Then why don't you leave her already?"

"I have."

"Oh, really? Then you're asking me to take you in?"

"Yes."

"Overnight? For a few days? Indefinitely?"

I can't blame her for wanting to know where I stand with her, but I can't let her know until I know where I stand with my home, my wife in my home.

"Maybe we should play it by ear," I said.

"Maybe I should throw you out," she said, "but I won't. Though you're not as charming as you once were, I think you could improve without so many disasters in your life. Besides, I believe in redemption."

She's not exactly complimenting me, but I'm not about to ask her whether by redemption she means that she intends for this reunion to become permanent. I'm thinking about here and now and very happy to be spending tonight beside her.

Chapter 7
A Man From Nowhere

I would have loved to stay on with Denise for the weekend and past, perhaps indefinitely. By Sunday brunch I had gotten her to commit to helping my fight against Borak. But before she could officially take me on as a client, I had to promise to make a good-faith effort to come to a settlement with him. A reasonable deal between us, which I did not want to jeopardize by overstaying my welcome and giving her a chance to change her mind.

I'm not afraid to meet Borak face-to-face again on his own territory, as soon as possible, rather than set up a formal meeting and give him time to develop a strategy to combat me. I probably should have dropped in on him months ago, before Denise's demand that I try once more to talk truce terms with him. But now when I find him I may as well find out how responsible he is for the lies about me in *The Sun*. They make me out to be a big-time polluter and swindler, rather than an honest businessman hired to clean up other people's mess! He's pushed me too far this time!

The federal office building, downtown in the capital, built of monolithic stone. Ten stories of columns on three sides, like a Greek temple, housing him and generations of bureaucrats like him in dignity, constructed of materials and in a style far more substantial and noble than any other building. Granite on the outside to withstand a thousand years of weather, smooth and workable marble on the interior, architecture no doubt designed to impress the citizens into compliance, not myself though. A building designed to show the state's power over them, to make them comply by paying their tribute on schedule.

Jacques D'Amour, my grandfather, a stone mason from France, a country full of cathedrals, helped build this place late in the nineteenth century, when the railroad finally arrived. A fine artisan with twenty generations of D'Amour stone masons before him. All those generations of my forbears, far more religious than I'll ever be, even if I could find reasons to become a churchgoer again. My family of cathedral builders, skilled in shaping, moving and setting thirty-ton stone blocks, fitting them a hundred feet above ground like a child's jigsaw puzzle. I wish I knew how big Grandpa Jacques' talent really was, whether he was as great as the best of the master carver D'Amours. In the old world his forbears would have carved medieval gargoyles, hideous enough to scare off those devils lurking in the corners. Or to capture the positive side of the imagination, he might have illustrated in three dimensions of stone the Bible tales the peasants were unable to read. But this being the cold end of America and a federal building rather than a church, Jacques as the chief of the masons labored with his crew of artisans to carve to government specifications New World themes, designed to encourage obedience not to God, but to the officials residing inside this stone temple of the bureaucrats. It was all part of a grand design in which they also created the state capital, the state supreme court and a couple of churches in the same columned Greek style. As I'm standing before this massive building with Borak inside, if I'd brought binoculars I could look up ten stories to the roof where I could see better the figures I remember of justice, obedience, duty, and service. Grandpa's handiwork, figures with an instructional civic purpose.

The doors are eight feet tall, with heavy brass hinges. These are permanently shut, so I go through the modern glass entry, where the guards can see me before I can set foot inside. They may think I want to proceed to the left to the post office side of the building, but they're wrong. I haven't come here to buy stamps or mail letters. I have more important business in mind in one of the offices on the top floors. I'm going to see if I can catch Commissioner Borak in his office right now.

The guard's handing me a plastic basket for the contents of my pockets, as they do in the airports, before I'm allowed to pass through the metal detector.

"Please place any keys, coins or other metallic objects here."

I could ask this guard a lot of questions myself, like whether he got that scar on his cheek by accident or fighting in the streets. He's not a young man, could be a retiree from the police force or the military who has to go back to work to pay his bills. A rent-a-cop, I'd guess, not a full-time government employee with a cushy medical and pension benefits package. An incredible security apparatus here, ever since the Oklahoma federal building was bombed. If these Feds weren't running scared of their constituency, they wouldn't have a Checkpoint Charlie like this. Grandpa Jacques would have never believed the electrical equipment installed here in his federal cathedral.

"I see you've written *Environmental Persecution Agency* as your destination, Mr. D'Amour. I must alert you about federal law regarding jokes."

I can see he doesn't care for my sense of humor. He has a grim look on his face as he points to a posted sign warning against jokes about bombs. Evidently he doesn't like the name of the destination I've written on his identification sheet. If I want to pass through here, I better do things his way. "Sorry, didn't mean to offend, Mr. Spinello," I said.

"That's better. Now if you'll fix your spelling here to *Environmental Protection Agency*, you may proceed," he said. I complied by crossing out the offending word in the register at his inspection station and replacing it with the right one. "And you need to write in who you intend to see. That's better: *Wynton Borak, EPA chief.* Hold it there, sir."

Wish he'd make up his mind. First sends me through the detector, then stops me at the elevator.

"I'll ring up Mr. Borak's office first."

Now he's retreated behind his glass partition, probably bulletproof, to watch me while I make my call.

"I'm afraid the receptionist has no record of any appointment for this morning."

"I didn't say I had one. I was just going to pop in on Wynton to say hi."

"A social type visit? With the chief? During business hours?"

"OK, Mr. Borak's too busy, how about his assistant, Moretti? Will you ring up Mr. Moretti and tell him I've got some news for him?"

"Mr. Moretti says that Mr. Borak doesn't have time for you now, but wants to know what kind of news."

"Tell him it's sensitive news. I can't explain it from here in the guard shack, because it's something visual."

Once again Spinello's relaying my message up to Borak's office, but this time he's called up a replacement at the guard station so he can ride with me on the elevator. He punches in the fifth floor button, though the EPA is on the top floor.

"Penthouse, please!" I said, punching the tenth floor button. He punched the fifth once again.

"You must know we allow no residences, penthouses or otherwise, in any federal office building. We're not cleared yet for tenth floor Environmental Protection. Watch your step," he said with menace in his voice as I leave the elevator on the fifth floor, with him a couple of steps behind me.

This overzealous soldier's determined not to let me out of his sight, waiting for me to make my next move. I can see I'm dealing with a highly disciplined professional sentry who's trick of the trade is to dump out the contents of his mind for the duration of his shift.

"Very good advice," I said.

An uncomfortable situation I need to defuse. Before we go any further, before we get to Borak's office, I need to talk to him man-to-man, to try to get him on my side. "But does your advice about having fun work with your wife or girlfriend? I mean do you know women? Do you have children by one or by more than one of them, Mr. Spinello?"

"What are you getting at, Mr. D'Amour?"

"How many have you got?"

"Six. But only five are living at home."

No wonder this guy's so stressed out, too little money and too many mouths to feed. I wonder whether he's ever figured out the connection between making the babies and supporting them. Leaving the house and coming to work probably seems like a vacation to him.

"Let's say you come home late from the swing shift, or even later from the graveyard shift and everyone in the house is sleeping. Except for your old lady or young lady, whichever the case may be, who shares your bed . . . Of course, it's none of my business, but isn't it OK if she's in the mood to make fun with her before she changes her mind?"

"If she's at work, she wouldn't be home, right? What are you getting at?" he asked again, looking at me suspiciously.

"Oh, nothing, just the truth. But before I get to that, how about giving me some advice about when you prefer to make fun —before work, after work, or in-between? Strictly off the record, what would you suggest?"

He's not answering me, but staring, trying to make sense of me. Now he takes off his hat and is scratching his head. I wonder what kind of notes he's writing about me in his pad.

"I would advise that you quit fooling around and work harder. That's how I got where I am today, sir."

A ridiculous advertisement for himself, but I don't dare crack another smile. A strange man. A good-looking man with a square face and thick, wavy hair, except for that impressive scar on his cheek. I would guess if he didn't get that cut in the military, then he was in a knife fight as a young man. Either way, he seems to be a tough guy at his core. Why is he nodding at me now? Actually he's not, but looking over my shoulder at Moretti, Borak's right-hand man, a man who can fill a room with his dignified presence. With his tall, cultured, haughty looks he could play the part of an ambassador. I don't know how long Moretti's been standing behind me, observing me. Stealth is part of his bag of tricks.

"Good to see you, Mr. D'Amour," Moretti said, shaking my hand. "This visitation comes as something of a surprise. Our calendar's quite full, I must tell you. To what do we owe the honor? I haven't seen you since we were at your office for our discovery."

I remember his *discovery*, running it for his boss like an Easter egg hunt, rummaging through all our papers and trash baskets, even our used napkins. To accomodate them we had to assign Rachael to him for a week to pull files and copy them for him. I know full well what the EPA was looking for then and what they're looking for now: a treasure map leading to a smoking gun that would make me a criminal and Borak a hero. Of all the Potentially Responsible Parties they've identified, it looks like they're coming down hardest on Resolutions, Inc., and me personally. These Feds have infiltrated my office and are even turning my employees against me! I know the games the EPA's been playing. But if I want to get anywhere with Moretti today, I must make him feel he's important. A player rather than a briefcase carrier for Borak the chief.

"While we might not agree on every issue, I've always had a great respect for your sense of fair play," I said. "That's why I'm coming to you policymakers right now. Though we could let the court sort it all out, I've always made it a policy to do business with the principals like yourself, rather than with your staff."

"Yes, absolutely," Moretti agreed with me. "Everything else being equal, like you I prefer to operate under sound principles. Of course, as a practical man, dealing with people on a daily basis, I always look at both sides. Reminds me of the time a wealthy man, a district manager in the private sector, told me once you lose your principles, the rest is a piece of cake. Don't you agree? My philosophy is there's never a right and a wrong."

It's clear to me Moretti's has no principles in dealing with Resolutions and would love the chance to rip me apart. A perfect man for his government job a self-righteous yes-man in a position of responsibility far above his level of competence. I'm not quite done with him yet.

"Was this wealthy businessman a friend of yours?" I asked.

"Not exactly. We were working with him to clean up his act, so to speak. He mistakenly thought he could set the foundation of his shopping center in an historical site without calling in the archaelogists."

"What does that have to do with the EPA?"

"You understand that everyone needs to get our approval first. But he thought he could bypass us, and we wouldn't notice. No problem, time's on our side. In his case we ended up working with the Historical Register to shut him down. In the end we got to keep our wetlands, which he was filling in a dumpload at a time without permits."

"And what happened to him, if you don't mind my asking?"

"Sure. It's public information at this point because we've long since closed it out. Let's just say we redistributed some of his assets to public coffers."

"I'm asking what happened to him!"

He's saying nothing, maintaining a diplomatic poker face, leaving me to imagine what they did to ruin his life. Moretti's a predator in a worsted suit. No doubt he scored bonus points with the agency for squeezing big fines out of that businessman. Wonder whether the EPA drove him to insanity, divorce, or at least bankruptcy? Either this creep operates with the ethics of an IRS agent seizing a widow's house, or else he's invented the story to serve as an example of the treatment I can expect if I don't settle their fraudulent claim that I'm responsible for the toxic seepage at Medford Pond. But I don't dare show him what I truly think of him. This guy's just the right man to assist Borak because principles don't matter to either one of them. Or maybe I'm giving this flunky credit for having far more power than he actually has. Borak's the player, and it's him alone I need to see.

"So let's see what you have for us," Moretti said. He was reaching for the new Medford Pond documents in my hand the General found showing the government's responsiblity over the past fifty years by knowing all about the hidden extent of the pollution at the site, long before Resolutions was involved in the clean-up contract.

"I'd love to share this with you right now," I said, "but this is privileged information, for Mr. Borak's eyes only."

"That will be all for now," Moretti said to the guard with a frown on his face.

"I have someone covering for me downstairs. I don't mind staying."

"We have things under control," Moretti said, "but stay at your station, just in case."

Moretti's once again sticking close to me and won't just send Spinello and me alone into the elevator. The three of us ride to the tenth floor.

"Now this must be where the important environmental business for the entire region gets done, Mr. Moretti," I said, once we were standing outside the EPA office. Moretti held the door open for me.

"Now if you'll give those papers to me, I can copy them right now," Moretti said, once again grabbing for my evidence without my permission.

"Not so fast, Mr. Moretti. Like yourself I prefer not to discuss privileged information, except with the principals."

"I promise to return the originals immediately after I burn the photocopies."

"*Burn*? Set them on fire. Would you do that in a metal wastebasket? Wouldn't that trip the fire alarm," I asked.

"No! I'm talking about burn a copy, making copies, giving you back everything you came with, damn it!"

"No need to get excited, Mr. Moretti. No, I'm afraid I couldn't take that chance because they're originals and very dear to us."

"Who's this *us* anyway?" Moretti asked.

"My defense team. We're pretty optimistic about our endgame strategy."

"That remains to be seen," Moretti said with the trace of a smile. "Did you have something so pressing to show us that you had to force your way through security without an appointment? You haven't picked a good day for a presentation because we've been quite busy."

"Of course, if you weren't so busy you wouldn't amount to so much."

So far so good, Spinello's finally gone, which leaves me up-stairs in the EPA command center, where Borak and Moretti have their quarters here in a suite separate from these drone workers. In this open space offices are defined by partitions that don't go to the ceiling, probably better for monitoring their conversations. It seems very quiet in here, not quite five o'clock, yet almost everyone has gone home early for the weekend. Besides Moretti only the receptionist remains. Now the phone on the desk in one of these cubicle offices is ringing.

"It's Mr. Borak," Moretti said.

Why's he muffling the phone against his chest? Something he doesn't want me to hear?

"You can tell Mr. Borak we found us a new Potentially Responsible Party," I said.

"Who?"

I'm tired of waiting for this guy to relay messages to his boss, so I pick up a blinking phone line myself in another cubicle.

"Mr. Borak, I'm ready, willing and available. Let's get on with it," I said to him on the phone. "I'll be there before you can say *Little Jack Horner sat in his corner . . .*"

"Suit yourself," Borak said.

Finally Moretti has no choice but to bring me to the chief. First through the anteroom where the receptionist is waiting for me. A dignified lady, salt-and-pepper hair, looking me over close-ly as I drink the coffee she's prepared, looking at me like she can't trust me. Then walking past her, led by Moretti, I come to Borak's door and knock on it, but no answer.

"Anybody home?" I called.

"We don't honor verbal clearances here, except for authorized personnel or for visitors with scheduled appointments," Moretti explained. "Please stand over there."

He's put me twenty feet down the hall so I can't see the code number he's punching into the keypad by the next door, lead-ing me, I hope, to Borak's innermost office suite. Now that he's punched in the code, he signals me back so I can pass into the anteroom, bringing me closer to the chief's quarters. Nineteenth-century dark paneling and wainscoating of mahogany, matching love seat and wingchairs. Victorian floral upholstery. The work of a decorator with good taste, as well as taxpayer dollars. Hail to the chief! Now I need to find him to hail him.

"You don't know how helpful you've been. Be good. I'll be right back. Don't go away," I said to Moretti.

I try to move farther inward, but Moretti blocks my progress. I hear a toilet flush. That's where the emperor is, on the throne. I bet he has a bathtub in there too. Maybe he's taking a bubble bath. Perhaps he believes if he stays in there and ignores me long enough, I'll get tired of waiting and go home. Meanwhile, I'll have a closer look at his working conditions.

"Very curious, Mr. Moretti, this formica podium."

"Why's that?"

"I doubt Mr. Borak would give speeches here in his office."

"Precisely, it's his practice podium."

"And, furthermore, it doesn't match the rest of the wood-work."

I knock on the wainscoating at waist level here, not the genuine article.

"Hollow, doesn't sound like real wood. Is this plastic?"

"I can assure you, we have nothing faux here!"

"I didn't know Mr. Borak did any public speaking. Do you have sales rallies for your select agents in order to encourage them to meet your quotas?"

"Nothing like that! We're not part of the private sector. Here our mission is to protect America's environment, not produce revenue. We're not nearly as well-funded as we should be and don't have the resources that the IRS has, for example."

The IRS stays alive by seizing what doesn't belong to them, and Moretti would like to be more like them!

"None of my business, but why's this podium in front of the mirror?" I asked.

"For Mr. Borak to know how his audience sees him."

"Naturally."

"And why this little step stool by the podium?"

"For a little step up," Moretti said. "Put yourself in his place." Judging by his barely perceptible smile, I've said something to him that he must know is true. Once again the phone rings, and he goes off to another room to answer it. Now I'll use this opportunity alone and position myself behind the podium, bending myself over to better imagine a lower perspective, Borak's. I try to imagine myself in his place, a foot less than my height. Not quite enough shortness yet, I need to bend a little more—make that a foot and a half less. And now I have to imagine myself straining, a tiny man standing on tiptoes in front of an audience and still unable to view the front half of the room. It would seem to be easier for Borak to do away with the podium altogether when he speaks to meetings, but then they'd see him revealed as a little person and might not pay him as much attention. Which could prove a dangerous loss of credibility. From my dealings with him, I'm beginning to suspect he may be an emperor with no clothes. Now for his stool which raises him up so he can see over the podium: I get up on it, while trying to lower my legs and bend myself over a foot and a half smaller. Instantly my stature has improved in the eyes of the audience, and I've transformed myself out of the land of the munchkins to normal range. In the mirror I see the object of my imaginings, Borak himself. At ten years old my boy Ryan was bigger than him, who can't stand any more than four-ten.

"I hope I'm not disturbing you or taking you away from something important. Sorry for any inconvenience," I said.

"And I hope you didn't come here to socialize, because I wouldn't want you to waste the little time I'll set aside this morning to review your petition. Shoot."

I hand him the article from *The Sun*, which he takes by the corner, as if he were afraid of catching a disease from it. He then retreats to his desk and reads it with his magnifier. Moretti's back with us again and stands tall right by him, more as a bodyguard than as an assistant. I use my opportunity to study Borak at close range, starting with his feet, which don't reach the floor. He swings them like a restless child, maybe to keep up the circulation. The pair of them, an unlikely combination. Moretti standing over Borak like the puppeteer with his marionette. I can imagine Moretti picking up his boss's body, controlling it by ropes and throwing out his own voice.

"I thought you needed to see this first," I said.

"So what do you think this is all about?" Borak asked and looked over his glasses.

"Here, let me help you," I said and came behind the desk, right next to him. "You know, I always prefer to read the headline first. They generally tell me what to expect."

"Obviously," Moretti said.

"Let me read this one to you," I said, and took the article back to show Moretti. *"COAST GUARD PLACES BOOM OVER MOUTH OF MEDFORD CANAL.* See the date? This article was written in 1952, a long time ago. The way I figure it, the Coast Guard put that boom across the mouth of Medford Pond for a reason."

"He must be calling to our attention the portable dam they built to lower the level from the high rains that spring," Borak said to Moretti nervously.

I caught him off guard. He wouldn't have such a quick answer for me if he wasn't familiar with that procedure. *Portable dam*, no way. The Coast Guard wanted to contain the pollution they knew about in 1952, long before I came on the scene, and that boom was a quick fix.

"In that news picture you can see all the warning signs to keep people away from the danger zone," I replied.

"Not a place where I'd care to swim," Moretti said.

"Thanks for sharing that with us, Mr. Moretti," Borak said with a stern glance and began escorting him out of the room and toward the reception area. "Hold all calls until I'm done with Mr. D'Amour."

"I'll be out here if you need me," Moretti said as he was leaving.

"Mr. D'Amour, you caught me at a particularly busy time. Unless you can show me how this old news clip might apply in any way, shape, or form to the remediation plan to restore Medford Pond, as well as to the adjacent impacted land and the contiguous water table, I'm afraid we have no further business to discuss now."

That's what he'd like to believe, that he can get away with blaming me for Medford Pond, conveniently forgetting that the Coast Guard had tried to contain the mess with a flimsy dike, long before I had anything to do with it. But if he thinks he can dismiss me as easily as he can that lackey of his he banished to the next room, he's wrong. Now that I'm showing him this copy of an old bill from the Coast Guard to the EPA, there's no way he'll be able to deny the connection between the Coast Guard boom and the EPA.

"Where did you get this?" Borak asked.

I've got the goods on him with this receipt from my friend Bill Haig's plumbing business, which was the main source of materials for the Coast Guard pollution dam. A receipt for materials for construction of the boom they built to hold the pollution from leaching out of the pond and into the broad lake a few hundred yards away.

"From friends in high places, like yourself," I said.

"Obviously you took this from our internal files. If you obtained this information without proper authorization, it will not be admissible. By the way, just the other day I read about your son's accident. Was he drunk or under some other influence?"

"Funny that you speak of my son without actually knowing him. Have you heard about him secondhand? Inaccurate second-hand information can be very deceiving. Like the kind of story the editor Adrian Beardsley at that scandal sheet *The Sun* wrote about me, implying that I'm criminally negligent, based on your interview which picked on me, rather than any of the other Potentially Responsible Parties. Familiar with it?"

"I trust you have not arrived at our doorstep to tell us what newspaper we should be reading."

I don't care about Borak's reading habits, so much as about his bedmates, particularly when he's in bed with Beardsley and his reporter, making up profitable lies about me, ruining my business and my name. And not content to hound me, he could be moving on to my son. But I must stay on track and find out whether he knows any more about Ryan than what he's read in the newspaper, and if he's snooping, what he intends to accomplish.

"Yes, he was involved in a car wreck, which the newspaper reported. Is that what caught your attention? Or did your source have a bigger story that caught your imagination?"

"That one, as well as one or two others. I know what I'd do with him if I were you."

"Mr. Borak, I don't know where you're from originally, but I know it wasn't from down east Maine. So why on Earth would you have any interest at all in the shennanigans of our local kids?"

"Because I live here now, and so do my children. And because my son Henry's picked up some bad habits from Littlehale, the car body man, as well as from your son Ryan. Frankly, I don't plan to ever see my son's name in print like yours, not if I can help it. Before that can happen I'll pick myself up and move from here to give him a fresh start where he can find better companions!"

When he tries to make himself sound righteous, he's even more ridiculous than Moretti. I'd have to assume that if he were moving out of the area it would be to pursue to the big promotion that they spoke of in the article. A promotion helped along by the editor who he must have in his pocket, Borak's trying to take me down in the process of building up his career.

"So you plan to head for Washington, if you play your cards right?" I asked.

"Do you know that on his chest, Littlehale even made my son tattoo the gang name they gave him Little Boy, Little Banger, Little—"

"You wouldn't mean *Little B*?"

His mustard-colored brillo hair, the same as Little B's—how could I have failed to see the resemblance? And now that I'm looking at another Borak family trait, the weimaraner light gray eyes, and, of course, the same short and muscular build! It seems to me that Little B was the one who recruited Ryan into the gang, not the other way around. Ryan has never been violent, but as far as I know it's Borak's son Little B who's the true thug.

"Little B, yes, a shorthand nickname for Little Bastard, I believe, which, thanks to your son, doesn't reflect very well on the Borak name!" Borak shouted.

Of course—Little B and Wynton Borak, father and son! How could I have missed it?"

"I hope you didn't get the impression when I let you in my office that it gave you carte blanche to give me all your opinions."

"You probably should have thought of that before you offered your lousy opinions about my son Ryan."

"Admit it, you've been meeting regularly with my son Henry!"

"Once, I just told you."

"No, for the last year you've been meeting him along with Ryan and Littlehale, training him to be a better criminal! Admit it!"

Now I understand! His mistaken belief that Ryan and I have corrupted Little B, a perfect reason for his vendetta against me! And if he can make all the newspaper readers believe that he has stopped me, the criminal responsible for Medford Pond, it would most certainly boost his career, a double benefit for him!

"If you really wanted to know the true story you would have met with Ryan by now and asked him yourself."

"I know all I need to know, and if you think you can get away with—!" Borak shouted, but interrupted himself to answer the ringing phone.

It's OK . . . I have it under control, no problem yet. I will if it comes to that, Borak whispered. He then hung up.

"In other words, Mr. D'Amour," he continued, "it will be in your best interest to voluntarily stay away from this Little B monster you and your gangster son have created. Tell me, does your godfather Littlehale pay you well?"

"A reasonable enough question," I answered, "but first answer me this: did you take stupid pills this morning?"

"Now I see why the only people who will work for you are incompetents who haven't abandoned you yet. If you're lucky, you'll go back where you came from, laying bricks instead of that pretty little lawyer Pendergast. Did you have to find yourself a new lawyer after you couldn't pay Chip Thompson anymore?"

"I'm curious, Mr. Borak, not so much about your sources of information and misinformation, but where did you come from?"

"I'm a man from nowhere."

Was he born of a mother, crying like the rest of us, or did he start out chirping because he was hatched?

"So that might explain why you've been spending so much time looking into my private life, because you don't have a life of your own."

"We don't have to explain what we know, Mr. D'Amour. I'm only seeking the truth"

"My personal affairs are none of your business!"

I shouldn't have said it quite that way. He's must be taking my words literally, smirking, no doubt, at the image of Denise and me in his dirty little mind.

"Very well. Since we have nothing further to discuss, you can let yourself out and someone will see you to the street. By the way, Mr. D'Amour, we didn't have to spend much time researching your background. In effect, you've saved us the trouble because you're careless and negligent, an open book. Now if you'll excuse me . . ." he said and moved away from me to look out through his window at the gold dome of the capital building which was gleaming brilliantly at the warm-toned sun low in the sky.

Now that he sees I'm not leaving he thinks he can simply walk away from me after insulting me! Trying to hide from me just around the corner into his entertainment center. What's he doing? I hear a financial reporter touting the stock market. And now I see him sitting on the couch watching the TV. He's crossed over my boundary line, and the time's come for him to account for himself directly to me. I won't let him get away from me. We are going to finish this conversation.

"You, know, Mr. Borak, I like your setup back here. A refrigerator, snacking table, and microwave. Very homey. I'm thirsty. I see you're drinking orange juice. If you don't mind I'll join you," I said, poured myself a glass and sat on the loveseat in front of the television.

"You must leave here at once!" he shouted, pointing to the door.

"It must be nice to have a job like yours where they let you watch TV in the middle of the work day if it suits you."

Borak then went to his desk and began opening his mail with a dagger-like letter opener. "So if that's all we have to discuss—"

"No, you haven't even started to explain this to me!" I said and threw *The Sun* article before him.

Borak reviewed it with his magnifier silently for a minute or two. "You know private citizens, but especially public agencies like us can't be held responsible for any errors of fact or omisions by the press. So if you have a gripe, go take it up with them." He got up from his highbacked leather swivel chair, guiding me to the door by pushing at my waist. "So if you'll excuse me . . ."

"You've already pushed me about as far as I'm going to allow! Now cut that out!" Immediately the phone began ringing.

He reached for the receiver, which I pulled away from him. "I figure it's about time you gave me your undivided attention," I said.

"I have nothing more to say to you."

"But you have plenty to say about me, '*EPA CLOSES IN ON CANAL POLLUTER..*'"

"If the shoe fits, wear it."

"You're pretty bold about pinning the blame where it doesn't belong!"

"I resent that remark. I serve notice that you are now trespassing on private property!" Borak said, pushing a button on the telephone which must have made it to function as an intercom.

"You're the bold one, Mr. Borak, trying to protect that sawed-off loudmouth son because he hasn't the guts himself!"

"And now I see where your jailbird son gets his audacity, but if it's the last thing I do, I'll shut down the pair of you lawbreakers! Now if you're smart you will be gone before Mr. Moretti and security must take action," he said, pushing at me with his short but powerful legs set at a steep angle, grabbing my arms to try to dislodge me from the couch. "This is my last warning: I want you out of my office now!" Borak bellowed.

Only when he took his hands off me did I stand. He rolled up his hands into fists and began circling me. I let him land a few exploratory jabs, until one tricky punch caught me in the abdomen, knocking the wind out of me for a moment. He then used his advantage to catch me off-guard, pushing me backward into a freestanding set of shelves. Travel souvenirs and books crashed to the floor and the half emptied case crashing into the wall, somehow trapping me beneath it. Borak came closer to stand over me and laughed.

"Did I mention I've taken lessons in self-defense?" Borak asked.

"Because the big kids in school picked on you? Is that why you've grown into such an obnoxious adult," I asked, then quickly lunged and tackled him. But once I was holding him, I wasn't letting go. I ran around the office with Borak flung over my shoulder. The more Borak pounded with his fists, the harder I laughed, since it was my turn to win. Finally I stopped. "If you can't run with the big dogs, then you should stay on the porch!"

"I insist you put me down and leave the premises immediately!"

"Immediately, if not sooner!" I answered, and without looking backward, threw him off my back. He went flying into the dark glass separating his office from the reception office, shattering it into pebble-sized pieces. Borak lay on the floor dazed as he brushed the glass off his suit. Moretti raced in and tried to determine the extent of the damage to his boss.

"I can stand on my own two feet, damn it!" he insisted as Moretti tried to help lift him to his feet. "And I can hold my own."

I can hold my own. If I didn't know better it would seem he's boasting that he's potty trained.

And I bet his mother, whether she has feathers or scales or breasts that produce milk, is proud of that great accomplishment. I'm hearing two-way radios, coming closer. Now why do I get the feeling that we have some uninvited guests?

"Mr. Borak's injured!" Moretti shouted. He brushed his hand over Borak's bleeding temple.

"If I were you, I wouldn't touch that blood. You don't know where it's been. Here, let me help." I then went to the glass wall and kicked in the rest of it.

I don't watch my back for a minute, and now the storm troopers sneak up on me. Not one, but two guards. They're probably expecting an explanation.

"My friend and I were roughhousing, and we got a little carried away," I explained to Spinello, "but we both can see Mr. Borak is not really much the worse for wear." I showed him the first aid kit Moretti had taken from the bathroom of the inner office. "Of course, if you can find any wounds, you might want to help dab on some iodine."

In his last call Borak could have called in more security men. If so, I have no time to waste and must get out of here very soon.

"Sorry for the accident, Spinello. I know you're here to fill out an accident report or something," I said.

"From the minute I laid eyes on him, I knew he was trouble," Spinello said to Borak who wouldn't let anyone help him and was pressing tissues on his arms to stop the bleeding. "We already got more than enough on him, sir." Now Spinello motioned to Moretti to take a position in front of me while he maneuvered behind, setting the trap I feared.

"Unauthorized entry. Illegal trespass," Moretti suggested to Borak. "Destruction of government property. Assault and battery. And I think we might have threats against a federal official, as well as tampering with a federal investigation. Is that correct, sir?" Borak soberly shook his head in agreement. Spinello, was sitting behind the receptionist's desk, telephone in hand, reporting the incident again, as if those two guards plus Moretti weren't enough at his beck and call. He was rocking back and forth in the chair like an impatient judge at a tedious trial.

"How's this supposed to work, boss: you lie, and like good boys they'll swear to it?" I asked. "They used to do that during the Inquisition."

"We've had more than enough for one day. Now get him out of here," Borak ordered.

"No problem. Consider it done," I said, rushing to the door, which unfortunately was locked. "Mr. Borak didn't give you permission to skip off by yourself," Spinello said, rattling his big chain of keys provocatively.

"If you're detaining me I want to know why, because someone's going to be held accountable!"

None of them's answering me, a good sign. But I don't care to see Borak and Mortetti huddling with Spinello.

"I'm going to see a doctor, and you're going downtown," Borak said. "To ask you a few questions. Mr. Moretti, bring his file with you to the station in case they need background on this felon. Meanwhile, Mr. Spinello, you can hold him downstairs."

"A holding pen. It sounds like you're taking me to the feed lot. This little piggy's not going to market! Why don't you forget about hauling me anywhere and let me just go home."

"Resisting arrest? We'll see about that," Spinello said, drawing his 9mm pistol.

"Give me that!" Moretti ordered. In seconds he grabbed it, removed the clip and shoved it into his own pants pocket, a man familiar with firearms. "Our policy is to keep that sort of thing to a minimum."

Excellent. I'm winning this campaign. A loss of face for Spinello, who's turned very red. And now he's getting back at me by grabbing me by the back of the collar and pulling upward. Damn him, I'll make this make-believe storm trooper wish he never laid hands on me like that.

If I don't get out of here now, I never will. Here goes: a little step sideways, I drive my right elbow hard into my would-be captor's stomach! Now that he's doubled over and not breathing so well. I swing leftward half an arc and pound his head with my right elbow, firmly enough to put him out of commission, but not hard enough to drop him into a coma! There! The deed's done, and Borak's looking at me wide-eyed, like I might lose my patience one more time and give him the same treatment!

"Halt!" Spinello strained to call to me, his breathing shallow and fast, as I began running from them all.

I don't think he can stop me yet! I don't challenge him or waste words on him, but try putting as much distance between him and me as possible before he can regroup!

"I said halt!" he repeated.

He's spraying something at me! Ducked in time! Red paint! Red pepper! Terrible stuff! I'm coughing, not critical, but Moretti's right behind in this corner of the corridor where I've been trapped, and he's choking, along with Spinello!

"O-O-Out of h-h-here, Spin—!" Moretti struggled to speak. "G-g-get h-h-him!" he ordered.

"Yes, sir! Sorry about your office, sir," Spinello murmured, speaking through a hankerchief he held over his face.

Spinello has no gun and can't shoot me. They have no real charges against me, and I'm not going to let them shift me to the real police where they'll invent some. I have nothing to lose, everything to gain by getting out of here now. With all my strength I launch myself between them to get to my escape route, the stairs, which I take two at a time! I know he'll be waiting to intercept me on the ground floor, so I go only as far as the fourth floor, where I can go to the back of the building and take the fire stairs instead.

"I knew where I'd find you! Welcome!" Spinello said, waiting for me behind the sixth floor fire door, surprising me and tackling me to the floor. "You're fast, but not fast enough to outrun the elevator! You can run, but you can't hide from me! We have monitors everywhere! Now you're mine!"

I fight him off long enough to get to the elevator, which I can't get to open. "It's no use, you can punch the up button or the down button all day and you won't get one of the elevators, because I have them all locked up," Spinello said, jangling his keys. "Now we can do this the easy way or the hard way, your call!"

He comes at me with his night stick, which I seize and use on his head, knocking him cold. This rent-a-cop with no authority over me pushed me too hard. Now with him out of the way I should be able to get out of here! But on the fourth floor I hear a man talking into a radio. If it's another guard, does he know my location here, or do I have a chance of getting out of this building? I stop, put my ear against the door, hear him coming down the hall, but not sure if it's toward me. That leaves me with nothing for my self-defense but a fire extinguisher, which I take off the wall. I stand behind the fire door and wait! My heart's beating fast, head pounding with the beat. This one kicks in the door like a drug-buster. He has tattoos, one with an anchor, and a big moustache. He's watched too many TV raids, but he'll see I'm for real! I spray him, douse him good with the chemical foam! I'm careful not to hit, punish, assault him any more today, but leave him wiping his burning eyes and move out. I run down the stairs, but he hasn't given up. Let him try catching this empty extinguisher! He intercepts it with his hard head, which knocks him to the floor, too bad! Meanwhile I'm off like a greased streak!

I fly down to the third floor and across the corridor to the main stairway, where for a second I look over the railing, and see where I'm headed, and all seems to be clear to the open door of the lobby. Now for the home stretch! Nearly home free! But now it's another guard waiting for me, this one younger than Spinello, maybe not even fifty, a very big man with a thick neck, a good six-four, grinning, baton in hand! No way I'm going to let this gorilla get in my way! I'll charge into him like a twenty-ton snowplow, freewheeling without brakes down an icy mountain road!

He's holding that black baton raised high to beat me! I push it aside and slam his soft body into the wall with both hands! Big as he is, I cannot use all my strength and risk knocking him unconscious, but a couple of steps past him, and he's jabbing me with that stick, lik0e I'm some kind of a dog. Now I have no choice, must teach them about fooling with an innocent man, the final lesson of the day.

He doesn't give up! He's lunging at me with it, trying to block my way, driving me against the stair railing! Like a fencer in search of a partner, only we're now playing my game, not his. I grab the baton out of his hands and pull it away from him.

He's holding on to his stick as if his very life depended on it. I don't have time to play with him. This time must kick him in the tibia hard enough to break it. No other way to stop him. I focus on his leg; he tries to tag me with his stick, which is wrapped to his hand with a strap.There, see my opening, launch my kick. But just before I plant it, he touches me with this baton.

ZAP! An electric shock! It's a cattle prod disguised as a nightstick! An electric club! Not just a sting this time, but he's taking a bite out of me and chewing on me, no mercy. *ZAP!* I want to fight back, but muscles won't take my orders anymore, and my head's overloaded to busting. He has me in his power, body and mind. Vision blurred and distorted, like looking through a smear of Vaseline. Head exploding! *ZAP!* All control gone! Pants wet, I think, but can't tell. Massive electricity scrambling up my nerves. Sending them into spasms. Whatever I do, I must never let him win.

I'm holding on to the railing and must stay on my feet at all costs! That's what my mind wants, but his assaulting electrons have jammed brain, muscles, and the pathways between. This bully's not done playing with me though. He shoves me backward hard into the railing, and I'm like a boxer knocked against the ropes! The match is over for me, but not for him. He's coming at me, teeth bared in a mad dog smile! He hoists me up above the railing, looking at me with a different kind of smile now, more like a happy little girl inspecting her favorite doll. His mood changes. He's angry at me, his limp rag doll. His smile now turns ugly, and he comes at me like a boxer now needing one good blow to finish the match, with a slam into my gut! Completely helpless, I can't stop him! He wants me dead! He sends me over the rail! I'm falling backwards! Tumbling down the stairwell! Soft falling body gaining speed toward my destination! I imagine Martha, Ryan, Erica and Denise watching me from those stairs as I fall, past them in slow motion! Falling to my destination fifty feet below! Falling toward the concrete landing! Falling!

Chapter 8
Twilight Sleep

*L*izards sooted up and down the rough plaster walls, across the floor and on the ceiling as I lay on my back. If they pass in my line of vision slowly enough and it's daylight I could recognize them by the different markings on their tails. The people would come briefly to take care of me, but the lizards were with me all the time, my companions. Nothing but twilight sleep, no telling how many days and nights. Thick wooden shutters on the windows instead of glass. When the nights came, candles in sconces lit the room a pale flickering yellow. People in dark gowns with rope belts chanted and cared for me. Mealtimes they'd prop me up and use a bamboo tube to siphon soups or porridge into my mouth and down into my stomach. Also down the tube bitter medicines they'd ground and mixed in bowls.

I don't believe they took me from the room and moved me outside because the medicines, or prayers, or leeches weren't working. I have to believe that if the matador hadn't arrived, they would have kept me in the room for a while longer. They weren't set up to handle more than one visitor in distress at a time. After all, they were holy people of deep faith, not healers. Devoted to prayer, teaching, winning new souls and keeping up the grounds, not to mending hurt people like myself who'd been deposited in their care.

The matador's violet silk shirt, plastered with two shades of blood, his own and the bull's. Torn, revealing a hole in his side, which they filled with dried grass from a bird's nest. Had we both fought monsters stronger than us, and would either of us survive after we'd been beaten? They had reasons for working with him more than with me. Good reasons or not, I was scared to be alone now in the dark back corridor with no windows.

When they finally did remember to feed me again, they didn't give me the usual porridge, but a very deep bowl of the most sublime pudding, specially made to run freely, which they took turns siphoning to me with the bamboo. After that soft and memorable meal, they changed me into a gown of the same violet silk as the matador's, but with the hole miraculously mended without a trace of damage. I hoped they didn't give me the delicious treat because he'd died and couldn't use it anymore.

By then I was resigned to being on my own and prepared myself for the move. Finally they removed me from the stone building, carried me out in a reclining chair to the very center of the courtyard, and set me underneath an umbrella.

My eyes are not used to the natural light and the brilliant color. My gaze fixes on the intense purple lilacs outside the cloister gates. I know how sweet they would smell to the average man, but I also know I'm different now. How could I have failed to notice before now that my nose isn't working right! If a man can't smell he can't taste, so why did my last meal seem to please me so much, unless both my smell and my taste have failed me immediately afterward? And what will be the next part of my body to fail?

If I want to live, I must first get myself on my feet. Through many sunrises and sunsets I imagine myself out of my recliner. I test my weak legs, holding my arms tight to my chair. I stand a little longer day by day, until I walk steps, finally all the way across the courtyard. I try opening the heavy iron gate, but don't have the strength yet. Oh, God, if I can only pass to the other side! Free me from this compound!

Just a prayer, a wish, but by a miracle my body accommodates my desire by changing me to a new spirit form, allowing me to seep through the space between the iron bars. Leaving me recreated on the other side, standing outside the walls of the monastery, beside the lilacs. The lilacs I should be smelling if there's enough life remaining in me. A crucial test, my life hanging in the balance. I need to know just how much I might be able to smell in order to gauge how much life I have left, if any.

It must be a thorough test, a true reflection of reality. I start by picking lilacs in full bloom and gather them up into a bouquet. I haven't been breathing, but now I will myself to breathe again like living people, expecting to smell the lilacs as sweet as I remembered they should be. But my willpower isn't strong enough to allow me to draw breath again, much less smell this bouquet! I can't fill my lungs anymore, and the lilacs are turning to shades of gray in my hands! Even the grass is turning gray, the green leeched from it, leaving me in a world without color, or smell, or without anyone at hand to help me anymore. I don't really mind though because now I'm in a better place where I don't have to spend my days resting and waiting. I may be alone, but I'm no longer dependent on the mercy of others.

Since I'm not really breathing anymore and I've lost my smell and taste and can't see color, I'm walking away entirely from those well-intentioned people whose cures haven't worked for me. With nothing much more to lose, heading for where the road might take me. I have no provisions, no shoes on my feet, nor do I have a watch with me. Time doesn't matter to a person like me without people to meet and appointments to keep, yet I'm hearing something ticking or beeping like a clock. I don't know how long I've been walking, but it seems like a long time, the loud clock beats following me all the while. That brings me to evening, another sunset, in black and white, and then the confusing darkness, making it hard to see where my feet are taking me all the time, to know where I'm going. I am traveling beside a dense forest. From within it on my right side, a lady's voice calls to me, "Ned, welcome!" I want to answer, but now in addition to my other losses, I have no voice.

Searing light overwhelms my weak eyes, blinding manmade light. BLEEP, BLEEP, BLEEP, BLEEP, BLEEP measuring for me a beat at a time my living heart.

The woman who's been following me and kept herself hidden must have a good reason for wanting to speak with me. If not an angel and not a devil's assistant, then she must be a person, alive.

"Welcome back, Ned! Welcome home! I've been praying for you and for the young man you struck. Rest now. Don't try to talk. Now I have to tell everyone that you'll make it!"

Sister Beatrice her tag says, pinned to her white nurse's uniform. No color either in her black hair. But her skin is ruddy and her lips are pink! Colors—I can see color again!

"Please tell Ryan about me first, then my daughter Denise! You can tell them I've come back! Tell them I think I'm here because I cheated death. But please don't tell everyone, promise?"

"That's OK, you rest."

"I mean it! Promise I'll only see who I want!"

From the first moment he met me, Dr. Garcia had it in for me, as if I were really a criminal. He doesn't seem to care whether I recover or not, so much as I heal up enough to get out of here and be punished soon. He's encouraged the police officers to try to interview me only one day after Sister Beatrice's visit! Good thing today she hasn't quite gone off duty, so she can help get them away from me. Fitch's at my bedside with a couple of cops, one in a uniform different than his, as well as one man in plain-clothes on crutches with both a leg and arm cast and a badge on his shirt.

"Police business, Mr. D'Amour, assisting today for the third district," Fitch said, grim-faced, not looking directly at me. He shows me his badge, as if I don't already know him too well, and the other uniformed policeman follows suit and shows me his. I'm ambushed here without being able to defend myself. I have my leg and arm in casts, an infection in my damaged kidney. They tell me I hit my head hard enough in the fall that I'm lucky to be alive or even to speak, that I'd been unconscious for two weeks. No one could tell now by looking at me since the head bandages were removed, but I don't concentrate and don't remember nearly as well as before, and I still have to learn how to walk much better. I know I'm not ready to answer a lot of questions. When I squeeze the buzzer by my bed for help, thank God Beatrice promptly responds and escorts them out of her hospital. Close call. I'm glad to be left alone, for the time being at least.

A week or so later I've finished a meal requiring a knife, fork and spoon and have dozed off during the television news of a flood and a war when I wake up hearing an argument not far from me.

"No, I came to see him right now! If you think I'm going to turn around now, screw you!"

I'm in twilight sleep, between life and death again. Or else that voice I'm hearing could be the echo of my own, as I'm stand-ing alone in the lobby of the empty federal building. I need to know what business I must complete and whether I'm talking to myself or to living people.

"Dad, get up! They won't give me much time! I don't have time to play around anymore! Time's money, remember? Only a dead man needs to sleep as much as you have!"

"Ryan?"

Ryan's laughing at me. I haven't seen him since I've been in the hospital because I've had no way of reaching him directly, and I'll be damned if I'd send someone to find Little B to deliver any message to him to visit me. He's wearing a leather vest and a high-collared white shirt and shined boots, not bad-looking today.

"What's so damn funny?" I asked.

"Time to go now," a young sister nurse insisted, holding my hand, looking suspiciously at Ryan's huge maltese cross.

"Nothing personal, Dad, but look who's talking about being in the wrong place at the wrong time."

"I don't remember."

"Of course you don't, Dad. That's why I'm here, to give you the true story, because none of these bootlickers around here will. I'm telling you that you could have landed square on your head on the concrete instead of sideways."

"Please, we can't allow this sort of thing during your father's recovery," the nurse interrupted.

"What sort of thing, the truth, miss? Well, I'm not done. Picture this, Dad—you would have been in even bigger trouble if that poor cop that was here with Fitch a couple of weeks back hadn't been in the wrong place at the wrong time, breaking your fall just enough to let you come back from the dead."

"I don't remember hurting anyone, just myself."

"Nothing critical. He broke a leg and an arm, gave him a scare. They discharged him while you were still in la-la land. But sounds like they're trying to make a big deal of it to shake you down for some money. Next time why don't you pick someone better to squash? This one was in a guard's uniform, but he was a municipal cop moonlighting from somewhere else. The municipal ones you don't want to mess with because they have too many buddies in and out of the courthouse. I bet he'd be a lot nicer to us if he was one of Fitch's deptuies."

"You've got to go now. Your father isn't up to all this stress," the nurse said.

"Friends?" I said, "Don't concern yourself, Ryan, because I have plenty of good friends. I'm not worried. But wait a minute. What about *your* enemies? Didn't I save you from someone who hurt you?"

"A long story, and they don't want me around here long enough to tell it. But don't worry about me right now, because now you have me on your side to take care of you. Why are you grinning, Dad? Think I don't know how to take care of myself, much less you?"

"Ryan, don't ask me a bunch of questions, because I don't know what to think lately."

"That's why you better get strong in a hurry. Like this you're no good to anyone."

———————

Strange family I have. There's Ryan trying hard to make a living as a criminal, always on the verge of being thrown in jail for a long stretch. And then his mother Martha, still my wife, the mother of my two children, yet she hasn't had the interest or even the curiosity to visit me on her own accord. Ryan's surely been in touch with her and told her about my accident weeks ago. Not that I'd care to confront her inevitable questions and accusations with these big holes in my memory. On the other hand, I can't afford the luxury of waiting to deal with her until I might be in better shape, not with Denise *insisting* I report to her my intentions toward Martha. In a way Denise is backing me into a corner, but at least with her it's a familiar corner.

And then there's Erica, who doesn't seem to care much more about my accident than her mother does. Though I haven't heard from her and know I shouldn't be the one calling, I do:

Oh, Dad, It's you. . . . What a surprise. . . . They let you call out already? No, I'll leave a message for her. . . . No, she's busy now. . . . Just busy; I don't know. . . . I can't promise anything. . . . No, I doubt she'll call you back. . . . Me, what for . . . ? Some of us have to work, you know. I'm so busy this week, tax time, inventory and all. . . . And the baby. Good sitters aren't easy to find. You understand. . . . You don't . . . ? I told you I can't just pick up and leave. When I see you next I hope you look better than when they first brought you in and your head was as big as a watermelon and you were all black and blue. . . . Nice talking to you.

I'm surprised when she shows up a couple of days afterward, not just by herself, but with her husband Derek.

"Feel any better, Pops?" Derek asked me.

He's shaking my hand. Now he's presenting me with a big get-well card with a stand-up center display of a bedpan, a greeting card writer's bad joke. Derek's more sociable than either of my own children, a guy easy to like, a good balance to artsy-craftsy Erica. In his high school basketball-playing days he never had much speed to work with, nor raw talent, but still a solid team player, reliable for defense. Not that the sport means that much to me anymore, but the way a player approaches his game gives me some insight into his character. Derek's blonde locks make him pretty as a girl. As for my daughter, she has the same pretty nose and fair complexion as her mother's, though she's allowed her appearance to slip. Erica's fortunate to have found someone as loyal and good-tempered as Derek. They're a handsome couple, even if oddly matched. He's even brought me a disc player, along with music retrieved from my collection at the house.

"I thought this would cheer you up," he said. "Here's the luau, minus the pig with the apple in his mouth. We could have brought you the dancing girls with the grass skirts, but we didn't want to upset the nuns here at Sisters of Mercy Hospital."

From that canvas satchel he's laying out both fruit and music. But Erica's looking through first the pears, then the peaches and plums, organizing them in some fashion, returning most of them back to the bag.

"That dark green color of your dress looks good with your blonde hair, Erica," I said, "Quite dignified."

A startling resemblance to her mother of about twenty years ago. Wearing a loose dress, good for hiding the weight she put on and never entirely lost since her pregnancy last year. Now that she's done taking back half the fruit, she's doing the same with the discs he brought me. She's never been very generous to anyone.

"Got this outfit at Derek's store, 15% employee discount, on top of the 30% off inventory reduction price. They sold out to Allied, the big clothing chain, but they promise not to fire anybody, though we're not sure whether they plan to gut the old building, during which they might lay everybody off for a couple of months. If bargains like this keep coming my way, Derek, I may never let you leave the store, that is if it continues to exist, and even if they never promote you past department manager," she said and gave him a kiss on the cheek.

Unbelievable how little she knows about restructuring these days. She doesn't seem to have a clue that he's most likely done at that location, that they really plan to take down the building and that they wouldn't be up and running again for the better part of a year. I'll have to talk directly to him sometime and see whether he understands his situation.

"Now are you going to tell me why you're rummaging through my recordings?" I asked.

"I'm returning those that belong to Mom, the Broadway musicals, as well as classical pieces with a lot of strings in them. Don't worry though, I'm leaving what's yours."

An old memory returns to me: when she was a youngster she'd hide her toys so Ryan couldn't find them. Never very willing to share anything with her friends, whether toys or food. A bean counter by temperament, good at counting other people's money. Comes by it naturally from her mother, even though they both think of themselves as artists.

"You did say you came by to visit earlier. But why did you wait so long to come back a second time?"

"I told you, Dad, a scheduling thing."

"And what about your mother? She's got a scheduling problem as well?"

"I don't want to talk about it now. Derek, could you get me a Diet Coke and a small bag of chips? Oh, and Dad likes to read the business news. It would be great if you could find him a couple of business magazines."

"By the way, did your mother ever come with you to see me when I was in the coma?"

"She didn't need to because I report back to her on your condition every time I've checked your progress. She was really very concerned about you."

I'll bet she was concerned, especially with all that life insurance riding on me if I don't make it. Now that I'm in my right mind, I should remove Martha as a beneficiary. That is, if I truly decide to remove her from my life.

"That's why she wanted to wait for the right time for me to contact you," Erica said.

"Can't your mother speak for herself?"

I didn't ask for these weird hide-and-seek games, and I don't appreciate Martha sending my daughter up here to report on me.

"Dad, you don't make this any easier for me! I didn't ask to be the one in the middle! If you'd been more sensitive to Mom's needs, it wouldn't have come to this. Here."

So that's the purpose of her visit, to give me this letter from Martha. By the looks, on Martha's best stationery. I should feel honored, the champagne colored engraved paper, usually reserved for correspondence with a couple of her out-of-town friends who moved to other cities. One is a former debutante who has the money and time to do charitable work; another, an equestrian friend who travels the horse show circuit six months of the year. But why are such unimportant details coming back to me, while

I still can't put together the important picture of where exactly I stood with my wife before this accident?

Derek returned with her snack. He himself began munching one of the apples he'd set out for me. "If we are what we eat, what does that make Erica, feeding on that junk?" Derek whispered into my ear while Erica was snacking to the other side of my bed.

"Didn't you think I heard that?" Erica said. "You men can be so insensitive."

So his funny little comment gives her the license to insult not only Derek, but me along with him? I don't think she'd be speaking to me so boldly if she hadn't been getting her cues from her mother. I'm sure she's read this pretty letter she's brought me today, and has been instructed to report to her on my reaction to it. She hasn't been here but a quarter hour, and she's already putting on her coat.

"Where are you going?" I asked her.

"Someplace else where I won't get indigestion."

"Be quiet, Erica. He's your Dad. If I talked to mine like that, I'd pay the price," said Derek.

"You mean he'd get physical, he'd get abusive? I'm sorry to tell you guys, but we don't have to tolerate abuse any more."

Derek's just smiling at me. I can see what he's got to overcome with his wife. I'll break the seal of the letter and see what glad tidings Martha has posted to me. Now if Erica already knows the contents, and if Derek is playing on my team, there's no reason I can't share the contents with them. After all, they're family, and this is family business. I want to read it before my impatient daughter leaves. Since I fell and my eyes don't focus as they should, I must point to what I'm reading, which she follows as she looks over my shoulder:

Ned, I trust that when you receive this message you will be of sound enough mind so that you understand the emotional distress I have suffered over the last months.

"Not all of Mom's distress, just most of it, Dad," Erica said.

Martha's assuming not only that I'm not thinking right, but that I'm responsible for all her troubles. In case I had any question which team Erica's on, now I know.

I can only guess as to why you have been so negligent in your domestic responsibilities, although I will assume it results from the mismanagement of our business.

"If instead of assuming that I don't know how to run my business your mother would look at the bureaucrats who have screwed up—"

"Dad, face it, you're absolutely paranoid about the government. Look at all the money you've lost, running away from the government, which really isn't out to get you. It's pretty scary for Mom."

You've saddled me with increasing debt that you've been unwilling to pay. You've made yourself completely unavailable to talk to your creditors, leaving the burden on my shoulders. Moreover, you have abandoned both your home and your wife, commencing September 3rd, for a period of six months.

"Wait a minute, Erica, I'm trying to remember something important about September third."

I heard knocking at the door, but before anyone could answer, Ryan burst into the room.

"Look what the cat dragged in," Erica greeted him.

"I heard that," Ryan interrupted. "That was the day Fitch busted me and Dad posted my bail and brought me home."he interrupted.

"Clean white shirt, pretty tie," Erica said, rubbing the tie between her fingers. "Silk."

"Well, what the hell do you expect, rayon? You think you're the only D'Amour with a decent paycheck?"

"Then you must be working," Erica said. "Has your job something to do with gasoline?" Ryan shook his head no.

"I'm between jobs, not that it's any of your business."

"Weren't your last jobs over a year ago, making sandwiches, hamburgers, fried chicken, milk shakes?"

"You remember only what you want to! I had a MacJob, OK? I was an assistant manager! Now shut up!"

"Both of you be quiet, or leave!" I tried to shout, but my voice was too weak to stop them.

"They just called you that so they could pay you salary instead of overtime," continued Erica.

"Anything else, sister?"

"That was last year, but what about now, after you served your sixty days for stealing the computers? They must have just let you out. Just let me know when you're in our neighborhood, so I can lock the doors."

"You seem to have all the answers."

"I hope your next employer doesn't leave you unsupervised. That would be like the fox guarding the henhouse," Erica said.

"Maybe you're trying to embarrass me, but that won't work because I take responsibility for what I did ever since Dad began to save my sorry ass."

"Began?" I asked. "What do you mean, son?"

"I mean it's not over quite yet. I may try to get back into the food business after I free myself up. That's my problem, not Mom's. If she's looking for someone to blame other than me, she can try herself, but she doesn't have to blame Dad, just because he was close enough to catch the flak when Fitch found me and brought me in cuffs to her, understand? Now give me that letter!" Ryan said and snatched it from me. "We'll look at the rest of it later, Dad. Meanwhile, Erica, I see you have on your coat. They keep these hospitals so damned hot. Better go before you get overheated, bitch!"

She left the room quickly and waited in the hallway, while Derek stayed back in the room with Ryan and me. "Has my sister ever made you a pie, any kind of pie, apple, cherry, peach, blueberry?" Ryan asked. "She's very good at baking pies from scratch, with no bake mix. I remember the kind of pies my mother would bake with Erica for Mom's gourmet-class guests, rather than trusting the maid to make them. I'd love to come over sometime when Erica's in a mood to bake for me. Second thought, that could be a long time away, seeing how she's never invited me inside your new house. Meantime, why don't you tell my sister you know from reliable sources how well she bakes and ask her to make one for you? If she does that for you the first time gladly and without complaining, you'll know she cares about pleasing you, and you should regard yourself as a happily married man. If not, I'd try to do something different."

"Ryan, you're full of wisdom for a kid who's too smart to finish school," Derek said.

"Thank you. Everything I am today, I owe to my father."

Ryan's making a poor joke at best, but at least he's trying to be sociable. Given a little time, the kid might develop some charm.

"Quite a recommendation, Pops," Derek said to me.

"Don't forget to give little Dave a kiss for me," I said. "And remember you can stop by anytime by yourself, even if Erica can't schedule it."

———

Since regaining consciousness, my sense of time changed, and it became harder for me to measure. For the next days, or perhaps a week after Erica's visit with her husband and her brother, it seemed I was being visited by people I don't know, or perhaps should have known, only didn't remember. There was the priest who offered to take my confession, apparently knowing more about why I fell than I do, but I told him I wouldn't know where to begin, that I didn't recall whether I was a sinner or a saint, but promised to ask for him when I managed to figure it out. There were other patients and their visitors who popped in, addressed me by my name, and introduced me to theirs, which in many cases just didn't register. There were the doctors who were collecting and measuring my brain waves, repeatedly telling me how lucky I was, but that I wasn't out of the woods yet. They must have been talking to the General, because when he visited me he seemed to be walking on eggs, treating me as if I were sicker than I was feeling. His approach had always been no-nonsense, but now I couldn't get him to tell me much about the state of my business, except he had things under control, and that I shouldn't concern myself with anything until I was able to go to the office and see for myself.

By the second week of my consciousness Denise had come a few times, but she was reluctant to talk business with me. Instead she brought me games, as if I were a kid needing to be entertained: the first evening, chess; the next, Scrabble. She seemed to be studying me carefully when I was making my moves, as if determining how much of my edge I had lost. But I showed her, winning the chess matches by strategy, always my strong suit. With the word games, however, she seemed to have the advantage, doubtless from her training as a lawyer. When she'd read articles from the paper then question me, I had trouble remembering the silliest things, like the location of cities and states and famous people's names.

Ryan must have talked to Denise about what she was doing to get me to remember, the reason why he's been bringing me old photo albums, a composite of my life with Martha and the children. Page by page pointing out pictures of birthday parties, anniversaries, graduations, vacations, boats, day outings, house pets, horses, friends, and relatives, quizzing me. I recognize better than two out of three pictures The picture story of my life, up to my close encounter with death, makes me think about whether I've seen more defeats or more victories. I can't show him how desperate I am to remember the missing details, but for the life of me I can't! Like the reason for Borak's vendetta against me. Why exactly Ryan ejected himself from the house in the first place, as well as why Martha then insisted on ejecting me. And why Erica seems every bit as hostile to me as is her mother.

It's come to this sorry state after I've worked hard to provide more than enough opportunity for my family, my two children in particular. I've done well for them. But of the three of them, Ryan seems the one who understands me the best lately.

"Ryan, your mother's letter you grabbed from me the other day—I'd like it back so I can finish reading it."

"Oh, that one. Mom says she wants to meet with you and Doctor Grandpa sometime. But if I were you, I'd ignore it."

"Thanks for the advice. But I'd like to read the letter myself."

"Trust me. You really should, because like I told you before, not everyone means you well."

The kid sounds much more cautious than he used to be. Maybe life on the street has taught him something useful after all.

"Just the same, I want to read my own mail."

"No problem, Dad. I promise to show it to you very soon. Maybe the day after tomorrow, after we get you out of here."

"Get me where?"

"Out of here. You've hung around here long enough. You look pretty good to me now. The doctors say you're out of danger. Yet they plan to keep you here another few weeks, just so they don't get sued in case they turn you loose and you drop dead."

Now he's playing doctor He's not stupid; he speaks with a mad kind of logic.

"And where were you suggesting I go?"

"Your home away from home. Our place, roomie! Actually, I could get you out tomorrow, but not before I take care of some business first. By the way, you don't mind if I bring another visitor for you tomorrow morning?"

It's early morning and still dark. Into my mind returns a familiar dream of travel through dark space. I've been in transit for at least a lifetime and need to land, yet I want to keep traveling forever. I have wonderful eyes, my ultimate vision more powerful than the greatest optical telescope. But I ratchet my eyesight way back to a more normal power, enabling me to plainly see a world of forests, rivers and pure, breathable air, the paradise at which I now must stop. I know how to pilot my ship, but my controls don't respond as they should! At last I find the world I've been seeking for so long, but now I'm disoriented. I'm quickly passing the window of opportunity to place myself in a trajectory that would take me safely down, an opportunity never to be repeated. I need directions, but I'm a one-man mission, utterly on my own. Now suddenly through the void I'm receiving a communications signal! A signal guiding me where I want to go: *Base to car four, base to four, where are you now, chief?*

"Unit four to base. Fitch here, and I'm not on duty until 8."

But where are you now? Can you get to a land line?

"No can do, Olmstead. I'm at the doctor's."

Not feeling well?

"I bet he thinks I'm getting a physical with a man's fingers in a rubber glove shoved up my ass," Fitch said to me as I was coming back to reality. To Olmstead on the radio he said, "Me? I'm seeing the doctor about a horse."

A horse, chief?

"Idiots," Fitch said to me, "I've got a crew of idiots. A horse with worms," he continued, speaking into the handi-talkie. "Got a tube down the horse's nose and the horse don't like it. Trying to kick down the stall. The vet's got her by the bridle, I got her by the tail and the bung hole, and she don't think I should be so friendly. Got to go now."

I realize I'm listening to a conversation between the dispatcher and another policeman. Officer Fitch turns down the radio.

"You know, by the end of the day this squawk box gives me a headache. If I could turn off this goddamn radio and never hear it ever again, that would suit me fine."

"There's something I know I should thank you for, Mr. Fitch, but I can't quite remember."

"How about for the time Ryan boosted a car? We never dug as deep as we could have to determine whether he stole it or borrowed it, and just took it away from him and returned it to the registered owner. Or the last time we nabbed him for breaking and entering and put him in your house under house arrest? If I had my way he wouldn't have served any time, but your wife's lawyer got him a better deal than he deserved, to tell you the truth."

"The garage, not the house."

"Then you are remembering better all the time, Mr. D'Amour."

"But that's not why I'm here. I have it from reliable sources that tomorrow about 1 P.M. you will have a couple of familiar visitors. Remember the cops I came with a couple of weeks ago, including the one you fell on? They'll be back, this time loaded for beer, now that the judge thinks you're sensible enough to answer questions."

"What would you suggest that I do, Mr. Fitch?"

"I couldn't say. The county doesn't pay me enough to be fixing your problems. But I did notice you get around pretty good on those crutches. If it was me, I might be taking a long walk. I wouldn't hang around this place a minute longer than I had to. Terrible bugs fly around hospitals, and we wouldn't want to pick up a dangerous bug, if you know what I mean."

"Turn my back on my problems? That's not how I do business." I said. Fitch was done talking, and now walked away. I was following him on my crutches, as fast as I could move. "And *we*, doesn't that mean Ryan's at the bottom of this? Take my directions from Ryan? Let the tail wag the dog? You're kidding!" I called to him.

"We expected you'd have a thousand reasons to do it your way, but I expect you'll smarten up and do it ours," Fitch said. "We'll see."

Chapter 9
Unfinished Business

"I'll stay with you overnight, but no longer, because tomorrow I've got to take care of some business, understand?" I said to Ryan as we drove away in Little B's van full of mops, buckets and cleaning supplies. "And another thing, I don't know where you got the key to the hospital service elevator, or why we headed out the back entrance. That's like eating a meal at a restaurant and dashing out before getting the bill. That's not what I taught you, and that's not how I behave. So I'll have to return in the next couple of days to properly check out."

"OK, Dad, knock yourself out."

"Excuse me?"

"Go ahead. Do it by the book, and let them throw the book at you. But before you head out anywhere, let me know, so I can make sure someone drives you."

"Don't bother, I can get myself there. By the way—my silver car, the Cadillac, can you get it back to me?"

"That's between you and Mom at this point."

Just the sort of evasive thing Erica might say, only I know she hasn't been able to control him for a long time now.

"And what's she got to do with it?"

"Because right after you took the fall, Mom took it out of storage."

"Then where is it?"

"She didn't want you to snag it some evening when she wasn't home."

"So it's home in the garage now?"

"Not exactly."

"Where then, Ryan?"

"Don't get hot with me, Dad. I can only guess."

"Guess then!"

"I guess she needed the cash and had to sell it, especially since she didn't think you were going to make it. Either that or she made a deal with the insurance company to get paid after I stole it that night Fitch hassled me. A stolen car, the report she spread around your office. All I can tell you, it's gone for good."

"Then I'll use this rig you're driving. But first tell me where you want to set the soap and the buckets."

"I hate to break this to you, but they won't let you drive anywhere by yourself because they don't think you're able."

"Who the hell's *they*? What other hair-brained schemes has she hatched for me?"

"Now don't get angry at me for what the Department of Motor Vehicles won't let you do, Dad. Actually, it was the doctors that forbid you from getting behind the wheel for six months. Just in case you have a fit, or something."

"Did your mother arrange that with the doctors?"

"Actually, I think she got the doctors to write the note to Motor Vehicles to get them to suspend your license."

"For six months!"

"Yeah, six months, or maybe it's a year. But even aside from the license thing, I couldn't lend you this van because I'm borrowing it from Little B, and he needs it for his work. He's in business for himself. He's got pretty good connections. I'd like my job a lot better if I got paid about triple. That's why I might have to leave it soon, because he made me an offer and I can't turn it down."

Little B I remember as a little thug with a lot to prove. I can't remember his exact connection with Ryan, but he couldn't be a good influence.

"That's your business, but I've got some of my own business to straighten out," I said. "So now that you've released me, how am I supposed to get around?"

"That's what I'm here for, Dad. I'll be hauling you around from now on."

The kid's annoying me, trying to take charge of me, while he can barely account for himself. I've been giving him the benefit of the doubt for a long time, but no matter how much he's improved, I know I can do a lot better on my own than relying on him.

He brings me to Rail City, built by the old railroad tracks, now Welfare Row. I remember the last time I was here his girlfriend coming out to greet us, eating ice cream straight from the carton. I'm also remembering their nasty apartment, stinking of old trash and a ripe cat box, the fabric of the sofa in tatters from the cat's claws. That last apartment had a sagging porch and a rickety wooden stairway running up the side to the third floor, but this has no porch and no stairs and only two floors, which means he's moved to a different place here in Rail City, unless my memory's playing tricks on me again. But I'm sure this one's the same girl, spooning her ice cream onto her tongue from an ice cream container with the cows on it. She's pleased to see Ryan, and she comes bounding across the lawn to the truck. A well-proportioned girl with long legs and plenty of bounce, nice nipples showing through her blouse.

"Someone's awful glad to see you, Ryan. Fresh from the dairy bar."

"A matched pair of spigots, heh, Dad?"

Crude. That's not what I meant to imply. She can't wait to get her hands on him. As soon as the van stops, she pulls him out of the car like she's grabbing for a Christmas prize from a stocking hanging from the mantle. And in the blink of an eye, they're hooked mouth-to-mouth in a very deep bedroom kiss, as if they were the only two in the world. But at least she seems glad to see him, which is more than I can say for my Deb Queen, who's certainly not waiting for me these days. Now the girl wants to come up for air.

"I didn't think you'd want to fool with us again," she said, came to my side of the van, opened the door and gave me a kiss. She grabbed me hard around the waist at just the spot where I broke my rib. As soon as she felt me flinch, she pulled back from me and looked me over as I eased onto my feet. "Shit, I didn't hurt you, Mr. D'Amour, did I? You look like you got into one hell of a fight! Was she worth it?" she asked me with a wicked laugh, then took my arm to help me into their apartment. "We got ourselves a better place since the last time you was eyeballing us. I guess you didn't like that shithole we was living in, but this place should suit you better. It's the best we could do for now. I wait tables, while Ryan's shift manager. We're trying to get a new start, but it ain't easy. I don't know what he told them to get that job, but he's doing real good for himself. I wish we didn't have to take in a roommate, but Borkman's cleaning offices are on the graveyard shift, so that we hardly see him anyway, except on the weekends. Ryan tells me you're going to crash here a while. Where are your bags anyway?"

"I'll catch up with them later."

"You didn't bring any bags so you could make a quick escape, like Ryan told me? Do outlaws run in your family"

"Put a lid on it, Annie! Don't pay any attention to her, Dad," Ryan said, stepping between Annie and me.

"Oh, fuck off!" she said to him with a smile, and took hold of my arm again, so that with my cane on one side and with her on the other, I was able to make good progress into their apartment.

Once inside, I lay back on the couch, extending my legs. "That must hurt so much. May I touch it?" she asked and tapped with her cigarette lighter on my leg cast.

I wish she weren't standing over me, circling me like a hungry vulture. She's leaning over, showing me her assets, either because she thinks I'm too decrepit to notice, or else to tease me. As she's been teasing Ryan, Little B, and probably every man she can get to look at her, young and maybe even some old ones. Wonder what category I'd fit in her mind? Now that she's made her impression on me, I wouldn't mind if she'd just leave me alone, but instead now she's poking at the bandages on my head.

"That must hurt so much Mr. D. It breaks my heart."

"No need to cry over me, Ann. That's your name—I'm remembering! If I were you, I'd put my heart to better use. Fortunately though, Ann, I can pretty much ignore what you're doing right now to my head, because it's numb where you've been pestering it with your fingers."

She pulls back her hand from my skull like she burned it on a hotplate. Now maybe she'll leave me alone.

"Ryan told me he's not sure whether you'll ever be all right again, but it wouldn't matter to me if you were fifty percent, I'd take care of you all the same if you were my old man."

"Why?" I asked. "What have I done to deserve so much attention?"

No answer to my simple question. She's on her knees, looking me straight in the eyes, and now she's leaning into me to give me a very encouraging hug. She smells like incense, or more likely it's weed. And I think I also smell patouli oil. An overwhelming combination of smells, but not entirely unpleasant. But if that's what Ryan wants in a woman, I hope he enjoys her. She's pulled back and is now standing behind me.

"If nothing else, Mr. D'Amour, you lit a fire under his ass," she said with a wink at Ryan, who smiled back meekly at him. "He got me out of that firetrap and finally got himself a job. Now if we can get out from under Blue, the five-hundred-pound gorilla sitting on us, then we might even get a life."

"Shut up, Annie, if you know what's good for you!" Ryan said, and jumped up to quickly close the door after a nervous look outside.

"I hope I'm not bothering you," she said, now having pulled up my shirt and touching my chest above and below the bandages. "I'm kind of affectionate. That's just how I've always been, and I don't think Ryan would want me to change now."

Ryan's now standing right behind me, alongside her, thinking I can't see or don't care what he's doing with her, tweaking that impressive chest of hers while she's talking to me. Not that I care, but it seems to me they should be retreating behind a closed door. This generation doesn't draw boundaries.

"Am I hassling you, Mr. D'Amour? I just want to get a handle on you to make sure you have everything you need."

"Hey, don't mind me, Ann, because tomorrow I'll be gone," I said.

"No way, Dad, no! After all I went through to get you here, I'm not about to turn you loose too soon! Now, Annie, go show him your stuff!"

Ryan turns on the stereo and settles on a hip-hop disc, his favorite type. I think the two of them met at a club dancing to it. To accompany it she's moved to the center of the room where she begins to entertain us with dancing completely unrelated to the music, starting with a Balinese sort of dance with small, delicate motions of her hands, then moving to one with her slow finale, long flowing arm motions and very fast shaking of her hips. She stops and changes it to another disc, a burleque. She entertains us with deliberate hip rotations, bumping and grinding, unmistakably a strip tease.

"She's got pretty good rhythm, don't you think?" Ryan whispered, sitting on the arm of the sofa beside me.

No shame, no boundaries. They seem to live for the moment's pleasure, a habit I know he never picked up from me. From when I was old enough to carry bricks, if nothing else, I've known how to put in a day's work. And unless my memory is playing tricks on me, I've always tried to teach him how to work as hard as me. But my example could be the very reason Ryan's run away for so long from honest labor, to rebel against me. At least until recently, if I'm to believe he's now supporting himself from his restaurant job.

"Outstanding, a natural talent," I said.

"You think that's good. Show my Dad something newer."

Now she's running through a medley of lindy, bugaloo, and disco. And I hardly believe this—she's back to the bumps and grinds, again.

"That's enough!" Ryan shouted.

"Self-taught?" I asked her as she took a bow.

"I'm not bragging, but either you got it, or you don't. Kind of on-the-job training."

"If I was you, Annie, I'd quit while I was ahead," Ryan said, signaling her to say no more.

". . . In a way I was always in the restaurant business every place I was dancing because they weren't serving just drinks, but food too. Now I'm waiting on tables taking and serving orders one at a time, while before I was kind of serving the public all at once."

"Serving them what?"

"You know, dancing and entertaining them so they'd keep eating, but mostly drinking. But to tell the truth, I like waiting tables better than professional dancing because people aren't looking at every freckle and you don't have to look good every night. Plus in the winter on nights when you don't draw a big crowd to fill the room with the heat from all those bodies, I'd get real cold, especially in between sets while my body wasn't moving. The drafts seemed to be coming from everywhere and gave me the goosebumps. And without a sweater on or nothing I'd get colds all the time, but still had to dance and look good, or else get replaced by some new girl. And I also like waitressing better in a regular family-type restaurant. I liked it when Ryan was working there in the kitchen, because there I could keep better track of him and keep him from running the roads. He was working there in the kitchen until he set a grease fire and they fired him."

Now I know why Ryan's trying to quiet her down; the more she says, the worse it gets. I can't imagine what her family must think, having a stripper for a daughter. Probably no happier than I am, having a petty criminal for a son. Or maybe her family doesn't know the whole story. Or see her much anymore. I'd guess she's a single-parent child, or an orphan.

"If you like waiting tables so much, how about whipping up some sandwiches?" Ryan said and answered the ringing phone, shielding it with his hand. "Just tell her what you want, Dad. I'll be heading out right now. Now don't be afraid to ask for what you need."

Oh, yeah, if you think I do, you're crazy . . . Ryan had taken the handset in the other room and closed the door, but he was speaking louder than he realized. *I don't owe you anything anymore. You win some, and some you lose . . . Not my problem . . .*

"No sandwiches for me, Annie," Ryan said to Annie and me when he returned. "I don't need anybody to wait on me. I can take care of myself."

"No need to have so much pride, Mr. D'Amour," Annie said, ignoring him. Hobbling around with all your bandages and everything, you don't look so good to me. And Ryan don't appear much better. Like father, like son. How come bad luck finds you guys? Maybe I'm stupid for hanging around you, maybe I should run away. Maybe someday we'll make us enough money to start a restuarant where Ryan can cook—anything but flip burgers all day, which is too boring to him—and I could keep the cutomers happy. You know Ryan thinks he's smarter than his bosses and likes to do his own thing. I don't know if his thing and my thing are the same thing, but I do know if he expects me to ever again live in an apartment like the rat's nest where you dropped in on us the last time, he can forget it! But this place ain't so great either with the vandals in the neighborhood. One in particular likes the blue paint. That's why I got busy with the white paint, to cover the blue, so Ryan wouldn't go ballistic when he saw it."

Says so much and so little at the same time. She talks to me about Ryan as if he's not standing next to us. Forgetful or intentional? She's complaining about the old apartment, yet she's not saying how they managed to move to this better place, especially since Ryan's been out of work so much. If she's a stripper by trade and wants to go down the road, she might be doing Ryan a big favor getting out of his life, not that I'd tell him so directly.

———————

Annie's very attentive, using most of her time off to watch after me. She's been cooking me three decent meals a day and plays board games in between, just so I shouldn't get bored. At checkers or Chinese checkers I can beat her every time because she can't think past the next move and uses no strategy. But for some reason she's especially good at poker and seems to want to raise the stakes from nickels and dimes, though I don't care to gamble for anything more than pocket change. A stripper and a gambler, and God knows what else, a dangerous match for Ryan, if he's ever going to turn himself around.

And she's been playing her Pink Floyd music all the time, stereo cranked high enough to shake the windows: *I got 13 channels of shit on the T.V. to choose from. I got nicotine stains in my fingers. I got a silver spoon on a chain. I got wild staring eyes. I got a strong urge to fly, but I got nowhere to fly to. I pick up the phone. There's still nobody home . . . Goodbye cruel world. There's nothing you people can say to make me change my mind. Is there anybody out there?*

I ask her to stop playing these same tunes over and over again. I turn her music off, and she turns it on, back and forth we go all day long.

"I'm young," she said. "You just don't understand where I've been."

She's right—I can only guess her origins: a motherless child, a fatherless child, an explanation for why now she's a partly grown child angry at the world.

"I can assure you, Annie, that if you feel sorry for yourself, the world, whether cruel or kind, really doesn't care about your hurt feelings."

"I've lived that Pink Floyd story, Mr. D, but I never regret anything I've ever done! You haven't seen the movie about Pinkie. I've seen it twenty times, and it's back in town. Ryan and I love it, because it's the story of our lives and the people who've fucked us over."

I've touched a sore nerve. It sounds as if she almost enjoys feeling like a victim. I wouldn't be surprised if she's convinced Ryan I'm the cause of his problems. But who cares what she feels or doesn't feel? This girl is either confused or crazy.

"Really? I certainly hope not."

"What's this sad song called anyway, Annie?"

"A title? First you need to know the story. There's the security guard who finds Pinkie sipping out of the toilet while he reads his notebook, the teacher who whips him on the knuckles for writing poems, and big mama who screens his girlfriends. People like them and like yourself—they always look for titles. If you really want to know the title of this Pink Floyd tune, it's *The Wall*, if you want a name. If you want to understand it, you better come see their movie about how we build walls and hide behind walls."

"We could get the video," I suggested.

"No, we need to see the big screen, the movie. Every time we see it I never sit further back than the fifth row so I can count Pinkie's freckles."

————————————

One of the five evenings of the week Annie was heading out with her working clothes in a gym bag. "Got to shake some ass!"she announced, kissing Ryan and me goodbye in turn, as usual. "Make sure he doesn't get loose and run the roads tonight,"she said to me, as if I could control his comings and goings. "Remember, you're on watch with your Dad," she reminded him.

"You're looking much better, Dad," he said, once the two of us were alone. "You needed Dr. Freunlich to get those bandages off and get you moving again," he said, referring to a naturopath who wouldn't touch me until I signed a disclaimer releasing him from any responsibility in case his care hurt me. "Now you can walk a couple of blocks without the cane. You're lucky he took you on. He did it as a favor to me. He's the one I always use. He's very discreet."

"I don't need anyone discreet. I have nothing to hide," I said. "What do you go to him for—to patch up knife and bullet wounds?"

"What's your point?" he asked me. "I can't continue helping Annie and myself, much less you, if you won't trust me."

That's exactly the point, the same one that Annie made, that left to his own devices tonight he'd be hanging around with gang boys like the mean-looking ones that came knocking on the door looking for him a couple of afternoons last week, while Annie was here babysitting me. I didn't like the looks of them and neither did she, who seemed jittery and scared afterward.

"I was just wondering what you do with yourself daytimes when Annie's here with me, if you're not working."

"What can I tell you, Dad? Sometimes a man's got to do what he's got to do. I got bills that won't quit. You know what that's all about."

A big difference, which my kid doesn't seem to appreciate: I've taken on debt for my family, and he's taken on debt for no better reason than to feed his bad habits. It's not my business what Annie's been doing to make the money for the rent. But I do have to give her credit for spending her time every day with me, feeding me, playing games with me, helping me get moving and talking with me. It seems odd that I've seen so much less of Ryan than Annie. If he's not working, where can he be going days and nights? If I stay here a little longer and get strong enough to be getting around without anybody's assistance, I could follow him for a day or two and find out for sure what mischief has been keeping him so busy. Or better yet, I should leave before I find out more than I care to know about Ryan's latest project.

"Ryan, tomorrow I need to check in at the office."

"Why? They aren't expecting you. I'm sure they're doing fine without you."

He says that with conviction and might know something that could be useful to me. But in business I know the danger of relying on secondhand information, especially from unreliable sources like my son.

"I want you to take me to tomorrow's staff meeting. We're going to take care of business, unfinished business. Dress sharp."

The next morning Ryan looks good, surprisingly presentable in his knit tie and corduroy jacket with leather arm patches, the sort of outfit I haven't seen him wear in a long time.

"You look like a young professor, Ryan, but from about twenty years ago. They were wearing leather elbow patches when I was a young man. Where did you get that jacket?"

"He rolled a drunk professor," Annie said, joining us in the kitchen in her frilly red panties. It's midmorning, but with her late-night schedule, this is the time she'd normally be asleep. Maybe she really is sleepwalking. Or have I become so familiar to her, she's not bothering with the formality of clothes? Or is she consciously showing me her assets to make me understand why Ryan's chosen her for a girlfriend? A body verging on skinny, her ribs clearly showing. Her tiny waist make her full breasts voluptuous, tempting to any man watching her, whether myself or the man at her floor shows.

"Don't listen to her, Dad. She has no respect," Ryan said and swatted her on her bottom. "Actually I picked this jacket up for fifteen bucks at a second hand shop. Good deal, huh?"

Years of labor for this family of mine, and my son's wearing other people's cast-offs.

"A bargain. I hope you took it to the cleaners before you put it on."

"Forget about how I look, you're looking pretty fair yourself, especially since we took off the last of the head bandages. You could pass for normal again, Dad. So if you're ready, I'm ready. Let's move out," Ryan said to me.

We had nothing more to say to one another until we were halfway to Gaylord. He was overtaking three cars in a row on the two lane road.

"Quit speeding!" I yelled to him. He ducked back in line a very few seconds before the tractor-trailer in the oncoming lane whizzed past us.

"I'm clean as a billiard ball! It's time you trust me! I've never done speed and never will!"

"I mean back off the throttle and pull over, Ryan. I'll get us there without risking our lives."

"Oh, safety, I can do that. I'm sorry. You want a safe chauffeur today? One who dresses sharp. I'm your man, Dad."

Ryan pulls into the parking lot of the office building where Resolutions, Inc. operates, just looking at it through the windshield, his hands draped over the steering wheel. "This place of yours is a concrete tomb. Or put bars on it, and it's a fucking medium security prison! If I was you, Dad, I'd turn my back on this place and never look back!"

"Thanks for the advice, Ryan, but I don't have the time to hear any more of it. Are you going to wait out here for me, or are you going to come up there with me?"

With no further insults or suggestions Ryan accompanies me to my office, which feels unfamiliar from the moment I enter. Someone's changed the color to a deep blue, making it much too dark. White or off-white would work better, giving them more light and the illusion of space. This dark and dreary blue must make them feel like the workers in Martha's repossessed *Five O'Clock Shadows* painting, like army ants. If I had been here the last few months as their chief, and if they'd been at least half-cooperating with me like they once did, I could have been motivating them, improving their outlook, boosting their morale. No, I shouldn't kid myself that my absence or presence would make more of a difference than a fresh coat of light paint!

We have a new cocoa-colored receptionist from a temporary agency, her hair in dozens of tight braids, each with its own bead. She couldn't be more than twenty and has no idea who I am, the chief. She wants to know who I'm scheduled to see, but I don't have the energy to keep explaining I don't need an appointment, that I've come to go through the mail on my desk. The door of what used to be my own office now has a plaque, *George Corbin Productions*. Inside I see decks, TVs, VCRs, an electric guitar, rock posters on the wall, and a lot of tapes and discs in what used to be the files room. But there's no sign here of my important files designated for my eyes or the General's eyes only. No one seems to bother consulting with me any more, not even the General. I must find out whether these have been moved, lost, or destroyed. Corbin seems to have some kind of music business going here by the looks of it. And a sweet young blonde girl on the couch, a notepad on her lap.

"I thought we were in the pollution business. So why are you here, George?"

"Why? I'm a booking agent. My needs are simple. Give me a fax and a telephone and some audio and video gear, and I can work anywhere. So why not here? I'd think you'd be glad to have me, with the big rent the General's been getting out of me for this teeny weeny little space."

His attractive artist is now on her feet. She's done inspecting herself in the mirror and along with Ryan is looking through George's music collection and pulling out an album. "I thought I heard everything Pink Floyd cut. My lady would love to hear this one. Can I borrow it?"

"How about showing me a copy of the lease?" I said.

"No, young man," George said to Ryan. "These CDs are my working tools." To me he said: "And, Mr. D'Amour, about the lease, you'll have to take it up with Rachael, because she's been in charge ever since you've been gone. This was just wasted space anyway with you being out of commission. It's not as big as I'm used to, especially when I have to see half a dozen artists at once, like this young lady, but it's convenient. But small space or not, I'm not moving from here, no way. It works out pretty good for Rachael and me, working out of the same office like this, because now we don't have the cost of running two cars to work in two different directions."

"Oh really? You want me to talk with her because she's in charge now?"

"Yeah, her and the General, but I don't see him around too much because he's too busy doing his own thing."

"And what might that be?" I asked.

"Playing in the dirt. But he stays out of our way most of the time. By the way, glad to see you pulled through. Funny, the last time I saw the General he told us you were close to dead. Rachael would have come to visit you in the hospital, even though you ate her up and spit her out at the last staff meeting, she said. But she didn't because your wife told her not to bother, that you were critical and in no kind of shape to talk to anybody. That's when the General came to her and talked her into hiring her back into your garbage business here. To tell you the God's honest truth, Mr. D'Amour, if Rachael thought you'd come strolling through the door like you did, large as life, I don't think he could have talked her into coming back, considering her health, no matter how much more money he offered her."

"What the hell was her problem, indigestion?"

"Actually, more serious than that, according to the doctor. He told her to avoid aggravation."

"That's unavoidable. I have no idea why you're here and what you're doing, but in our business, aggravation goes with the territory!"

"To be honest, Mr. D'Amour, the doc was warning her about you in particular, that unless she wanted her condition to progress to an ulcer, then eat a hole in her stomach, she shouldn't continue working for you. Running this place, for you in and of itself never really bothered her, but she was looking for better treatment on your part."

Yes, I remember now how she was always talking more than she should, especially to Martha, telling her about what went on inside this office, long after Martha stopped working here to stay home. And now evidently Rachael's been hanging out my dirty wash for George, probably her latest boyfriend, to see and sniff. A better, more loyal attitude on her part would have led to more preferential treatment on my part. Her lousy attitude gave me enough reason to get rid of her for good, but for some reason she's still here. This time I can't be hasty before I sack her permanently. But before I act I need to at find out why she wanted to come back if she has so little respect for me, her boss, the one who's provided her livelihood for so long.

"So where's your prima donna now, backstage somewhere?"

"I don't have to take this!" his pretty recording artist said, mistakenly believing my question applied to her, rather than to Rachael. "George, you can call me when you can give me your attention!" She flung her bag over her shoulder and quickly left, Ryan followed after her. They'd just left the room when we heard a scream. Ryan returned with an apologetic, embarrassed grin.

"Mr. D'Amour, if I may make a suggestion: Rachael's a sensitive woman, and she may be listening to us now. Open your eyes and take a look," George said, walking me to another office, though I couldn't remember whose it was last. It had pastel blue blinds and a carpet a complimentary shade of blue. "She also has a fine sense of color. That was part of the deal the General gave her to get her back, that she could redecorate with something more cheerful, so she wouldn't come home at the end of the day nerved up from the happy horseshit she had to deal with. Yeah, be a little more sensitive this time, and you'll get further." George shook my hand, as if I'd agreed to some kind of treaty, and returned to his quarters.

"With this Rachael woman, you got a tiger by the tail, or else she and George got you by the short hairs," Ryan said once we were alone. "One way or the other, Dad, I'd break away from the both of them."

I'm looking down the hall, Rachael spots me, stops in her tracks, stands staring at me, and rushes to the receptionist. Obviously she isn't expecting to see me.

"I don't know what I'm hanging onto, or what's hanging onto me," I said to Ryan. "I try to be fair. I owe it to her to hear her side of the story, son, right now."

Well-composed and smiling, Rachael returned with the receptionist. "Kunya, meet Mr. Ned D'Amour, the CEO of this company."

The girl looked puzzled. "CEO, what's that?"

"The boss, your boss," Rachael said. "Now why don't you write Mr. D'Amour's name down? Put it by your phone. It may come in handy in case someone's looking for him. I hear the phone ringing. You better get it now." Rachael gave her a gentle push toward the reception desk.

Now why is she seating Ryan in the chair in front of the desk, while she puts me on the couch at the far end of the room? It's as if I have no say around here anymore. Now it's her phone ringing.

"My phone never stops ringing," she said to Ryan and me. And to the person on the phone: "I'll have to ask you to hold just one more time while I can take this in a quieter location." She left her office for the unoccupied one across the hall, to continue her talk without our listening.

"I wouldn't trust that woman," Ryan said. "She sure acts like she's got some kind of side deal going, and like she wants to cut you out of it."

Though this kid talks like he's been making his living on the street for too long, I shouldn't entirely discount what he says.

"I'm getting tired of looking at the back of your head, Dad," Ryan said after we'd been waiting a couple of minutes. "You can wait for her as long as you like, but me, I'm going to check her out a little closer."

Ryan listened at the door to Rachael on the phone. He wanted me to follow him, but I wouldn't.

"It's none of my goddamn business," Ryan said as we stood in the hallway outside her office, where her door was opened a crack, "but it sounds like you owe someone money. She's not prepared to pay your bill right now. Are you really that broke, Dad? They're asking for you, but she's telling them that you're critical, last time she saw you. She's a pretty good liar, isn't she? And now she's telling them she can't do a thing without Langway—who's he anyway?"

"The General, my right-hand man. I'm sure you met him before."

"I never paid much attention to how you made a living and who with, but all that's going to change, I promise! Seems like here the right hand doesn't know what the left's doing. Man, if I was you I'd hunt up the General, so he could at least count up the bodies for us."

"You shouldn't be eavesdropping."

"Yeah, and she shouldn't have been telling people you're near dead. It's bad luck."

The door was opened suddenly from the other side. "Are you in the right place, young man?" Don Peters was asking.

"You bet your sweet ass! Tell him what we're doing here, Dad," Ryan said to me.

"Good Lord, it's you!" Peters said. "So good to see you again, sir. What a surprise. You're looking quite good actually, considering."

I don't know who to believe. I wish I knew who's friend, who's foe, or who's neutral.

"Well, I'm getting sick at what I'm seeing! What the hell's going on here, Don?"

He's shaking my hand, but instead of looking at me Peters is looking at my suit and rubbing the fabric in his fingers. Peters has always been something of a clothes horse.

"It looks like you paid plenty for this outfit of *yours*," Ryan said, in turn taking the hem of Peters' jacket in his hand. "Did your mother ever tell you you're a good-looking guy? Mine once told me my face could stop a clock. I took that as a compliment, and thought I was doing the girls a favor to look them over, and look where it got me. You have the same problem?"

"We don't have any problems here," Peters said.

"Sure could have fooled me. Doesn't look like no one knows nothing around here."

"Shut up, Ryan. Mr. Peters knows as much as anybody."

"Yeah, but I bet he can't show me who's in charge here today."

"Actually, nobody's in the office right now, not with the General off-site so much lately."

"Why's he out of the office—he doesn't have enough to do here?" I said. "Never mind, Peters. It doesn't look like anybody's in charge. So why don't you just show me whatever you're working on now?"

"Very bread-and-butter. Not much to look at," Peters said, pulling out a sketch of the interior of a store.

"I'll be the judge. Don't underestimate yourself, Don."

"Well, we've branched out from pollution project design to building interior design. I regard myself as a very good designer, and I've been enjoying working on the interiors of these buildings."

"Well, I don't enjoy hearing about this! Why the hell has Resolutions gone from pollution abatement to low-end drafting projects —piecework! How much could that sort of thing pay!"

"The going rate for one-man architect's shops for refitting and remodeling supermarkets. It's very competitive. They picked us because we bid less than any of the other known engineering and design firms would charge."

The word's getting out that we hire out at cheap rates. All those years working to build our reputation, and now the market sees us as a bottom-end shop. It sounds like a sweetheart deal for them, not for us, being able to reuse our interior layouts over and over again in their identical stores. I've heard more than enough. Now let's follow the noise to the coffee and lunch break room and see if someone else can answer some of my questions about the changes. Two young women drinking coffee and and one eating donuts, the other a sandwich. They stop cold before we even enter the room.

"They couldn't be older than me," Ryan whispered to me, "and you were always saying how educated I'd have to be to do the kind of work you do. So are you hiring them for minimum wage, Dad?"

"Why, you want me to take you on?"

"By the looks, there's no future here. Thanks anyway."

Not that I was making him an offer, but he's very quick to reject the business that's been feeding him for so long. Each of these girls is putting her hand over her mouth, hiding grins. I don't know what's going on here, but I feel as though I've paid for the party, only nobody's bothered to invite me. Is this lunchtime already? Who are they? They're saying nothing, looking at me like I'm interrupting them, waiting politely for me to leave. New faces, young oriental women. Resolutions has become a United Nations, but I'm not being rewarded for furthering the cause of world peace, if that's the new plan.

"What's your specialty, each of you?" I asked.

They giggled again and had no answer for me. "Never mind. Just passing through. Don't mind me. Carry on," I said and we left them alone.

"So, Dad, you were also saying how hard you work here. What did you actually do as a boss besides walking around and looking over people's shoulders, getting them all nerved up, and trying to get more work out of them?"

I can't believe he understands so little of what it takes to run an organization. This kid can be very obtuse when it suits him, but I hope it's not too late to re-educate him. No answer is the best answer to his foolish question.

I've probably already found out more than I want to know and needn't aggravate myself any more today, but now I've come across Lewis. I can never understand why he never uses his glasses to read, though he has to hold his books six inches from his nose. Barefaced without glasses I can imagine how he must have looked at fourteen years old. He's proudly told me that he'd stay indoors reading while the other kids were playing ball outdoors. Today he has the usual children's food: chocolate milk, red, stringy Twizzer candy, one peanut butter and jelly and one salami sandwich. And let's see what he's reading. On the cover the creatures have little bodies and large heads with bulging veins nourishing their big brains. I don't know whether I've found intelligent life here in Lewis. But I do believe Lewis is too childish and too literal-minded to lie well. That's why he could be the best one to ask for the news:

"Mr. Lewis, I'd like you to meet my favorite son."

"That's because I'm his only one," Ryan explained. "Did he forget to tell you that? No offense, Dad—about the forgetting, I mean."

"Enough said. I hope we're not taking you away from something important."

"Not really," Lewis said, looking at his watch. "I still have thirty-three minutes of the lunch hour remaining, why?"

"Because I was wondering whether you've noticed anything different around here lately?"

"I keep an open mind. To me nothing is out of the range of the possible. Like with your neuro-cerebral crack-up, I always believed they could put together the pieces, and here you are."

"Humpty Dumpty recycled," Ryan said.

"Shut up, Ryan!"

"As I said before, no offense, Dad."

"I was wondering about the different faces around here. Like those Chinese girls, for instance," I inquired.

"Actually one is Thai and the other Japanese."

"Whatever. What are they doing here?"

"They're new hires, the most qualified at the price the company can pay," Lewis said. "They're very talented in other areas with their hands, Mr. D'Amour."

"Good hands, man, would I like to find out for myself," Ryan said.

"So what exactly are they doing?" I asked. "Are they making paper roses, oragami, serving tea, dancing, singing?"

"None of the above, Mr. D'Amour. They're very accomplished in line drawing and can often work faster than anyone else on objects like bushes and trees they have such good eyes they can often draw freehanded while the rest uf us would have to use straight edges and curves. They've been selected by Rachael, but authorized by the General."

"Many are called, Mr. Lewis, but few are chosen. I still don't know why we need them here on the payroll."

"To help out Peters. He scouted around his old campus and looked for the best senior year draftsmen, without regard to race, creed, religion, handicaps, national origin, sex or sexual preference, made them offers, and here they are."

"Doing what?"

"Mostly convenience stores, fast food restaurants, interiors, renovations, redecorating. That sort of thing. We're taking pretty much what comes our way."

"Well, when all is said and done, are we making any money here?"

"Enough to pay my check every Friday. That's all I know. You're teasing me though. You must know whether we're making or losing it. Or don't you know, Mr. D'Amour?"

No, I'm not sure of anything at this point, but it would appear that the whole lot of them's been scrounging in garbage cans and feeding on scraps, certainly not what I had in mind when I started the Resolutions organization. I can't listen to him anymore. It's best to walk out of here right now before I say or do something I shouldn't.

"Mr. D'Amour, I still have some time, anything else?"

"You've been surprisingly helpful, Mr. Lewis, but the General's still in charge of this horse-and-pony show, isn't he?"

"You think this is some kind of performance?" Lewis asked.

"No offense, Mr. Lewis," Ryan said.

"Keep out of this!" I shouted.

"Mr. Lewis, what do you like to do with your family when you're not here?"

"Family? Come on, you're kidding. You know that I'm a bachelor. Besides, with all my books at home, how would I have space for a woman?"

"Beats me!" Ryan said, making an obscene gesture.

"So out of curiosity, what do you do with yourself when you're not here?" I asked.

"Read and think. Think and read."

"Well then, where do you think we'd find the General?"

There he goes, checking his watch again. For a man who wastes so much time, he certainly keeps good track of it.

"Mr. Langway while he was with us always took his lunch after the rest of us were through. I'd say he's shut down his rig, it being a little past noon time now. Like a male dog he may be looking for a tree out of his path of destruction which he's left standing."

"A tree?"

"Not to be fresh, sir, but he will either wizz on a tree, if he can find one left, or else sit underneath it in the shade to eat his grinder."

"Where?"

"They haven't told you that either? Conklin Farm."

"A farm—farming—has the General completely lost his mind? Or maybe I'm in the process myself. Now my right hand man's using my time to play on a farm! Show me!"

"Sure, I'd love to get out in the air and go for a tractor ride! But I've got to shut out the lights here in my office, just in case Rachael comes checking and reports to the General I've been wasting money on the job."

If Lewis could think for himself, I might give him a chance at running this asylum, but he can't, so I won't. Which means I'll never know if he'd do any worse a job than whoever else might really be in charge here. On the other hand, if he sticks around long enough, he might be the last one left.

"No, I wouldn't want to take you away from whatever project you're working on here."

"Don't worry, I've got nothing much going. They have me designing storm drains. Give me a roof and a building beneath it, and by now I can draw drains with my eyes closed."

It's come to this: supermarket shelves, fryolators, and storm drains. I never gave anyone permission to steer us away from pollution abatement. Then again, I wouldn't have gotten into the pollution business if I hadn't won my first contract and trained my staff who had no specialized background in that area. So it shouldn't surprise me that the first chance they get they abandon pollution for cleaner and more pleasant work, even if it doesn't even cover our overhead. No one in this region has developed the pollution abatement skills of Peters, the General and me, but we're afraid to use them and letting this EPA thing undermine us.

"So why don't you tell me how to get to this farm."

"I'm not much better at taking directions than giving them. Not in words anyway," Lewis said, then drew out a map on his lunch bag.

"Buried treasure, dig here," Ryan said and took the paper bag map the moment Lewis had finished drawing it out. He stuffed it in his pocket.

Once we were outside, Ryan looked toward the sun, closed his eyes and took a deep breath. "I got to hand it to you. Man, I could never work in an office like you do. The walls would close in."

"I'll take those directions now," I said, reaching into Ryan's pocket.

"Don't get so grabby, Pop. We're not going after the General, not today."

"Why's that?"

"Because I don't think you need any more excitement. Your skin looks a little gray," he said. "And besides I got some unfinished business of my own. Borkman wants me to see his new deal, what he does during the day."

"I don't think I care to know."

"Don't be so suspicious, Dad. He's a changed man. It's a good clean business, you'll see."

Chapter 10
Conklin Farm

It's probably better that Ryan waited a couple of days after our visit to my office to allow me to cool off before bringing me to Conklin Farm. We're having trouble finding it though. Maybe it's not such a good idea letting Ryan look for the General without a better map than Lewis has drawn. It's leading us through this back road hill farm country, where the roads intersect without signs and snake back and forth in unpredictable directions. Lewis's brown bag map lacks the important roads, yet is filled with hard-to-find landmarks, the work of a man who can't tell the forest from the trees. He's marked an old wooden grain silo, a narrow bridge and a clump of six mailboxes, but he's confused LaMothe Road with Gilead Road. We'd been traveling and re-traveling a two-mile radius, and still no LaMothe Road, but Ryan apparently wants to find his way himself. But ever since he's left the divided highway he's been lost, randomly checking all the roads that intersect it, as well as some that come off those roads.

"If we don't do something different, we'll be looking all day and all night. Now are you ready to let me help you get your bearings?" I asked. "I have a pretty good idea where we need to turn, unless you want to continue going up and down Cochane Road, then Symonton, then Gilead, then Adams."

"So, Dad, you knew all those names, even though the signs were down? And you've let me wander like a rat in a maze without even giving me a hint?"

"I thought you were taking me on a scenic route. You wanted to do it your way, without my help."

"I'll bet when you were a boy you also enjoyed pulling the legs off flies." Ryan pulled the map away from me. "You haven't seen the General since you took your fall, so why are you so anxious to see him now?"

"Because by now I'm just a wee bit tired of going around in circles."

"For christsake, Dad, we're right off the state highway, which runs in a line, not a circle. I don't have time to drive around in circles. If I wanted to show you something, I wouldn't have taken you on a road like a snake."

Logical in its own way, though not very sensible.

"If you have something to do more important than escorting me, don't let me hold you back," I said, once he had let me direct him to LaMothe Road. "But sometimes you so seem like someone who enjoys getting lost, rather than arriving. At one time I knew nearly everybody in the valley here, but Conklin—Conklin Farm? We haven't passed any businesses, except for Bud LaMothe's Salvage. Turn up his drive. Now if he doesn't know, then nobody will."

"Good idea, Dad. When we get closer you can get out and find where the hell we really are. If we can't get a better fix, then we're done fuckin' with this shit, and I'll go home and take care of my own business instead."

The kid's disrespectful, completely out of line, getting fresher by the day. I've been under his roof and on his own terms too many weeks, and now familiarity is breeding contempt. I need to move on very soon. I'm not sure though whether Denise is ready to take me on in my present condition. Before I can get back with her, I'll need to make good on my promise to her to deal with Deb Queen. For every pleasure, there's a pain, and Martha's a very big one.

Now we came to LaMothe's Salvage, which used to be one of the biggest hill farms. It set high above a field of a couple of hundred acres, probably scoured flat by the last glacier. The office was a travel trailer around which a wooden house had been built afterward. A good-sized dog was barking, waving his tail, alerting the owner, who stepped down from the porch to meet us by the car. "D'Amour, Ned D'Amour," I said, offering my hand to LaMothe, who wiped it on his pants before shaking it.

"I knew that," he said, surprising me. "I saw you last in the bank, about six months ago."

He's a big man in his forties with sunbaked skin and big working man's hands that look like they've wrestled with machinery, huge hands probably strong enough to break off the heads of bolts by turning his wrench too hard, arms powerful enough to carry off a transmission by himself."

"I never recognized you. It's been a long time since I last saw you in high school."

"No, I don't remember you saying hello in the bank," Bud LaMothe said. "Since you were busy counting out a stack of checks and cash which you were depositing, I thought I'd move on. My grandmother told me never to be counting other people's money."

"Your grandma and me probably would get along pretty good," I said. "I see now you have some cars on the lot with fewer years on them than you did when you started out, some less than five years old, a better inventory by the looks of things."

"I thought you was always driving a Caddie around town."

"Until recently," Ryan said. "That's because when he wasn't around my mother sold his Caddie to raise money."

"That's my boy Ryan," I said. "We're driving his rig today instead of mine."

"Me, I wouldn't ride in this thing," Bud said, kicking a tire of Ryan's old Honda. "A unibody car like this once it gets body cancer, it makes them hazards on the road. Yours got it bad in the rocker panels," Bud said, scraping paint with the big screwdriver in his pocket, reveal to us the hazardous rust. "If this were a full frame rig, I might buy it, if it could pass inspection. Terminal. She's a goner."

"Then why are you poking holes in it with that blade?" Ryan said.

"No one wants to hear he got himself a shitbox. But as a favor to your old man, assuming you got enough good parts I can sell, I'll give you five hundred bucks. I'll even give you a ride home as part of the deal. Want me to write you a check now?" Ryan frowned, looked at his feet, shook his head, no deal.

"I remember some of the rust buckets I was driving around in when I was your boy's age. One didn't even have bumpers, so I got me some railroad ties, cut them in half lengthways, drilled and bolted them down. As a matter of fact, they'd hoot and holler when they'd see me cruise by. Then when I'd ask some of the girls in my school for dates and they turned me down, you know what I did?"

I don't have time for this nonsense. I just want to get directions to where the General's working and get out of here.

"You found some in another school where they didn't know that ugly car belonged to you," Ryan said.

"I'm talking about the car, sonny! The better ones, they wanted to see better equipment. No girl worth a damn wants to ride around in a shitbox."

"They were looking for a guy with a bigger back seat?"

"There's plenty of girls quick to jump in a back seat! Then there's the girls that won't let you get too familiar."

"Mr. LaMothe, you must be married now with kids?" LaMothe shook his head yes. "So which kind of girl did you get?"

"You little dickhead! You got to smarten up this kid, Ned! My point being that I got into the auto retail trade so I could drive whatever car suited me, because it suited my kind of lady."

"Running a junkyard?" asked Ryan.

"You're looking at an automotive recycling center," Bud said. "There's a whole lot more money in the parts of a car than in the whole, sonny. OK, 600 bucks cash, just to get you the hell out of here." LaMothe took a big roll of bills from his hip pocket and peeled off that amount in $50 and $100 notes. "I saw a cash business here, a gold mine, and I mined it. The vein's nowhere near tapped out. The planners in the suits think they'll shut me down, talking about the highest and the best use for my land, damn them, and then voters like your father give them the power to take what doesn't belong to them."

"I know exactly what you're saying," I said. "Given half a chance, they'll chase after you like a pack of wolves, tire you out and bring you down."

"Dad's pretty paranoid these days too," Ryan interrupted. "But no need of bothering Mr. LaMothe with our situation. See, we just got ourselves crossed up, looking for a Conklin, a farmer, somewhere nearby and were wondering—"

"Well, if you have anything to do with that Conklin project, I want you guys out of here!"

"Why? I don't know a thing about Conklin Farm," I said. "Is he raising chickens, dairy or what?" I asked. "Why haven't I heard of them?"

"Don't tell me you don't know! Right now we're standing about dead square in the middle of three hundred acres of what used to be the old Conklin farm! But over in Town Hall they want people to forget about me and my salvage yard. So to confuse everyone, don't it make sense they name this big project after Sean Conklin, a man who's dead and gone?"

"What project?" I asked.

"As if you don't know! Those bastards you hired are bull-dozing closer to my line every day. They don't want to pay me but a fraction of what my land is worth, which is more than what the figures show. I ain't about to explain a cash business to them, which would just give them an excuse to shoot up my taxes."

"My father's hung up on money like you are," said Ryan. "It seems if you're losing the business, you shouldn't worry about how they'll tax you. You got to look on the bright side, or else you'll get crazier."

"Ned, your boy here thinks he's a comedian. I think you're one of the money boys behind this goddamn Conklin Farm shopping center!"

"Shopping center?"

"Now don't play dumb! The operator running that big Cater-pillar bulldozer tells me you own it and a good part of the other equipment."

"We don't own anything Caterpillar, just John Deere, and I certainly don't own any part of a shopping center!"

"So why'd you show up today, to see how many more of my acres they cleared off since the last time?" Bud La Mothe asked.

"I have no idea what you're talking about," I said. "We just came here for directions, not for insults."

"Your father's for real?"

"Yeah, he has a thing about the truth and telling the truth."

"Either I'm a fool, or you're one hell of a good liar!" LaMothe said. "I'll tell you what I'll do, take you for a tour of Conklin Farm in my personal hot rod here. No one else gets to drive it," he said and took a seat in an all-terrain vehicle. "Ned, you ride shotgun. The boy can wedge himself in the cargo bay." He helped us position ourslves. "Now hang on! We wouldn't want to lose you!"

He's tearing away from the trailer like a horse out of the gate, now flying down this hill at dirt track speed. If we hit a big chuck-hole just right, this kiddie car's bound to flip over. Good, we're off the hill and down to the level ground now, traveling the cleared perimeter of the lower field, just inside the remaining woods. But now he's picked up considerable speed, running fast as a racer on a paved road, banking into the turns. He's scaring Ryan enough so he's holding me tight, like a frightened little boy. If we fly out of this machine, my son and I go together. A big joke to LaMothe, who's hitched himself in with a safety belt and is looking over at us, laughing.

I know he hears me yelling for him to stop, but he doesn't care. We make several mile-long loops about the field, for a good quarter hour, and I shut up, keeping my fear to myself. Now he's dropping in closer to the center of the field, racing in smaller and smaller and even faster circles. He has a destination for this wild joyride, coming closer to the logging machines. We are now close enough to see how they're stripping the land, starting with a couple of chainsaw men dropping trees. We pass no more than thirty yards from them and see them in a fast blur, removing branches, dragging them in chained bunches with a skidder to make a big pile for the logging trucks. The bulldozer, a big one, easily pulls the newly cut tree stumps and flattens everything in its path in subsequent passes. A bucket loader follows the dozer, picks up the debris, loading it into dump trucks. A well-organized machine, this two-hundred yard operation, turning woods ultimately into the pavement and buildings I can't really blame LaMothe for fearing and hating. LaMothe's real destination, is this bulldozer, a forty-ton beast, a Caterpillar D-9 with the General at the controls! He could have told me that before he brought us on this kamikaze ride, nearly tossing me out a half dozen times already! LaMothe leaves the other equipment alone, but circles the General's dozer with a crazy vengeance, at less than twenty yards, targeting it, a hornet buzzing a bear's head. He has a gun in his hand, which he holds in a ready threatening position!

"Those bastards have crossed over my side of the line now! Don't you think I have the right to defend what's mine! Pleasure having you aboard, Ned! Last stop!" Bud was shouting, waving the pistol over his head.

"On second thought, Bud, how about we forget about Mr. Langway. If you don't mind, you can take us back up the hill to Ryan's car."

"Sorry, pal, too late now. My yard man's probably flattened the shitbox by now!"

"That's OK. Take us back any way that suits you."

I must be careful not to challenge or provoke this guy in any way. Ryan, for some reason attracts firepower. The boy looks as panicked as I'm feeling, but at least he has the sense to keep his mouth shut, not provoking him further. Bud's firing test shots at the sky.

"I've been waiting for this chance for long enough, Ned, and now we're within range!"

Bud began shooting at the bulldozer from behind, and was hitting it on either side of the cable winch. "Stop!" I shouted and tried to grab the gun from him. "They can ricochet and kill someone!"

"I don't care!" Bud shouted back to me over the din of the powerful engine of the bulldozer, the metal to metal of the turning steel tracks, as well as the scraping of the twelve foot blade on the ground. He was driving us in a circle so tight we could reach out and touch the enormous machine. Now suddenly the Caterpillar wasn't going forward, but swinging sideways pivoting on its braked left track, directly at our four-wheeler, a maneuver that caught Bud by surprise.

"Abandon ship stern side!" he ordered, jumping off to save himself. Somehow Ryan managed to pull me out with him before the gigantic machine caught the empty four-wheeler in a track and pushed it over on its side. That done, the General climbed down from the cab of the bulldozer towering over us, hit stunned Bud LaMothe hard enough with the bottom of his fist to his temple to knock him to the ground. He then retrieved Bud's pistol from the ground, placed it in front of the steel track, climbed back up to the controls and ran backward and forward over it, until it disappeared into the dirt. He jumped to the ground to rejoin us.

"What a pleasant surprise! Glad to see you're up and about," the General said. "I see you got the boy with you, Ned," he whispered. "Trying to rehab him, or just taking him out riding with this cowboy?"

"Who you calling names?" LaMothe shouted, back on his feet once more, his fists clenched as he stood before the General.

"Better one than you deserve, shooting a man from behind! Consider yourself lucky—the way I've been trained, if a man with a yellow stripe shoots at me from behind, we usually don't bother taking him prisoner."

"You wouldn't be calling me a coward now?"

"Cut it out you guys!" Ryan said, stepping between them and pushing them apart.

"Hitting you from behind, bullshit, Langway! Are you telling me you took it up the ass, or did I strike something else soft? See, he won't answer me because I didn't shoot within six feet of him. I'm sick and tired of this guy and the whole bunch of them ignoring me! Did you stop when I pulled up to warn you beforehand, plinking warning shots—no! I was trying to warn you to get the hell off my land, not kill you outright!"

"Should I send him back where he came from, sir," Langway said to me.

"Oh, I get it," LaMothe continued shouting, "he won't talk to me but to you, Ned, because you really own him. So don't tell me you don't know nothing about this project. As far as I'm concerned, I've given plenty of warning to your operator about what I'm going to do with him if he keeps tearing up my land!"

"I have work to do, Ned, and I'm running behind schedule." Langway said, then signaled to Ryan to help him right the precariously balanced four-wheeler.

"Get your mitts off my ATV!"

"No problem, we're all done!" Langway was walking up to him with raised hands, palms outward. "See, mitts off your toy! Now why don't you get your butt in that seat and your mitts on the handlebars of this kiddie car and get rolling before things get ugly for you."

At that point the General swung his fanny pack to the front of his waist and unzipped it. He pulled out a shiny chrome weapon. With a look of terror in his eyes, Bud LaMothe jumped on his four-wheeler and left in a cloud of dust.

"The clown comes after me with a varmint shooter cartridge gun and thinks he can rattle me," the General said to me, as we watched LaMothe putting distance between him and us.

"What the hell do you think you're doing here! We don't do landclearing, and I never hired you as an equipment operator!"

"It would appear that way, Ned, but things aren't always what they appear," the General agreed with me.

"You got that right!" Ryan agreed with him. "But whatever you're packing in your fanny pack, it's a real gun, not a cartridge pistol, and it sure scared him shitless."

"I didn't know what he was pointing at me until I could see it close up, and I don't like to take chances," Langway said. "He saw pretty quick I don't play around."

"You always carry a sidearm when you play in the dirt?" Ryan asked him.

"Just as a precaution. That's because the cab of the dozer sits so high over the scraper blade, sometimes I can take down a deer, raccoon, beaver, or whatever without even knowing it. That's why I have Mr. Smith & Wesson with me, so I can put a critter I hit by mistake out of his misery. I hate suffering, especially when I can end it fast."

"But this tank moves so slow, how can you possibly hit a deer?" Ryan asked.

"The does like to lay in the grass, and in this big rig I hired here, you can't see a whole lot down below from the cab. You know I started out in the army engineers, running dozers in the days when we had cables and pullies lifting up this big blade, instead of hydraulics. That worked OK, unless, of course, you got stuck in the mud and couldn't get yourself lifted out, since if you don't have any hydraulics, you don't have any down pressure on your blade, and you have no way of lifitng yourself out of the mud. That's why a smart operator would try to stay on dry, safe ground, unless he had a backup, another dozer with a winch that could pull him out, one dozer operator helping the other. I always believed in the buddy system, no matter how good you are."

"I have no idea what you're talking about, Mr. General," Ryan said.

"Then you both better ride with me and see how it looks from where I been sitting lately." Ryan broke into a grin and seemed pleased to take him up on his offer. Without asking my plan, they both helped me up into the cab, and the General shut the door.

"Funny how the more things change the more they remain the same," the General was shouting over the idling engine. "When I was a young enlisted man, I had to get off the heavy equipment if I wanted to advance. Now here I am a retired commander, riding the big Berthas again."

"But wasn't Big Bertha a bomb? Or was that Fat Boy? I remember about that from history class."

"No, you half-remember," Langway said, "which is often worse than not recalling at all, because then at least you should know that you don't know. Sometimes we're educated beyond our intelligence. That's always been my challenge as a leader: how much I really need to know. Remember that military intelligence isn't the same thing as civillian intelligence, though the same principles apply."

"Dad, I'm sorry, but the General here's making no sense to me."

"Actions speak louder than words, so if you gentlemen want to know what I'm doing, let's roll," Langway said, threw the machine in gear, which seemed to have the power of a locomotive.

"So how do you know what you're doing if you can't see?" Ryan asked, leaning forward, trying to see a dozen feet down past the enormous pusher blade.

This is a very big machine, big enough to push out of its path good sized rocks like they're pebbles and snap young trees like twigs. And what the blade doesn't push aside we roll over as we grind it beneath us into the dirt."This is how I know what I'm doing, same way you tell how the wind's blowing." The General licked his finger and held it in the air. "Ooops, almost hit my oak."

"I thought the woodcutters were supposed to take them down, not you," Ryan said.

"Woodcutters?" the General shouted back to Ryan, cupping his hand to his ear. "Once again, the boy's half-right. See, these trees are softwood and small, just good for pulp. These chainsaw jockeys are too slow removing these good-for-nothing smaller trees, which means I've got to take them down if we're going to meet our deadline. I'd go around them, but the paving crews are ready to go. I've got some contouring to do before I can break for lunchtime."

"Let me remind you once again, I never hired you to move dirt!" I said.

"Dirt's important stuff. If you don't build on good soil, sir, properly graded, you'll pay the price later when your project's completed and your tenants have moved in."

"But we don't have a project!" I shouted.

"Now you do, Ned!"

"Park this thing so I can find out about this goddamn Conklin Farm of yours!"

"I'd prefer not, Ned, not until I break for lunch. In the meantime, let me get one of the trucks over here to give you a ride to your car."

"Forget it, I'm riding with you!" I said.

I've given the General a direct order, yet he's ignoring it, continuing to flatten the landscape. I don't believe he'll stop until he's good and ready. But when he shuts down, he's going to tell me exactly what kind of crazy plans he's been hatching for Resolutions. But in the meantime we're captive passengers.

Two P.M. and the General's taken us back to that oak he nearly leveled. We get out of the hot cab and sit beneath the tree. He shares with us a cooler full of sandwiches and drinks and fruit, more than enough for just himself. Why? I bet if we weren't here he'd be eating with the truck drivers and the equipment operators.

Once I was sure he was in my corner, that he had a management rather than a labor viewpoint, but I'm not sure who he's loyal to anymore.

"I want some answers, General, now," I said as we were eating.

"Where were we? Yes, why I'm here at Conklin Farm instead of in Gaylord. Do we really want to discuss this here and now?"

"Right now."

"With a third party present?"

"My son's here. He's a party. Yes."

"Ryan, with all due respect to your father, you must swear you won't broadcast the news that he's a broken man. Broken in the sense that when the doctors first got hold of him, they couldn't tell me he'd be OK. Not to mention dead flat broke. We've been floating on minus figures, Ned."

"When I get to be your age, I sure hope I don't get hung up on the numbers like you guys are," Ryan said. "I can live on peanut butter, rice and beans, next to nothing. Money's for food, a roof over your head. You make it, you lose it, you make it again, no big deal. When you're standing on the railroad track and the train's coming at you, if you don't pay attention and get out of the way, you're bound to get squashed. Go with the flow."

"Ned, I could show your son how he's been sucking on the sugar teat for too long, and that you should have weaned him about ten years ago, before he started getting too big for his britches. Now to make a long story short, our creditors take their money very seriously. So does my wife. When you have to raise cash, you do what you have to do."

"Keep him out of this, General!" I said. "That's family business, not your concern!"

"Raising cash," Ryan said. "I know where you're coming from. I've been there, done that."

"I'll bet you have, young man," said the General, "but I don't ever do anything that isn't legal, ethical, and moral. Ned, I looked at our resources at Pollution Resolutions and maximized them."

"Let's get down to specifics," I said. "Tell me why Resolution has to get into low-end shopping center remodeling and now excavation work? Tell me how much do we get per hour for Peters' new oriental girls?"

"Market price. More than it costs to keep them."

"And what about this dozer? If we're renting it, then hiring it out with you as the operator, seems to me we could hire us another operator by the hour for a lot less than we're paying you. Not the best use of your time."

"I'm out here for a good reason, not for fun and games. You got to understand that while I'm here on the job, and especially after hours, I get to meet the money players in this project. They like me well enough so I'm able to line up work for our new girl draftsmen. It's all about cash flow, about keeping the wolf from the door."

"You guys are still complaining about money," Ryan interrupted again. "Why don't you just give it up and go to work for someone else?"

"Because your father's enemies want us to fold. But I assure you, if it looked like we did it on purpose they'd crucify us for non-performance of the Medford Pond cleanup contract."

"And that's another thing you guys are hung up on—performance. So what's the deal: are you out to save Dad because he's so good, or because your wife wants to redecorate your family room or take her on vacation to Florida?"

"We used to have guys like your son here come into the service, Ned, full of piss and vinegar and running their mouths. When I was done with them though, they'd become respectful."

"That's a great advertisement for your reserve unit, General. That's why I would have never enlisted under you, not that you could have ever been my commander, seeing that they already put you out on pension."

"Shut up, Ryan!" I shouted.

"If I talked to my old man like that, he'd take it out on my hide," the General said.

"That's because you can run, but you can't hide," Ryan said, smiling at his pun, "and that includes you, Mr. Langway."

"You owe Mr. Langway an apology."

"No more than you do, Dad. Why don't you tell him what you do with fuck-ups like he's made with your business?"

"If you can't shut your mouth, Ryan," I shouted, "you can start walking out of here now!"

"Forget it, too far to walk. And you're stuck with me for the time being too, Mr. General, unless you can call us a cab up here."

"Ned, I'm a patient man, but with all due respect, I don't want to see your son anymore," the General said, turning his back to Ryan and taking up his handi-talkie. *"Langway to Conklin number five. Request to evacuate two guests to ground zero . . . As a courtesy as per my request . . . No kidding, we're all busy . . . So I'll owe you boys one . . . No good, not in half an hour. We got a situation right now."*

"See, Ned, I got friends in the right places," the General said, pointing to a dump truck racing toward us in a cloud of dust. "They'll get you out of here pronto. I'll catch up with you later." He shook my hand and was climbing back into the bulldozer, until I held him back by the hem of the jacket.

"As far as I'm concerned you're done with this project," I said.

"No can do, sir. We're tied into all phases at this point, by contract."

"I'm the one who signs the contracts!"

"Of course, Ned. But I had to act in your absence as your agent while you were incapacitated. I'm pleased to see how well you're coming along though. But first things first. The concrete boys are getting ready to pour."

"I'm not interested in any more excuses or evasions, General! I want you back at the office tomorrow first thing."

"First thing, sure, got it covered," he said and removed his plaid woolen lumberjacket. "It's hot riding next to the engine, but nippy out in the air. Careful with your resistance down not to move too fast between hot and cold. Why don't you borrow this fleece from me? Better put it on, Ned. You need to take care of yourself." He put it in my hands, but I threw it back at him.

"Nine A.M., and I'll be checking!" I shouted over the bulldozer, which he fired up once again.

"You both know you don't have a scab to replace Mr. Langway with, so I wouldn't be calling on him tomorrow morning," Ryan advised me, once the General was moving away from us.

"Scabs bust unions, and we don't have a union, so that's impossible."

"Don't get technical on me, Dad. You know damn well he's got you by the short hairs. Since we can't do any more good here, let's hop in before we lose our ride," Ryan said, then helped me up into the cab of the dump truck the General had summoned to take us back to Ryan's car at LaMothe's Salvage.

Chapter 11
The Black Cat

The more I find out about Ryan, the less I seem to know. Perhaps it would have been better if I hadn't asked him about his real connection with Little B, whether they'd been criminal partners, as Wynton Borak was accusing that afternoon I took my fall in the Federal Building. He still holds to the same story that he and Little B have put all that behind them. I'm skeptical, and I don't care very much to be now seeing so much of young Borak, as if telling me that story somehow makes their association legitimate.

Once, maybe twice a week—Saturdays and Sundays—Little B's over here for breakfast. As usual the four of us watch the TV news while we eat. Little B loves current events, even though he appears so unlike his political boss father. This morning we're watching a clip of soldiers executing revolutionaries on crosses on the beach of a Latin country.

"It seems to me," Ryan said, "if we wouldn't sell these dictators our best weapons, we wouldn't have to track them down and punish them when they don't act right anymore."

"Wouldn't you like to put Blue on one of those crosses?" Ryan asked.

"Only if I could tie Diablo on one right next to him," Little B said.

"You guys make me nervous,"Annie interrupted, changing the subject. "What do you think, Mr. D'Amour? Do you think these dictators are being executed because they're butchers, or because they don't know how to build hotels, parking lots, boutiques and golf courses like civilized, democratic people like us do?"Annie asked me.

"There's nothing wrong with democracy," I said. "By the way, are you old enough to vote?"

"Why the hell would I do that?" she asked and replenished her bowl of dry cereal.

"She's a vegetarian. Notice she won't take her rice puffs with any milk," Ryan pointed out to me, "but that doesn't stop her from eating Ben & Jerry's ice cream all the time."

"I'm trying to get away from all animal products, but I'm not there yet," she said. "I don't believe in killing animals either because we're human animals, and we don't eat each other, unless we're cannibals."

"Me, I take whatever comes my way," Ryan said, eating a donut.

"Yeah, wouldn't you like Blue and Diablo to come our way for payback time," Little B said, staring intently at the TV, which had changed from world news to a helicopter shot of a Jeep perched on top of a butte somewhere in the Western desert. "If we could tie him to a couple of those stakes, wouldn't you like to send them back to hell where they belong!" He'd always cook his own breakfast. He was mopping up his eggs with Annie's specialty, oatmeal bread.

"If you're talking about hell, your folks made you go to church," Ryan said.

"How did you guess?" Little B asked.

"That's how I grew up, going to church. Right, Dad?" Ryan asked me.

"Then no one taught you guys about forgiveness," Annie said.

"Forgive what?" I asked Ryan.

"You really don't want to know, Mr. D'Amour,"Annie said, pleadingly.

"Your old man *needs* to know. You show him first what the bastards did to you, Ryan!" Little B said.

Ryan leaves the kitchen and returns without his shirt. I see at the very edge of his chest a small red scar that's not continuous, but exits out the rear in a similar round scar. A bullet puncture, most likely—I feel a pain in my own chest and for the moment stop breathing. I hug Ryan, an inadvertent reaction, comforting myself as much as him, glad my boy's survived.

Ryan pulled away from me and nodded to Little B, "That's the last time Blue's ever going to do that to me! Your turn now."

Like Ryan has done, Little B goes to the bedroom to shed his clothes. He returns with a towel around his waist. Solidly built, though no muscleman, he nevertheless struts like a bodybuilder on review, his chest expanded and his arms held away from his torso. I don't know how I could have failed to see the similarity of his mustard hair with his father's, a consistency somewhere between wool on a lamb's back and steel wool, the color of new-born baby scat. He couldn't be much taller than his father—a good foot and a half shorter than me. He looks to each of us in turn, as if to see whether we're paying sufficient attention to him, and he drops his towel. With a sense of pride he moves his arms up and down his thighs massaging himself. His penis is stouter and longer than normal, but how much more, I can't tell, because it's in proportion to his testes. Testes bigger than apricots, the diameter of plums, or maybe nectarines! Testes enclosed in a sack that looks like it's been sliced open and sewn back together!

I've seen enough of young Borak, but Annie's eyes are still fastened resolutely to him. She puts her arm around him as an old friend, which makes me wonder whether he and Ryan have been taking turns in her bed.

"I'm so sorry about what Blue's done," she said.

He takes her other hand in his own and brings it down to the long scar across his navel, which I realize is the same one running through his scrotum and across his thigh—probably done in one slice of a knife! I can see the wound on his body, and now I'm beginning to understand the wounds he and my son have been carrying inside. I'm not sure I blame them for wanting revenge, but I do blame them for the stupidity of thinking they can do it without even worse consequences to themselves. Then again, after nearly paying for my vendetta against Little B's father with my life, I'm hardly the one to offer them advice.

"They'll wish they finished us off, I swear!" Ryan shouted, raising his fist to their enemies.

"But Ryan, don't you think we would be safer if we moved far away from here?" Annie asked.

"There will be a time when we can come and go free from them! But now it's payback time! " Little B bellowed from the bed-room where he was dressing.

"Can't you see they're waiting for you?" asked Annie. "Now that you won't do jobs for them, they have no use for you! Next time I might not be able to get you guys to a doctor in time! The more you fight them, the more you become like them!"

She's the most reasonable one of this strange menage, but Ryan and Little B aren't listening to her. I think they want to start a new life, but Littlehale wants to drag them back to his gang. It would probably be a smart move on my part to leave them before they fight any more losing battles. "Get in here!" she called to Little B.

When Little B rejoined us, Annie took him in one hand and Ryan in the other to the kitchen table. Then without releasing either of their hands, she sat at the head of the table and they sat to either side. "Well, Mr. D'Amour, do you want to be part of our circle?" she asked. I took my place at the opposite end and held her hand and Ryan's. "Since you're the oldest guy here and might have more sense than these guys, maybe you can put some positive energy into our ring."

"Excuse me?" I said.

"Say something positive."

"The greatest misfortune of all is not to be able to bear misfortune," I said.

"He got that right," Little B said, altogether missing my point. "They should know by now we can take whatever they dish out."

"And their big misfortune is pushing us too far!" Ryan said.

"You guys are hopeless!" said Annie. She broke the chain, came back to the table with a spoon and a pint of ice cream.

Since I've been a guest of Ryan and Annie here in Rail City, this is the first time I've been alone and unsupervised. Annie's the reader, not Ryan, and she has shelves and boxes of books everywhere. Pocket-sized books with handsome men and glamour girls painted on the covers, as well as the gothics with the pictures of the pretty young heroines in danger, pursued by a relentless enemy and saved by brave, manly lovers. Books that I won't waste my time reading. I know I'm an honorable man, in spite of what Martha and Erica and the newspaper readers may mistakenly believe about me, though not a religious one, someone who wouldn't under better circumstances be reading the Bible. But I've discovered this collection of a hundred Bibles boxed up and in the basement—finally something for me to read with some substance. I look over the rest of the collection of Bibles and see they've been taken from from the Weeping Willow Motel, Crimson Canopy Cabins, Thatcher's Cottages, the Best Western, and all dated within the last twelve months in Annie's handwriting. Some people take snapshots or buy postcards to remember their holidays; she and Ryan evidently bring home Gideon Bibles. But what Bible story to read first, the tale of the rebellious rabble wandering through the wilderness with Moses as a guide for 40 years, as long as it took for them to lose their evil habits? Or something more immediately useful to my situation, like Proverbs for a plan how to face down enemies once they've won the early battles. With my eyes still not focusing at close range as well as they should, I take up to the living room an edition that's illustrated and easy on my eyes. I read about Job, how he dealt with his losses.

Perhaps I'm being punished as a test, but a test for what I wonder and begin to think of reasons. The lights go dead, and with a flashlight I try checking the circuits of the main circuit breaker box. I kick over a boot that falls over, dropping something heavy on my foot, a 9mm Glock automatic with a full clip of bullets. My son must believe he lives in a dangerous neighborhood. I flip the all the breaker switches, but still no electricity. Probably will come back on soon. What else is Ryan hiding here? On a hook in the front hall closet I find a keyring hanging behind a coat and which solves a little mystery that's made me curious ever since Ryan first removed me from the hospital—why the utility closet off the kitchen has a padlock. Now that I have the key to open it, I discover what Ryan doesn't want me to see: a 25mm Beretta, just right for his pocket, or her purse.

I move my chair by the big window, closer to the light, and return to my easy chair to read the Gideon Bible. With time alone, the down time I've had so much of lately, I'm searching for relevant tales, in particular the section in Proverbs about how some very bad men may prosper and that God does not punish them in this life, no more than he rewards those who behave well. Though I'm eager to find some kind of a short-term answer in a Bible episode, I have trouble concentrating, thinking instead about how Ryan and his girlfriend may be using their weapons, about who's pursuing them and why. So I set out to resolve a more practical problem, how to restore our lost power. But first I need to see whether anyone else has been affected as well. Most of the neighbors are off to work. Either that or they're not coming to the door as I ring, but I do find a young woman caring for her own children rather than working out of the house, a rarity here in this better block of Rail City where the majority seems employed during the day. She tells me she has electricity and calls a couple of friends who do as well. It seems off that this unit is the only dark one. I need to take it up with the power company:

"Yes, I do live at #3 Westwind," I said on the phone to the power company representative. "Why else do you think I'd call you about the blackout here?"

"Your zipcode please . . . ? Your phone number . . . ? And who I am speaking with?"

"D'Amour, but I'm a guest of my son, who's renting."

"Sorry, we can only talk to the owner of record about the status of the account."

"I don't care what he owes or doesn't. I want to know why this is the only unit without power."

"I just had a look on the grid board, and we show no interruption. We're only responsible up to the service entrance, and from that point and through the interior of the dwelling the owner's responsible for maintaining his own wiring. I would suggest that you call your son's landlord, and that he arrange for a licensed electrician."

"So who's his landlord?"

"That's not really public information."

"Am I supposed to sit in the dark until my son comes home this evening and wait until tomorow until we can get this fixed?"

"I'm very sorry, sir. That's just our policy."

"Let me tell that to my 87-year-old mother who is lying in bed with a bout of flu she can't shake and is under three comforters and is getting damn cold in here? Not only that, but we have a hundred-gallon tank full of tropical fish, and without the electricity to heat up their water, they'll be belly up in the morning."

"Mr. D'Amour, I think you're really telling me you're cold and uncomfortable. I may work for a utility, but I can feel for our rate payers, even if you're telling me a tall tale. Why don't you call your son?"

"He could be anywhere, but we're here in the dark!"

"OK, then why don't you try contacting a Timothy Littlehale, senior or junior, co-owners. But if anyone ever asks, you didn't hear it from me."

"And speaking of paying rates, you wouldn't be shutting him off for a back bill?"

"Not without ample notice. We deal with people's lives. Shut-offs should never come as a surprise to either the owner or a tenant. Perhaps Mr. Littlehale cut off your power for a reason."

———————

No power, no lights, and I'm sitting alone in an apartment one step up from a slum, the left half of what used to be a one-family two-story home. After the fall I was suspended between life and death, and ever since my problems have been multiplying in my absence. And today, now that I finally have a day off from my keepers I would like to use the opportunity to find a bit of enlightenment in this stolen Bible. I can't seem to concentrate on the great lessons of the past. In order to build my endurance I go outside and walk briskly for half an hour around a two-block square, the safer part of Rail City near these duplex houses rather than the four and six-family rundown tenement section at the Yard, where the old railroad repair buildings used to be. When I return to the apartment my late afternoon headache returns, a very mild form of it, not nearly as intrusive as the ones I had when I first awoke from the fall and the doctors were doping me with intravenus painkillers. A mild headache, which sends me looking for a bottle of aspirin, other than the one I expect to find in my bureau, but which I have finished. Leading me to look through all the cupboards, including one padlocked in the bathroom, which I open with another key on the keychain. I find my aspirin, as well as an ammo box, much too big to hold Q-Tips and cotton balls. But a perfect home for this Smith & Wesson .44 Magnum and a couple of hundred rounds, exactly like the one I had to quit using at the range with the General or ruin my shoulder for shooting hoops. If I ever get back into my house I'll have to see whether it's still there, or whether Ryan stole it from me!

Not a good situation, staying under the same roof of my son who keeps an arsenal, but won't tell me who he's fighting! I'm looking through this bay window, sitting on its big sill, facing onto the track, the dangerous Welfare Row side of Rail City. Too bad this house couldn't be turned backward and face behind us toward the more pleasant and safer two blocks of responsible home owners with something to lose. When Ryan and Annie return I'll tell them my intentions firmly, to be out of here very soon. And I have a way out of here today, Ryan's Honda parked safely in the back yard. I have no idea who picked him up this morning, whether it was Little B, another friend, or a restaurant co-worker, whether he's really at the restaurant like he's been telling Annie and me. I get the feeling she doesn't ask too many questions as long as they have enough money to cover their expenses, but I'm determined to get some answers from him about the source of his income.

I hear a couple of shots, which are hitting the house, right, left and above the window. Maybe I'm a sitting duck! As I'm backing away from the window to the center of the room, it shatters, an explosion of glass, then silence! I'm the target, under attack! I retrieve the automatic from the bathroom, load it, and cautiously work my way toward the living room to defend myself, safety released. Before I get there I hear a crash into the living room wall, then running footsteps on the porch. The damage: a blood-spattered hole in the living room wall, and on the floor below it, a rock with a bag attached, air mail stickers pasted all over it! I see a blue Corvette at the curb, its big engine revving, and in it Tim Littlehale. He's tooting his air horn. He's past my gun's 40-yard range, so I won't even attempt to blow out his tires. Now he waves at me through the sunroof as he burns out of here.

In this bag, Littlehale's thrown through the window, a black cat! Its fur nicely brushed and shiny, probably somebody's living pet an hour or two ago. Fresh blood around the hole in its neck, still warm, probably killed on the way here. And a message in indigo blue, one tone brighter than his car: *ACCOUNTS PAST DUE. SECOND NOTICE.* A dangerous way to collect money, and evidently this isn't the first time he's dunned Ryan.

I was hoping I'd never have to see that bastard again, not after running into him at that rat-infested tenement he was renting to Ryan and Annie before. Why are the Littlehales still their landlords here in this second apartment? And does Littlehale Jr. think he can use this place for shooting practice because he owns it? I wonder what his next stunt might be. But that's going to be between Ryan and him if Ryan's crazy enough to stay under his control, certainly not my problem. I don't plan to be a sitting target by hanging around here. I'd like to just walk away from this mess, but first I have to batten down the hatches. I'll use the cardboard box from that big TV they bought last week, split it down its seams and hold it to the wall with the roll of duct tape I saw in the garage. It should be good enough to seal out the weather until they can get it repaired, maybe with hoodlum-proof glass next time!

It's still hard for me to believe that Denise didn't know I was in the hospital in a coma, though that's what she told me when I regained consciousness and she answered my call. I believe she could have visited me much earlier, no matter how busy her schedule. I can't help but feel that she blamed me for the accident, as much as she did Borak's strongmen, her real reason for keeping her distance. But now that I've sealed up the window, I must move on. But first I must patch things up between us and let her know where I've been since Ryan so quickly pulled me out of the hospital.

"Hi. What are you doing?" I asked her on the phone.

"It's Wednesday, the middle of the day, and I'm talking to my favorite client: you. I'm here in the office working, like you used to do, remember?" Denise answered me brusquely.

"Working on my case? By the way, I've been staying with Ryan."

"Would you be insulted if I said you're a hopeless case?" she laughed. "One that no one is stupid enough to handle but me, and I'm beginning to wonder why. Where in God's name have you been? I've been very worried about you."

"You're just sore because I haven't been very good about staying in touch."

"Your touch part seems to be the last to go. It's your brain that baffles me. If I didn't know you since we were very young, I might have given up on you by now. If you're insane these days, perhaps Mr. Borak's driven you to it. Do you want me to forgive you, Ned, for ignoring me and for almost destroying yourself? What's on your mind?"

"Staying warm."

"Has it come to that? Are you on the street, rubbing your hands together over a 55-gallon oil drum filled with burning trash?"

"Actually it's not much warmer in here than in the great outdoors. No heat, no power."

"But you wanted to stay with your son rather than where you had it good with me, probably too good."

"Which I appreciated at the time, a place I'd like to revisit," I said. "I'm very sorry if I haven't let you know how much you've done to help me."

"Visiting hours are over though," she said. "Not your visiting hours at the hospital, but my visiting hours at home."

"I can't blame you for feeling hurt."

"Please, I can't tell you how I feel, not here."

"OK, may I come over to the office to talk business?"

"I don't think you'd be too welcome here. Did I mention that Chip's cut you loose, though by default you're still tethered to me, I suppose."

"Then can I meet you after hours at your place?"

"Only if you've done the homework assignment I set for you, Ned, not before. Regarding Martha, remember?"

"How about for dinner?"

"I'm on a diet, and I've got to get back to work."

"OK, you name the place."

"How about the disaster zone?" she suggested.

"Excuse me?"

"Some time, Ned, we're going to have to meet at Medford Pond. We've got to get down to the bottom of your troubles, or you won't be fit company for anyone."

"Are you really on my side, Denise?"

"You better realize by now I may be your last friend. OK, you win. You can see me here at the office, three o'clock sharp, sweetheart."

I don't know whether I'll be returning to the apartment, so I do some essential housekeeping first. From the ammo box I remove all of Ryan's weapons and throw them in a garbage bag. I throw the dead cat in another bag and put it all in the trunk of the Lincoln. I'm relieved to get out of Ryan's apartment.

Denise sees me for our meeting in a conference room at the Thompson law offices. When I try explaining to her about the cat flying through the window, either she doesn't care to hear the details, or else doesn't believe me. She seems far more interested in my progress with Martha and me, and tells me flat out that I'm going to have decide between the two of them, that until I do I won't be invited to spend the night with her.

I suppose I could call my wife first to let her know I'm on the way to settle up with her, but instead I decide to drop in on her unannounced. Her car's in front of the house, and I verify that she's inside by stepping back to the edge of the driveway until I can see her blonde head through the window. She's in the library on the second floor, just after five o'clock, probably just begun watching her afternoon TV talk show. That means I have an hour to retrieve some of my clothes from the first floor master bedroom, clothes which I can use now that the seasons have changed. I quickly let myself in. I'm in luck, finding a couple of her empty leather Louis Vitton suitcases in which I can put my own things.

It has airline stickers to Lexington, Kentucky. Evidently, she's been to bluegrass country to visit her socialite equestrian friends. Working fast I'm throwing in my own things when I hear footsteps in the hall.

"Is that you Erica?" Martha called. "Did you find that mauve cashmere sweater I wanted to give you?"

In a minute she'll be in here to check on Erica. With the window open I can bail out of here in a flash. No, not a good idea. These are my clothes, this is still my house, and I'm going to stand my ground.

"Hands off my luggage!" she shouted, the moment she entered the room. "Get away from my wardrobe now! You have no right breaking in here and taking my things!"

What's she doing now, rooting through the top drawer of her dresser, counting her cash then stuffing it into her pocket?

"Excuse me, but, as I recall, this is my house."

"By my count, I'm short three-hundred dollars, Ned," she said with her hands on her hips, staring at me angrily.

"Any other claims?" I asked.

"It's been longer than six months, so as far as we're concerned, you've given up all claims! Now go!" She clasped her hands over her ears, shutting out any anticipated response and walked away from me with her dresses. Erica had heard the yelling and was standing beside her mother facing me. She yanked a suitcase from one hand, and Martha simultaneously grabbed the other, as if they shared a secret signal. "Do us all a favor, Ned, and leave now, before I have to put you out."

"You think you can wear my pants, but I'm taking what's mine, whether you like it or not," I said as calmly as I could manage.

Martha's playing out our dispute in front of Erica to win herself sympathy. For me this is a no-win situation. I've got to get out of the house with no more unpleasant words in front of our daughter.

The cell phone rang, and I took the call. *Hello, it's you, Ryan . . . Where? Here at the house . . . New window, portable kerosene heater? All the comforts of home. I'll be back at the apartment in a little bit. Don't bother, no need of you hanging around here . . . You don't think I should be driving at night? Not a problem because your mother sold my car, remember?*

She has it all figured out: she takes everything, I get nothing, and now she accuses me of of rifling through her petty cash drawer. The Deb Queen's doing her best to undermine me in front of Erica, doing her best to hide her master plan of running away from this marriage. And to justify it she can always blame me because Ryan took to the streets. But her real reason is financial, that lately the business hasn't generated enough to keep her in club memberships and overseas holidays. Denise is right: the time's long since overdue to find out what she wants, so I can figure out how to either deliver it to her, or else cut my lossses.

I'm here alone in the bedroom. They must have left when I first began speaking of the cell phone with Ryan. Are they being considerate, or have they just left me to hatch a new plan in private?

Erica returned downstairs by herself and said to me, "Mom says she wasn't expecting you, so she wasn't prepared for you right now."

"Really? What else?"

The damn cell phone's ringing again. I realize how much I've enjoyed the months I haven't used it, and now I wish I didn't have it with me. "You always answer that phone, no matter what, Dad. I think you love business more than us." Once she saw me turn off the phone, Erica continued, reading her notes from the back of a credit card envelope. "Mom's under a lot of stress, through no fault of her own. She says she's had a hard day and is tired now."

"Are you forgetting any other messages from her highness?"

"It's just that kind of attitude that we see getting you into trouble with Mom all the time. I hate to be the one in the middle of you guys, but Mom also said if you think a home's a railway station where you pass through on the way to somewhere else, then you don't deserve to live in one."

"Erica, I have to assume you really want to help," I said. I put my hand on her shoulder, which she removed. "If you do, can you tell me where you took those suitcases of my clothes?"

With her eyes closed and her arms crossed, she shook her head no, like a stubborn child. I didn't want to continue the argument with my daughter. "You're absolutely right, Erica. I can't blame you for not wanting to be caught in the crossfire. Excuse me while I find your mother."

"Martha, I came here to talk to you and no one else." She was back in the second floor library, catching the end of her show in which grown adopted daughters were being reunited with their biological mothers with tears and hugs.

"Not now, please."

"This is real life, not a show!" I shouted and pulled the television cord out of the wall.

"Don't you dare talk to me like that! And as long as you don't have any more respect for family, I'll never have any more reason to hear from you!"

She's looking for apologies, sympathy, concessions, or God knows what, and I don't plan to leave here without finding out what exactly she's demanding. Now she's jumped up from the chair and is heading back downstairs, waving me to follow her. This could be progress. She leads me back to the bedroom, where she locks the door behind us.

A knock on the door."Are you OK, mother?" Erica asked.

"Don't worry, honey, I'll be OK," Martha assured her. "You can stay here," she said to me, seating me like a guest in our mauve reading chair with the matching ottoman.

She's retreated to her walk-in closet, leaving the sliding door open about a foot, just enough so I can see her pull off her clothes. She puts on the black lacy pegnoir she knows I like better than any other of her nightclothes, the sheer one she hasn't worn for me in years. She still has an incredible body, quite firm. Her three sessions a week at the health club have yielded visible results. She stares at me with the start of a smile. I want to grab her, carry her to the bed, see if the old fires could be rebuilt. No, not a good idea. I'm putting it out of my mind, because afterward I'd then have to pay her more tribute. She's pacing and drops an ash on the carpet without noticing any more than she notices me. After she stops to stretch, a holdover from a dozen years of ballet lessons, she moves into a flattering stationary dancer's pose, her pelvis forward, the gateway through which both my children passed, reminding me of the countless times in our years of marriage I popped in there. And then she adjusts her pose, pulling her shoulders back, extending her chest. I seen her pinkish, familiar nipples. Finally she turns to me, with a bitter smile. I can't tell whether she's teasing me or mocking me, but as she passes close to me, I reach out for her and touch her derriere. She smiles, which I take for an invitation, then I touch her breast. After parading naked in front of me, she instantly draws back from me. A sudden change of heart, she seems ready for me and quickly bends my arm. I must blame myself for even considering that we could make up our differences, for falling into her trap. She makes me angry and sad at the same time, but I'm careful to remain calm, not to get into a pushing match with her. Just the same she slaps me hard across my face, catching my nose in a stab of pain.

"Help me, Erica! Help!" Martha deliberately yelled, as if I had hurt her, and unlocked the door. Erica responded quickly, bursting into the room, Ryan behind her. "What's going on here, father!"

"If you take a look at Mom's outfit, you don't need to guess," Ryan said, "unless you're pretty naive, Erica. I mean how the hell do you think you came onto the Earth? Or you think you're so good you got here on earth the same way Jesus did? My take on it, if it feels good, Dad, go for it!"

"Erica, Ryan, everybody, for the record, I have not seen your father—personally—for longer than six months," Martha said.

"You never change, Ryan," Erica said. "For someone who fails at everything, you have all the answers."

"Dumb bitch, you get ahead because you kiss up to anyone who can add a few bucks to your cash register at the end of the week!"

"Ryan, dear, if you can't clean up your mouth," Martha said, "I shall have to wash it out for you."

"OK, to Mom, I say I'm sorry," Ryan said, kissing her, then holding his arm around her shoulders. "But to you, Erica, I say go fuck off!"

"Hate to see you go, Ryan, but someone's out there waiting to carry you back where you came from," Erica said, looking at the driveway at the tooting vehicle. "Let me guess where you're headed tonight: to a bar, or a friend's to get stoned, or some trampy girl's, or if you're short of cash maybe break and enter, or if you're flush maybe you'll get yourself messed up enough to where you forget where you wanted to go and just end up on the street, passed out."

"You know, I feel sorry for your old man, having to put up with you every day," he said.

"I expect you to apologize to your brother this instant!" Martha shouted.

"No way, Mom, not until he cleans up his act!" Erica said pointing accusingly at Ryan.

"If you can't be kinder to your brother, out—out of my room!" Martha shouted and unsuccessfully tried to push Erica out the door.

"None of that's true anymore, is it?" Martha asked Ryan directly. "But honestly Ryan, I still worrry about you every night. Promise me that you won't get into trouble tonight."

"You know that Erica will tell you anything you want to hear, Mom. If you can't trust me, Mom, there's no one left, now that you're shooting poison arrows at Dad."

"No need to take it out on me, just because Ryan's acting like a jerk!" Erica began yelling again. "Why don't you let that moron out there who's leaning on the horn take Ryan away already, Mom, so you can sort it out with Dad?"

"Your brother's come a long way, and we're proud of him, now that he's training as a chef," Martha said, kissing Ryan on the forehead.

"That's news to me," Erica said. "I thought he got fired from flipping burgers."

Ryan made an obscene gesture at her, which Martha didn't see.

"Don't worry, Ryan. Your father and I plan to sort it out, only at a better time."

"No better time than now," I suggested. "That's why I made a special trip here."

"In case you haven't noticed," Martha said defiantly to me, "I march to a different drummer now, and he doesn't play your requests anymore."

As if to make her point that her time was more important than mine, Martha leaves the bedroom, walking out on me, taking Ryan with her to the library, where she and Ryan pull together the two big leather easy chairs. She's making an effort to behave as if I'm not in the room, but I'm not about to oblige her by hanging back and missing the conversation between her and my son.

"Ryan, you've got to promise me that after you've dropped off your father," she said, "you'll come back and sleep here tonight."

"You want me to drop Dad off like trash to the landfill?"Ryan asked, looking at me across the room. "He deserves better treatment from us than that."

"Speak for yourself," she said in a very low voice.

"No, Mom, speak up!" Ryan said. "There are too many secrets in this family already."

"Don't kid yourself, Mom, Dad's not the one breaking up what's left of this family," Ryan shouted, gesturing to me.

"You couldn't truly feel that way about your mother?" Martha said in an even tinier voice than before. Then she turned away from Ryan to wipe tears from her eyes, and she dabbed her eyes with the tissue Ryan offered her, her voice became stronger and more confident. "So don't let me stop you if you and your father and that little orphan Annie girlfriend of yours all have one big party. Don't give a second thought to your mother back here sitting home alone worrying. So never mind, I'll—I'll try to get—get on . . ." Her crying had overwhelmed her so that she couldn't speak.

Erica now came up from behind me in the living room and tapped me on the shoulder. "Maybe Mom wouldn't feel so left out if you weren't so mean to her, Dad," she said. "And it didn't help that you terrorized her in the bedroom."

"Why don't you quit fanning the flames? Hasn't there been enough hysteria without your contributing any more?" I said in a discreet voice, directed to just her.

"Hysterical, as in hysterical woman, Dad?" Erica all but shouted, as if I in some way had genuinely offended her. "Are you calling Mom and me hysterical?"

In the meantime, Little B let himself into the room uninvited. That tattoo of the death's head and bones bother me. I can't be sure whether he had it needled into his arm for its decorative value, whether to annoy his father, the senior Borak, or whether he means it to advertise to all bystanders like me that he's a force to reckon with, more dangerous than his size would indicate.

"Excuse me, sister," Ryan said, after having rushed over to him with a high-five greeting, "but I didn't hear Dad say any such thing about my Mom. What did you hear, Borkman?"

"I been too busy looking at your sister," Little B said. "You never told me she was so good-looking. Glad to meet you, Erica, especially since I'm between girlfriends. Now you wouldn't object, Mr. Ned, if I went out with your pretty daughter?"

"Forget it!" Erica bellowed in her own defense.

"Why not? I got the cash, if you got the time. Payday!" he said, fanning out his wad of bills.

"First of all, I don't know what you and my brother did to get you that dirty money," Erica said.

"Touchy, isn't she?" he said to Ryan.

"And, second, you shouldn't be asking my father's permission because I'm nobody's property."

"Except, for Derek, her husband," Ryan said, "He's a nice guy. She henpecks him, so I wouldn't worry too much about him."

"And, fourth, I don't like your attitude any more than Ryan's."

"You forgot third," Little B said.

"Oh, yes, third. Your face. I don't like it."

"Why not?"

"Because you have a fat head, or maybe it appears that way because the rest of you's so—compact, close to the ground. Or maybe if I could stand to look at you more closely, I'd find everything about you really is in proportion, and that you're a child who's never going to grow up."

Little B said nothing and began walking away from us, except for Ryan who was following him toward his van.

"I'm not done, Ryan!" Martha called to him, in turn following Ryan outside.

"Mr. D'Amour, you got a sweetheart for a daughter there," he said to me and pointed to Erica. "Does she like insulting everybody, or just me?"

"She doesn't have to take that abuse," Martha said and pulled Erica back from Ryan, young Borak and me.

"The point is don't talk to me about my looks, if you don't want me to talk about yours!" Erica turned and hollered. "Not that it's any of your business, but I'm married to a great husband, no matter what Ryan would have you believe! And I don't appreciate being judged by a hoodlum like you!"

"So we meet again, Mr. D'Amour," Little B said, cheerfully and shook my hand. "Ryan, you shouldn't have told me to come back in half an hour. You guys weren't half done fighting. I don't know about you, but I'm getting the hell away from your sister."

"Dad, are you with us?"

"Not exactly, but you can give me a ride anyway."

As I was stepping into Little B's van, Erica came running out with two dufflebags, which she threw in the car after me. "Mother asked me to bring you your clothes in case you need them, wherever you're going."

"But I had them in the suitcases."

"Those are hers. She needs them for visiting friends," she said and left us before I could ask her anything more. She rushed back to the house, where her mother was waiting for her in the front hall. Little B punched the gas and jolted down the driveway throwing up pebbles.

"Ryan, I'm amazed at how fast you showed up after speaking with you on the cell phone," I said after we were traveling for a couple of minutes. "If I didn't know better, I'd say you've been following me."

"And I'm amazed at how fast you managed to trash my apartment, Dad," Ryan said.

"You got that wrong, son. It was Tim Littlehale's doing. If I were you I'd find myself a new landlord."

"I'm just pulling your chain, Dad. We really do have things under control," Ryan said, exchanging smiles with Little B. "There's a new window and the power's back on."

"That's not the point. I was almost the target, not the window."

"Not to worry, Dad," Ryan continued. "It's easy to set the power company straight when you know the right people, and it's not very hard to replace a window when a glass man owes you a favor."

"Just one more mess to patch up," young Borak said. "Like the night I was with Ryan at Melissa's café and I find my work truck busted up and setting on its axles, minus the wheels. That's how come I replaced it with this blue one. Soon as I get the chance I got to put a sign on it for my cleaning business so the world knows what I do for a living."

"Did you tell him Blue threw blue paint over your old white van?" Ryan asked. "What do you call this color—violet, purple, or what? It's not a man's color, and not my favorite. Why did you buy it, because you got it for a good price?"

"No, because I want to be ready next time Blue comes after my truck or my cat with his blue paint. If there is a next time, Mr. D'Amour, Ryan and me are going to bury him."

"Blue?"

"No, I'm talking about my fat old black cat," Little B said. "Show him." Ryan put a work glove on his right hand, then held up by its tail a very big, stiff cat with some blood at the corner of its mouth, which didn't look like it died of natural causes. "Not like that, dickhead, or you'll break it off. Good thing my father didn't see Rufus here sprayed blue or see you flinging him around like that. Eighteen years old. In his younger days, come springtime when the mice would sneak into our house, he'd go on patrol all around the foundation, inside and out, sniff them out and nail them. Only way to do it, one shot, wham bang, snap their neck! This cat was Dad's favorite pet of all times, not only because he was a good hunter, but so smart he could jump up to a door knob and twist it open.

"Rufus was staying with me in my place, keeping me company until I could find me my next woman," Little B continued. "I don't think Erica and me hit it off too good, Mr. D, that she'll be my next one. Now I'll have to tell the old man Rufus died normally, of old age. Dad loved this fucking rat-catcher. He was so patient with him he didn't even get angry one time when he was taking care of business with Mom before he had to get up for work, and Rufus jumped up to the doorknob and opened up the door and scat under the sheets with them. Dad never had much of a sense of humor, or anything, but he thought that was cute, even though they had to throw out the bedsheets. But in the last couple of years old Rufus got too big fat and middle-aged to hop off the floor. Goddamn, this is a hell of a way for Rufus to die, the second cat Blue killed and threw our way!"

"So Blue must have thought that cat he threw through my window was Rufus," Ryan said.

"Then Blue he must be thinking he's dealing with a couple of wimps!" Little B hollered, pounding his steering wheel. "Old Rufus had the right idea how to deal with those pests running wild where they didn't belong!"

"Does he think you're wimps, or is he really trying to provoke you and lead you into his snare?" I asked.

"No matter. We're not afraid of him, and we're ready to go head to head with him, once and for all. We'll leave you off at the apartment, so you can keep Annie company until we get back later this evening," Ryan said.

"Ryan, take me back to the house," I said. "I don't dare leave the General's car here because it might disappear, like my Cadillac did."

"I can get it tomorrow."

"That may be too late. Your mother saw me arrive in that Lincoln, and if she thinks it's mine, she may have it hauled off and sold like she did the Cadillac. I left the keys in the ignition."

"If she does, then she'll have to pay me for it. If I'm not worried about it, why should you be, Dad?"

"I have my reasons," I said.

"And we have our reasons for dropping you off and getting on with it."

"OK, what would your mother think if she found a black cat in the trunk?"

"So?"

"So we bury both cats together."

"Not next to Rufus!" Little B said. "Your alley cat can go in the dumpster."

"And, more importantly, Ryan, what would your mother and her pals assume if she were to find that .44 magnum I took from the cupboard in there with a dead cat?"

"It's my car, and I'll take my chances," Ryan said.

"OK, leave me at the apartment, and I'll figure out how to get the car without your help."

Right then Little B hit the brakes hard, locking up the wheels. "Are you trying to get us killed!" Ryan shouted, turning his head to the truck behind them, sounding its air horn.

"Not yet! Hang on!" Little B said, then made an abrupt u-turn. "I got bigger fish to fry than listening to you two fighting over the car."

"Stop here," I said, a hundred yards short of the house, and got out.

"Wait here, and I'll follow you," Little B said, and made his way through the shrubs and trees, rather than on the lit driveway itself. Ryan was right behind him. "You heard Ryan. We got some big fish to fry. I don't have time to drive you around."

"Good, I was planning on driving myself anyway. I'll just follow you."

"OK, Dad, but only if you promise to drive yourself directly home," Ryan insisted.

Chapter 12
A Public Service

I was relieved to be out of Ryan and Annie's cursed apartment and to have regained enough strength to be able to begin swimming laps at the Sunset Motel, where Dimitri gave me better quarters, a two room suite. And I was pleased to return to Resolutions, where I was working hard to bring order to my unruly office, traveling back and forth in the ten-year-old Lincoln the General insisted I borrow from him. I was very busy working and seeing Denise as much as our schedules coincided, but I always made time to see my son.

One evening while Denise was working late at her office, I used the opportunity to check in with Ryan at Rail City. Rather than ask Ryan questions while we were in the apartment, where he knew I wasn't comfortable ever since the afternoon the cat came through the window. This evening Ryan's been acting strange. It's Monday, Annie's night off, and she has lasagne in the oven, which she makes better than any I've ever tasted, but Ryan won't have any of it. He won't touch it, and instead grabs our jackets, all but pushing me out the door. He insists on taking me driving with him to the other end of Gaylord to a Subway sandwich shop. It doesn't take us more than fifteen minutes to finish. He frequently looks at his watch, not rushing, but lingering slowly drinking a soda, then a couple of coffees afterward.

"If you're ready I'm ready," he said nervously. "Or if you want to stay out of this thing with Little B and me, I can drive you to the cab stand so you don't have to be involved. Your choice."

He's not asking me directly, but there's something bothering him, and he wants me to stay to help him with it. He's been very secretive and agitated, and I can't account for why he so suddenly left Annie and her fine dinner, other than to protect her from some venture tonight. But I've learned by now questioning him is worse than useless. I sense he's afraid of something, that he needs me, which is why I'm going to stay with him the rest of this evening, if necessary.

Now that we're in Gaylord's old city negotiating the narrow streets where the buildings huddle on either side, creating canyons, there is an overwhelming racket coming out of Ryan's car, worse even than the last time I was in it. With each turn of the steering wheel, especially righthand turns, the clunking in the front end of the car echoes so loud that the few people walking on the sidewalks stop to stare at us. Finally we come to Central Avenue, the wide thoroughfare of old Gaylord, now a street of large railroad and timber boss houses, long since broken up into apartments and commercial offices. Ryan stops and pulls over to the curb. He looks at his watch.

In a couple of minutes Little B pulls behind us in his blue van, but tonight he's removed the magnetic *Interstate Maintenance & Cleaning Services* signs. He seems to be waiting for all the traffic to pass before he gets out and quickly slides into the back seat.

"I didn't think we'd have company tonight," Little B said, tapping me on the shoulder.

"I shouldn't have brought you, Dad," Ryan said to me without conviction.

"You can drive yourself home in my rig if you want, Mr. D'Amour," Little B said, trying to hand me his keys, which I didn't accept.

"No, I'm not about to cut Ryan loose now," I said.

"If you ask me, even though Ryan's my friend, you don't want to be hanging around with him, especially tonight." Little B said. "Even though Annie tells me he's not worth much, he's still my friend, so I'll do the best I can to bring him home safe and sound."

"Keep fucking with me, Borkman!" Ryan shouted.

"Pretty much Annie's exact words to me not too long ago," Little B burst out laughing. "Too bad she doesn't respect either of us a whole lot, no more than Blue does."

"How could you compare Annie to Blue, you dink!" Ryan shouted. "If you can't say anything good about Annie, stay the hell away from her!"

"Forget about her for now!" Little B hollered. "Even my old man knows it's Blue we got to deal with now! Ryan, you know damn well he would just as soon kill us off with a pizza full of arsenic, if he could find the right delivery man. Remember how ugly he got when we were 45 minutes late to do a delivery? I don't have time to talk. We got to get moving."

"Deliver what?" I asked.

"We're talking about no more than delivering pizza, right?" Little B asked me in a strangely soft, conspiratorial voice. "We don't do that kind of cash business anymore, but we have one old acount to straighten out tonight." And to Ryan he said: "Next time you leave your old man behind, or you can count me out!"

"I'm going to ride with him, Dad," Ryan said, starting the engine in the Honda for me before he took off in the van with Little B.

I don't care for this half-baked plot the two boys seem to have hatched. Their vague warnings mean nothing to me; I'm following them. I don't get it. This venture doesn't feel right. Could the senior Borak be encouraging Little B to make my son take a fall?

They now lead me out of Gaylord altogether, then fifteen minutes further to Rail City. So far it seems as if I've been going around in a circle without a purpose. We're about where Ryan and I started the evening, on Farrington Street, a couple of minutes west of Ryan's apartment. Farrington Street, Rail City's main road, set on the old railroad right-of-way, a street of dozens of story-and-a-half railroad worker houses, attached. The workers who came from rocky New England farms for steady wages in the days Rail City was a train hub with mile-long trains of timber, coal, potatoes and milk running from the rest of New England and to the West and the South. A boom that lasted until the Canadians built their own track and undercut the market on the American side of the border, eliminating Rail City as a hub.

And now we come to the Yard, with tracks that go nowhere anymore, tracks the heirs to the old Maine Central won't remove for fear of diluting its old right-of-way claims. The Yard during the boom time had employed over a three-hundred men for equipment repair and maintenance, and had four turntables for turning around locomotives or cars, as well as a pair of cranes. The half dozen hundred by five-hundred foot repair shops have long since disappeared from the Yard section of Rail City, and in its place, built in the 1920's four and six-plex apartments, each with a steel roof. The front porches were built deep enough for straight-backed chairs, but not for rockers. Though the buildings were not attached, they were set close enough together to touch two of these houses with outstretched hands.

The hard-working railroad families have long since moved out, conceding these apartments to displaced farmers and others without work as the twenties yielded to the depression thirties, the start of the downward slide for the Yard that even the War boom and the federal money couldn't stop. All of which has opened the way for a new and bad kind of entrepreneur, dealers like the Littlehales, who have made this their base of operations.

From two blocks away I can see the blue glow of the Blue's Coach Works sign. Little B has killed his headlights and signals me to pull over behind him.

"If you drive any closer with that rattletrap, Mr. D," Little B said, "you'll let them know for sure we're in the neighborhood. We'll get more out of them if we come up on them slowly, and let them know we're serious about making peace."

"We thought it would be best to talk to them one at a time," Ryan said, "so they know, once and for all, they can't walk over us. Starting with Littlehale, Sr. He's about your age, Dad. What do you think?"

Ryan seemed so resolute earlier this evening, as if he knew in advance exactly the mission he wanted to acomplish. Now I see fear in his eyes, that he's looking to me not so much for advice as for direct help. I don't like the way this is unfolding, but I can't walk away from him now.

"Then you think he might listen to me better than to you? If that's the case, why don't I see what I can do," I said.

Here I am walking alone toward Blue's Coach Works, my son and his cohort not with me, but safely behind me in the van. It's ridiculous for me to still be stepping between him and thugs, but he's repeatedly drawn to destruction as a moth is drawn to a flame. As much as he might deserve it, I can't let Ryan just fly and burn. I'll do what I can to save him from his suicidal instincts. For their sake, I hope their hunch is right, that they can get somewhere with his father. It seems to me that if Tim Littlehale, Sr., can handle bookwork, maybe he's the brains of the operation, more reasonable than his useless son.

I see the light on in the office, a light at a desk where it must be the father working. I need to compose my thoughts and am not quite ready to present my petition for my son. There are streetlights here, but with the globes shot out of them, none work. The only light, aside from those from the apartment windows, comes from the blue neon of the Blue's Coach Works sign. And lighting the perimeter of the Littlehales four-house complex, mercury vapor lights, set on the corners of the outermost buildings, throwing an intense and unearthly bluish light. For the moment it's Blue's Corvette, sitting in the lot on the far side of the building, away from the man in the window—that interests me much more. I know the color's a violet blue, but in the powerful security lights it looks black. In it I see a couple of stereo speakers, big as toasters. Two-way radios on the back seat, probably to coordinate his hirelings for theft operations.

I'm just looking, careful not to touch anything, but I step too close to the car and set off a siren! I hear running steps—time for fight or flight. I decide to make myself invisible again and back off quickly into the shadows, and see it's Blue himself who's arrived to defend his car. The alarm won't stop, not until Blue kills it, finally. From where I'm hiding, behind some drums of solvent, I can see him, but he can't see me. In the blue light he turns to me the damaged side of his face, which he smashed in a wreck so that it appears permanently blue in the daylight, but in this eerie mercury light closer to black. And the blue tattoos on his arms, they looked like they've been burned into his flesh with a branding iron. He's cursing, checking for the intruder or animal that set it off. He walks around it a couple of times. But there's someone walking behind him like a servant— Little B! Whose side is he on! I just left him a few minutes ago, and he's reappeared! Blue wanders away from the buildings and into the woods of a vacant lot, when young Borak pops open the passenger door for a second, but setting off no siren. Either the alarm wasn't reset, or Little B knows the car well enough to bypass it. I can't make any sense of what Little B's game is, but I know I don't belong here and have to get away from Blue before he finds me and I have to fight him off with that two-foot iron pipe in his hand. I'm relieved when they quit poking around the Corvette, and the both of them get into an old Lincoln and drive away. This would be a perfect time to get out of here, but it's also a window of opportunity to pay the senior Littlehale a surprise visit. With no further hesitation I walk to his office.

"Hello!" I holler, pounding on the door. "This Blue's Coach Works!"

"No, we're all closed up. Come back in the morning."

"This cutomer service?"

"No service this time of the night. I know you from somewhere. Ain't I seen your picture in the paper?"

"No service? You don't have a wrecker?"

"Where are you located?" Littlehale asks, finally unlocking the door and stepping outside to meet me. "By the way, was it you prowling around that 'Vette, setting off that wailing?"

"Here I am, right in front of you."

"I don't care about you. Where's your rig?"

"Way down the road."

"So what name should the wrecker driver ask for, if I was to call one of my associates for you?" He pauses between words in order to catch his short breath, which had an odd whistling overtone. Asthma or emphysema, I'd have to guess.

"OK, you saw Ned D'Amour in the newspaper, but the name Ryan D'Amour should be more familiar to you. I'm his father."

"Sure, the one who dumped all that shit in Medford Pond," he says with a smile. "I read all about that screw-up. The inspectors trapped you good, and now they got your nuts in their hand, and they're squeezing, ain't they!"

"I didn't come here to talk about me, but about my son Ryan, who's told me a great deal about you and your son's enterprises. I'm here to straighten out my son's problems, Mr. Littlehale."

"You can call me Senior," Littlehale interrupted."

"In all the time Ryan was living upstairs here in your apartment next door, I never knew what he was doing to pay you the rent, Senior. At first I thought he was learning bodywork, but one day I looked at his hands, and they were smooth and clean, not a working man's. Are you sure he wasn't helping you guys out around here some other way?"

"I tried to teach him how to mask car body trim and windows, run a sander, a grinder, but I gave up because he don't have no common sense, as far as I could see. Blue was doing your boy a favor, taking him on, keeping him here, teaching him the auto body business, showing him the ropes."

"Yeah, you gentlemen are nice guys, giving Ryan enough rope to hang himself," I said.

"I'm not talking about your useless son," Littlehale Senior continued, "but about my years in the auto body business. The expenses are pretty heavy because these days you have to set up a special paint spraying room, and every time you overall spray a car, you need to do it in a special oxygen suit for breathing. No, the auto body trade hasn't helped me none, the lousy way my lungs are working these days. Before they came out with the real toxic paints, it used to be if you had a compressor and a spray gun you were in business and you could make a decent living."

"That's very interesting, but it has nothing to do with my son. Before he was hanging around this place he didn't have a hole blown clear through him!"

"I don't know nothing about it," the senior Littlehale said. "If he got hurt, he must've got himself in the wrong place at the wrong time!"

"I want to know who hurt him and the Borak boy."

"It seems to me like you and your boy Ryan have the same problem, sticking your goddamn noses where they don't belong!"

"And it seems to me that you couldn't be as dumb as you'd have me believe, or blind. I hear you're married," I said. "Do you mind if I ask your wife what she knows about how Ryan got hurt?"

"You come in my place the middle of the night and insult me about my wife? You D'Amours—your son's as big a pain in the ass as you, which might explain why those Italians from down-country might have put the lead through him."

"Mafia gangsters—what are you talking about?" I asked.

"I'm talking about my wife, who's gone ten years now, and you expect me to hunt her up to talk to you!"

"Forget about your wife, I want to know about the Italians."

"I might be able to forget about her if you wouldn't keep reminding me! I'd love to forget how she left me when the manufacturers started turning out the new toxic paints and the government come in and told me I had to buy me new equipment if they wasn't to shut me down. That hit me hard in the wallet. The wife needed to take a job, working in a bank, and she ended up making more than I was pulling out of the shop. So she figured she don't need me any more. You better believe it wasn't easy losing my wife, not that she ever had much respect for me and the auto body business anyway. But Blue and me's blood, not like the wife and me. A son you can depend on, raise 'em right. But a wife won't stick around if she can find a better deal somewheres else. What's my life to you anyway?"

He's really telling me that he's sacrificed his health, lost his wife and turned Blue into a hustler, all to save Blue's Coach Works. This lousy business hasn't even made him decent money until recently. Money that came too late to keep his wife from walking out on him. A lethal business, leaving him bitter and huffing and puffing through battered lungs. Time now for him to give me the rest of the truth rather than more pitiful excuses.

"I want to know how my son and Little B got tangled up with the Mafia and Blue? What was Ryan doing around here for so long, if he never amounted to anything. Was he a bag man? Delivery boy? Crow bar specialist?"

"I have no idea what you're talking about! If your boy has a beef, let him take it up with Blue!"

Ryan lets himself in the room slowly and quietly without Littlehale hearing, a cat and mouse game to him. First Little B playing his hide-and-seek game, sending me out alone to make a truce with the old man, while meeting unannounced with Blue. And now Ryan reappears after knowingly sending me to the front line. They're both playing games with me, and I don't like it!

"So now I know that's what you think of me, Senior!" Ryan bellowed. "Maybe Blue thought his guys could beat on me and get away with it, but you're going to have to show me a little more respect!"

Maybe it wasn't Mafia gangsters from out of state, but Blue's thugs who hurt Ryan. Either way, the kid's probably in more trouble than he's been telling me. Ryan then walks up to Senior's desk and sweeps the papers over to one side. In the empty spot he's created, he throws down a plastic bag of white powder. "Last week I found this planted in my car, Dad. I told you I was done with this crap! These two clowns know I'm clean and wanted out a long time ago!"

With one hand Senior clears his throat into his handkerchief; with the other, rummages through his drawer until he pulls out a Glock 9mm, which he lays on top of his desk. "I'm going upstairs to sleep, and I don't want to hear no more from you guys tonight!"

Without speaking we hurry back to the van. "I'm worried about Little B," Ryan said once he was in the driver's seat and I've locked both our doors. "We planned that he'd back you up as you were talking to Senior, but I guess instead he ran into Blue and got hung up along the way."

"Littlehale is too trigger happy for my comfort. We need to get out of here, and right now!"

Ryan's not listening to me, but instead he's rooting around in the boxes in the back of the van, coming up with aerosol cans and a mallet, which he throws into a dog-eared leather doctor's bag. I should have disposed of all of Ryan's firearms the night Blue threw the black cat through the window. Now he's trying to be discreet, draping a towel over a Glock 9mm, just like the one with which Senior threatened us, probably the one I found in the ammo box in the cabinet. By now he must realize I have a pretty good idea of the criminal life he keeps claiming he's putting behind him, yet he invites me to talk to the criminal family that still controls and terrorizes him!

"Now where are you going?" I asked, grabbing Ryan's arm through the window as he was leaving with his black bag like a cat burglar.

"Remember when I was little, Doctor Grandpa gave me this doctor bag? Well, now I'm making a house call. Blue called on us when I wasn't home, and now that Little B's keeping him away from here, I'm going to use the opportunity to give him a taste of his own nasty medicine. I guess he'd be liking me better these days if I was following in his footsteps, instead of yours. But if him and Mom and Erica don't understand us, Dad, that's their problem," he said and shook himself loose from my grip.

My foolish son's disappeared, heading right back to the blue light of Blue's Coach Works! I can't just sit in this truck and wait for him. I see he's slid the keys under the seat, and when I retrieve them I find his .44 Magnum! No way does he have a permit for this gun, not with his record. I'm amazed he hasn't been arrested by now for carrying firearms. But that's the least of his worries right now, prowling though that yard on a mission to somehow get even with Blue. I'm going to ease the van closer to the Littlehale compound, no headlights, and grab him, if I can find him. No chance spotting him now, because as I come to the side of the building blind to Senior's window where the Corvette sits, the mercury lamp lighting it goes dead. Ryan must have found the kill switch. Now I can ease the truck closer, near enough so that if I listen very carefully from the direction of Blue's car I can hear the hissing of discharging spray cans. Now I hear tap-tapping, metal on metal, maybe a hammer on a chisel. I look at my watch, seems like a very long time waiting here, though it's just seven minutes before his flashlight picks out this truck, and he's back again with me. He has a big grin across his face, and seems quite pleased with himself, and displaces me from the driver's seat. I'm ashamed and angry with him, but won't tell him here and now.

"Don't put on the headlights until we're out of harm's way," I say as Ryan starts the engine.

For once Ryan does as I say without questions, running slowly down Farrington Street, headlights off. Then for a minute or two we're heading westward out and away from the Yard, when Ryan suddenly begins pounding the steering wheel. He's laughing so hard, his eyes close, and he brings the van to a stop.

"What are we doing sitting here!" I yelled.

"Let's make a U-turn. What goes around comes around!" Ryan shouted and swung the truck around back toward Blue's Coach Works.

"Stop! This time I want out!" I shouted.

"Too late now, Dad. Can't let passengers off between stations." In less than a minute we're in front of the Corvette again. "Here we are, last stop!"

He's backing up so we're in the lot alongside the blue Corvette. Now he's bringing me to the back of the van, cracking open the rear window, and shining his flashlight over Blue's car. He's showing me the holes he had driven into the fiberglass body, as well as the blotches of paint he's sprayed on all the surfaces! Not a pretty sight.

He's laughing, happy, nervous, insane—I don't know anymore! This is no time to figure him out. I must get to the driver's seat of the truck and get us moving out of here. I grab him with both hands and with all my strength pull Ryan away from the wheel and take the position myself, anxious to set us on course away from here! But what's this coming directly at us, on the wrong side of the road—my side—they're headlights getting bigger, coming closer, coming right at us! I swerve to the far side of the road, and he swerves with me, like a torpedo homing in on a target! *BAM!* We're hit, bumpers are locked. Now we're traveling backward, accelerating, shoved by this enemy vehicle! *BAM!* Another collision, this one behind us, our mini van, rammed backward into the Corvette, leaving us sandwiched between Blue's Corvette and Blue's Lincoln, the car attacking us, our engines both still racing, but mine blowing steam from under the hood ! I can't go forward, nor backward! We're trapped, locked in on both sides, not going anywhere. Ryan may be right we're at what could be the last stop! Check! Or maybe checkmate!

Blue turns on his interior lights to show us himself in the driver's seat of the attack car. He also shows us his bright stainless pistol, which he's pointing left to right across his chest at his passenger, Little B! And now that he's gotten our undivided attention, he picks up his handi-talkie: *Blue to Diablo. Blue to Diablo. What are you doing? I thought you were holding down the fort. Twenty minutes? I need you right now. I don't care; fix her up with a broom handle in the meantime. Yup, a direct order. Zip it up, and get down here pronto,* I can hear him saying through the open window of the Lincoln.

"You're in my territory, and I'm the law around here, understand, you shitheads!" Blue shouts at us, standing outside the van, with Little B before him.

A very bad miscalculation of Ryan's, turning back after we were out of his reach, delivering ourselves to this hoodlum. I step out to see if I can talk to him, resolve this peacefully, but he answers me with two shots, rapid fire close to each foot!

"Now get back in that baby truck where I can keep an eye on you, Mr. D, if you don't want to become Mr. Dead!"

My heart's accelerated to double speed, my knees weak, now that it's registered in my brain I've come within inches of having holes shot through my feet! A show of force, trying to rattle me, threats more than intention, I hope. True assassins act, don't boast. I can't panic and push him further than he intends.

In a couple of minutes his backup, Diablo, the man on the handi-talkie, arrives. He has tattoos everywhere, up both arms, his chest and neck. He wears pointed boots with chrome tips, and a chrome chain running from his back pocket. He's armed with a .22 rifle.

"You sure going to have a job putting your plastic pig back together again, Blue," Diablo says, walking around the Corvette, spurting out long flames with his flame-throwing cigarette lighter in order to see the damage better. "Whew!"

"What the hell you bring that long-barrel deer rifle for? To draw attention to yourself? Or is your freezer empty, and you're looking for some deer to jack? Get over here. Make yourself useful," Blue says to his man, and has him take over guarding Little B and the rest of us.

Diablo lights his cigarette with his free left hand, keeping the barrel in Little B's side. "Figured out you can run, but you can't hide, Borkman?" Diablo asks. "You know damn well we come up short on cash on the last assignment you done with us, and some of it come out of my pocket! That short-weight shit can put me back on welfare!"

"Shut up! I want you to hustle into the shop and get me a couple of rolls of duct tap pronto!" Blue shouts to Diablo. "And next time you talk private business in front of strangers, you won't have no privates!" He shoves me alone into the van and rolls up all the windows.

When Diablo comes back with the heavy gray cloth tape, Blue peels some of it off, using it to seal the rear and side windows of the van. From the outside he attaches three-foot plastic fasteners on the door handles, the kind the telephone company would use to bundle overhead wires, binding the handles to hinges wherever he can. Then at the driver's door he builds up a chain of a dozen fasteners, making a chain that passes through the right and left door handles over the roof and ratcheting it tight back onto itself, fastening the front doors shut, then the side door. He also binds my arms behind me with the tape, then the electrical fasteners to one of the fixed shelf posts in the rear.

"What are you doing!" I ask.

Without answering Blue pushes me aside. "Ryan, get out here now, and bring the key with you. Your daddy won't be going nowhere!"

"How long are you going to keep me in here!"

"Could be forever, Mr. D. I'm tired of your questions."

"And what are you doing with him?" I shout. I can see through the rear door window Blue has his gun in one hand pointed at Ryan, his flashlight in the other. In the deep shadows of the reflections of his searchlight he looks a violet blue, more monster than human. With Diablo guarding Little B and my son, he's walking around the wreck of the Corvette, looking over the damage.

"You wanted to get my attention by trashing my car!" he shouted at Ryan. "Well, you got it, motherfucker!"

"You know as well as me, all you have to do is tap that fiberglass piece of shit and it cracks and splinters. You know damn well you did most of the damage yourself, ramming your truck into it."

"Shut up! First you steal money from me. Next you destroy my car, and now you want me to let you get away?"

I don't like what I'm hearing out there! He's getting ready to beat Ryan, or worse, and the same's in store for me, unless I free myself. Time's of the essence. I've got to get out of this death trap! I've been working on this tape binding my wrists and have finally unwound it. Now I'm able to work the plastic fastener back and forth on the steering wheel, until finally I slide out of it. It's a good thing he taped up the windows, because he can't really see me in here, but I can see out between the gray strips. As careful as he was about the windows, he completely ignored the sunroof—my escape hatch! Great, Blue is distracted by his man Diablo, yelling at him to stay in the Lincoln with Little B, which gives me the chance to stand on a five-gallon cleaning supply can, and then hoist myself through it. If Blue shines his light on me, I'm a dead man! I'm in luck—Blue's too busy threatening Ryan to notice me.

I jump off the roof of the truck, and the moment I hit the ground I hear a shotgun blast. I don't move, in case they're shooting blindly at me in the dark. Then I hear another blast, this one coming from the Lincoln, where Diablo's been guarding Little B! Someone, just one person, leaves the car, but I can't see which one. Ryan uses this distraction to knock Blue on his back. Blue takes some of Ryan's kicks and punches before finding his feet and retaliates by whipping Ryan's head with the barrel of his gun! I don't know if Little B's wounded or dead, and how much more Blue's going to punish Ryan! I can probably slip out of here undetected and get some help, but if I do, I may never see Ryan again! Now that Ryan's not moving, Blue leaves him lying on the ground and heads for his shop. He's declared war not just on my son, but on me. This is a matter of self-defense. I trail him ten or fifteen strides ahead of me, using the back of the big neon Blue's Coach Works sign for cover, which he's shut down so the neighbors can't witness his attack on us. Now that we're at the Lincoln and it's quiet inside, I duck behind the side of the car opposite from Diablo. I'm about ready to play my last card, the loaded .44 Magnum Blue overlooked when he rummaged through the van. This is life and death, my target human. As at the firing range, I need to stay calm, firing in the spaces between my heartbeats to keep my grip steady and true! If I miss my mark, I doubt we'll have a second chance!

Blue opens the door to the Lincoln, Diablo's body flops out, then he pushes him back behind the door. "Oh, Christ, Diablo! How can you do me this way! Goddamn, Diablo!" Blue said to his dead assistant.

Then from across Farrington Street I hear the main door of the shop slam shut. Blue walks toward it, slowly and deliberately, as if stalking human game. I've kept myself deep into the shadows to avoid detection, but now I must make myself known before he attacks.

"Blue, I'm right behind you!" I shouted with my Magnum fixed on him. "Drop that gun right now, and give us free passage out of here! We don't want to hurt you!"

"You and who else?" he said and spun around on his heels, his gun pointed at chest height, my heart his target if I let him spin a second longer.

So he revolves a little more than half the circle he'd intended when I get off my shot. The Magnum has a very loud report and launches a powerful bullet, which finds its mark. Blue drops in an instant.

"You and me, that's who, Mr. D!" Little B shouted.

He's the one in the shop, emerging from behind the door that gave him away and saved him. I'm amazed Diablo's shotgun hadn't finished him off in the Lincoln. "God, thank you! You saved my life!" he said with a startled look.

Now his bewildered look changes to a smile. He's regained his life, but in the process I've become a killer. I'm glad Blue's lying on the ground, not my boy, me, or young Borak, but I'm scared that the blame will be laid on me!

"Is Diablo still in the car? Dead?" I asked. He looooked down at the ground, unwilling to account for himself. "It didn't have to come to this," I whispered.

Little B bent over Blue, confirmed no heartbeat, shook his head to me in the negative. "He got tore up pretty good. You're shaking. But first of all, I'll get rid of this for us." He took the gun out of my hand. "He won't be bothering anyone else. My man Ryan OK?"

"No one's OK now!" I hollered. "We're murderers here, every one of us!"

"Quit talking crazy," Little B said, soothing me. "Now I want you to hustle down the road, drive Ryan's car, not my truck, go home, and don't dare tell anybody anything. We'll catch up with you."

"I could have moved Ryan out of town, and you could have gone with him, and none of this would have happened! I'm responsible! I can't just leave Ryan here!"

"Listen up, Mr. D'Amour, I'm bringing Ryan home myself! Don't worry, I'll tidy up around here! Go now!"

A .44 magnum, a potent weapon packing a big charge, a wrist breaker. If Blue knew I had one fixed on him, that it was my weapon of choice on the firing range, wouldn't he have had the sense to drop his own gun? I could have told him I had one pointed at him and knew how to use it, and given him one more chance to live. But then afterward, after I let him go, wouldn't he have found a replacement hit man for Diablo and trailed us and blown us away the next chance he got? I saw one big wound in the right side of his chest where he was turned to me, the other one smaller, in the front and center of his chest, the smaller one where the blood drained out of him like a hole in a bucket. A wound not unlike Ryan's, only his was an inch or two closer to his heart. I thought I fired one shot only. It seems an impossible trajectory from where I was standing. Maybe I got off two shots. It looks to me like the bullet traveled, deflected off bone, and exited through the front of his body. I had no choice, but fired at him in self-defense, by instinct to stop him before he had the opportunity to murder us.

I've killed a man, and I don't know what to do with myself! I should probably get away from this place as fast as I can before we have more company. Senior could show up here any moment —unless he's been sleeping through the shooting, or else ignoring it as nothing unusual in this neighborhood! It doesn't feel right walking away from my son, leaving him in young Borak's hands, but I can't do him or myself any good if I can't spring myself from this trap! It's not as if I should be ashamed of what I've done! What better reason could I have than defending Ryan's life and my own. Just as Little B had to defend himself from Diablo, the thug Blue intended as his hit man, I believe. Not that it matters now that Diablo's dead and gone.

Tidy up? Does Little B have a cleanup assignment? I wonder if he has special detergents for removing blood, scrubbing a killing clean. If only he had a special solvent to take out all signs of murder, remove all specks down to microscope-sized! No, some sign will be left. Somebody's bound to pay for this. Most likely me, but maybe one of us guilty ones, Ryan, will get lucky and be able to walk away from punishment for this bloodbath.

If only I could turn the clock back to before I let the boys talk me into joining them in the Yard! I'm alone, sitting here in this junker of Ryan's, going nowhere, shaking. I need to get moving, so I turn the key, put the car in gear. Being in motion isn't enough to help me—I need a plan, other than to put some distance between these bodies and me. I could drive to the airport, book a flight to somewhere the coyotes outnumber the people, a place like the big forests of Idaho, find an hourly job in logging if I were ten years younger. No, I don't dare to run too far and too fast to appear as if I'm escaping.

I need to be careful to keep a low profile and keep my speed down. I'm holding myself to the slow lane, letting everybody else on this road overtake me. In an instant, with the pull of my trigger I've cut myself out of any pleasant destinations forever. That leaves me with no rush to get to the next station on my new journey to God knows where! Probably to a very hot destination where the furnaces are fueled through an everlastling night, where the fires are stoked by killers like me condemned to pay for their crimes with continuous pick and shovel work, enforced by regular beatings. That is, if I'll truly be judged a murderer rather than a protector.

I see spinning colored lights, coming in my direction, toward Rail City! Immediately my heart's accelerated to overdrive. A half minute later a car with a red pulsing volunteer firemen's lights follows in its wake. Then following these firemen a couple of minutes behind them, fire trucks, two of them. Now, instead of red lights, I see blue lights, police lights, state police markings on the car as it moves along right after the firemen. I'm relieved the procession has moved right past, with no one having taken any notice of me.

But right after I turn off the divided highway, a truck follows behind me in my direction for a minute, then on go blue police lights! It's all over! They got their man, and Blue's blood isn't even cold! But I must do the best I can to stay calm, and tell them nothing. Let Denise deal with them. No, that's impossible, because if she ever finds out about this shootout, it's all over between us. Whether I go to jail or not, she'd certainly want to keep a killer far away from her.

"Good evening, Mr. D'Amour, glad we caught up with you," the cop said after emerging from the police truck.

If he's been following me, either someone reported the shooting, or else he's been monitoring me beforehand for some reason, waiting to entrap me. Or maybe he's no more than gotten my name from reading Ryan's license plate and thinks I'm Ryan. I don't recognize this one, must be a new recruit. By his uniform I see he's a county cop, one of Fitch's men, not much older than Ryan.

"The state police didn't stop you for any reason, did they?" he asked me.

A strange question. He might already know the answer, but he could be trying to confuse me, make me contradict myself. I don't have to answer anything. Instead I'll answer his question with a question.

"Why are you stopping me?" I asked.

"Your front end don't sound so good. You need to get it fixed before you hurt someone."

"I'll see to it tomorrow. If that's all, can I go?"

"No, sir, we'd rather you stay with us."

"If you're detaining me, then I have a right to know the reason."

"You do, but I think we'll be keeping you under observation."

The policeman returns to the police truck. *Chief, we got him. . . . He's at Blake Road, where it intersects, about half a mile before the condo, and I was wondering. . . . Yes, sir. I didn't know you wanted me to phone you instead. . . . Signing off right now, chief.*

"He wasn't too pleased that I was talking to him about you on the radio, Mr. D'Amour. Anyone with a fifty buck scanner could be listening in on us," the cop explained to me. "And worse, the state police, who always want to be on the scene first, like tonight at that big fire—they eavesdrop on our frequencies all the time. So I'll call up Mr. Fitch on the phone to let you talk direct to him. But when you're done talking to him, don't forget to give the phone to me, if you don't mind, Mr. D'Amour."

Though he hasn't written me up for anything and told me he's not detaining me, he never told me why he stopped me. I don't know why he's being so accommodating. At least I'd know what to expect if he had read me the boiler plate speech about my right to remain silent, the speech they always read to Ryan whenever they arrest him.

"We understand you've been keeping a close watch on Ryan," Fitch said to me, as I spoke to him on the cell phone in the police truck. "Just what the boy needed, at least until he learned who his friends were and who weren't, if you know what I mean."

"I appreciate your concern, but I don't understand why you sent your deputy to intercept me."

"For your safekeeping."

"And one more thing, Mr. Fitch—why did your man ask me about the state police?"

"Goddamn state police! I do business the old-fashioned way and stay tied into the community. Forget about those grandstanders. We were just trying to get your bearings relative to them and the big fire they were chasing."

"What fire?"

"Sorry, can't hear you on this end. Battery's running low. You're breaking up. Hold the thought."

I don't know what Fitch and his man want from me, but unless they come up with a charge, I'm giving this cop back his phone and leaving right now. I'm not interested in their rivalry with the state police. County police or state police, it won't matter who catches me. I haven't gotten another mile, when once again I'm intercepted by another cruiser with blue lights and a quick burst of the siren! This time it's Fitch approaching me. How did he get here so fast? He must have been on the way as soon as this cop reported my location, then stalled me by chatting with him on the cell phone.

"Ned—I'll call you that if, from now on, you call me Bud, now that we'll be working more closely with you. I had to talk with you face-to-face.

"Listen, I'm here to give you some friendly advice, so you don't embarrass yourself. I suggest that you slip into a fresh outfit. You look like the morning after the night before."

Fitch is shining his two-foot flashlight on me, over all my clothes, stopping at each red stain! A simple match: these bloodstains against Littlehale's blood, no contest! He knows! I'm done! He has enough right now to arrest me, pull out his cuffs, shove me in the back of his car, and throw me in one of the cells where Ryan's been so many times!

"You look like you been playing football in these clothes. Showing the boy your stuff, playing a rough game, got a little cut, by the looks. But someone would have to wonder how that little slice in your head made such a bloody mess. Now you can use the back of the truck to change, instead of out here in the open. That's why I had General Langway ride along with me in the cruiser, because he knew what you required, all your sizes, etcetera. Got to run, gentlemen."

With Fitch gone, the General leads me into the back of the police van. "Go ahead, why don't you get undressed now?" he said, cutting tags off the new clothes with his pocket knife.

"I'm ready now," I said, once I stripped down to my shorts. "How about at least giving me a pair of socks?"

"No can do," the General said, handing me a robe instead. "Only when I've bagged up every item you're wearing, then I'll issue you a new set."

"What kind of a game are we playing?"

"A life-and-death game. We can't afford a mixup, an old sock with a new sock, for instance. You don't want to be walking around with any of these old clothes."

When I was finally dressed, the General handed the bag of clothes to the young officer. "Make sure the chief gets this so he can process them. Pretty big blaze, isn't it?" The General then stepped closer to the scanner, which was picking up transmissions from the fire department and the state police.

"They've run out of firetrucks to send up there," the cop said, "and they might have to call up for Dale county rigs. The flames are burning pretty hot on those old wood buildings, dry as kindling, plus feeding on those solvents and car paints. It would be a public service if all of Farrington Street burned to the ground, along with all them pushers and thieves, instead of just the couple of them who got trapped!"

This cop has to be talking about Blue's Coach Works, burned to the ground! The cops must suspect someone set the fire— perhaps me! Fitch might not know exactly what happened in Rail City this evening, but he wouldn't have been trailing me so closely if he didn't think I was involved. And whatever Fitch might know, then most likely so does the General. And, of course, after seeing the blood on my clothes Fitch and his deputy must believe their suspicions about my part in the bloodbath have been confirmed!

"It's been a long day, and I'm going home, if you don't mind," I said to the patrolman. "I wonder if you wouldn't mind giving Mr. Langway a ride?"

"That's between you and him. I got my orders we don't take any riders, except prisoners. So if you're a free man, I shouldn't be doing any more favors for you tonight," the cop said and left me with the General.

"I don't think that gash in your head's going to give you a very big headache. And, Ned, if you don't mind my saying so, you look like hell, so I'll take those keys," the General said and snatched the keyring out of my hand.

"I don't care, as long as you get me down the road and safely in my bed."

"*Safely?* You should have thought of that before you set out tonight. A man goes on a mission, danger goes with the territory.

My way of thinking, you're a hero, but we're not going to tell anybody about that public service you performed. That rat's nest of
the former Littlehales—we think you best put some distance between you and it. And you must stay away from Ryan too. Safety?
This is a dangerous car he's driving. I'll have to take care of it
tomorrow."

The man who's worked for me all these years, is giving me
his opinion of how I appear and on what I should do. The former
Littlehales? By my count, only Blue Littlehale's dead, unless the
General knows something I don't. The General seems to know
some answers, but I have no time to pick his brains, not now.

"So where does that leave us?" I asked.

"At our place. My wife's expecting us. Have you lost your
appetitie, or do you care to eat?"

A peculiar question. I've arrived with blood in my clothes, and
he probably knows how it got there, yet he's ignoring all that and
wants to feed me. He's getting very personal, but at this point I
suppose I've given up all rights to privacy. If I did something terrible, maybe I should feel repentent enough to forget about my
stomach. I'm just a man, and now I'm hungry, but I'm afraid to
yield to my appetite right now. I'd like to accept the General's
compliment that I've completed an heroic mission, entitled to a
hero's dinner, yet I can't help see myself as a killer.

"I wouldn't want to inconvenience you," I said.

"It's much too late to worry about that. You've made me late
for dinner, following you around all night. We've got a great blueberry pie sitting on the counter, if you'd like to feed on something
good."

Chapter 13
LaMothe's Salvage

*A*ll eyes are fixed on me. I'm in the final round of the shooting
competition. My arm's sore from the recoil of the big handgun,
my ears hot under the ear protectors. I've been shooting at all
kinds of targets as they pop up from everywhere in the field, targets of full-scale men. Then come the real-as-life 3-dimensional targets,
dead ringers for men. I shoot at one of these targets with tattoos of an
eagle or a vulture, at another one wearing a leather jacket. I blast one
with motorcycle boots, then another with a snake tattoo. Have I come to
the end off the match, or not? I wish there were a judge to tell me where
I stand, or at least a scoreboard I can see. But if I've already gathered
enough points to win this game, then why are all the spectators still
watching me, as if expecting more to come? So I don't stop, but keep
shooting. That leaves me one more target, the most humanlike one, of a
big man. I fire two quick shots at it, and both hit home. He drops hard,
dead weight! A mix-up, mistaking a manmade target for a man! No one
in the audience moves to help this man lying on the ground; they are
waiting for me. I kneel over my target and see a man with a face of two
colors, one side deathly white, the other side blue. He lies in a pool of
blood, dead at my hand.

Standing in a circle around the dead man and me, the crowd of mur-
muring watchers divides in two parts. On one side stand his enemies,

glad I killed him, chanting PUB-LIC! SER-VICE! And cheering me: HE-RO! WEL-COME! But then the handful of hecklers, his friends booing and cursing me and threatening me, as they carry his body out of the shooting range.

If he hadn't come at me so fast, if he hadn't been where he didn't belong. . . . Wonder if he's leaving behind a girlfriend, family. Shouldn't be worrying about such details, whether it's really my fault or an unfortunate accident. But where have my supporters gone now? Why am I alone on the empty firing range? I have my gold-plated marksman's trophy, but did I have to take down a living target to win it?

And from nowhere a man in a hooded robe snatches away the award I worked so hard to win. "You had no right," *he says to me,* "so now you must sit before us." *Because I don't like the looks of this troupe of men in white robes and don't trust their plan for me, I try running from them, but they immediately encircle and grab me. Now that they've made clear their control over me, they lead me to a huge, very bright room. It is lit with piercing sunlight falling from the skylights, as well as from an unnatural, even more intense light pushing inward through the walls. They've taken me directly into a light a thousand times brighter than than the brightest beach or field of snow, a powerful magic light such as I've never seen in my life. But instead of overwhelming my vision, instead of blinding me, my vision becomes more acute, enabling me to see what I never could have before. With the aid of this supernatural light from a hundred yards away I can see the finest detail, which should be invisible to the naked human eye. With my new vision I can see dry red microscopic specs of blood in half a dozen of their hems. If they had brushed past their dead friend I had shot, then I can't understand why they weren't smeared with his blood, unless they were truly holy people and had magic powers of purification.*

They take their seats at a long walnut table so brilliantly polished it reflects back on them like a mirror. The walls, floor and ceiling are translucent and pass light of changing pastel colors. Their chief with long flowing white hair sits at the head of the table. They ask me to speak, defend myself, but I'm frozen, and have nothing to say to them. They won't accept my silence, but instead they keep waiting for me to explain myself, acting as if they have all the time in the world behind them. I have no idea how long they keep me, because here I can't tell day from night and because, for some reason, I feel no hunger anymore. My fear of these judges in white turns to boredom, I doze off, and am awakened repeatedly by blasts of brass horns. Now I really want to say something on my own behalf, to explain why I don't think of myself as a hero. I'd like to convinve them that I'm not a villain either, but no words seem to pass my throat in my own defense.

"We were wondering whether you were still with us in the land of the living" the General said, "because you've been sleeping like the dead."

I'm in his office on the sofa bed, the one he converted from the old summer kitchen in his two-century old Federal era house. For a man who's spent his career with airplanes and other high tech equipment, he has a geat liking for not only this old house, but this antique furniture. I believe he once told me he inherited this house, though I can't remember whether from his relatives or hers. My memory's improving, but still it's not quite as good as before my fall. He opens the blinds of an eastward facing window, even though it's still dark outside, well before dawn. He probably wants me to accompany him on his customary three-mile walk. This room has photos of military planes, a glass case of medals and awards a file cabinet, and an oak rolltop desk.

"Welcome to my command post," he said. "My father gave me this desk before he died. He worked as a railroad clerk and sat behind this desk for thirty years. You like it here, Ned?"

"I haven't been sleeping very soundly," I explained. "Bad dreams."

Not that the General hasn't tried to be a good host for the last week, but there's no escaping his good intentions. The way he's been standing watch over me, he makes me feel more like a house prisoner than a house guest. But guarding me seems no better use of his time than his running the bulldozer at Conklin Farm. This reminds me of my stay at Ryan's after I fell, receiving far more attention than I needed, and that visit didn't turn out very well!

There's no need for me depend on his hospitality or to take up his time anymore. If I can only get out of here. He's driven me everywhere I've needed to go, but now I'm ready to take control once again of my office and my life.

"What's the matter with Ryan's car?" I asked once we were inside in the living room, away from the women's running argument. "They've had it in the shop for a long time and should be done by now."

"The mechanic tells me it's not worth repairing," the General said. "We'll find you some better transportation."

"Maybe so, but meantime he needs it to get him to work. Let's see what he wants to do with it. Let's go see him."

"We don't have his new phone number and no one knows where he's staying."

"Then he must have moved out because you gave him the same advice you gave me, to stay away from the Littlehales' condo, right?"

"Actually, no, I personally haven't said a word to him since he . . . you know."

"No, I don't know."

"Frankly, Ned, you've done more than enough already for him, including putting your life on the line. Because you're the key man in the organization, I'm far more interested in your personal outcome than anyone else's. And the good news is I'm working on a breakthrough that will put Pollution Resolutions back on the map. So are you going to get suited up, or do you plan to sleep in this morning?"

Breakthrough? Nonsense. Could he just be trying to give me a little hope, now that I've cut myself off from not only my business, but my family? Not a good situation, putting my life in the hands of another man, no matter how much I've been able to trust him. And who's he to judge whether Ryan's worth saving or not? Ryan's come a long way, and I'll never give up on him, no matter how precarious my own immediate situation. Someday my trust in my son will pay off in a big way. In the meantime though, I don't care if I'm the only one who understands his potential.

"About Ryan's car, give me the number of the garage. I've got places to go."

"I wouldn't go anywhere in that road hazard. The shop didn't think it was worth salvaging."

"Who cares what they think?"

"So I got a second opinion from a friend of mine in the business."

"Just take me to whoever has the car!"

"You're in charge, sir. I'll bring you there right now so you can see for yourself," the General said.

"Good to see you, Langway," Bud LaMothe greeted the General with a smile and with his arms outstretched.

The last time I saw the two of them together, they were at each other's throats; now they're the best of friends by appearances, very happy to see one another. In fact, LaMothe is so focused on the General, he doesn't notice me until I put my hand in his and make him shake it.

"What's your program for today, playing with your dozer over on Conklin's side," LaMothe said to the General, "or did you come here to trade? And I see you've brought a friend. Word-of- mouth advertising's the best kind, if you told him good things about me."

LaMothe's wise guy manner annoys me, so I tune him out by looking away from him. Instead I watch the Payloader shoving the forks of its big bucket into a pile of cars, picking them up one by one, dumping them onto a press, where another man runs the machine that compacts them, reducing them to piles inches tall. That done, the loader picks the flattened car off the press and sets it in a rising pile on the truck trailer for shipment to the steel recycling plant.

"Yes, we were just in the neighborhood and thought we'd pay you a call," the General said.

"I know you from somewhere," LaMothe said to me, looking at me more closely, "but I see so many people here, I can't place you."

Can this nice-acting guy possibly be the maniac who took Ryan and me for that wild ride on his ATV buggy, sniping at the General on his big Caterpillar, nearly getting us killed under those big steel tracks? Then he was beserk, fighting the General as if he were his mortal enemy, defending his territory, from the advance force for Conklin Farm. He's a changed man, declared a truce, all friendship and smiles now. This change in his attitude confounds me.

"No matter, I didn't bring Mr. D'Amour for a social visit."

"Well, if you're not here to trade with me, General, you and your friend are going to join me for a coffee."

Perfect. Now that he's in a coffee-drinking, friendly mood, I should be able to find out from him about Ryan's car. I see grease on Bud's pants and shirt, which shows me he's not a businessman who cares too much about his public image. It's a different story though for this clean and neatly organized parts room through which he's leading us. And manning the parts desk, rather than the typical backyard mechanic parts man, a very presentable young woman. She's checking the computer's exploded detailed mechanical diagrams for parts numbers, availability and model-to-model crossovers. This attractive and well-dressed woman doesn't look as if she belongs here in the salvage yard. She could pass for an agent in a big accountant or insurance office.

Then LaMothe brings us to one more room, which serves as his office and kitchen. Once he has all three of us inside, he hangs a red stop sign on the outside of the door warning *In Conference. Off Limits Until Further Notice.* This room he keeps clean as an examining room. He makes us take off our shoes before we enter. Big Bud LaMothe with gray bristles on his cheeks and tattoos on his arms, serves us fresh pastries on a gold leaf china platter. Between customers, the golden-hair parts girl has taken a break to bring us a tray with our drinks.

"I'm drinking tea, since the last few weeks anyway. I used to drink a dozen cups a day of that heavy caffeine you're taking, but it made me jittery. Most anyone would rub me the wrong way, and I'd tell them what I thought of them. Like your loud-mouthed son," he said, pointing his finger at me.

"Glad to see you do finally remember that I've been here recently," I said.

"And I'm glad, General, you moved Conklin Farm in a new direction," LaMothe said. "At least for now you guys quit contaminating my water supply with that oil that one of your jokers was dumping by the barrel, leaving it oozing from about where you'd park that big Cat every night. Thanks to you guys, my well isn't fit to flush a radiator. It looks like it's going to cost your project plenty to keep hauling me water from their clean source up there on the hill above me, the tanker load at a time."

"Actually, you can thank the EPA, not me," the General said, "for shutting down construction on the western end of the project, your side. But it was just as well. My kidneys were taking an awful beating, running heavy equipment all day."

It's about time that the General returned to the Resolutions office where he was most needed, but I can't believe that's the true reason he's so suddenly stopped working at Conklin Farm. There must be a specific reason the General isn't telling me, why the EPA or their regional representative would have taken such quick action on Bud's behalf. It would seem the order restraining the Conklin project at some point must have come across Borak's desk. No matter how slipshod the excavation company's operating practices, I can hardly believe they wouldn't notice costly barrels of motor oil overturned, unless afterward an operator covered over the mess with dirt. I knew nothing about this project in the first place, yet now, thanks to the General's involvement, we may be defending ourselves once again against the EPA over another contaminated water supply.

"So you're a Lincoln man," Bud said, looking out his window at the General's car outside. "Looks like you're trading down. That dark blue one you just brought me, the one that took the hit in the front end, was the newer model body style, not so boxy as what you're driving there. I could have sold you a newer

one than the rig you're driving, if you told me when we compacted the other Lincoln. And for sure I would have given you a
couple of hundred more if you let me pull off the good parts. But
I'm like you fellows, a man of my word. A deal's a deal. One
hand washes the other."

"What deal?" I asked.

"Yes, General, it's coming back to me now. Didn't you tell me
D'Amour was your boss, or was it vice versa—you're his boss?
Don't you tell each other nothing? No matter, I don't give a shit
about titles. I don't care if that Lincoln was the undertaker's, the
company car, or what the President used for his party girls. You
stood there while I flattened it, and you saw we never poppped
open the trunk, so I hope your mother-in-law wasn't in there!"
Bud laughed. "If she is, by now she's probably on a barge on the
way to Korea or Japan, and she'll be recycled and come back to
America in a Daewoo or Subaru or Hyundai!"

This is not good! LaMothe seems to know much more than
he should. I bet he also knows about the Rail City fire from the
paper or from the TV or radio, or neighbors. And if he does, then
he'd have to be a fool not to make the connection between the
Littlehale's disappearance, the fire, and the car he compacted for
the General. More than likely that was the deal: in exchange for
making the Lincoln disappear, the General must have promised
LaMothe he'd push back the Conklin Farm project! But I don't see
how he could have done that without the cooperation of Borak,
the man bound and determined to break me.

"Ned, you don't look so good," Bud said, suddenly remembering my first name. "Something on your mind, something bothering you? I been doing all the talking. Why did you come here
anyway, to pick up the check for that shitbox of your son's we
compacted? Same deal as the Lincoln's: we pressed it while the
General was watching, and I promise you we didn't crack it open
or pull off no parts either. Or you want to do the deal off the books,
no check, no nothing, never happened like we done on the blue
Lincoln?"

I've got to find out what's really going on between them, but
I can't do it with LaMothe listening. I take the General out of the
building, then fifty paces beyond.

"Did you destroy Ryan's car?" I asked the General. "Did you
and LaMothe pull the license plates off it? Tell me the truth!"

"Affirmative," he said. "The operation went real smooth."

"I didn't ask you to do that, any more than I asked you to involve yourself in this project! Now I want you to get me back the plates."

"No can do, Ned. The plates were shipped out with the rest of the car . . . I believe. But let me verify that. I'll be right back."

Now I see LaMothe standing inside the door, with it cracked open. I wonder if he's been overhearing our conversation. There's no doubt in my mind that thanks to the General's scheme, now I'm in bed with LaMothe! Sounds like the General's told him a joke! LaMothe heads back into the office, then returns with a sealed envelope.

"Next time you're in the neighborhood, you know where I am," LaMothe said. "I'm sure I'll be talking to you, General, if the water hauler gets behind on his deliveries. Meantime, be good."

"See if these are the right ones," the General said, tossing me the envelope.

Inside the envelope I find what I'm looking for—Ryan's plates. But now I'm not sure why I really want to see them, other than to confirm that they destroyed his car, the evidence, which brings even more people into my crime! People who now have the power to cover for me or to destroy me. I don't like depending on others, and right now I must get away from these two before I show them how much they bother me. The worst thing I can do right now is appear to be on the run. Perhaps the best thing I can do is report back to work.

"I don't need any of this!" I said. The General was a couple of minutes into his drive back to his house. "I'm ready to go back to work. I want you to turn around and take me to the office."

He turns to me and looks at me indulgently, as if I don't know what I'm saying. Or worse, like I'm crazy.

"No, that's out of the question for now," the General said.

"So for how long would you like to keep me away from the office?"

"Until we make a breakthrough."

"I wish you'd quit teasing me. You know as well as I my prospects are dim at best."

"I may not know as much as you think. But you might want to enlighten me by telling me what you and Ryan and Henry Borak were doing on Welfare Row with the Littlehales and their lieutenant."

He's far too curious about too many dangerous details, but he's not telling me what he really knows, the details of the plot he's cooked up with Bud LaMothe. LaMothe seems to have seen ghosts and seems to know the players in my life, a couple of which they could have compacted in the trunk of Blue's Lincoln. If the General and LaMothe somehow prevailed upon Ryan or Little B to tell him something they should have kept to themselves, they've spread their web of influence. I hope LaMothe is on the General's side, my side, but right now I really don't know who my friends are, if any.

"LaMothe was right, you don't look so good," the General said, pulling off the road to the shoulder to take a closer look at me. "I understand how difficult mop-up operations can be, especially civilian, outside a battle theater. If you must know, I'm working on a final liquidation of your outstanding obligations. I can't promise anything."

Final liquidation? Could the General intend to remove someone else, maybe a witness? I never intended to hurt anyone, but maybe he's so loyal he'd do anything if he thought he could protect me. He might be losing perspective, forgetting that as an ordinary citizen he's going to have a lot harder time getting away with murderous tricks than if he were on the government payroll, military or civilian. But if I can't trust him, I'm probably a dead man. For now, though, I must figure out how I can put some distance between us, before he gets me into even deeper trouble than he had at LaMothe's, destroying Ryan's car.

"OK, you don't think I should go to the office; take me to the airport, General."

"I wouldn't recommend that either. You can run, but you can't hide. At this point even the appearance of flight to avoid—"

"I want you to take me there so I can rent a car. I've taken advantage of your hospitality long enough. I feel like I'm on my back with a truck on my chest! I need to get free right now!"

"Forget how you feel, renting a car in your name's a bad plan. I don't want you to sign any car rental contracts or use any credit cards. We're cleaning up a bloody trail, and we don't need a paper trail."

"I'm not a criminal!"

"If I believed you were, would I have invited you to my home?"

"It's time for me to help myself! I'm not asking you, I'm still your boss, and I'm telling you!"

"OK, wherever you go let me sign for your room, rather than you. I'll use Lisa's car, and you can use this one for the duration."

"The duration, General? How long did you have in mind?"

"Until you don't owe anybody who doesn't mean you well, Ned, or until your biggest debts are paid, whichever comes first."

Chapter 14
Doctor Grandpa

The General had loaned me his Lincoln and was following me to the Sunset Motel with his daughter's car. "This is the last place I'd pick to stay, if I were you," he said, having stopped at the curb behind me. He slid into the passenger seat beside me. "The trouble is they know you too well here. I'd prefer you were staying further away from Gaylord—Augusta, or better yet, Bangor. If I were you, I'd be keeping a lower profile and circulating somewhere new every week at the most."

"I told you, this is my deal, not yours, General."

"Our deal. You'll be signing in on my charge card."

"No, Dimitri, the motel owner, already knows me. I always pay him cash. Besides the tail shouldn't wag the dog."

"Who? How so?"

"I've paid my own freight and yours, I might add, for as long as I care to remember, and I don't need you as one more creditor."

"It's not like you haven't gotten more than your money's worth out of me!" the General said.

"Then I wouldn't want to take advantage of you anymore."

"Fair, unfair? That's how wimps think," the General said. "I believe in delivering the goods and in service. We both know I've been more loyal to you than anyone, except maybe your mother, rest her soul. I've served you too long to let you get on the wrong freighter."

"But still it's my trip, not yours."

"Teamwork as well as service, Ned. I've got too many years of service invested in our team to allow my leader to shipwreck. An SOS might not do you any good if I couldn't find you in time."

"Couldn't, shouldn't? And speaking of my mother, quit trying to mother me, General. Who are you to give me advice about the high seas? Let me remind you that you're land-based. Don't talk to me about the law of the high seas because you're completely out of your element!"

"Is that all, sir?"

"I told you that you don't have to loan me the car. I can rent one."

"Afraid, fearless? That's how I always sorted out my men," the General said, helping me with my bags and, leaving me off at the entrance.

I mean to tell him he's acting strangely toward me, quoting my own words back to me. But I don't have the chance because he quickly leaves me after giving me his habitual salute.

"Dimitri, this is like a home away from home," I said a few evenings after the General left me at the motel. I had just returned from a movie.

"Where's your real home, Mr. Armor?" Dimitri asked me

"Not that far from here, but too far to drive, at least until I'm done with this project I need to complete first."

"I knowing exactly what you mean. We's doing anything takes to survive."

Dimitri's from Armenia, a Greek Orthodox, who tells me some of his family permanently disappeared after they were caught practicing their religion. His eyes are sad, the lines in his face with heavy lines like contour plowing. Maybe I'm reading too much into his appearance, but looks like he's seen hard times. I should end the conversation right now rather than share my own troubles, but he seems to me a man who's learned how to keep secrets. I'll try approaching him gently, first making sure he wants to share the details of his story, before I can even consider confiding in him.

"It looks like more rooms are filled than empty since the last time I was staying here. You seem to be surviving here."

"I make my living best I can, Mr. Armor. This place it's a killing me. Know someone who buy a motel what need a little work? I have it on the market. When it's gone, Dimitri's Lounge get all my attention. I hire better band, feed a good food, better customer. At end of week peoples paying a lot of money for to amuse themself in my lounge. Here in America make money, and no one can take away what's yours. Where I come from too easy to making enemy, specially you have something the men wearing the high boot like for theirself. Then they can take away from you, or shoot you in the back. That's why I sell my boat, and my family and me come America with nothing. You a lucky American. Everyone working survive in America."

"It sounds as though you've made it on your own though."

"A man think he need no friend, nothing but a fool. Poor man like me not find powerful friend do me good in my country, so I land here. Here it easy do business without knife in a back. But everywhere, America too, can make enemy. I tell a dangerous one by the eyes," Dimitri said and looked more closely at me. "Running from dangerous enemy, the reason you lay down alone here in my motel?"

I wonder what could he really know about my enemies? Has he been reading my mind, heard rumors about me, or is he simply making wild guesses to satisfy his curiosity? Now I'm having second thoughts about enlisting him as an ally.

"I hardly get to see you here at the motel. I'm glad I finally caught you, Dimitri."

"Why, something bust in your room?"

"No complaints. I was wondering about the pool. When does the swimming season start here? I kind of enjoyed it last summer when I was staying here."

"Last summer, you like lost in a woods, no compass. Now you find way back to Sunset Motel and wish all the peoples pretend you dead and forgetting about you. But I won't, if I be your friend. So this pool I heat nice and hot, only you promise swim in it every day, return my investment. Storm or sun, day and night, I heat for you warm like baby bath. Keep you in a good shape for when time come fight again."

"No, this is much too soon to open up your pool, and will cost you too much."

"Mr. Armor, I have money, I spend money, and when you ready, my friend, we make business."

Dimitri's extending me his hand, refusing to take *no* for an answer. I don't know what he's expecting from me in return in

the future. With a handshake we seal our new friendship or agreement, or whatever it really is.

"Hello! Time out, Ned!" the General called, crouching at an end
of the pool to catch my attention before I could duck back into the
water and execute my turn by pushing off against the wall. It was
about 9 P.M., a couple of weeks after he left me.

"I wasn't expecting company," I said squinting into the flood-
lights. I hoisted myself over the edge, got a hotel towel, wiped myself dry and stood before him.

"If you were a Navy SEAL and training for cold water duty,
OK, I might expect you to be swimming now, but you're not in
training. Ned, what are you trying to prove?"

I took the General's hand and put it in the tepid water. "This
is pleasant as a baby's bath. No need to worry about me. When
you have time to stay longer, you can join me."

"Just the same, we don't need you to get sick, so don't just
stand there in the cold."

"I wouldn't want to seem impolite by walking away from
you, but excuse me," I said and walked past him.

It's Saturday night. I wonder whether he was at a party with
his wife tonight and had to excuse himself because he was so
worried about me. Or perhaps he was at home with nothing better to do than to check up on me. I wonder how much he's been
thinking about me the last couple of weeks, whether he realizes
I'm on my own now, not dependent on him any more. I should
have ignored his advice that I continue to stay away from Pollution Resolutions. No matter what he may think is best for me,
Monday morning, I'm planning to return for good to take back
the duties he's assumed. He's acting strangely this evening—
agitated, persistent as well, following me into my room. And now
he seats himself on my bed expectation in his face, like a young
girl taken to a motel rendezvous for the first time.

"So what can I do for you, General?" I asked, once I had
changed into my walk-around clothes.

"Here," the General said, handing me a telephone message
slip. "Martha wants to see you."

"Why? The last time I saw her she seemed anxious to get rid
of me!"

"Look, Ned, Marlene and I make it a policy not to interfere in
our friends' marriages. On the other hand, it might help if I had

a better idea of what happened when you were eyeball-to-eyeball with her."

"I saw Martha I was getting some clothes out of the closet, OK? She wasn't too happy to see me, and we didn't accomplish much."

"Just as I thought! That's why this time we set up a working meeting."

"What makes you think it'll be any more productive this time?" I asked.

"Because now we've lined up all our ducks and you'll use a superior strategy. I have you scheduled for twelve noon at Martha's this Saturday. She'll feed you lunch, I presume. I don't believe she and her advisors would poison you, though they may give you indigestion."

"That's just the way she operates, surrounding herself with her boosters! But I don't care who she's been listening to and where she's been getting her advice! This time I want to see her alone! Either you tell her, or I'll tell her it's got to be just her and me!"

"Too late now. We're dealing with some busy people, and scheduling wasn't easy, except in Ryan's case. This is an oppor-tunity, Ned. She seems to be in a talking mood, perhaps in a bar-gaining mood. If you wait to negotiate with her until after we see the results of the breakthrough I'm working on, you might not be able to strike as good a deal with her. I'd let them see you're the captain of a listing, rusting, leaky wreck of a ship with an empty hold, not very valuable to them."

———————

The General insists that I go through with his arrangement. Every evening he returns to tell me how important the weekend meeting will be, playing out different scenarios for my negotia-tions. I've always been a man in charge, quite able to make my own decisions, which now he seems to want to make in my behalf. But just because I don't appreciate his intrusion, that doesn't mean I should ignore him. I missed my chance by not dismissing him the first evening he came at me while I was in the pool. Now, for better or for worse, I find myself agreeing with the fact that I probably have nothing to lose and possible something to gain. He's an insistent and aggressive tactician, so I find myself yielding to his judgment, agreeing to show up at the conference he's set for me. Though the General has prepped me for what he thinks Martha will demand and what in turn I can win, I'm nervous when I arrive alone at the house. The rooms look different than the last time I was here—smaller, closer. It seems that now that I've been out of her way, the Deb Queen's been using the opportunity to have everything repainted in rich blues and greens and golds. No more of the plain white walls and ceilings she knows I liked, but instead, either to spite me or to please her decorator, she's switched to dark colors that suck up light, rather than reflecting it, just as her pal Rachael did to my office. She can continue to remodel with me gone, probably to match her new paint with new upholstery. She probably doesn't see me fitting into her new decorating scheme. In the meantime, Chip's been standing by the dining room entrance, waiting for me, like a beefeater guarding her majesty's residence. And at the further end of the room, I see Ryan for the first time since the fire.

"So glad you could make it!" Chip said to Ryan, shook his hand, then looked towards me. "And I see you've brought the brains of the operation."

"You a lawyer, or what?" Ryan asked.

"An attorney by trade, yes."

"I once knew someone who had a lawyer for a friend."

"Has this friend needed one as much as you do?" Chip asked.

Ryan responded with a dark look at Chip, then a mischevious glance at me. "My friend and the lawyer are walking down the street one day and see this dog on the porch . . ."

"They must have been coming or going from the courthouse," Chip said.

"This dog's mangy, with patches of bare skin where the fur was gone. Fleas are jumping off him. He sits there, licking his balls. *'I wish I could do that,'* my friend says. *'Me too,'* the lawyer says, *'but I think I'll have to pet him first.'*"

The color's drained out of Chip's face, and now it's red. In any event, he's not letting Ryan leave, holding him by his belt so he can't walk away.

"I heard that egregious joke before," Chip said, "and I didn't appreciate it the first time any more than now. You must have forgotten who kept you out of jail not too long ago, Ryan. I hope you've managed to stay out of trouble in the interim."

"What's going on here gentlemen?" said my father-in-law. As he walked Chip away from the dining room, Martha, Ryan and I followed.

"I'm quite pleased that you could join us, Dr. Aldrich," Chip said. "We really need to have all the decision makers present before we can come to an actionable decision."

"Now I'm confused," my father-in-law said to Chip. "Don't I recall that until recently, you were representing me? Which side of the street are you working?"

I know he's certainly not working for me anymore, but his interest in my family remains undiminished. He goes where he thinks the money is. In particular Chip seems to have an affinity for Aldrich's and Martha's side of the family, which his firm was handling a good thirty years before Martha and I were married.

"Regarding this marital matter," Chip said, "we need to think win-win."

"No need to hedge," Aldie said. Let's get the cards on the table. Isn't Martha retaining you?"

"Way to go, Grandpa Doctor, getting the best lawyer money can buy!" Ryan shouted.

"That will suffice now, Ryan!" the doctor said. "Our apologies, if he's spoken disrespectfully to you."

"I've got a couple of boys myself," said Chip. "They know so long as they're in my house I won't take any nonsense from them."

"Over the years that would have been a good policy for you to follow, Ned, rather than turning a blind eye to his escapades," Aldie advised me.

"Time out! Foul!" Ryan said, rejoining us. He made the referee's sign to stop the game. "I don't like you guys trashing me! If you want to get rid of me, say the word, and I'm out of here!"

"Firstly, you don't begin to know what you don't know, young man," his grandfather answered. "Secondly, your father and I were conferring privately."

"Well, excuse me if I'm not deaf!" Ryan said and made his way from the three men over to the table, where Martha and Erica were waiting.

That mahogany Chippendale dining room set was given to Martha and me for our wedding by Aldie's parents, who were then alive. The tweed fabric chair with the chrome trim where Ryan's sitting seems big enough for two people, oversized and modern, quite a contrast from the Chippendale dining room lighted by the crystal chandelier. Not modern, not traditional, and certainly not unified—a mix-and-match style that doesn't hang together, very much like the members of my family.

"What are you doing here?" Erica called to her brother, leaning back on the awkward low-slung seat, the tree-sized philodendron, not bothering to walk any closer to him right then.

"Well, if I weren't here," Ryan said, "it would be you, Mom, Doctor Grandpa, and the lawyer versus Dad, four against one. I'm here to remind you guys how to play fair."

"I wish you'd both told me in advance you were joining us," Martha said and gave both him and his sister a peck on the cheek, then sat on the edge of Ryan's stuffed chair.

"But, Erica, now that you're both here, would you mind setting places for you and your brother? Then directly after lunch, I'm afraid you'll both have to leave us."

"Help out, then leave—I understand. No problem, I have a date afterward," Ryan said.

"I wouldn't be bragging about it, if I were you, not if you're seeing Little Orphan Annie," Erica said with a wag of her permed blonde curls as she passed him on the way to the kitchen.

"If you don't have anything good to say about my friends, shut up. Besides, she's not my only player," Ryan said and went off to make new arrangements, now that he knew he wouldn't be staying for the principal meeting.

"So what's it like to be retired, Dr. Aldrich?" Chip asked.

"I may be seventy-five, but I'm not ready to retire, not yet. My partners like to have me come in a couple of days a week."

"Do much boating this past season?"

"Not so much now that I lost Lillian. Our summer home at Boothbay isn't the same without her. Of course, Martha's situation has been occupying much of my attention the last several months," the doctor said, turning to me, as if I were the source of her trouble.

"Don't look at me, Aldie," I said. "Ever since I was issued my exit visa from this little castle, I've been a persona non grata and haven't been permitted to come back."

"If you think you're going to get out of it that easily—" Martha said.

"If you think I'll let you suck the blood out of me—!"

"Not in front of Ryan and Erica. This is unseemly," the doctor said.

"Halt! You two must desist immediately!" Chip said rising from the table. "We'll address these issues in an orderly fashion shortly."

Ryan continued eating his lunch by himself. Chip cut a sliver of cake for his own plate, then took a bite. "Mmm. Wonderful. Chocolate layer cake?"

"Fallen chocolate souffle cake," Martha answered.

She half turns away from him, and I see tears in her eyes. I wish I knew what's set her off. A great performance on Martha's part, sobbing, but not entirely obvious, turning away from us at the right moment. When all else fails, tears prevail, an effective stragtegy for winning sympathy.

"Now look what you've done!" Erica said, the first besides me to notice. "What are you laughing at, Dad!"

"Nothing, I see nothing even a little amusing today."

"You don't have to be so cruel to mother."

"How about letting her speak for herself, Erica," I said.

"She's not exactly in the mood."

"Time out!" Ryan shouted again, after Erica led her mother into the kitchen, away from the men. "So, Mr. Thompson, since you're running this event, mind cutting to the chase? I mean what's everybody fighting over today?"

The way Chip's looking at Doc for guidance shows how much Ryan's questions have rattled him. The kid's fearless, though a bit obnoxious. I still don't know why the General arranged to have Ryan here with me, other than so that I don't have to face the whole lot of them all alone.

"Can you tell your son it's none of his concern, that we'll be sorting it out directly?" Chip said to me.

"It seems everywhere you look there's another lawyer looking for work," Ryan said. "Like yourself. I know a guy who figured out how he might find a new use for some of you extra lawyers. He has a lab where they do experiments, so instead of using white rats he began using lawyers. They had to go back to mice though. The trouble with lawyers was #1 the lawyers multiplied faster than the rats and they didn't know what to do with the spare lawyers. #2 some of the technicians had become attached to the white rats, but none could ever get attached to a lawyer. #3 there were some things lawyers would do that you just couldn't get a white rat to do."

"This is outrageous, Ryan!" I hollered. "I want you out of here! I want you to apologize to Mr. Thompson immediately!"

"Sorry, very sorry, Mr. Thompson, to embarrass anybody. Now Grandpa Doctor, you're not going to threaten to disown me again or anything, are you? Not that I care because I'm on my own, and I got nothing to lose. So, you and Mom and this lawyer of yours can try busting up Dad, but I'm sticking close to him, no matter what lies you want to throw at him!"

"If he'd finished school, Ned, he wouldn't speak in terms of *bust ups*," Aldie said. "And if he had a better example at home, he'd behave—"

"Fuck it, I don't care what you think of me. We're out of here," Ryan said.

Why did the General bring both of them together? Ryan's been snapping at Chip and at his sister like a pit bull. This isn't much of a family anymore, maybe not salvageable. Maybe I shouldn't be too quick to give up on Erica, though. Some time if I can get her alone, away from her mother, I just might be able to reason with her. Maybe the General sent the kids here as a warmup to the main event, either to distract us from our own differences, or to encourage us to settle them.

To call the dining room meeting to attention, Grandpa Doctor was ringing a spoon on one of the crystal glasses. "Be that as it may, we request that you two young people take a raincheck," Martha said. "Here, this should be enough to cover today's lunch for you and your sister, now that you'll be making new plans." She handed Ryan some green money. This he stuffed into balls and threw over his shoulder, one bill at a time.

"Thanks, but no thanks! No more, Mom! You don't have to bribe me to get rid of me!" Ryan said, and Erica followed him out of the house.

That left me at one end of the table; Martha at the other end, with her two advocates flanking her. "Together at last," Doctor Aldrich said and bowed his head. "Supreme Judge of all mankind, grant us today enough wisdom to give unto Caesar what belongs to Caesar. Amen."

What a spin the doctor puts on God's word, comparing him to an emperor provoking his own assassination!

"Excuse me, Aldie, could you be referring to how Caesar was able to wring tribute out of his citizens by terrorizing them?" I asked.

"I think we all know why we are gathered here," Dr. Aldrich said, with a glance at Martha, ignoring me.

"No, I'm not sure," I said. "Why don't you tell us yourself, Martha?"

"You still don't get it, do you? I can't take any more of this abuse, and I don't have to!"

"*Abuse*, really? A pretty strong charge against someone who hasn't been near you for the better part of a year now."

"It was your choice to abandon your home. I'm sure you've been having a grand time, fun and games with Ryan. "

"And what else, my Deb Queen?"

"See, there he goes again, making fun of my heritage!" she said, looking to her father for his response.

"I won't attempt to address the personal differences between Martha and my son-in-law, Ned, but I feel I must speak as an advocate for their—my grandchildren. Whereas the eldest, Erica, has been successfully employed for some time and is a mother of a charming two-year old, Melanie, Ryan, on the other hand, in his idleness has developed a lengthy police department resume," the doctor said, looking at Chip.

"A rap sheet," Chip added.

"A police record caused, in large part, by his father here who has been unable and/or unwilling to offer himself as a proper role model.

"Be that as it may," Chip said, "I suggest we look at the substantive issues and develop a preliminary agreement prior to obtaining the final divorce decree."

"It sounds like you have it all figured out in advance," I said. "I don't care if you're not being fair to me, but I don't like you tearing into Ryan while he's not available to defend himself."

"How can you possiby question my father's motives?" Martha asked. "If you cared so much about Ryan, you wouldn't have taught him how to get in trouble, showing him by your example how to be in the wrong place at the wrong time!"

She could be referring to the Littlehales, but no way could she know about the showdown, Ryan's part or mine. None of them at this table with me has my best interests in mind. I don't need to share anything new with them, which they might use against me.

"I concur with Martha," Aldie said. "If he hadn't the idle time, with yours to match, then you two wouldn't have humiliated the family name."

"It's a good thing then that neither Ryan nor me's an Aldrich," I said. "I'm getting a little tired of third parties interfering."

"If you're suggesting that my father has been interfering in any way, shame on you, not after all Dad's help since you've made yourself scarce!"

"Wait a minute: you were the one who wanted me out of here! At least try to keep your stories straight, Martha!"

"And what story do you have explaining what you were doing chasing young girls from party to party a few weeks back?" Martha said, looking to her father, who nodded in agreement. "Father has it from an unimpeachable source."

One lies, and the other swears to it. Someone must have seen me with one of the General's daughters at a party, drawn the wrong conclusions, then reported it to Aldie. "I can't imagine what you're talking about, or who would spread such rumors."

"Sorry, Ned, but that's privileged information," the doctor said.

"Nevertheless, I move that we get on with the business at hand," Chip said. "If I can speak for Dr. Aldrich and your wife, we're looking for an equitable arrangement, an agreement in principal, a meeting of the minds."

"I'm not sure what you're gagging on, Aldie. Did you bite off more than you could chew with me, when I married your daughter? I asked."

"Not more, but frankly less," the doctor said.

"I got a whole lot less than I bargained for with you, Ned," Martha said. "I should have listened to your advice, Father, the first time I met him."

"If my memory serves me right, Martha," I said, "that was right after you campaigned for Belle of the Jewelled Ball in Boothbay and lost."

"And how would you know, if you weren't invited?" she reminded me.

"Of course I wasn't invited to such an event because I came from a working family and didn't have enough money to pass the scrutiny of the judges! Not your concern though, because the D'Amours never cared what you fakers and pretenders demanded for entering your club!"

"Wait a minute!" Aldie interrupted. "For the record, Ned, the screening committee has always sought young people from substantial families exhibiting good character. No one can buy his or her way into the cotillion, which is just one event on our calendar. Many are called, but few are chosen."

"And even fewer are chosen from the wrong families, right?" I asked.

"As I said, the committee supports the best families, yes."

He's a relic from a dead age, and my mother-in-law Lilly was an even worse snob than him. When I first knew Martha she must have been using me to rebel against the both of them. Not that it matters at this point, but I'm curious what he really thinks of me, and if I don't find out right now, I never will.

"No one can blame you, Doctor," I suggested, "if you weren't too pleased when the D'Amours got in bed with the Aldriches."

"A union, nevertheless, from which Erica and Ryan issued," Chip said. "And in the agreement we draw up, we must take them into consideration."

"Not so fast!" I interrupted. "I want your client to tell me, twenty-five years after the fact, here and now, why he and my mother-in-law have been willfully turning my own wife against me."

"I can't speak for Martha's mother, who's no longer with us," Aldie said, "nor for Martha."

"But you can speak for yourself, and this time you can do it directly to me, not behind my back!"

"As you wish. In particular, Martha and I have come to the conclusion that you are no longer acting morally, legally, nor responsibly in your clandestine dealings."

I might be the one who's bitten off more than he can chew! Is he close to the secret, or am I imagining it? My heart's beating fast, my temples pounding. If fear's overcoming me, then I better control it before I tip my hand. Doctor Grandpa never liked me, has never meant me well, so I don't need to give him the opportunity to settle old scores with me. Who could have told him my secret anyway, the General, or was it Ryan, or Fitch or Little B? I've got to calm myself down and remember he has no authority over me and probably knows nothing about what happened in the Yard.

"Let me ask you this, Aldie: when you have a very old, very sick patient you know who's dying, do you do the best you can to keep that person alive?"

"You don't have to respond to that, Doctor," Chip whispered. "I know how stressful this sort of situation can be, so we'll ignore that last provocation."

"To answer your last question, my patient records have always been confidential. However, I fail to see any comparison between my medical career and your clandestine off-the-books refuse dealings."

So that's what he means by *clandestine*! No mention of my Rail City disaster. So far, so good, he's far off-target. He's a self-righteous man, who I won't have to deal with much longer, more annoying than dangerous to me, who's held me under his magnifying glass too many years, but he hasn't been able to set me on fire. I deal with the stuff people like him would rather forget about. I clean up other people's messes!

"Frankly, we've wondered why with your personal and family background as an artisan in the building trades, you've given up more constructive pursuits in favor of that sort of thing."

"The trash thing?"

"Yes, you traffic in the flotsam and jetsam of life, in debris and cast-offs. As night follows day, we become what we do."

"Just as we become who we associate with . . . or marry, Aldie?"

"If one trades in detritus, one begins to associate with—"

"*Detritus*, meaning junk?"

"We always thought French was the mother tongue in your household, was it not?"

"Not."

"And through the wrong associations, before we know it we no longer submit to the rule of law and can find ourselves resorting to chicanery to consummate our business transactions."

"I think you're a little confused, Doc. Are we still talking about my business or about yours? Not that it's any of my business, but what did you do lately of any consequence? Write unnecessary antibiotics to appease patients coming to you with sniffles?"

"Or send the 300 pound guy with the 100 pound gut over to your heart colleague for a big referral?" It was Ryan shouting at his grandfather in my defense.

"I thought you and your sister were gone!" I said.

"You got that half right, Dad. I'm not about to sit down in a restaurant with her. She's a pain in the ass, and she'd give me indigestion. I turned her loose so I could check up on you."

"Ned, you've irrevocably revealed your ignorance, and your malice, as well," the doctor said, his voice quivering. "To wit, I make it a practice, never to accept gifts from vendors, nor to pay nor receive rebates, considerations, barter, referral fees, nor do I split fees, as a point of honor."

"Ned, you wouldn't be so jealous of Dad if he weren't so successful! He always helps out others, while you just run away from your responsibilities!" Martha shouted.

"At the United Way, in particular," Chip said, "we certainly believe so, given the high level of your ongoing support over the years."

"Your appreciation always meant a great deal to me, Chip." Aldie said. "For your part you've also done a great deal, keeping the United Way Board on track and in the black, giving your valuable time gratis to sit on that board, as well as on others," said Dr. Aldrich.

I wish they hadn't called me here to sit in on this mutual admiration society debate. They appreciate each other far more than they do me. It's turning ugly, and I wish Ryan weren't overhearing their nonsense.

"Do you mind telling me why you wanted me here so urgently?" I asked.

"Because I haven't spoken to you since your last publicized confrontation with the authorities," Aldie said. "The acorn doesn't fall far from the tree. It seems that if I'm not reading about you in trouble, then it's Ryan. Your son has clearly learned the wrong lessons from you."

I see Ryan rolling his eyes, but at least he's keeping his mouth shut.

"Perhaps not wrong lessons, Aldie, so much as wrong conclusions, based on hearsay!" I said.

"And speaking of wrong conclusions, why have you and Martha's mother been manipulating her mind against me all these years?"

"Ned, you're so paranoid, I can't stand living with you anymore!"

"So what else is new? We can talk about this later, alone," I said.

"Us, alone?" Martha hollered. "No, I'm tired of keeping your secrets! Give me one reason why I should continue to wait for you to get off your Trojan horse!"

She probably means get off my high horse, rather than my Trojan horse. Or she could mean I should present her with a big gift to buy peace. Martha's a history major, trying to dredge up an old lesson she's long since forgotten, educated beyond her own intelligence. Unlike her, I had to go to work before I finished college, but at least I can remember most of what I was taught.

"I'm looking at a breakthrough," I told them.

That was the General's word, and it just came out of my mouth! I've said too much. Now she's prepared for details, note pad and pen at hand. This is the closest she's come to me in a long time, close enough for me to notice she's wearing her string of real pearls, the ones I bought her for our tenth anniversary. I wonder why she's overdressed herself for this grim occasion, to tease me or to impress the pair of escorts she's dragged in with her? It's time for me to take care not to try to reveal secrets to those who don't mean me well. I must try to get back to business, steer them away from my dangerous personal issues.

"What kind of breakthrough?"

"A break-in would surprise me less," my father-in-law said to Chip.

"Quiet, father! I need to hear what he has to say. I'm all ears." Martha said.

"Second thought, I don't think this is the time or the place. The atmosphere stinks here. I don't even recognize this as my house any more."

"Situations change," Chip said, "I'm here to help ease the transition for all parties concerned."

"Then why don't you and Aldie go home and leave Martha and me alone to take care of it?" I asked.

"You still don't get it," Martha said. "there's no *us* any more, Ned. I don't expect much from you anymore, much less miracles."

"Don't fool yourself," I said. "I don't depend on miracles, though a run of better luck would help."

"You'd need more than luck to pull yourself out of this colossal failure at Medford Pond."

I haven't failed! It's not over until I win! I'm going to fix Medford Pond and get paid handsomely as I deserve, not be blamed as a scapegoat! And after that, who knows, maybe I'll take my expertise offshore, but must be very careful not to let them suspect I'm looking forward to any sort of a victory from which she could extort a bigger settlement.

"Ned, you create your own bad luck, and everybody around you shares it with you," Martha continued.

"OK, Martha, you're absolutely right. Borak's going to gobble me up and spit out my bones."

"This is no place for you, young man!" I heard Ryan's grandfather yelling downstairs, and shortly afterward Aldie came up by himself without Ryan.

"Excuse me, Father, but I don't have the heart to speak anymore," Martha said. "Now that Ryan's not here, would you please tell him what I must do."

"Ned, as a small shopkeeper might say, one who's been disappointed by the poor delivery record of his supplier, it's obvious to us that you can no longer deliver the goods," Dr. Aldrich said. "That's why we're giving you the option to withdraw yourself, so to speak, and to nullify your contract."

"My contract? You're talking about my marriage, not a set of living room furniture bought on time."

"We don't have a marriage any more!" said Martha, "Your time has run out!"

"Chip, Aldie, before this gets any uglier," I said, "why don't we postpone this for a better time, if you wouldn't mind leaving now."

"No, I insist that you stay!" Martha shouted.

"No way, there's no place for both you guys and me today," I said. "I've already heard enough!" I quickly rose from the table, in the process breaking a dish and a glass on the floor.

"That piece was irreplaceable. It was in my mother's family five generations. I'll never be able to buy a match. Now look what you've done!"

I can't reason with these people any more. I can't win arguments with fools. If I attempt it any longer, perhaps I'd then become the biggest fool myself.

Chip meanwhile had caught up with me just before I was out the front door. "OK, Ned, walk! But if you do, you'll lose, no contest. Time's on Martha's side, but time's running out for you. If you walk away now you'll be fighting another long-term, losing battle that none of us needs. Trust me."

"I don't know why I should," I said.

"Why you should trust me, or why you should negotiate with us?"

"I wish I had a pair of tweezers, Chip. You've jumped across the fence so many times, you really need someone to pull out those deep splinters lodged in your butt."

Chip and Martha and her father shouldn't get the wrong idea that they can overpower me. I'm not afraid of them. I've certainly laid my cards on the table, yet they haven't done any more than insult me. Aldie now knows I've been onto his cotillion and prestige game for a long time. And whether Deb Queen believes that I'm a pitiful loser, that's her problem, since long ago she counted herself out of a life we can continue to live together. As for Chip, the chameleon, I've just spotted and identified him in the last of his disguises. So now I'm done eating with them, hearing their complaints about me. It's time for me to return to them, not to the dining table, but to the negotiating table. I'll see exactly what they want, maybe give them some of it, if only to get them out of my life more quickly.

"Oh, Ned, we weren't expecting you to double back or to see you again," Aldie said, once again trying to keep Ryan away from me.

Just the same Ryan gave me a hug, whispering, "Tell that lawyer to stick it in his ear if he tries to clean your clock, Dad."

"No, sir?" Without knowing what exactly I was going to do, I walked away from Ryan and back into our great room, as Martha preferred to call it, where she was sifting through the remains of the glass and the platter on the table, putting the broken pieces into separate plastic bags. "All the kings horses and all the king's men couldn't put Humpty Dumpty back together again," I said to her.

"Everything you touch seems to break,"Martha said to me. "Is that all you have to say for yourself?"

"Deb, don't try to put it back together, but find yourself someone with a steady hand and a good tube of glue. Why don't you put that aside so we can continue. Last chance."

"You don't own me. You never have and never will. I don't have to do anything on your schedule. You can't—"

"Hold on, Martha! Ned's returned in good faith, I believe," Doctor Grandpa said. "We're wasting valuable time. I have a five o'clock commitment I must honor, so we must begin in earnest right now,"

Finally we get down to particulars, agreeing on what items I would be permitted to take from the house, and which ones would become hers. The dollars should be easier to divvy up, assuming as Chip, Martha, and her father did that my liabilities exceed my assets. They seem eager to cut me loose with my business debts, aparently believing I'm personally a far greater liability than an asset. They're severely underestimating me, not believing in my breakthrough, and evidently not in me! But I must remember, as the General predicted, this could work in my favor to strike a better deal. It seems that Martha plans to go back to work and let Aldie move in, so that together they'll be able to make the payments on that house I had built for her, which we used to call our house. Whatever piece of this home, if any, I'll be able to keep, today I'm relieved to walk away from it with Ryan and take him to a restaurant for the pleasant meal neither of us could eat here.

Chapter 15
Trial by Water

Before Dimitri took off for the weekend, he could have left better help at the front desk than this kid, nineteen or twenty at the most, his voice squeaky and changing. He never seems to know where anything is or how it works in the motel, yet he's been hired for the most difficult graveyard shift starting 11 P.M. Then at 7 A.M. relieving him arrives a teenage girl with braces, even younger-looking than the boy. These kids must be working cheap, for close to the minimum wage. Not that they haven't been doing a decent job with routine check-ins and check-outs, but everytime I go up to the desk to ask them to do something about the carousing they don't seem to know what to do about a situation they obviously can't handle. A couple of hundred hell-raising dart players have arrived for the Eastern Regional National Dart Championship, being held 8 A.M. until midnight in the Kennebec Municipal Auditorium across the street for the entire weekend.

A male dart thrower's tee-shirt reads: *A.C. Marcelino Paving. Pavers Do It In The Road!* And a female player, a big girl with a belly that might or might not contain a baby—hers says: *Men Are Like Drugs. It's Only Good If You Have the Right Pusher.* These dart throwers began arriving yesterday, Saturday morning. From noon through Saturday midnight they kept themselves busy across the street in the elimination rounds. Then as the defeated players are weeded out, they begin drifting off from the competition in the hall across the street. They make up for their losses by partying hard well into the morning.

The eliminations continue, and by late Sunday afternoon I understand there are parties all through all the motels where the players are staying, though I'm in the middle of the chaos here in the Sunset. The tournament's winding down and the non-stop parties in the hallways, the grounds and the rooms are steadily building momentum.

To help unwind those men who haven't brought their own female companions and who are willing to pay a fee, the professional girls have been presenting themselves throughout the motel for hire. Not that I care, since they seem to go about their business quietly, or at least I don't hear them through my wall when I'm in my quarters. Free enterprise efficiently at work. One slips messages under the doors, including mine: *MISTY. Magic Fingers, Ltd. Professional Massage. Your Place or Mine? 24 hours a day. Call 374-9222.* Another markets herself by placing her calling card underneath the wipers of the newer cars in the lot: *Paramount Escort Service. Satisfaction Guaranteed. Ask for Cindy, Personal Consultant. 374-COME.* Word of the good response to their advertising must have spread through town to the other working girls, who join the first ones in increasing numbers. One of them I spot at 12:30 A.M. wearing a halter top, even though summer's gone; another one with tiny brass bells tied to her ankle.

Every time I fall asleep, I'm awakened by someone slamming into the wall, by a woman in hot pants and an ankle length coat knocking on my door with an offer of her services, or by the bouncing and squeaking of bedsprings through my ceiling from the room above me. And once when I do manage to sleep, I dream that this building has caught fire, that I can't find an exit. When I awaken I check the outside walls and believe that they're concrete block, that the motel probably won't consume me in flames. It's 1:00 Sunday morning, and this party shows no signs of ending! I've been seeing the dart men and women and their companions running in and out of rooms with six-packs and coolers, and the drinking spreads into the lobby and throughout the grounds around the motel. There's shouting and laughing everywhere. I hear put-downs and insults traded back and forth, as well as cursing. But when it spills over to the parking lot, even though they seem happily drunk, not inclined to fighting, the first of the police cruisers arrives to disperse them.

I wish these dart throwers weren't drawing attention to themselves, and perhaps to myself along with them. After the mishap in the Yard, I have tried to avoid the police, and now through the glass of the lobby I see them out in force, patrolling the parking lot of the motel and checking licenses. They're not yet in the interior of the motel, but they're close enough to make me uneasy. The cops leave, and the fun continues unabated. Some of the men break out street hockey sticks, using a special kid's street hockey puck. This puck, made for the pavement has ball bearings to make it slide faster, as if it were on the ice. But here in the hallway as their arena, with the carpet as their playing surface, that puck won't slide. So they modify the rules, firing their street puck into the air as a projectile. Through the night I hear their sticks and puck slam into the walls and into my door. I must have asked them a dozen times to cut it out and go to sleep, but they have far too much energy to ever quit.

2:00 A.M., and I'm awakened by one of the floor hockey players slamming his body into my door. Then as I'm sitting on the bed, getting dressed to try to talk reason to the human projectile and the rest of his impromptu team, a round life-preserver flies through my window and lands at my feet! For a moment this scares me more than it should, like the black cat Blue had thrown at me. My window's completely gone, pieces of glass scattered about the room. I'm wondering how I can move to another room with the motel already filled to capacity.

"Man overboard!" a man yelled from the vicinity of the pool.

I quickly break out the remainder of the window and climb through it. I can't see who's in distress, because we're in a dark spot in the back yard where the lights don't cover. In a moment though I hear something metallic jangling, coming closer, then realize the noise is the chain on a belt, which is securing this dart man's fat trucker wallet.

"Billy knocked his head, fell in the pool, guy!" he shouted at me. "I can't swim, but if you can swim, go get him, pronto! I'm calling up the medics."

"How'd he do that?" I asked. He smelled like beer.

"Last I saw Billy, he wasn't none too steady on his feet," the man in the half-dark said to me, "he took a fall, hit his head, then dropped in the water like a lead sinker! Do him a favor, fish him out first before he gets too waterlogged, then ask him yourself! I'm calling the rescue boys, bye!"

"Wait a minute!" I called as he was leaving me.

This dart thrower drops this terrible news on me and then just walks away! He's moving in slow strides, like a sailor on a heaving deck, probably as drunk as his buddy who must have fallen into the pool. While I don't have to believe him, neither can I just ignore him. Nor can I wait for a rescue crew that he might or might not call.

The pool lights are off, and there's no time to find the switch. With no lights I can't possibly see if anyone's in the water. Maybe the man with the chained wallet just misplaced his buddy, after drinking together with him in one of the rooms. But if he's telling me the truth and his friend Billy's really lying at the bottom, some-one has to go after him right now! I don't know the depth of the water. Maybe I'm too late and he's dead, but I must find out for sure. There's no way of telling if it's shallow or deep, so I just peel off my pants and shirt and jump into the pool feet first. Once I touch bottom, I roll myself over ninety degrees, hold my breath and search the bottom in the dark, feeling my way with my hands. I must be careful not to swim forward too fast, to ram my head into a wall, and drown with this guy Billy, wherever he is. A dozen more times I carefully pass back and forth at the bottom of the pool, until I feel something soft—clothing!

I pull this man halfway to the surface, but his sleeve rips loose and he falls backwards, out of my hands! I go after him once more, making several passes before I can grab him again with both hands now. This time with all my remaining strength I'm able to hold onto the ladder with one hand and with the other maneuver his emormous body far enough out of the water so his head and shoulders are leaning over the edge. Out of the pool I hoist myself from the water and am yanking on his arms, trying to get his large belly to clear the edge, when I realize help is at hand. A woman's grabbed one of his arms, and together we inch him completely out onto the concrete and roll him face upward. Immediately she drops onto him, face-to-face, begins to breathe into his mouth, until he begins to cough and choke. She pauses, turning her face to me, but it's too dark for us to really see one another.

"Just because he owed you a few bucks, you think you can get away with it?" this Florence Nightingale warned me.

"You must have me confused with someone else."

"Don't play stupid. I don't have to see your face to know who you are."

"What are you talking about?" I asked, now trying to keep my face turned away from the distant light, against the chance that she could see me well enough to ever identify me.

"I mean why don't you get your ass in gear!" she said. "Bobby told me all about how you and Milt here got to fighting and you knocked him out and dumped him in here. The ambulance is on the way, and they're going to save him, no thanks to you. If he lives through it, or if he dies, you're going to pay for this, buddy!"

He's stopped choking, and maybe stopped breathing again. She clears out his mouth and resumes her mouth-to-mouth, alternating with pushing on his chest, and once again he begins to cough.

I see flashing lights, either cops or medics! I know I've done the right thing, but I can't afford to hang around and let them interview me and decide whether I'm a hero or a criminal. Once she's out of sight, I climb back through my window, change out of my wet clothes, throw a few things into a bag and get away before I have to answer questions and find myself any more involved than I already am. I need to put a few miles between myself and these drunken dart chuckers, so I take a drive down the Maine Pike twenty miles south to Biddeford. It's 3:30 A.M., and I wake up the proprietor when I sign into a motel on old US 1 with a chainsaw carved statue of a lobster, the Lobster Trap Motel. I don't feel at all tired, and could dispense with sleeping altogether, but know I must. If I can only have a good dream rather than a nightmare, that might give me a direction, help me decide what I ought to do next.

I do manage to drop off for a few hours, dreaming I'm a man under water, drowning. I awaken to hear a motor running outside my room, the refrigeration unit of an idling fish truck. I wonder why his rig is just sitting there, why he's not driving down on the road, traveling in the daylight. It makes no sense why he's hanging around when he should be on the road delivering his perishable load, but then I look out once again and understand why. His cab's tipped open, exposing the engine, and a mechanic's repairing it. I wish my problems were as visible and repairable as that trucker's.

I fall back to sleep, this time with dreams of the kids when they were little and we'd spend the day fishing in Sebago Lake and I had to bait Erica's hook, but not Ryan's. This time though when I awaken, the fish truck's gone. I follow his example and check out. Like the fish hauler I should be paying attention to my vehicle, my business. I've let Ryan, then the General scare me for

too long from going near the office. But since I haven't done anything but help people, nothing wrong, I refuse to live in fear any
more. Besides no witnesses have come forth, no criminal charges
have been pressed against me. If anyone has any suspicions,
they're unproven. I'm tired of feeling like a fugitive. It's time to
get myself on 495, destination Resolutions.

I shouldn't be worrying about meeting my crew here on a Sunday. If it's so hard to get them to work during their normal business hours, there's precious little chance they'll be putting in extra
hours on their own time on a Sunday afternoon. My first order of
business: to get into the files, to know what they've been accom-
plishing, if anything, without me. The old alarm switch cover's
off the wall, the wires hanging out of it. This is no way to run a
business, and I can't believe a careful military man like the
General overlooked this breach of security. He wouldn't have
given me the key to the new locks he installed if I hadn't insisted,
which means he probably takes me, his boss and his best friend,
as a security risk these days.

And in Lewis' rabbit warren, in his wastebasket I smell before
I see the remains of his last sandwich, peanut butter or liverwurst
—I can't tell—as well as cheese. Lewis, one of the simpler employees, quite predictable, always knew where he was headed, a Han-
sel looking for his Gretel, the reason for this trail of crumbs from
his desk into the hallway. I guess I shouldn't complain if he still
prefers to eat his brown bag of lunch alone, rather than to hang
out for an hour by our lunch table, fridge, coffee pot and microwave and gossip with the rest of the crew.

I hear something moving, which sounds like it's running between the walls. I wonder if Lewis has been feeding not only himself, but pests, or whether he's bribing them with food to make
them better friends than he can find in this crazy office. While the
boss is away, the mice shall play! Now I hear a noise, the creak-
ing of floorboards, a human noise. It could be someone walking
around in the office above this office.

I didn't think anyone would be working here today, but I
don't believe I'm alone. There, I hear it again! This time though
the source seems to be the drafting rooms the General set up for
his new hires, which I'm going to check. Here on a drawing board
I see a charcoal sketch, one-third life size, of one of our lovely new
oriental drafting girls, minus her clothes. From her likeness I see

she has small breasts and narrow hips, a delicate oriental beauty that for me right now is warming up this whole room.

The noises continue. By standing very still and placing my ear to the supply closet door, I believe I can hear the creature moving. I've found this can of insect spray, which Rachael bought when she noticed a hornet's nest hanging outside her window. I open the closet door a crack, spray a fog, and close the door up again. Suddenly the intruder is acting very human, throwing his weight against the door, coughing as if he's dying.

"Help! B-b-bully!" the intruder gasped, stumbling out of the closet, his back toward me.

When he stops sneezing and coughing into his handkerchief, I finally get to see his face. It's Yankovich! He's wearing a leather jacket, leather pants and heavy motorcycle boots with chrome hardware. I wonder where he's going in that outfit? If not a biker's rally or a dart tournament, then what sport is he playing today?

"You poisoned me! Wouldn't you like to kill me?"

Another one of Yankovich's false accusations against me, assuming I knew he was in the closet! I'm not a violent man, but he's pushed me beyond my limit! I can't stand listening to him any more, and without my realizing what I'm doing, I slap him backhanded across his face.

"You'll pay for this, Mr. D'Amour, I swear to God! Witnesses to your behavior are on the way!"

Witnesses to what? Defending myself in Rail City? Rescuing a drowned man at the Sunset Motel? I have no way of telling whether Yankovich is trying to bluff me, or whether he's heard rumors. I'm confused. I don't know why he's here, whether I've met him by coincidence, or whether he's been following me for a purpose.

"Face it, Francis, you're a thief, and *I'm* the witness."

"I beg to differ. I'm a consultant, Mr. D'Amour."

Yankovich consulting with who? With Borak? Did he break in here to do his dirty work and scavenge records for him?

"If you're no longer with Resolutions, this is breaking and entering! What the hell are you doing here since you've been fired!"

"Fired me, really? You're so out of touch. I told you I was a consultant."

"Consulting for Mr. Borak, you little weasel?"

"If you weren't so paranoid, you'd blame yourself instead of me. But I refuse to discuss anything more until my witnesses arrive."

I gave Yankovich a sharp push out of my way as I was leaving the room, which sent him careening backward into one of the drafting tables, on which lay a ruler, pens, drafting curves and a big set of pointed dividers, as well as an open utility knife on which he managed to cut himself.

"You can't get away with this anymore!" Yankovich protested.

"Get out of my sight now!"

I'm giving him a chance to scurry out of here, but he's not taking it. It's time now to motivate him to move out of here faster. I grab him by the waistband and pull him out of the drafting room. But as we pass a window he digs in his heels, and points to the parking lot and street.

"You've pushed me around one time too many, Mr. D, you'll see," Yankovich said. "If I were you, I'd run as fast as my legs would carry me, because help's on the way!"

"And if I were you, I'd get the hell out of here before I really lose my patience."

Again he's balking, fighting me every step of the way as I try to remove him. He's an accident waiting to happen, this time crashing into the drawer of the filing cabinet, which I have to believe he came here to ransack.

"Are you proud of yourself! Now I'm bleeding again!" he said to me, mopping the cut on his forehead with his calico handkerchief.

This struggle isn't just between Yankovich and me—I'm confronted with more uninvited company! This guy in jeans, our guest, looks familiar. He's off-duty and flashes me his state cop's badge! I've met the law again!

"Frank, where have you been? It must be half an hour since you dropped me off," Yankovich said. "My boss here's been terrorizing me! You must arrest him!"

If I had known his boyfriend was a state cop, even though off-duty, I would have never let him in the office while we had the meeting with Yankovich to terminate him.

How could I have forgotten Frank Sizemore's face. "You have a right to remain silent," he said.

"Mr. Sizemore, I think you're forgetting I own this place," I said. "Your friend has been rifling through my files. You were with him when we fired him months ago. He doesn't belong here, and the police certainly don't belong here."

"Frank, don't listen to Mr. D!" Yankovich shouted. "Mr. D'Amour is conveniently forgetting Resolutions has hired me as a consultant. I'm surprised Rachael hasn't ever shown you my receipts. Or maybe Mr. Langway didn't want to bother you with the facts. I don't think he likes me any better than you do, but he wanted to give me some hours so I couldn't sue for damages if he fired me for the wrong reasons."

Sizemore's speaking on the radio, calling for help. Why? What's going on here? Maybe Sizemore didn't know that his friend Yankovich was up here rummaging through the files.

"A blue Lincoln. You found it? Go ahead and crack it open," I heard on Sizemore's state trooper radio. "Need some help opening up the rocker panels? I'm on my way!"

It doesn't take many minutes for Sizemore's buddies to arrive. I can see them through the window, one of them picking the lock of the General's car, while a second one's taking flash pictures of it. What if they have a lead on Blue's Lincoln and they're confusing the destroyed car with this one I'm borrowing from the General!

"What the hell you think you're doing, busting up my car!" I shout.

"We both know it's not yours. Don't worry, we're pros, Mr. D'Amour, we'll crack it open without a scratch."

"You can't search that unless you have a warrant."

"Have it your way, Mr. D'Amour. I knew we'd run into you one of these days. We can charge you, cuff you and arrest you now, if you won't cooperate. We don't need a warrant, since we're responding to an assault in progress on Francis Yankovich. Plus, as I'm sure you've guessed, we're looking for some answers about that bonfire at Rail City. If you behave yourself, though, we might just let you sleep in your own bed tonight. But first I must use the facilities. I'll be right down the hall. Don't try anything foolhardy. Francis, holler real loud if you need me."

Once again I've fallen into a trap, this one in my own office. Has Yankovich been trailing me with the police, and are they using him to set their snare?

But now down there by the car, four stories below, I see friendlier cops looking for me! Fitch and a couple of his men are yelling at the state cops who are dreaming up reasons to take me away for questioning. It's time to let the county cops hear from me, but I have to act fast, before Frank Sizemore rejoins us. I grab the nearest heavy object, which happens to be a folded steel chair, and smash it through the window.

"Fitch, help me!" I shout through the broken window.

"Later! We'll catch up with you later!" Fitch shouts back from ground level.

"No, come get me out of here now!"

Fitch sees me and hears me, waving at me to come down, but he's not budging, and he shrugs his shoulders. It looks as if the state police have won this round over Fitch's county department. I can't let Fitch walk away from me and put me out of sight, out of mind. I need to get down to tell him I've been captured by Sizemore. Now what's this fool Yankovich doing, blocking me, guarding me in my own office, grabbing me by my shirt!

"A lot bigger men than you have tried to hold me back, Francis. I'm done playing around. Now get out of my way," I said softly to avoid attracting any further unwanted attention.

"If that's meant as a threat, Mr. D'Amour, I'm not impressed!"

"I'm surprised you haven't yelled out for Frank to help you," I said, hoping he wouldn't do as I was challenging him.

As I'm trying to pass, Yankovich is holding onto my waist with his eyes closed and his arms locked around me, as if his very life depended on restraining me. Even after I release myself by prying his fingers apart, with all his might Francis is shoving me away from the door. I then push him back, but with a force so great, it sends him flying backward into the steel reception desk. One of its side drawers is open. The corner catches his shirt, ripping it off, leaving a gash on the side of his chest. When he falls, he hits his head on the hard floor. He doesn't seem hurt too badly though, yet he's walking around in little circles moaning, holding his head as I charge out of our suite.

"Halt, D'Amour!" I hear Frank Sizemore call after me as the elevator door closes.

Another chase with me the fox and they the hounds! They have no legitimate charges against me, and I can't stop now before I get to Fitch's men! My heart's pounding to burst out of my chest! My last chase at the federal building, they caught and dropped and shattered me like a glass bowl, but I won't let them break me like that ever again! Nasty little man-hounds, nipping at my heels, trying to run me down, bring me down! Once again I'm running for my life! A dangerous business, fighting for what belongs to me! Today they're loaded for bear and won't rest until they take me down!

I know every corner of this old building, before and after it was remodeled. These steel stairs welded on site, replacing the wood ones have an eighteen inch open space between them and the outside brick wall. I wait in the gap between the original building and the stairs on the first-story landing, letting Yankovich and Sizemore race down after me, not leaving my tight refuge until they charge past me in the reverse direction, back up the stairs.

I'm on my escape path, open the side door a crack, when I see Sizemore's men coming at me. I have to move directly for the hatchway at the rear of the building. I'm then able to elude a couple of Sizemore's reinforcements by sneaking to the basement. I race to the utility room, through the vault under the sidewalk and out the steel hatchway doors! I'm free on the street, alone, undetected! I must get to Fitch before the troopers catch up with me, but he's gone! I don't dare stop until I get to his county police office, and I'm moving as fast now towards it as my legs will carry me! I need to change course right now, get off the main street where the drivers see me running as if my life depended on it, and work my way into the alley between the Crocker Bank with its granite window keystones and the old stage coach hotel, now a restaurant.

I hear footsteps behind me and see a man in a white shirt and tie following me about fifty feet behind. I'm on Skowhegan Street, the main street of Gaylord, and there are a few people in Sunday clothes walking to a restaurant on a side street for after-church supper. When I suddenly change course and take a left and zigzag through them, so does the man behind me.

"Mr. D'Amour, stop, you're under arrest!" this bulky man yells.

I'm not about to stop for this guy who has no uniform and no badge. He can't keep up with me, so he stops entirely to talk into his walkie-talkie. He may be a part-time deputy, one of Fitch's men, an ally. Rather than take that chance, I run for my life away from him, taking quick turns into some alleys! But as soon as I emerge onto Skowhegan Street, I see a state police cruiser, reverse myself and race through more downtown alleys, until I'm on grass, racing through residential yards. I run as hard and as fast as I can until I get to the Kennebec River. I drop from the bridge fifty feet below to the riverbank where I used to play hide-and-seek in the high grass, and where now I just hide! I should be able to stay here, unbothered, until dark, then through the night, if necessary, until they figure out they have no good reason to chase me.

How have I come to this, hiding in this tall saw-toothed grass, pursued for trying to rescue my son and Little B, then trying to rid my own office of a spy? I'm not in the grass more than a couple of hours, watching the traffic clatter across the bridge, when I see a vehicle parked on my side of the river, going no further. I begin to inch away from the bridge, farther south down the riverbank, but as I begin to move out again, I spot Yankovich on my side of the riverbank, with Sizemore and the deputy strung out over a couple of hundred yards downstream on the other side! Yankovich, barefoot, his leather pants rolled to his knees, is walking back and forth through the mud and the grass, advancing directly toward me, his eyes half closed, as if in a trance, drawn in my direction, though there's no way he can see through this high growth. He has both his arms extended like the hands of a divining rod, following his own lead. Unless I make a preemptive strike, I'm left out here vulnerable to a squeeze play. I'm done backing away from Yankovich. As soon as he walks within my reach, I grab him and in an instant take him down into the grass and the river mud with me. He tries to scream, but I'm lucky to find a Kentucky Fried Chicken bag, which I stuff into his mouth. I don't think he's so eager to have found me!

Now I must quickly baptize this liberal sinner, washing the yellow baby poop mud off his black leather. At this point with all the cops and deputies so close at hand, my only hope is to distract them with trying to retrieve Yankovich while I make my escape to Fitch, so I toss him into the water.

"You-you'll pay!" Yankovich gasped swallowing brown water, sinking and disappearing.

What have I done! Without intending I've put him to a life-or-death trial by water! This could be the first time in his life he'll sink or swim, entirely on his own effort. After a minute I'm relieved to see his head again. He's back on his feet, walking back to shore. I'm afraid in a minute trooper Frank will be all over me with his huffing and puffing deputy in tow.

Yankovich loses his footing and slips far enough backward from the riverbank so that the current carries him downstream as he flails and chokes on on this dark yellow river water. He's failed the test into which I pushed him, unable to swim for his life, leaving himself at the mercy of the river! He's being pulled away from my side of the shore over to the other side. There the deputy's swum into position to intercept him. On the road above I see another state police cruiser—Sizemore's. He flings himself from the cruiser, slides down the bank, landing on his butt, then chases on foot after me who's trying to evade him by running underneath the bridge. I can't get up to the other side of the bridge before I see him behind me, gun drawn, pointing to the sky. He has me.

"You're under arrest, and this time I'm not fooling around, D'Amour."

"Mind telling me what for?"

"Manslaughter, and now we have the evidence. Let's go for a ride," he said, as I struggled up to the bridge leading me to the cruiser. "You have a right to remain silent, because anything you say may be used . . ."

Maybe Yankovich wasn't bluffing about witnesses against me! How could I have assumed that I fired those shots in Rail City with nobody noticing? Either real witnesses or manufactured ones! The state police couldn't have had too much trouble finding someone scared and desperate enough to testify against me. Maybe this witness with which they're threatening me was one of the neighbors looking out his window toward the shootings, curious whether the next gunshots might come through his own window. Or maybe the state cops coerced one of Blue's flunkies, any of those he might hire on an as-needed basis for stealing, driving, deliveries, enforcement. It could be a bum on Blue's payroll, scared and desperate enough to say anything about anyone for a price. Or maybe this trooper thinks he can scare me into believing he's found the smoking gun so that out of fear I'll fall in line and give him all the details.

"Sorry I'm getting your back seat so muddy and nasty," I said. "It's lucky for you these seat covers are plastic. After I'm gone, you should be able to hose down this paddy wagon and remove all traces. Then you can forget about me and do something useful like find yourself a criminal."

"I'm looking at one," he said, looking at me through the steel mesh of the cruiser's prisoner's cage that was separating us.

"You're looking at a businessman who was working overtime and who happened to catch your boyfriend running barefoot—"

"*Boyfriend*? I have no idea who you're referring to! So far we've been very easy on you, but that could change in a flash, mister," he said, bringing the car to a sudden stop as he turned up the police radio.

"Come again," Sizemore said. "I couldn't hear you over my prisoner chattering."

"He must have took enough river water to drown him twice over," the trooper back at the riverbank said over the handi-talkie.

"But is Francis now safe on dry land?" Sizemore asked. He was nervously tapping the mike on his teeth as he waited for an answer.

". . . He looked like a reptile in that wet leather suit. The zipper froze up, caught his weiner in it trying to work it open, so had to cut his britches off him. Lucky we got him out when we did. Able to get him breathing in fits and starts. Don't think he stayed down long enough to hurt his brain much, but can't tell the way he was babbling before we put the dope to him. We're on the way to the hospital. Over and out."

". . . I meant that Francis was running barefoot through our files, OK?" I explained. "So you can get moving now."

"You better not be giving me advice, jailbird!" Sizemore said to me. "I saw what you did today to Francis, with premeditation. And there have been several witnesses this afternoon to assault and battery, as well as attempted manslaughter. If I was you I'd be some worried!"

So this is all about Yankovich, no mention of Littlehale, or the dart thrower in the pool. Thank God Yankovich didn't drown on me! It doesn't look like they found a gun, or any other new evidence linking me to the accident.

"Just the man we we've looking for!" the state police sergeant MacNab said when I stood before him at the booking desk, a beefy man with a thick neck and powerful arms. "We've been looking forward to hosting you for some time. We missed the chance when you were laid up in the hospital, with your man Fitch and his boys getting in our way. Nice going, Sizemore. Now you can strip him and scrape the crud off him and throw this uniform on him so we can process him."

"No, I'd rather stay in my own clothes," I said, grabbing the prison suit and throwing it back on the sergeant's desk.

"What's the matter, Mr. D'Amour, too bright a color? Don't you like orange?"

"Yes, but not blaze orange. That's for prisoners. I want to make a call. Where's the phone?"

"Here," the sergeant said, handing his phone to me. But as soon as I touched it, he pulled it back onto his desk.

"What number?"

"I'd rather call myself."

"No, I dial all the outgoing calls here myself," he said, taking the number I had to write out if I wanted to get any help. "Who's this, your lawyer?" I nod yes, not wanting him to know I'm trying to track down Ryan so he can in turn figure out how Fitch can get me away from the state police. "No one's home. Anyone else . . . ?" I gave him another name. "Too bad, but no one's home there either."

"Wait a minute, there's another person I'd like to call."

"No, mister, around here it's you who's going to get used to waiting! Now suit up, and afterward we're going to have a little chat!"

He thinks he's bagged a trophy, outsmarted Fitch. He still seems bitter that he was outdone and couldn't yank me out of Sisters of Mercy hospital bed for an interrogation. Now he seems pleased to have me here in his lockup.

Sizemore, for his part, makes me uncomfortable watching me strip off my clothes. I wish he wouldn't hang around me at the shower. I wonder if he has eyes for all naked men, or just hankers after Yankovich exclusively.

"These license plates, they look familiar?" MacNab asked me once I was in my orange uniform and Sizemore had taken me back to the front desk again.

With his gloves MacNab's removing a pair of plates from a plastic bag. When I try taking them from him to check the number, he yanks them away from me before I can touch them.

"You must have pulled those out of my car. They're my son's."

"Where's his car?"

"His car was a hazard on the road, so I had it junked."

"Very convenient, destroying evidence."

"I must be stupid, sergeant, but I have no idea what you're driving at."

"See those red smears? Human. The lab's finding a nice match with Tim Littlehale Junior's blood. Appears you and your boy have been hanging out with a bad crowd. What do you have to say for yourself?"

"Nothing, because you know damn well it would take weeks for a lab to run that kind of test, and you know we don't have that kind of lab anywhere near here! And nothing because you still haven't let me make my call!"

"Is there another number you want me to look up?" MacNab asked, looking through my address and date book. "The name Denise comes up a lot of times in here. You could let me look her over, and if you both cooperate, I may be able to arrange a conjugal visit between now and the Fouth of July."

"I want you to dial 872-9304."

"Just a second,"MacNab said, looking through the list of numbers in the back of my book to cross-check it with a name. "Langway, another associate of yours, or a personal friend?"

"872-9304, got it?"

"Just one more moment," the sergeant said and with his white gloves removed a charred automatic out of its bag. "We pulled this out of the fire on Farrington Road. It's registered in your name." He put that gun in the bag, then produced a machine gun. "And this one, we're taking bets whether it matches up to your son's or to the Borak boy's weapon."

He has burned guns, a smear of blood, and wouldn't surprise me if he could produce a witness to piece together all these shreds. Nothing for me to say. He has all he needs. God help me! At last he allows me to make my telephone call.

"General, I've never been so glad to hear from you."

"Figured you'd be sending me an SOS about now. Have they been beating on you, Ned?"

"Nothing like that, not yet," I told him cautiously.

"Good, then I'll collect you tomorrow, first thing."

"Hang in there until we make the breakthrough, Ned. Tonight I'm meeting with the big guy."

"I don't know what you mean! Can't you get over here and get these monkeys off my back!"

"Monkeys, are we? Hear that, Sizemore?" MacNab said, disconnecting the phone from the wall, leaving me holding a dead instrument. "I believe a wise guy like him respects boxing gloves a lot better than kid gloves."

The sergeant's looking me over carefully, now that he's on his feet. This man's tall as a commercial freezer, built like a front line offensive football player, the ones who I had to figure how to out-maneuver and outrun. On the playing field if I'd get close enough to a hulk his size for him to get his hands on me, no amount of finesse would mean anything against him. Brute force prevails, the bigger man taking the smaller to the ground, inflicting injury and pain in the process. But I've never played my game based on fear, and won't begin now.

MacNab calls in a trooper to relieve Sisemore. "One way or the other, you're going to answer me some questions," he said to me.

They want all the details from me, and they won't leave me alone. They don't let me sleep through the afternoon, the night, through the morning, then until the late afternoon. MacNab whacks me awake every time with his fat sock filled with beans, intended to leave no marks. He and his deputies are careful interrogators, taking turns roughing me up without ever hitting me hard enough to leave marks.

They've given up the grilling for now, having dumped me in this cell with a hoodlum, his jeans halfway down his buttocks. I don't like the way he keeps smiling at me, as if the turnkeys have deposited fresh meat for his feasting. Every time I begin to doze off, he comes a little closer to me, until I shove him off me. I'm beyond exhaustion, but I don't dare try sleeping, afraid to let him get the jump on me and wake up with him lying on top of me. He has scars on his arms, a big gash across his cheek. I wonder if he enjoys inflicting damage on others, and himself is immune to pain, or whether the scars are the occupational hazards of a thug.

"Psst, it's me!" Fitch called to me, startling me from my half sleep. "Visiting hours at the zoo? Ah, they have you caged with that gorilla, Flash Gannon."

"Don't call me that!" my cellmate responded to Fitch. "I don't do that no more!"

"Damn lucky it wasn't me who collared you, Flash. Still think you can outrun the law?"

"Fitch, you don't have no jurisdiction here, and I don't belong here", my cellmate said.

"Yeah, where do you belong? Where do you come from? You, your mother, and your father, if you could ever find him, all swim in a gene pool that don't have a deep end. Flash thinks he's a mean dude, but he can only win a fight by taking cheap shots. If a felon like him gets his hands on a shiv and you don't watch yourself, he'd just as soon put it to you between your ribs as give it to you in the ass."

"Fuck off, pig! You're out of your territory here, and you're sniffing around the wrong pig sty!"

Then to take out his anger out on someone, Flash catches me off guard with a smack to my head. When I regain my composure, I stamp on his knee, hard enough to drop him, but not quite hard enough to break it. Flash tries to stand up, but hobbles over to the bottom bunk bed where he curls up in a ball, biting the pillow so the others won't hear him moaning in the pain I now know he can feel as well as I can.

"Good thing you didn't kick him in the crotch, because Numb Nuts would have never noticed," Fitch said. "We got to find you a safer cage where the animals aren't so aggressive."

"What brings you here, Bud?"

"I have to take care of my friends, so I keep my ear close to the ground."

"And your eye in the keyhole?"

"I'm not a snoop, but the General believes in good intelligence, and we do whatever it takes."

Fitch left me, returning with Sizemore, a tough twelve hours since his previous shift. "I understand you don't like the accomodations, Mr. D'Amour," Sizemore said. "You should have thought of that before you went on your first rampage. This must be your lucky day though. You should be glad to know I just saw Francis Yankovich, and he's on the mend. He'll be OK. Not that you deserve preferential treatment, but come along."

Sizemore then transfers me into another cell, where a fresh set of street clothes in my size has been laid on the bed. For some reason, ever since Fitch arrived the state cops were more accomodating to me.

"What the hell you done, letting Fitch in here?" MacNab bellowed to Sizemore all the way from the booking desk to my cell, where I could see neither of them. "Time to get back to work! I want to find out what the hell Fitch wants! And I want you behind this desk while I get to the bottom of this crap!"

"Before I forget, sir, someone called me about an hour ago to visit Mr. D'Amour later afternoon. I told them it was OK," Sizemore said.

"Well, call them up and tell them to forget it because we're not running a goddamn hotel here!" MacNab said throwing his hands in the air. He was now directly in front of my cell, pacing back and forth, keeping Fitch in his vision at all times. "And you, Fitch, what the hell's your interest in D'Amour? I sure hope while you've been roaming around my station, you haven't been teaching my boys any of your short-weight tricks! We don't have a place for rogue cops like you!"

"Who the hell are you calling a rogue, MacNab?"

"You, the cadet at the state police academy they booted out for cheating on your exam."

"That's a damn lie you're spreading, pal! But I wouldn't want to embarrass you in front of your boys, so why don't you just let me set you straight outside!"

"Glad to oblige you, Fitch!"

They leave together, and I can't see them again through the bars of my window until they're at the driveway leading to the underground garage where they park the state cop cars. There MacNab takes off his belt and holster and sets it on the driveway.

"You wouldn't know what to do with yourselves if you wasn't writing speeding tickets!" Fitch shouted.

"Oh yeah? At least we don't operate for private gain! We make you county cops nervous because we work to state standards!" Mac Nab shouted back.

"Bullshit, you work for the state politicians. Private gain—what the hell you getting at? I can't believe you didn't get the word from your keepers to get off the D'Amour project!"

"We never terminate a state police investigation, unless for good cause. But state business shouldn't concern you counties!"

"So you think you can do this D'Amour thing solo?" Fitch asked him.

"We're going to split this thing wide open, and we're going to see who's had you in his pocket all these years!"

"Before you do that, I'm going to split your fat head wide open!" Fitch said, jabbing at MacNab's shoulder with punches.

Fitch is surprisingly agile on his feet. He's able to hop and duck, easily avoiding the punches MacNab directs at him. Then Fitch lands one solidly in MacNab's chest, knocking the wind out of him. When he recovers, he throws another at Fitch. But their fight goes no further. I see a couple of military officers, who restrain each of the fighters!

"Officer MacNab, Officer Fitch, you must cease and desist!" one of the officers yelled.

"Sergeant MacNab, meet Colonel William Nelson," Sizemore said, helping separate the two fighting cops. He saluted the man in the Army colonel's dress uniform.

As they move past my window I see rows of bars and some medals. I hope they'll come close enough to my window so I'll be able to see their faces.

"At ease, Lieutenant Sizemore," one of the intervening officers ordered.

"In case you haven't noticed, this is a police station and I'm the one in charge of giving the orders here," MacNab said. He then paused to look at the scar across Billy Nelson's chin, then at the other military man, the one with the white bristle cut hair and sunglasses. "Wait a minute, you're Navy!"

"I'm Commander Sal Pignaro, and I'm here assisting Colonel Nelson!" Sal introduced himself.

"Since when does the Navy work for the Army, except on big missions?" MacNab asked.

"Gentleman," Commander Pignaro said, "I come here in the capacity of an observer in order to assist with damage control and/or containment, only to the extent, if it truly has, to which Navy security has been violated,"

"In any event, Mr. MacNab," Colonel Nelson said, "this matter, on the face of it, may indeed have fallen outside of your jurisdiction."

"I don't believe so," said MacNab.

"The Army operates on facts," the Colonel said, "not on beliefs, as my Army reserve man Sizemore can tell you. According to these papers you have Army property on the premises. Ditto for Mr. Ned D'Amour." The colonel turned in my direction and winked at me.

"Excuse me," MacNab said, perplexed as I was.

"We're going to debrief him along with you, Mr. MacNab," Colonel Nelson explained.

"You can't just come in here without a warrant or something."

"We're not secure out here," Commander Pignaro said. "Follow us. We have something to show you."

In just a couple of minutes Sizemore released me from the cell. Once he escorted me into the front office, he locked me inside with MacNab, Fitch and the military men. Billy Nelson laid on the desk in front of MacNab the Army papers authorizing his visit.

Then to Sizemore, Colonel Nelson said, "I don't believe you have enough rank to pass clearance, so I'm going to have to ask you to check out a cruiser and hit the streets. We'll let you know when we've completed debriefing the sergeant and Mr. D'Amour. Dismissed!"

"And what about him?" MacNab asked, pointing to Fitch.

"Oh, he's been cleared. Officer Fitch, why don't you help Sergeant MacNab retrieve the impounded firearms, all of them."

"Starting with MacNab's service pistol?" Fitch asked, grinning at MacNab. He removed it from MacNab's holster and tossed it to Pignaro.

"Interesting," Pignaro said. "A military weapon, not meant for you cops." He removed the clip containing the bullets. "Certainly not the kind of gun I'd expect to be circulating in your department."

"That's because it's my own sidearm, which I never lend out. Now give it over here!"

Colonel Nelson kept it in his hands, turned it over and inspected it. "It looks like we have an M-9, Army issue. A cop would normally be carrying a 9 millimeter."

"Chevrolets or Fords, same difference," MacNab said defensively. "My boys have been using .40 caliber Colts for about five years. Personally I prefer to use that piece in your hands. It seems to me, law enforcement or military, we're after the same thing, more bang for the buck."

"So can you tell me, Officer MacNab, about the guy who owned this military weapon before you?" Colonel Nelson asked.

"I was in the service fifteen years ago," MacNab answered. "Now give it back to me!"

"Not so fast!" Colonel Nelson shouted. "Light-fingered grunts like you are responsible for most of the inventory shrinkage I've witnessed over the years. The petty thieves go after gallon cans of paint, cases of beans, truck parts, bags of cement, silverware, most anything that isn't nailed down. But it's the criminal element in the service, the ordinance thieves like you, who tend to favor the weapons they can carry off in a duffel bag, such as this M-9 you've appropriated."

"Colonel, this gun has memories," MacNab pleaded. "Thirty years ago I was off duty and visiting a girl in what I thought was a friendly village, when some gooks tried to take me out. When I come out of there blasting, next thing I remember—"

"If that was your darkest hour, you might want to keep it to yourself, so it doesn't prejudice us either for you or against you," Commander Pignaro said. "But if you expect us to show you any leniency, then you'll have to produce for us each and every one of the other weapons you've stolen. We can move this along now if you'll allow Mr. Fitch to assist."

Fitch returned with the weapons, which he laid on MacNab's desk. "Sal, check out for a numbers match of the submachine guns," Colonel Nelson ordered.

"I already did that, but I can't trace any of them to any owner in any of our data banks," MacNab said.

"That doesn't surprise me, since these are both AR-15s. They're military, not civilian, and you wouldn't find anything about them in your computer," Pignaro said, handing both machine guns to Fitch.

Meanwhile, MacNab grabbed Fitch as he was carrying them out of the station to his cruiser. "What the hell you think you're doing, removing evidence!"

It looks like another turf war. First one between MacNab's and Fitch's departments, and now one between MacNab and the US Army and Navy.

"We can do this the easy way, or the hard way," Colonel Nelson said to MacNab. "We have been assigned to retrieving all the property stolen from us! This is a matter for military intelligence. We'll find out one way or the other how this ring has been organized. When you return Mr. Fitch, you can take this weapon," the Colonel said, pointing to a third machine gun.

"Bullshit!" MacNab protested. "That one's foreign, an AK-47, which has nothing to do with the Army, Colonel Nelson!"

"Does .223 caliber mean anything to you? That's the US designation."

"But this is a Russian AK-47, and you don't have a right to it!"

"Or, if you prefer the international NATO designation," Commander Pignaro said, "you're looking at a 5.56 mm piece, American-made, a lot better quality than that cheap stamped metal AK-47 hardware. It fires like a .22 with a big charge of powder behind it."

"Who cares about what bore it is and who made it?" MacNab asked. "I got a man here we've linked to arson—"

"From what I heard, that paint garage was like a Molotov cocktail with a lit wick," I said.

"From what you *saw*!" MacNab said. "We all know you were right in there, burning up the evidence after you blew away Littlehale and his friend!"

"Mr. MacNab, you must stop accusing Mr. D'Amour," the Colonel said. "And I find it highly irregular that you waited so long before letting him make his outside telephone call."

"He had his chance to contact anyone he wanted, but no one was home!" MacNab insisted.

"One more reason, aside from lack of jurisdiction, that you've disqualified yourself from this case against Mr. D'Amour," the Commander said.

"I don't get it," MacNab said. "Are you running the show, skipper, or is the Army man?"

"This has become an interagency matter," Colonel Nelson said. "In any event, it's out of your civilian hands. Commander Pignaro will be impounding the .223. In the meantime, Mr. Fitch, you can escort Mr. D'Amour to your cruiser for safekeeping."

"If you think I'm going to allow—"

"MacNab, you allege that thirty years ago you were blasting your way out of a hostile village with this M-9 and that you've kept it as a kind of good luck charm," Nelson said. "That's impossible, because these were first issued only about fifteen years ago."

"So?"

"So you got this from another source," the Colonel continued. "On the face of it, this is a smuggled, illegal military weapon. A serious offense, any way you look at it, crossing state lines. It would be better if you'd cooperate so we don't have to let the FBI hunt down the civilian gun violators. MacNab, I think you could help to get us to the source of these illegal weapons that we've found in your possession. Do you follow?"

"Not exactly."

The Navy man Sal Pignaro sat down on the desk, his back turned to MacNab. "Billy, I think our friend MacNab's going to help us find out exactly how the Littlehale gang has been trafficking in military ordinance, certainly domestically, perhaps internationally. In our investigation I wouldn't be at all surprised if we were to find a connection between the ring that steals our military weapons and these military weapons of the Littlehale gang and your own military weapon, Officer MacNab. If I were you I'd begin cooperating with us, starting right now!"

"If it's connections you're looking for, go ask Fitch!" MacNab said.

"Bud, I don't think your colleague here gets it," Colonel Nelson said with his arm around Fitch's shoulder. "It's going to be in MacNab's best interest to cooperate with his military counterparts, exactly as you've been doing, Officer Fitch. That way when we need either of you as a witness, we can call him in to tell us what we don't already know. But in the meantime, if I were you, I would forget this meeting ever happened. So Mr. Fitch and Mr. MacNab, that means you don't say a word to anyone about this incident. We've instructed Sizemore to do the same."

"Then you've been using Sizemore as a mole in this department!" MacNab shouted, the veins popping on his neck.

"And I would suggest that in no way, shape or form you question or harrass Mr. Sizemore about this matter," the Commander said.

"So what do you plan to do with D'Amour here?" asked MacNab.

A good question, what these military men plan to do with me next. Are Pignaro and Nelson here at the General's requests, as his friends? How could they have known I was captured by the state police, if not through the General? This is no time for me to be cheering though, because I'm still in great danger. If they're serious about solving this gun-running conspiracy, they'll certainly find out I did the shooting. Since I'm not military, then they'll probably turn me over to the feds.

"Mr. D'Amour's not your concern anymore," Billy said, dropping the red-flecked license plates into his briefcase.

"What are you doing with those plates?" MacNab asked. "There's prints on them, and you haven't used gloves!"

"We'll take that under advisement. Stay out of trouble, sergeant," said Colonel Nelson, saluting him as he left the state police station. Along with Pignaro he carried off the remaining confiscated weapons, driving off in a government sedan. Fitch opened the front door of the cruiser for me, as if I were his honored guest, a gesture that annoyed MacNab, judging by the angry look on his face as I was driven away from the state police station.

"I thought you were taking me home," I said to Fitch once we cleared the sentry at the gate of the National Guard armory, about half an hour outside Gaylord.

"Home, where would that be? I didn't think you were living anywhere in particular anymore."

Where exactly in this compound are they taking me? To the base? To their brig? It looks like we're at the biggest building here. A few dozen tanks, with some trucks and trailers to move them. Now that we're on foot, Colonel Nelson seems more relaxed, proud to show Fitch, the Commander and me the equipment. He claims he has a thousand times more firepower at the base's disposal than was used in all of World War ll. Like the General and the Commander, the Colonel has made himself a career preparing for or avoiding Armageddon. These old military men refuse to die or fade away. The Colonel's definitely past retirement age for active duty, but it seems odd to me that he has free access to this restricted Army compound, that he could bring an inactive Navy man to it, much less us civilians.

"It's OK to take a closer look, unless you're some kind of spy or gun runner or assassin like MacNab makes you out to be," the Colonel said, as if reading my mind. "Any questions?"

"Can these tanks fire smart bombs?" I asked, not because I cared, but to appear interested.

"You mean laser-guided, the kind that can hit a dog or a man or what-have-you at fifty kilometers? Yes, if that's how we decide to set them up." Colonel Nelson then looked at his watch. "We still have a few minutes before the boss gets here. I'm sure you've never been inside one of these tanks. To play tank jockey you've got to be a whole lot more limber than a couple of old warhorses like us. Can you do me a favor and drop yourself down the hatch? We got some mice in this building, and I want to make sure the boys haven't been leaving their lunch in there. Go hop down there in the cockpit." I did as he said and climbed into the tank. "Tell me if I need to call the clean up crew . . . What do you see?"

"No food, just a little bit of trash."

"Toss it all to me," Commander Pignaro said from topside. He caught the styrofoam containers and wadded-up wrappers I tossed him.

"If that's all you find, good. Don't come up just yet, because I need you to help me practice closing and opening the latch," the Colonel said and secured the lock.

"Get me out of here! It's dark as a tomb! I can't breathe!" I shouted, realizing a moment too late that I'd been trapped.

They've locked me in the tank, brought me here to pump me for information, or maybe to eliminate me! The steel plates on this monster must be a foot thick! Wouldn't I have had a better chance surviving solitary in the jail, or maybe even in a double cell with Flash, the mankiller! I don't know who's worse, the prisoners, their jailers, or these crazy military men! There's not a crack of light anywhere, and I'm sealed in here like in a thermos! It's a matter of time before I use up my oxygen! The bastards—they're afraid to confront me head-on, have tricked me, and are now squeezing the life out of me! I trip on something, which drops me on the floor of the tank. I feel in the dark it's a heavy three-foot long wrench. I now use it to pound on the hatch hard enough so they have to be hearing me, but still they're doing nothing to release me!

"Turn on the radio to the front and center!" Colonel Nelson shouted to me. Through all the steel I have to strain to hear his muffled voice. "Turn on your receiver for your instructions!"

In the dark I work every control I can touch to no avail.

"I'm not having such good luck releasing him!" I faintly hear the Colonel say to the Commander. "He's rattling around down there, like a pea in a whistle, but muffled, like he's under a stack of wet blankets."

"To me sounds like a jackass in a tin barn in open country, from a quarter mile off, him flinging around in his cage," Commander Pignaro concurred.

"Let's remember, if anybody ever asks, that on his own free will he accepted a ride from us and that he wanted to sit right where he is in the cockpit."

"Now that we got him here, we better do something, even if it's wrong. See if you can get hold of an acetylene torch set pronto!"

For several minutes I hear nothing, then a new voice: "Colonel, the sea captain here tells me you want me to cut into the tank with my torches. Are you sure, sir?"

"Affirmative, Private Brown," Nelson said. "Get cracking!"

"But, sir, even without armament each of these rigs still got to run a few million. I don't think we have the authority to pop it open."

"I'm in charge here, Brown," the Colonel said. "You can leave those torches right there. I'm requisitioning them right now. I can write up this incident with your commanding officer, or you can get cracking!"

"Sir, yes sir, do you want me to get to work now, sir?"

"No, we'll handle it, Brown. I don't write you up, and I want you to forget you saw any of this happy horseshit here today, understood?"

"Ned, listen up down there below decks!" Pignaro yelled after some time. "You might smell something, because we'll be doing a little torch work from topside."

During what seems like hours, the cabin begins filling with smoke from Colonel Nelson's cutting torch. Then I hear him ask Pignaro to try his luck, though mine seems to be rapidly depleting.

"I'm working the flame around the latch," Pignaro shouted to me. "I'm trying to free it up with my maul. How's it going down below?"

"I can't breathe! The fumes!"

"Then put your shirt over your face, or something."

"And how are you doing up there?" he yelled to Colonel Nelson.

"Not so good. The latch is bending, not breaking off."

The fumes are getting worse. I'm losing consciousness.

"What the hell are you doing, sabotaging Army property!" I heard the General's unmistakable gravel voice. "Where the hell's Ned . . . ! Sal, you just set my coat on fire!"

"Then next time don't be wearing polyester near welding operations and making yourself a fire hazard," Colonel Nelson said. "I always preferred wool or cotton near any kind of flame."

"Damn it, Billy, you and Sal are the hazard!"

"This isn't part of the plan!" the General shouted. "What the hell are you doing here anyway, sabotaging Army property! Where's Ned . . . ? Tell me how long's he been sealed up! Five minutes . . . ? Ten . . . ? Twenty . . . ? More . . . ?"

"Yeah, that's why we're taking measures now," Billy Nelson said.

"Do you know this is a tight sealed unit, made to keep out nerve gas and anthrax, and you're using up his oxygen! Step aside! Get out of here! I'm going to pop you, Ned!" the General bellowed so loud I don't even have to strain to hear him.

"I can help," Pignaro said.

"I don't need any more of this kind of help! You've done too much, and you have no clearance for the Army, much less on classified tanks!"

I have no idea exactly what the General's done, but he's the one who frees the latch and opens the hatch for me! When I see daylight I scramble toward it so fast, I bounce off the steel track and onto the floor! There I stay on my hands and knees, choking, gasping for breath, dry heaving!

I sat on a crate, my heart racing, my breathing very fast. After a few minutes I was able to raise my head from between between my knees. "Where have you been, General?" I asked.

"Sorry for the snafu, Ned. If I were here__"

"But you weren't because you were too busy and sent Mr. Pignaro and Nelson instead! They acted like good commanders, trying to complete this mission, whatever the hell its purpose, but—"

"They got the weapons and you out of the wrong hands, didn't they?"

"Good for them! They don't seem to care one way or the other whether I died in the process!"

"I can appreciate that, but you do seem a little worked up over nothing."

"Nothing, General, nothing? First they lure me into the cockpit, lock the hatch behind me, and leave me in there long enough to suffocate me, then try to finish the job by pumping in gas fumes! What's so funny?" I asked when I saw a perplexing response on the General's face—a look of amusement or satisfaction—I couldn't tell which.

"A brilliant maneuver on their part," he said. "Was it Billy or Sal who convinced the State boys?"

"Don't talk to me about them! I don't want to see them ever again! Just get me back to the Sunset!"

"And what would you plan to do there?"

"I don't know—I'll soak my head, I'll try sleeping off this nightmare, or maybe I'll just shoot myself and get it over with!"

"You don't mean that, do you, Ned?" the General asked, kneeled before me and picked up my head up by the chin and looked very closely into my eyes as if I were his kid.

"I'm dead serious! I can't take this anymore! Don't bother looking for me tomorrow because—"

The General stood up walked around me slowly and then slapped me briskly across the face once. "Believe me, that hurts me more than you, sir. You must snap out of it! I won't let you give up now! We have too much at stake!"

"Forget it!" I shouted, enraged. "You don't have a goddamn thing at stake, any more, General, because as far as I'm concerned, from this point on, you're kaput! Hit the road! Sayonara! Fired!" I say, standing up straight, feeling woozy from the fumes.

"That's better. Your old spirit's back!" the General said, with a pleased look on his face, missing the point.

———————

I've asked the General, Pignaro and Nelson what the next step is, as if they really have any control over me, and the General tells me once again about his *breakthrough*. I know that's a fanstastic lie designed to appease me, but I can't get him to tell me the truth. So with no alternative for the moment, I do it their way and get into the General's car with him. I sit there alone, watching the retired military friends tell jokes and laugh—jokes I can't hear but which I suspect are at my expense. I still have no idea where I've been led, or why. Just as I'm about to get out of the General's car and join their reunion, too late, the General sends them on their merry way. Surprise, another car, another visitor for me, Denise! The General must have brought her, but why? I don't need her feeling sorry for me, and don't want her to see me like this at my worst. If she begins to think I'm just another criminal for her to represent, it's over between us.

Here I am beaten up and dirty and not in any mood or condition to speak to a stranger, much less my best friend Denise. She comes to me, all smiles, hugs me as if she's noticed nothing wrong with me. Is she blind, misinformed, or just very forgiving? Reunited, we make up for lost time, our kiss growing deep, neither of us seeming to notice or to care the General's watching us, who I finally see out of the corner of my eye smiling like an indulgent chaperone.

"Excuse me," the General said, looking at his watch, "we're running behind schedule."

"I thought I told you that I won't be needing your services anymore!" I reminded him.

"Don't be foolish, Ned," he said wrapping his arms around each of us, as if we were all a happy family.

"No, we haven't carried you this far to drop you," Denise said, resting her hand on mine, smiling at me, trying to calm me.

I haven't gotten where I am by asking for help and depending on anyone. Like the General's men, it seems even Denise, no matter how good her intentions, has also been talking about me behind my back. But this time they're going tell me the plans they built around me.

"I think you have it backward," I said. "So long as I pay the General and you, whether as a consultant or an employee, I carry you."

"If you think that's all there is between us, Ned—" she said, "I needn't continue working on the breakthrough."

"If you think of us as a couple of your working stiffs," the General shouted, his face red with anger, "if that's all we are to you after so many years, then we can quit right here and now!"

Now he also has her talking about his breakthrough, contagious wishful thinking! I'd love to get rid of him once and for all, but if I take him up on his offer now, I'd probably lose Denise and can't take the chance.

"What did you have in mind?" I asked.

Denise has brought me a fresh set of clothes—once again other people insisting on dressing me up, like the night after Rail City when Fitch and the General insisted on destroying my incriminating clothes.

"And we can't afford to be late and lose what credibility we still have," the General said. "I have just the place where you can shower and shave, and with any luck you will no longer look like the police just hauled you in for breaking and entering."

"I thought you had more faith in me, or at least common sense," I said once we were underway in the General's car. I'd calmed down, realizing, as much as he could annoy me, he'd always be on my side. Denise was following us in her car. "A person doesn't just break into his own property and burglarize it. Or maybe you know something I don't know, like the reason Mac-Nab's troopers came after me, just for checking in on my own business? And can you tell me why the burglar alarm was hanging loose on the wall?"

"I understand MacNab had an all-points bulletin out for you," the General said. "Either Sizemore came upon you by accident, or else MacNab figured he'd catch up with you eventually."

Or else I'm going crazy!

"Then why didn't the police show up right after I entered? How did Yankovich get in if we've fired him? He must have set off the alarm when he broke in."

"No, he has a key, and he knows how it works. I put in a new silent alarm so we could catch any intruder by surprise. Didn't you notice the old alarm key mechanism hanging dead by the old wires? I'm sure it was you, Ned, who triggered the alarm, no one else."

"And now I'm sure it was you who rigged it up to snare me! You didn't really hire Yankovich on as a consultant afterward, just so he wouldn't make trouble, did you?"

"Not to snare you, in particular. I was just tightening up our security. But wasn't Sizemore waiting outside the office while Francis went in to pick up the coat he'd forgotten?"

I notice the General completely avoids owning up to whether he took on Yankovich as a consultant without telling me, but I'm not about to challenge him on it right then.

"I don't know anything anymore, General! You tell me!"

"Let's just say you happened to be in the wrong place at the wrong time, once again. If you recall, I did suggest you keep a low

profile and stay away from work until we could make our breakthrough. Sorry for any inconvenience."

Inconvenience? I'm struggling for my life, gone under twice already with no help in sight, and that's very inconvenient! Thanks
to stumbling through his new jury-rigged alarm, I delivered myself into MacNab's hands for a day's interrogation. Giving the
state troopers another incident for which they can convict me.
Trial by water—Yankovich and me fighting it out in the river—
and they're finding me guilty enough to push under more and
more, until I can't fight any more! Not so long ago I saved a man,
a stranger, from drowning, but there doesn't seem to be anybody
who can save me! I've been sabotaged once again, this time not by
Yankovich's treachery, but by the General's incompetence! I need
to talk to Denise about the General, but I believe she's been hypnotized by him with promises of a pie-in-the-sky breakthrough.

I don't know where we're going now. We come to the Road
Warrior Truckstop on I-495, not traveling directly toward
Gaylord as I'd expect, though I'm not going to ask him once
again to explain our destination. The General pulls next to a
dozen tractor-trailers, Denise driving directly behind us.

"I still don't know where the hell we're going, but didn't you
tell me you were running late? If you need gas, then why don't
you pull up to the pumps, instead of hanging back here with the
big trucks?" I asked, if only to see whether he'd follow any advice
I gave him.

This is the biggest truck stop between Montreal and Massa-
chusetts. It stocks jumper cables, mudflaps, spotlights, tire chains,
pepper spray, tire irons, rope, tie-downs, canvas tarps, air horns,
reflectors, girlie magazines and videos, tire gauges, radar detec-
tors, CB radios, air fresheners, as well as beef jerky, candy and convenience groceries. There's a connected trucker's motel posting
at the sign-in desk: *NIGHTLY, WEEKLY, AND HOURLY RATES.
SHOWERS.*

The General takes Denise and me to the restaurant. There is
a woman at the counter chatting with a trucker without much
flesh on his frame, who's so keyed up he won't sit down, as if he's
had a lot of coffee or some other booster to keep him awake for
long hours behind the wheel. He and the woman stop their conversation to look the three of us up and down. I don't care for the
attention of the strangers in this restaurant, so I don't join the

General and Denise at their booth for a cup of coffee. Instead I move on to a far corner of the building, curious about the bleating and ringing video games. From here I see the back of a familiar looking head. It could be Ryan! Maybe I have Ryan too much on my mind. This young man I can see from a distance is wearing a tie, while Ryan never does. I move close enough until I can see his neck, the scar from the time he fell out of the apple tree onto the barbed wire fence! I know about scars and have a few of my own. Scars aren't such a bad thing if they remind of us of where we've been.

"What are you doing here?" I said, embracing my son, startling him.

"Oh, Dad, God . . . ! I'm waiting for them to come back with some more quarters."

"I mean why are you here?"

He better not tell me this is a coincidence!

"Dad, I would have come after you sooner, but the General didn't think I should. I mean he told me I'd do you more harm than good if I saw you too soon, before he made a breakthrough."

Like Denise, he's begun to talk about a breakthrough! The General knows something that I don't know, or he's brainwashed the both of them! Now here comes Annie, not in Ryan's company, but hand in hand with Little B! They're smiling at each other, a happy couple. I wonder whether she'll remain his bedmate as long as she had with Ryan. She's wearing a modest dress, no breasts hanging out this afternoon, with an ordinary neckline. And Little B, like Ryan, is wearing not only a tie, but a jacket.

"You guys got all dressed up to play these games?" I asked. I walked them away from the noisy machines to a quiet spot in the hallway, away from the restaurant, store, hotel and game room.

"Mr. Ned, I'm real glad to see you," Little B said, embracing me. "I would've looked you up sooner, but Wonder Boy Ryan's running scared to let me near you."

"Why don't you leave him alone already, Little B!" Annie shouted. "He was just waiting for the right time, you asshole! And I didn't see you in any rush to be talking to your old man. It seems to me if you got to your old man earlier, Borkman, those fuckers wouldn't have been pounding on Ned. You do look like shit, Ned. Haven't you found a woman yet to rub you down?" Annie took my hand and kissed me on the cheek.

Denise arrived and handed me my clothes. "I don't think we met before," she said, extending her hand to Annie.

"So Ned didn't tell you about me? I'm the one who tucked him in every night after he split his head open."

"Annie's Ryan's close friend," I explained. Denise noticed Little B's hand resting on Annie's buttocks. "And, more recently, Little B, Borkman, Borak's friend, or whatever you want to call him." While keeping his right hand possessively on Annie, Little B shook Denise's hand with his left.

"We'll be waiting right here for you, Dad," Ryan said.

Without saying any more, Denise took me towards the shower she just rented for me. This must have been planned out beforehand, but for what purpose? I quickly cleaned up and dressed, but when I returned I saw that the General had joined Denise and was speaking with my son and his Rail City friends. With my arrival he gathered Ryan, Annie and Little B and walked them quickly out of the building and into the fuel plaza, with Denise and me following.

"A change of plans," the General announced. "Mr. Borak wants to meet with us one at a time," he said to Little B.

"Yeah, you do better with the old man one-to-one," Little B agreed.

"You already know the way to Dimitri's Restaurant, heading north a couple of minutes from his motel, the Sunset?" the General asked. "Mr. Fitch will be expecting you there."

"Couldn't we have held this at Borak's office?" I asked as the General, Denise and I were traveling from the Road Warrior to Dimitri's Restaurant.

"Yes, except that he insists that we keep this off the record and unofficial."

"Why? Did he get cold feet meeting at the truck stop?"

"I'm not about to question his reasons, especially now that we may be able to break through with him."

"More breakthrough talk! Remember what happened to me the last time I tried talking to him!"

"Wynton called me half an hour back to reschedule," the General said. "He's a busy man, and I didn't want to lose him. I think he was afraid of someone he knows walking in that truckstop and discovering us."

"Isn't that nice you're on a first name basis with that hidebinder!" I said. "Apparently I choose my friends more carefully than you do! You know I regard Dimitri as a friend, and I think it would have been better to use any place other than his for this meeting!"

"At this point, Ned, I don't care what you like," Denise said. "Either we go ahead with this conference, or I pull your name permanently out of my personal Rolodex . . . !"

She's looking at me very intensely. I'd like to find out how angry she is, what she really means, but can't with the General there. My options seem to be steadily decreasing So without challenging her, I concede, simply shaking my head in agreement. "And by the way, Ned, speaking of personal preferences, did you complete your homework assignment?"

Denise is really asking me whether I settled up finally and irrevocably with Martha, but she doesn't want to say so in front of the General. No doubt she's growing tired of waiting for me. Without her earlier ultimatum though, I probably wouldn't have had that meeting with Doctor Grandpa and Martha, but I'm not about to tell her that now.

"Assignment completed. Now we can think about commencement," I said, "if you'll be my honored guest and share a very important day with me."

Denise looks confused at first, then breaks into a radiant smile and gives me a kiss, very pleased that a major obstacle to our life together has been removed. I know she's taken my report as a personal offer, and in her heart has fully accepted me, finally, trusting the details to follow.

———————

When we arrived at Dimitri's restaurant, Fitch was waiting in the parking lot to greet us, as soon as the General, Denise and I got out of the car.

"Little Borkman and Annie have been talking with Mr. Borak for about a half hour now," Fitch reported. "It shouldn't be much longer. Dimitri wanted me to tell him the second you arrived so he could come out and say hi to you."

Borak! What the hell are his son and Annie doing with him? Since the two of them have already turned on Ryan, I wouldn't be surprised if next they turn on me! Is this some kind of setup?

"That's OK. We'll wait inside, get a cup of coffee," I said.

"Sorry, but Mr. Borak doesn't want to speak to anyone but the kids for now. So what'll that be, three coffees? With cream? Sugar?"

We try to follow him into the restaurant, but he blocks us at the doorway and walks us back to the car. I can't believe my friend Dimitri doesn't want to see me. This order could also be coming from Borak.

"It's too busy in there right now. You need to stay right here where we can find you," he said.

In a few minutes a waiter returns with the coffees on a tray, as well as Greek pastries, as if serving the last meal before the execution. Once he sets the tray on the front seat between the General and me, Dimitri himself then takes a seat in the back of the car alongside Denise.

"You got better looking lady than bad boy like you have right expect," Dimitri said to me. "I know a man by eyes. Ned good man. Miss, you still be a lawyer when you marry this man . . . ?" he asked her. "Don't worry, Mr. Longway," he said to the General, "I good with secret, drive wife crazy who want yak-yak all a time, knowing everybody business. But don't matter what I say, since I work all a time and never home. I give your little government man friend underground room for talking to Ned's boy and his friends. Not to worry because I have no windows and no one ever come down there without me inviting first. Got to go now to the restaurant and make some money."

In a few minutes I see Ryan, Annie and Little B getting into Little B's work truck. They must be done with their meeting with Borak. Did Borak cut a different deal with his son than with Ryan, and is he now in the process of finalizing some dirty master plan with three separate meetings? I'm done waiting in the car and head over to find out exactly what they've said to my son, Denise right behind me.

The General followed us. "I wouldn't, if I were you. I promised Wynton no debriefing. Don't screw up the breakthrough, Ned."

There he goes again, making promises on my behalf without asking me first. The General's catering far too much to Borak, which puts me on the defensive. What kind of deal could he expect to make on my behalf if he lets Borak set all the rules up front? He's nuts if he thinks he can continue to separate me from my son.

"Oh, Dad, we were just heading out," Ryan said as Little B put his cleaning van in gear. "See ya."

"Hold it! Not so fast! Care to step out?" I said, opened Ryan's door and tugged him by the sleeve. He reluctantly got out and strolled with me away from the van so that just the two of us could talk. "So what did you tell Borak? I wish you spoke to me before him. Was he pumping you for information?"

At that very moment Fitch came at us from behind and placed a hand on each of our shoulders. "I lost sight of you for a minute, Ned. Glad I caught up with you. Mr. Borak couldn't see what the hell's going on out here and wanted me to check in on you."

"What else does he expect, hiding down in his bunker without windows?"

"That's why now I'm his spare set of eyeballs," Fitch said, out of breath. "Glad I spotted you in time before Ryan said something you might regret!"

"Bud, what I say to my son has nothing to do with you."

"Yeah, but the deal seems to be that the three kids answer Mr. Borak's questions first, then it's your turn to meet with him. He doesn't want you to influence their answers and vice-versa. And he tells me if he doesn't find out the true story, he won't talk with you. Guaranteed."

"We'll catch up with you later," Ryan said, apparently anxious to leave.

"Not so fast!" I said, grabbing my son by the sleeve.

"Dad, listen to Mr. Fitch. I can't—"

"Never, never, never run scared if your cause is right! Remember no more excuses not to stay in touch with me after today." Ryan hugged me, which felt good. As Ryan hurried off to join his friends, I now saw Denise and the General moving back toward me from where I'd left them at Little B's truck, which was gone. Fitch looked anxiously toward Denise and the General, coming to me from where Ryan and I had left them.

"You're on next, Ned. I'll tell them they'll get their chance with him after he's done with you," Fitch said and rushed toward the General and Denise to intercept them before they could get back to me.

There's a steady flow of cars, people coming from work for happy hour at Dimitri's Restaurant, filling up the lot. In the bar the music's cranked up, every bit as loud as the customers' voices. But Fitch and I are just passing by the drinkers on our way down the stairs to Dimitri's office. Once we're in the basement I'm hearing little more of their party-making than the bass thump-thumping of the stereo, which is so loud they probably wouldn't hear the blast of a shotgun. Dimitri uses the basement not only as a storage room and workshop, but as his office. We're surrounded by electric wires, power meters and boxes, heating and air-conditioning ducktwork, furnace and workbenches. But Dimitri's restaurant supplies—his boxes of oil, vegetables, noodles, potatoes, flour and sugar—have been gathered up from all over the floor and are stacked against the outside wall like sniper barricades, covering up all the high little basement windows. The other end, the business side with the file cabinets, it has been rearranged so that Dimitri's highbacked rolling chair is between the desk and the wall. And sitting in it I see Wynton Borak who immediately rises when he sees me, shaking his head to me soberly. When he steps forward and begins pacing in front of the desk, I see he's wearing a dark blue and red-striped jogging suit and high sneakers with see-through shock absorbers.

"I didn't know you were an athlete," I said.

Finally Borak approached me and shook my hand, very slow to release it. In his other hand he held my necktie. "And I didn't know you were still a businessman."

I must be careful. The worst thing I can do is take his bait. He's testing me, trying to get me angry, to make me lose my composure and throw me off balance so he can better manipulate me. But he should know by now that short of killing me, he'll never beat me.

"And I didn't know you lost your sidekick, or did you leave him at home today?" I asked.

"Now you wouldn't be speaking of my better half?" Borak asked. "She's happily retired, thank you. I'm next."

"No, I'm wondering what ever happened to that big gray, crinkle-haired *schlub* assistant of yours who ran me through the mangle before I ever got upstairs to see you our last meeting!" Borak looked at me, perplexed. "You know who I mean!"

Borak turned his back towards me and looked through Dimitri's books, picking a Greek-English dictionary, which he threw on the desk. He began looking through it, then slammed it shut.

"*Schlub*—I can't find that name. Are you sure this individual exists?"

"You know I'm referring to that government hack backing you up that day your man threw me over the railing!"

"Ah, you must be referring to Mr. Moretti. It was time for him to move on. Off the record, I've come to believe that due to some of the misinformation contained in Mr. Moretti's reports vis-a-vis Pollution Resolutions, he was responsible for much of the ill will between us. Not to mention your most unfortunate accident in the stairwell. I have come to believe Mr. Moretti relied too heavily on Mr. Yankovich for his information, as well as what's her name—Rachael. I might have encouraged him to take early retirement for improperly gathering data, but instead I did the next best thing, transferred him out of our regional office over to the district unit in New Hampshire."

Incredible! I can't believe he's finally owning up to screw-ups in his organization. Maybe he's really trying to dodge personal responsibility by shifting the blame to Moretti. At any rate, he seems more approachable than I ever remember him. But even if this admission of his is an honest attempt to make peace, I still won't consent to anything until I know what a treaty with him would really cost me.

"So you think I'm not doing business any more? I know Ryan wouldn't have told you such a thing. From what you're telling me, you don't like to rely on hearsay. Then it must have been your son who told you I was on sabbatical. Not that I care, one way or the other, about your opinion of me."

"Actually, my son Henry told me you're a hero. I believe without a doubt that he would have been gunned down without your intervention. I didn't understand until now that both you and Ryan were cooperating with my son to get away from the Littlehales' extortion and intimidation. It's unfortunate for the Littlehales that they got in harm's way, through no fault of my son, your son or you." He then opened up Dimitri's little refrigerator. "Soda pop or beer, which do you prefer, Ned?"

I must be careful to take nothing alcoholic that could cloud my judgment in negotiating with him. Now he's seated me in Dimitri's padded desk chair in this jury-rigged office, while he himself sits on a box. I think he's trying to make me feel comfortable, giving me the seat of honor, going out of his way to make me comfortable. But he could be trying distract me in order to find out from me the particulars of the shooting. No way though will I ever tell another soul!

"What kind of *intervention* was Little B—I mean, Henry—talking about?" I asked.

"Shall we call it full reasonable force? Without embarrassing you, Ned, without getting more specific, let's simply say that Blue Littlehale had no charity in his heart. A bigger man than I once said he who has no charity deserves no mercy. I'm a GS-15 bureaucrat, not God."

"Are you talking about Blue?"

"Must we? If we could bring back the departed, would we want to? He's dead, gone, and, if I have anything to do with it, forgotten. Now I'm talking about you, Ned. As one of the better presidents, Woodrow Wilson, once said, if a dog won't come to you after he's looked you in the face, you ought to go home and examine your conscience. . . . I'm sorry you can't go home. Nevertheless, I can finally see now you're a man of good conscience. Otherwise, I might not have made the time and taken the effort to help Mr. Langway in his capacity as adjutant general with state and national security responsibilities. Do you understand?"

No, I don't understand why now he's acting so friendly to me, other than from simple gratitude that I saved his son's life. But I have to believe his motivation for peace must be genuine, that otherwise the General wouldn't have worked so hard to set up this conference.

"It sounds as though you may be able to work with Resolutions," I cautiously suggested. "Since General Langway is a public servant, like yourself, you might feel more comfortable dealing with him than with myself."

"Precisely," Borak said, smiling, "as well as working with your legal representative, Denise. However, let's keep in mind you, your General and I needn't share all we know with her. She's a lawyer, and a charming one. But lawyers, no matter how charming, can become loose cannons on the deck when they come untethered. Excuse me."

Then Borak spoke on his two-way radio to Fitch. "I'm ready to receive Ms. Pendergast and Mr. Langway now."

Borak tossed me a tennis ball. I tossed it back, and we were playing catch. Maybe we weren't on the same team, but at least we were playing the same game. When he heard knocking on the door, he pushed the ball hard onto an old-fashioned receipt holder made of a six-inch raised spike, destroying it.

"I better be careful, or someone might get hurt with that thing," Borak said to me with a weird gnome's wink.

"Do you want me here, as well, sir?" Fitch asked.

When Fitch arrived with the General and Denise, she at first seemed out of place in Borak's comandeered basement quarters, then was able to gain her composure and smile. Fitch set up folding chairs for us in front of the desk.

"I don't see why not, Mr. Fitch," Borak said. "I keep no secrets, especially with public information. After all, we're talking about a public project."

"If we can't trust you by now, Bud, then Lord help us," the General said, taking his place next to Denise, with me on the other side of her.

It's a stretch for Denise to reach down to Wynton Borak in his seat behind the desk to kiss him hello. I didn't know she was that familiar with him. Does she realize she's kissing the enemy, or is Wynton Borak really now a new friend to me, one who's had a conversion? But how can she represent my best interests if she's so cozy with him?

"How's the campaign going down in Boston?" she asked. "I heard you were planning to move back there soon and run for office."

"My plans have changed. There is no campaign anymore," Borak said.

"Sorry to hear that."

"Don't be, because I've decided to get out of civil service, and out of the public sector completely. I will be retiring shortly, probably spending summers in Wellfleet on the Cape for which my wife's been campaigning. But before, in good conscience, I can leave my post and hand it to my successor, I would like to have some completion."

"Completion regarding Medford Pond and Pollution Resolutions?" Denise asked.

"Yes, if nothing else you need to remember me as a man of principle, such as I've discovered Ned is," Borak said. "Unfortunately, until now our principles have clashed."

"Completion regarding removing Pollution Resolutions as a PRP, Wynton?" the General asked.

"Those unfortunate decisions won't be easy to reverse, but if we make that recommendation, I believe we can do so."

He sounds like he wants to end our fight! If I understand him right, this must be the General's breakthrough! If I'm no longer a Potentially Responsible Party, I can't be nailed for the massive fines and criminal penalties they've been piling up on me! And it sounds as though with Borak's help no one will be coming after Ryan and me over the Rail City incident any more! If only Borak had decided to get his claws out of me a few years ago, I might have more of a business left to salvage, but at least now I should be able to salvage myself.

"The way I have come to see it," Borak continued, "both the government and Resolutions have already spent enough money on studies on how to clean up Medford Pond. If money were no object, maybe we could drain off the 600,000 cubic yards of sludge and spend about $30 million making a stable landfill on the site. But I'm a practical man and believe we need to lay this whole matter to rest and have recently been working toward that end. My engineers have very recently suggested an alternative that would cost perhaps a third of that amount. Rather than disturbing the site and causing further migration of toxins into the groundwater, perhaps the least disruptive solution would be to do a minimum of dredging and cap off the residue with sand and silt."

"That's fine regarding Resolutions, Inc, but what about the outstanding court orders against Ned?" Denise asked.

"Ms. Pendergast, we'll announce individual settlements, sequentially. "

"I don't understand," she said.

"We'll work systematically to answer, eliminate, and nullify them," Borak said. "I am proposing, off the record, that we end the adversarial relationship between the Environmental Pollution Agency and Resolutions. On a personal level I will do what I can to lessen the challenges Ned continues to face."

He's guarding his words. Without saying so directly he must be referring to eliminating the case the state police had been building against me for the Rail City shootings and fire, as well as the assault against Yankovich. And come to think of it, I've heard nothing lately about the EPA case against me, which he'd be pursuing if he still wanted to try crushing me.

"Then what would you like in return?" the General asked.

"Would you like me to ask your forgiveness, Mr. Langway? I can't do that. But, as a man of principle, I can suggest that Ned finish up his Chapter 7 bankruptcy. I have very strong reason to believe that once he reorganizes he would no longer have to be concerned about any personal, civil or criminal suits against him."

"Then are you suggesting he eliminate the source of his live-lihood?" the General asked.

Not at all. I am suggesting that once Ned has reorganized, he may then be eligible to bid on government projects, big projects. At that point if a feasible bid were to come across our desk from him, particularly if Ned is not actively involved with the Resolutions Company at that time, we may look at it favorably. However, for obvious reasons, I must warn you, don't even think about going near Medford Pond again. In other words, Ned, you must stay away from Medford Pond once we release you. Better yet, you might want to consider moving out of Gaylord, and perhaps out of the state of Maine for a sabbatical. In other words, once I retire, you might be wise to keep out the public eye, especially during my successor's first year in the regional office. Again, whatever you do, don't even think about bidding as a subcontractor on any remedial work relating to this project, or, quite frankly, my successor may be obliged to bury you at the bottom of the Pond, if there's a bottom to it!"

I have little more to say as the General and Denise are chatting with Borak about his travel plans for retirement. He and I have been battling for so long, it seems hard to believe it's over!

I excuse myself, not wanting to do anything to intrude on the atmosphere of goodwill.

I had left the three of them in Dimitri's office and was walking down the road towards the convenience store for food, having not eaten for a day, when Fitch, riding in his cruiser, intercepted me.

"Your missus wants to talk to you," he said.

Does everyone in Gaylord know my business? Incredible! There's no place I can hide from the people I most want to forget. Why is Martha calling me?

Fitch handed me the cell phone in his car. "I'm kind of busy. What makes you think you can always find me near a cop, Martha?" I asked her.

"I don't anymore. I wanted to talk to you about where we go from here," she said.

I heard a new voice on the cell phone. "And this is Aldie, Ned. Congratulations on your breakthrough."

I wonder if Chip has been telling Aldie about my negotiations, or whether Aldie's network of friends has been reporting back to them about my sudden change in fortune.

"Apologies if I misspoke at out meeting," Aldie said.

"Yes, honey," Martha then said to me sweetly. "I'd like you to come home so we can begin where we left off."

"A family man belongs with his family," Aldie said. "We have reason to believe you'll emerge from your business crisis, and we would like to help you celebrate."

Evidently they're having second thoughts about our dinner table agreement. I bet they'd like to celebrate this breakthrough with Borak by striking a deal better for Martha than the one Chip's drawn up between her and me. I wouldn't put it past her to want to divorce me later, now that it looks as if I won't have to declare bankruptcy. She's probably worried that she's cut herself out of a bigger payoff! No, I've already signed off with her, and I'll be damned if I reverse it!

"A belated vote of confidence. You're right, I'm a family man, but now I've found a new one. Thanks for the offer, but no thanks."

———————

Once we're seated in Dimitri's restaurant for a cup of coffee, the waiter brings Dimitri to us, who insists that we have supper on him.

"The happy hour crowd's gone home now to spouses, pets, and kids, as you will, General." Denise said.

"Did I detect, Ned, from what you suggested to Denise that you and she may be making plans together?" the General asked.

Denise said nothing, blushing. Dimitri returned. "Our host is back," she said, grateful for the distraction. "He seems to be a nice guy."

Dimitri looked directly into my eyes. "You a happy man, Ned. Make a good stroke of business with the little man, hey?" Then to her he said, "And she get him sign on a dotted line?"

"Not exactly, Dimitri."

"I don't know you business, but have to be bigger money business than I do here at Sunset Motel, day and night serving public. You have nice lawyer who girlfriend, that smart. You make money and I never see you go to work. But when you find another good business like you have where you don't go to office, tell me when you need partner, because I ready to work like American work," he said, then left us.

"He knows I'm your lawyer; he thinks I'm your girlfriend, Ned. You talk entirely too much," Denise said, looking even closer into my eyes than Dimitri had. "I trust though that neither of you gentlemen told him about all your scandals?"

"Scandals—if you only knew the half of it," I said.

"This time you handled yourself fine without me," the General said. "Care to tell me why Borak was so friendly toward you by the time I got there, Ned?"

"Why? His conscience began working on him. But Borak's guilt met our persistence, not to mention fear. Someone better than me once said it's not so much that man has conscience as that conscience has man."

"So which of you, the General or you Ned, was the fearful one?" Denise asks.

"I can't afford to look back or remember. All you need to know for now is I'm your amorous one, if you care to let me take you home, finally."

Photo by David Abrams

Neal Graham earned his BA and MAsters in English from Columbia University and the University of Vermont, respectively. **_Blue's Coach Works_** is his first novel.